A pleasant death

Chapter One

Monday

The street ahead looked like a dirty black river that led nowhere, and I hated it.

The lamp posts hung their heads like suicides, their anaemic, rain-filled lights barely illuminating the flat, wet, surface, and as I walked wearily from one pool of pale, apologetic light to the next, all I could see curving away between the looming dead-eyed warehouses on either side was the all too familiar road to my own, personal hell, the deep, dark shadows thrown across it like black knives stabbing at me from the other bank, searching for a heart I hadn't got.

After two painful, drink-numbed years, I knew every black-bricked inch of that street and as streets went it was strictly second rate: Maybe even third. Yeah: definitely third. It was a third rate street in a third rate part of the city which meant that everything in it was third rate and that included me and my office.

I stood and swayed unsteadily, looking up to the fourth floor of the semi-derelict building where that tatty excuse for an office was situated.

Face it, I thought: You are worse than third rate: You don't rate at all. Right at that moment you are a busted button, barely able to hold anything together.

I'd told myself that over and over many times before.

I'd told myself that one of these tired, wet, life-sick days, I was going to crawl out of this toilet and go somewhere that was wide open and green and had big, fat lazy cows munching on grass in flower filled fields: That had bloody big bees buzzing around making golden honey and that had blinding, beautiful sunsets that spilt radiant yellow flavoured laughs into the sky and yelled 'Good night you lucky fuckers! See all of you dumb bastards in the morning!' as the smug, sizzling, searing hot faced daughter-of-a-bitch sun slid like a melting gold coin beneath the welcoming horizon, on its way to bring light, heat and fun to some other piece of this wild, God-loving world.

Somewhere where there was no booze and no women.

I swayed a little and snorted again: Definitely no women.

As usual, I was in a bad mood. My head was in a bad place, put there, as always, by bad drink and a bad woman, and I badly needed more bad drink: Brain-killing drink that would finish me off like the others I'd had tonight were meant to do but still hadn't, and up there, four flights away in the bottom of a drawer in my third rate office, there was a bottle of something that would probably do the job properly, which was why I was heading in that direction at almost midnight, tired and angry. Angry enough to want to kick in the rear lights of the few cars that were parked randomly against the pavement like abandoned boats on the soaking, black river. Except for one: A sleek, foreign coupe that looked completely out of place in this rain-washed street full of garbage and rusted wrecks: I stared at it for a few seconds with what passed for a curious expression on my wet, sliding-off-the-bone face. It was shining and slender and looked dangerously elegant, like a chromed rat-trap: Some lucky bastard owned it but it wasn't me, and that only added more bad feeling to the headful of bad feelings I already had.

Shrugging off the momentary diversion the car had been, I shuffled up the worn out steps to the paint-peeled door of my building, fumbled with the keys and opened it, the smell of dust, damp and decay hitting me as it always did. I was used to it but tonight for some reason it seemed worse than usual which made my mood even stinkier, and I began climbing the bare wooden stairs that led up to my office, dragging my feet from one step to the other, the thought of the golden bottle in my desk giving me the incentive I needed to keep going.

When I finally reached my floor, I walked unsteadily along the bare-planked passageway, passing all the bum-hole little offices where all the other losers played at being clever: An insurance agent; a publisher of cheap porn and an importer of whatever tacky crap it was that paid the low rent a dive like this demanded every week.

I got to my door, the last one right at the end, but instead of fumbling with the knob and going right in, I stopped because, despite only half my brain working, I could sense something wasn't right and after I'd stared at the out-of-focus picture for a few seconds, the part of my brain that was looking after me worked it out. There was a thin strip of white light along the bottom of the door, and a voice in the back of my fogged up head, my sensible voice, was telling me that I hadn't left any lights on.

I stood looking down at it, forcing my whisky-fuddled brain to work out the possibilities.

Did I owe Danny Cleaver anything? An old debt maybe? Had he sent some of his pay-roll around to collect on it? Cleaver didn't like people that didn't pay their debts and waiting wasn't one of his strong characteristics, but I knew for certain that I didn't owe him a penny. If anything, Cleaver owed me a clean one thousand pounds, not that I'd see that for a whole while longer. So: If it wasn't Cleaver who was it?

I put my ear to the door and listened for any kind of movement or the sound of voices on the other side. There were none of those things but I did smell something: Perfume...Good perfume. None of Cleaver's pay roll wore perfume, unless he was using 'Gucci Tony' again. No: Gucci Tony was dead, supposedly. No-one knew for sure, but he hadn't been seen for months now. I took another sniff. No...This was definitely perfume, not aftershave.

As carefully and as quietly as the handle would allow, I opened the door and stepped cautiously inside.

There was a woman sitting nice and relaxed in the old leather armchair I'd dragged out of the bankrupt office next door three months ago, and as I entered she looked up, coolly appraising me.

I looked at her.

Everything about her looked expensive: The two piece grey business suit, the long, black coat she wore over the top of it, her shoulder length chestnut hair, the gold and diamond rings on her long, manicured fingers, the very good, very big diamond clip brooch on her coat lapel and the pair of black kid gloves that lay across an impressively sized black handbag on my desk top.

The coat was well tailored and showed off a figure that she, or someone she was close to, had spent a lot of money on maintaining. Her hair shone like thick, silky chocolate, and on her slender feet she wore low heeled court shoes but not the type a lowly secretary might wear. These were the kind the wife, or mistress, of a very wealthy man wore.

Her face was long and pleasing to the eye: She had carefully made up eyes, a straight nose, a mouth that a fellow would willingly lose his fortune to be allowed to kiss, and a complexion that must have taken a very healthy budget to support.

Whoever she was, she did not fit in here. It was like finding a swan in a garbage can.

"Good evening..," I said, my words slurring slightly, slipping off my worn out raincoat and draping it over the broken hat stand I had found in a skip at the back of the building. Walking a little unsteadily behind my desk, I sat, no; slumped down into my creaking chair, switched on the tarnished desk lamp, took the half-empty bottle of McClallan's from the lower right drawer, unscrewed the lid and took a long swig from it, shuddering a little as it reminded me I hadn't eaten for thirteen hours, all the time looking at the swan sitting opposite me.

The lady seemed faintly amused.

"You are Mr. Carter I assume..?" she said.

I nodded and took the bottle away from my lips.

"When did you get here..?" I asked.

"About thirty minutes ago. Mr. Cleaver said you always came back to your office after drinking hours. He also said that he thought you would probably be doing a lot of drinking this evening."

I pouted and took another short swig from the bottle.

"Did he now..? That's nice of him. Why would he tell you all that?"

"He said you'd be very tired after doing him a favour."

I grinned.

"An understatement...," I said.

"Do you often do favours for Mr. Cleaver?"

I shrugged.

"Sometimes...," I said, casually.

She raised a long eye brow.

"What kind of 'favours'?"

I took another swig of the whiskey.

"The professional kind...," I said, wiping my lips with the back of my hand.

She smiled and pointed, elegantly, at my face.

"Did you get that doing him one of your favours?"

She was pointing at my left cheek. I touched it and it stung. So did my jaw. The bruise still showed obviously: I must be getting old: Losing my resilience.

"One of the risks of my profession..."

She moved in the chair.

"And what is your profession Mr. Carter?"

"Didn't Mr. Cleaver tell you?"

"He told me you..."rectified problems"."

"Did he now..?" I said carefully:" That's a nice turn of phrase..."Rectified problems"? Hmmm...I like that: Very classy. I'll put it on my web-site."

She pouted and tilted her head ever so slightly.

"What kind of problems..?" she asked.

"Problems that need rectifying..," I said holding her stare with one of my own. Where was this leading? What business was it of hers?

She gave me a half-smile that meant she accepted she wasn't going to get a more detailed answer and crossed her long legs, leaning further back into the leather.

"Mr. Cleaver also said that you are unscrupulous; cheap and for hire. Is he correct?"

"I'm certainly not cheap..," I replied.

She traced a finger slowly across her lower lip, obviously sizing me up before speaking again.

"But you are unscrupulous..?" she said.

"It depends..," I said.

"On what..?"

"On what it is I'm asked to do."

"Are you for hire?"

"Like I said; it depends on what someone wants to hire me for."

"Do you care..?"

I was about to take another swig from the rapidly emptying bottle but changed my clouded mind. I had been going to ask her to leave so that I could drain what was left alone, but then I decided I wouldn't. I needed to know why this good looking, well-dressed woman was sitting in my God forsaken office at midnight asking me if I was unscrupulous.

"Why are you here..?" I asked, replacing the cap.

She smiled slowly.

"I went to see Mr. Cleaver today, on the recommendation of a friend..," she said.

"Not a very nice friend..," I interrupted, grinning sarcastically.

"...to ask him to handle some business for me..," she continued, ignoring my attempt at humour:"...but when I told him what it was I wanted doing, he told me that he didn't wish to become personally involved in that sort of work but if I really wanted to have it done there were those of his acquaintance whose ethical standards were low enough for me to approach. You were top of his list."

"Again, very nice of him..," I said grinning again." I must be back in his good books. Mr. Cleaver always did have an over-developed sense of gratitude, but he also does nothing for free and that includes recommending people. How much did my name cost you?"

"One thousand pounds...," she said matter-of-factly, observing me through emotionless eyes, obviously looking for a reaction.

"Is that all..?" I said. "I must be going down in his estimation."

"Another thousand if you accept."

I sat looking at her. She was relaxed: Quite unperturbed by me, the surroundings or by what she was asking. I decided that the Coupe downstairs had to be hers. It figured. As I said; dangerously elegant like it's owner. I went on looking. After a minute she said:

"Well...aren't you going to say anything Mr. Carter?"

"About what..? You're not the first person he's pushed my way. Cleaver's an oily bastard that passes dirty work onto guys like me so that he keeps his broken nose out of anything unpleasant but still makes money. That's how I and others like me make my living: By recommendation. It's a mutual thing: Nothing to get excited about."

She raised her eyebrows at me. She had nice eyes: Clear and green: Quiet and unhurried.

"Why are you here..?" I asked. "What exactly is it you might want me to do?"

"Of course..," she said. "I haven't explained myself have I..?"

"No..," I said, wearily:" You haven't."

She re-arranged herself in the armchair, crossing her legs again. Her legs were very good. She could have spent all night crossing and uncrossing them as far as I was concerned.

There was a silence: One of those silences they say you could cut with a knife, then suddenly she got up and stood across from me on the other side of the desk, looking at me with a serious expression on her elegant, expensive face. She hesitated; then:

"I need help Mister Carter. The sort of help I think only someone like you can give me."

It was time for me to raise my own eyebrows.

"Someone like me..? What kind of person do you think someone like me is?"

"Someone who doesn't ask too many questions and who can make themselves understood."

I pouted again.

"Is that the impression I give..?" I said, wryly." That's a shame. I always thought I came off as the intellectual, home-loving type."

I laughed but she didn't which was a shame because I would have liked to hear her laugh. I was beginning to like pretty much everything about her to be honest, and I imagined her laugh would be nice.

"I think you're the type who can persuade other people against taking certain actions or continuing with actions that they might not wish to stop taking..," she went on.

I frowned. I knew what she was trying to say but I made a pretence of not understanding because I wanted her to come out with it: To spit out in plain English what it was she thought I did for a living.

"Forgive me..," I said, feigning confusion; "Persuade other people to stop taking actions? What kind of actions would those be and how would I stop them taking them?"

She sighed, pulled a slim silver case from her coat pocket and took a cigarette from it.

It had a gold band on it and looked like one of those you bought from swanky shops in Mayfair: Rolled in Turkey or France by peasant girls and smoked by men in bow ties and rich women like her.

She lit it and took a long drag.

"You didn't ask me if I minded you smoking..," I said.

She smiled, an amused look on her face.

"I'm sorry..," she grinned, waving a hand around the room." Forgive me but I rather assumed…"

"You should never assume..," I said, coldly.

She raised her elegant eyebrow again and nodded.

"Quite right: As I said: Forgive me. Do you mind?"

I shrugged.

"As it happens I don't but it would have been a courtesy to ask..," I said." Just because I look like a bum and have a shit-hole for an office doesn't mean I am."

There was silence again as she stared at the wall. I was getting impatient suddenly. I was also getting tired. I'd planned on emptying the bottle then crashing out on the beaten up sofa over in the corner, but those plans were being delayed and my eyes were telling me they didn't want to stay open much longer despite the pretty picture in front of them.

"Look. Let's stop dicking about, ok..?" I said, holding back a yawn:" It's late, I'm tired and if you go on being enigmatic too much longer I may just pass out on you, so why don't you just tell me what it is you want me to do. It must be something unpleasant for a woman like you to approach someone like Cleaver in the first place and then to come to a place like this on your own, in the dead of night to see a drunken wreck like me: Someone with bruises on his cheeks and who drinks whiskey neat from the bottle right in front of you."

"Cleaver told me you could be a son-of-a-bitch..," she said, quietly, still looking at the wall. It was bare apart from two pictures in broken frames. Both were of me in my army days: One was taken in the jungle, the other in the desert, sitting or standing in groups of other men, three of whom were dead now.

"Mr. Cleaver is right…"I said:" I can be a son-of-a-bitch at times but only when I am being played with."

"I'm not playing with you Mr. Carter..," she said, and I detected a little catch in the voice which was interesting:" I'm just finding it hard to actually tell you what it is I need doing and why?"

I settled further down into my seat.

"Ok. Take your time then but don't be surprised if you turn around and find me asleep. I've had a tough day and an even tougher night and I hadn't planned on doing any talking when I got back here which is why I drank too much."

She blew out a long column of smoke.

"Is that you..?" she said, pointing at the two pictures with her cigarette.

I nodded.

"Yeah: That's me; a few lifetimes ago. Cute wasn't I?"

She looked around at me and there was a small smile on her lips.

"You still are in a down-beat sort of fashion."

I picked up the bottle again and saluted her with it.

"Why thank you ma'am..," I said, unscrewing the cap and throwing back almost the last swig. I put the bottle back and crossed my arms.

"Now come on..," I said." Suck it up and let me know what it is you want and how it is you think I might be able to help you. If you can't, kindly leave and call my secretary in the morning to make another appointment. I have a very uncomfortable sofa I'd like to crawl onto and die."

She paused for another moment then sat back down in her chair, facing me.

"Is there anyone you are fond of Mr. Carter: Really fond of?"

I shook my head.

"No..," I said. "No-one: Not any more. There are people I've liked; even respected but there's no-one I'd rush home to. I've learnt to think about people very superficially. It makes life a lot easier."

I was lying of course. There was someone but it was none of her business.

I smiled at her in what I hoped was an endearing way but was probably more like a leer.

She moved in her chair and took another drag on her cigarette.

"You sound to me like a man who has been very disappointed about something: A woman maybe?"

"You mean this week or over the last few months..?" I said.

"That's very cynical."

I didn't say anything.

She went on: "I asked if you'd been very fond of someone because if you had you would understand the way I feel and what it is I am going to ask you to do."

"And how do you feel..?" I asked, stifling the first of several yawns.

"I'm unhappy..," she said. "Miserable in fact, but not about myself: Personally I've nothing to be unhappy or miserable about, but I'm very unhappy about a friend: She's younger than me and is, or was, a very sweet girl."

"And what has that to do with why you're here..?" I said.

She stayed silent for a few moments, as though trying to make her mind up about something, which gave me time to look at her and concentrate on the potential business ahead. I came to the conclusion very quickly that she was an interesting woman. I didn't often come across women like her. She had beauty, style and breeding, but she was also clever and in my experience that rarely came as part of the same package.

"It's a rather long story..," she suddenly said, breaking my thoughts; "...but best you hear it from the beginning, then you'll know how to handle it. You'll be able to advise as to whether what I have in mind is the best plan. Would you like to listen?"

I nodded, a little too heavily.

"Go ahead..," I said.

She began to talk and as she talked I got the impression she was trying to convince herself more than me that what she was about to ask was right.

"A few years ago, just before the last Gulf War, I thought I was in love with an officer in the Guards. He was a family friend, younger than me and..."

She broke off for a few seconds, took a breath then carried on: "...I had an affair with him. Now that I've had a lot of time to think about it I realise didn't actually love him. I suppose I just felt very maternal towards him, which I know sounds odd considering I had an actual affair, but somehow the two feelings became intertwined into one overwhelming fondness. Can you understand that Mr. Carter?"

I shrugged: "Why not? These things happen."

She went on: "The affair lasted a few months then he was sent to the Middle East with his regiment, but before he left he told me he wanted to marry me when he returned. I knew I couldn't do it but I was a coward and never told him that directly. I merely said that we could talk about it more when he returned. He was sorry to hear me say that, but said he understood. He was a very nice person: A lovely man."

She stopped talking and I could see her fingers clasping and unclasping in her lap.

"The thing is, he didn't come back. Apparently his unit was ambushed and he was captured by some militia men. From all reports he had a terrible time in one of their prisons and was only discovered when it was liberated by the Americans. He had been badly tortured and died of his wounds the day after he was found."

Her voice trailed away.

"I expect you can imagine that he must have had a pretty grim time before the end."

I drew a long breath, suppressing a sudden rush of memory.

"Yeah," I said, flatly." I can imagine that. Go on..."

"When I heard about his death I was terribly upset. I felt angry with myself and unhappy about everything. I left London and travelled everywhere I could think of to try and escape my guilt and give myself time to think. I ended up in America, taking a young friend, Charlotte, with me."

"Is this the young woman you are here about..?" I asked.

She nodded.

"Yes: She's eight years younger than me..," she said. "She was carefree, happy and had a very superficial, almost innocent attitude to life. She lifted my spirits, which is why I took her with me. I was very fond of her. I still am."

She fell silent again for a few moments before carrying on.

"After we'd been in America a couple of months, California to be exact, the sunshine began working its magic and I was getting over my depression so I opened myself up to the possibility of another relationship. That's how I met a man called Marcus Dexter. He seemed charming: Very friendly and had a very strong personality. He seemed to know an awful lot of people and introduced me to a much more relaxed way of life. He became extremely attentive, brought me out of myself which is exactly what I needed, and it wasn't long before we became lovers."

More hand-wringing and staring into middle space:

"He made me the centre of his world: 'Couldn't do enough for me. After less than five months, stupidly, we married and for another two or three everything was wonderful, but things began to change and I realised I had made a mistake."

"What kind of mistake?"

She gave me an apologetic half smile.

"I discovered that he had a bad history..," she said. "It seems that he wasn't a very nice person at all: Quite the opposite in fact. I found out that he made his extremely substantial living in several very seedy ways. One was selling drugs, the other was by blackmailing women. His charming character hid an extremely nasty and sadistic nature. His 'tendencies', I discovered, were very unpleasant and when he felt like it, he became violent: Increasingly so. It turned out he had married me purely for my money which, since the death of my father, had trebled."

"What did you do about it..?" I asked.

"I had a straight talk with him: told him that I knew all about what he did and that I was going to divorce him immediately."

"I'm guessing he wasn't very happy about that..?" I said.

"No Mr. Carter; he wasn't. He threatened me, tried violence once or twice and generally made my life over there very unpleasant but because I had money I was able to employ men of a certain type and expensive lawyers to keep him down. At first he just dismissed my bodyguards' warnings and laughed at the notices my lawyers served on him, but when they raised the threat level by telling him they would involve the police if he continued to intimidate and harass me, he backed away."

"His record was pretty bad I take it..?" I said.

"Very bad: When he was threatened with the courts he left me alone and agreed to a divorce. My lawyers forced him into admitting to some of the things I had discovered about him but I felt uneasy. He was being too submissive: Dexter was not the kind of man that allowed anyone to intimidate him. I knew that. I'd seen him up against other men and I knew he never backed down from anyone, so I had the feeling that he was planning some kind of scheme. He isn't the sort to be told what to do, and I suspected he might have a surprise in store for me. I really did fear for my own safety so I told him I was returning to London; that I had instructed my lawyers to bring the suit for divorce against him in my absence and that I would take steps to ensure he couldn't come near me. I did return to London, and brought Charlotte back with me but she had seemed very reluctant to leave which was odd as she was very fond of her family back here and had intimated to me that after my marriage, she may want to come back at some point, but it was only after I got back that I discovered she and Marcus had started an affair almost within a month of his marrying me: Like every woman he met, Charlotte was fascinated by him and believed anything he told her. She even believed that it was me that was making his life a misery."

"Does Charlotte have any money of her own?"

She nodded: "Her family own a private bank so yes, she was very well off. At least she used to be..," "she sighed.

I told her to go on with her story. It was interesting, or at least it was keeping me awake.

"In due course my divorce came through, but almost immediately, within two weeks of the decree absolute, Dexter came to London and made a big thing about being seen around town with Charlotte. She seemed to be obsessed with him and because she believed every word he told her, she began to distance herself not only from me, but from the rest of her family. They hated him as much as I did, but Charlotte couldn't, or wouldn't, see it. Six months after Marcus arrived in London, to everyone's astonishment, he and Charlotte announced their engagement. I was horrified and wrote to her telling her everything I knew about him. His past: His violence towards me and other women. His police record: I spared no details but she ignored me."

"Did she talk with you at all...?" I asked.

"No: She wrote me a long, rambling letter in reply telling me that I had concocted the whole thing about Marcus and his past because I was jealous of her happiness and that if I continued making trouble she would take me to court for slander. She refused to take my phone calls and returned all of the letters I wrote to her. Soon afterwards, they were married, in Italy."

"Are they still married?"

She nodded gently, staring at her fingers.

"Yes, they are but she is very unhappy."

"How do you know that?"

She looked up from her lap.

"Because she finally told me: She said she realised very quickly after they were married that everything I had told her was true. He started spending her money as though it was being abolished at midnight. He held wild parties, brought a lot of people over from America, sold one of her houses in Italy, bought a yacht out of the proceeds and used it as love nest for his numerous girl-friends. He was totally blatant about it: Didn't try and hide anything. She was miserable and tried once or twice to divorce him but kept changing her mind for some reason. For a while, at my insistence, she left him and came to stay with me. That's when I heard all the stories of his cruelties and violent conduct. I begged her: Pleaded with her to stay with me: Not to return but he had some kind of hold over her: Something so powerful she couldn't keep away from him…"

"Drugs..?" I said, flatly.

She nodded.

"Yes," she said, slowly. "He'd tried to introduce me to drugs when we married but I wouldn't have anything to do with them, so he turned to her and being the trusting, naïve soul she was, she took what he offered. Gradually the bastard hooked her until she became an addict, dependent upon him for her fixes. When she came to stay with me, with my help, she made an attempt to break away from him but it was only half-hearted and one day she gave in, caught a flight to the south of France and ran back to him. Since then none of her friends or relations can get anywhere near her. She is completely and utterly in his power."

She stopped talking and there was silence in the room.

"Is that all..?" I said.

She looked up at me, quizzically.

"Isn't it enough..?" she said.

"Maybe; maybe not: Enough for what though?"

She put her hands on the edge of the desk and I could see that her fingers were trembling.

"Enough for you to do something about it..?" she said quickly.

I frowned.

"What exactly do you want me to do about it..?" I asked.

She took a deep breath, summoning up courage or something.

"Listen to me Mr. Carter. I am awfully afraid for Charlotte. I think she has come to the end of her tether, which is what he's got tied around her neck. She is badly strung out. Something needs to be done and quickly or she will do something very bad either to herself or to him."

"Like what..?" I said:" Kill him?"

She stared at me for a long second, her eyes searching mine which must have been difficult because they were glazing over and half-closed.

"Yes..," she breathed:" I think she might. She talks about doing it enough and I know she has a gun. I worry she will use it one day."

"A gun..?" I said, slightly surprised:" Why would she have a gun?"

"Because Dexter has one..," she said:"...and the way her mind is working lately I think she feels he might use it on her. He wouldn't because, whatever else he is, he's not an idiot, but her thinking isn't clear anymore and I can see the drugs she's taking are making her more and more paranoid. I want to get him out of her life before she does something stupid in an uncontrolled moment."

"What did you have in mind..?" I asked. I was getting tired but I was also getting interested.

She sat back in her chair. Her voice was calm again but there was anger behind her eyes.

"I can't actually prove she is getting her drugs from him..," she said. "But I'm pretty certain he's supplying them, and not only for her. I'm almost convinced he is selling drugs to others; keeping them addicted and in his pocket for future use. Dexter is a very nasty, very clever man Mr. Carter. He uses people for money and for protection. He builds a wall of dependent, blackmailed people around him from behind which he twists and manipulates others for his own pleasure. I'm not the only one who is convinced either. So is her doctor and her friends but we can't find any direct evidence. The one thing I do know though is that Marcus is afraid of the law, or at least afraid of imprisonment. I'm positive it would help Charlotte if you went to see him, told him you were acting on behalf of Charlotte's relations and that you had discovered he was not only keeping her addicted against her will but was dealing in drugs: Tell him that unless he agrees to leave the country, divorce Charlotte and leave her entirely alone so that she could be looked after and rehabilitated, you would take the evidence you have to the police. That's what I want you to do Mr. Carter and I want you to do it immediately: At once. We need him to go: Now!"

I uncrossed my arms and leant forward, resting my elbows on the desk. The almost drained bottle beckoned to me out of the corner of my eye but I ignored it.

"That sounds a little too easy..," I said.

She took another pull on her cigarette and looked me straight in the bloodshot eyes.

"It won't be easy at all Mr. Carter..," she said. "As I said, Marcus Dexter is a very clever and unscrupulous man..."

"That word again..." I said, grinning. "You like unscrupulous men don't you?"

"Not all of them..," she said:" Only the ones I can use."

"Fair enough.., "I said, a grin on my aching face. "And you think you can use my particular lack of scruples?"

"Dexter has some very peculiar associates Mr. Carter. If he felt threatened, he could call upon them to come to his assistance and there might be severe repercussions."

I grinned widely at her. It made my cheek ache but I couldn't help it.

"I see. You mean I may have to look after myself?"

"Yes..," she said. "That's exactly what I mean, which is why you come highly recommended."

I sat back again, contemplating her and her story.

"OK..," I asked casually." I've heard you're story, now who are you?"

For the first time in what seemed a long while she smiled.

"You are the strangest man Mr. Carter. You arrive looking like a tramp, stinking of alcohol, find me sitting in your office unannounced, proceed to drink Scotch straight from the bottle in front of me, listen to what I have to say, and only then do you ask who I am."

"Doesn't sound strange to me at all..," I said. "Up until now, I wasn't interested enough in you or your story to want to know anything about you. No names, no bloody pack drills is one of my many mottos: Now I'm a little bit interested, so it seems reasonable to me that I at least know who I might be working for and whether they can afford my lack of scruples."

She looked at me and smiled again. Nice eyes, nice teeth.

"Of course: You are quite right..," she said. "Up until now it hasn't mattered who I am. I was just a woman who was keeping you from collapsing into your stupor. Now that you've become curious and it seems I might be of some financial benefit to you, you want to know. You must lead a very dull life if your only criteria for interest is money."

I shrugged.

"You could be right..," I said. "My life is pretty dull most of the time, but money helps make it a little less dull and the more I can get, the shinier my life could become. There you go, eh? Now: I'll ask again. What's your name?"

"Leonora..," she said. "Leonora Fitzpatrick."

I took a pad of paper with only two sheets left on it from the top drawer of my desk and wrote the name down.

"That's a nice name..," I said. "Better than Dexter."

I wrote her name on the pad, pushed it away and tapped the stubby pencil against my teeth.

"Have you got any money on you Leonora Fitzpatrick..?"

Her smile widened.

"I knew you'd help..," she said.

"I didn't say that..," I said, dryly." All I asked you was if you had any money on you: Cash I'm talking about: A lot of it."

She opened her expensive handbag and brought out a brown envelope. It was bulging nicely.

"Cash..," she said." I had a feeling you might accept the work and I guessed you wouldn't take bank transfer."

I looked at the fat envelope and grinned.

"Very pretty..," I said." Two pretty sights in one evening. You're spoiling me. How much is in there?"

"£5,000..."

"New notes..?"

She gave me a half-smile and slowly opened the flap of the envelope, pulling out five bundles of crisp, fresh notes, each bundle bound with an off-white wrapper belonging to an exclusive bank which proved she wasn't lying about being rich.

"Brand new..," she said, pushing them across the desk towards me.

I sat back contemplating the neat, sharp-edged bundles for a few seconds.

"You know, if I were an artist that would be my idea of a masterpiece..," I said, eventually.

"Perhaps you are Mr. Carter...," she said, raising one eyebrow in a way I was coming to like. "I can imagine you are a bit of an artist in what you do."

I snorted and grinned.

"Nice of you to say so but there's not much finesse in what I do..," I said, scooping the four bundles together and putting them in the only lockable drawer in my desk, slipping the small key into one of the button down pockets on my shirt." Occasionally I might have to be a little creative at times and from what you tell me, I may have to be a little artistic with this Marcus Dexter, although from what you've also told me I doubt subtlety is going to work too well with him. Where doe's Marcus live..?" I asked, picking up the stubby pencil again.

"He's renting a house on the outskirts of Brighton for three or four months, called, appropriately, 'Devil's view'. It's on the North Downs: Set in half a dozen acres. He likes privacy: A lot of privacy. He's not always there so I'm told, but I know for a fact he is for the next couple of weeks."

She tossed over a small card with the address written on it and I put it in the same pocket as the key.

"Is he alone when he's there..?" I asked.

She nodded.

"Most of the time: During the day he's in London but he usually returns in the evening, unless he's staying with a woman."

"What about staff..? Is there a housekeeper: Anyone living in?"

"The house has two women that come with it, to clean twice, maybe three times a week, mostly during the morning, and a gardener who looks after the grounds for the real owners but nobody lives there permanently."

I took a deep breath to clear my, by now, throbbing head and sat forward heavily. Suddenly I was really tired. My brain, realising it wasn't going to be put to sleep with whiskey had decided to go there on its own.

"Thank you very much for coming Mrs. Fitzgerald..," I said, rubbing my face with my hands and trying not to yawn." I appreciate your faith and trust in me, etcetera, etcetera, and I appreciate the five thousand pounds even more, but I need to sleep suddenly: A lot. I've got your number so when I've got something to tell you I'll be in touch."

I stood up as a signal that it was time for her to leave and for me to fall onto the sofa or the floor, whichever I reached first.

She looked up at me for a few seconds then rose to her feet, picking up her handbag and tucking it under her arm.

"What are you going to do now..?" she asked.

This time I did yawn, and it was a big one that threatened to crack my jaw apart, stopping me from speaking.

"Nothing..," I said, after a few seconds, rubbing my strained jaw bone.

She stood looking at me, wriggling her fingers into her gloves, and there was a cold curiosity in her gorgeous eyes.

"What do you mean 'nothing'..?" she said.

I smiled sleepily.

"I mean 'nothing': Not right now. Right now, like I said, I'm going to collapse onto that couch over there and sleep off a bottle and a half of very expensive whisky which if past experience is anything to go by, will mean I won't wake until the middle of tomorrow, then I'm going to try and recover what's left of the brain cells I haven't killed and put them back into some kind of order: My guess would be about two o'clock in the afternoon by the time I leave here. So, there you have it: Until then…'Nothing'."

There was silence; then: "So you don't intend going down there tonight..?"

She sounded unhappy.

I yawned again, partly as another signal to her that I really was tired but mainly because I had to.

"No..," I said, shaking my closing down head in disbelief that she actually wanted me to get on the case right then: Half past midnight? "No I am not. Look…You obviously didn't work out the clues I was giving you so let me repeat myself. I am tired: You get that? Very, very tired: Far too tired, not to mention far too drunk and thick-headed, to even think about getting in a car in the middle of the night and driving all the way down to Sussex to deliver a bleary ultimatum to a clear-headed and angry man who, if he is even there, has been woken from his cosy, probably shared bed at two in the morning by a scruffy, booze-soaked tramp and who would probably tell me in no uncertain manner to piss off, that's if I wasn't pulled over long before I got there by some bored policemen and arrested for drunk driving."

She said nothing, just stared at me.

I came around the desk and walked over to the door, a little more unsteadily than ten minutes before, opening it for her to leave through.

She was still looking at me and I frowned. She actually had tears in her eyes, and she was wearing an expression like a dog that had just been kicked. She took a step towards me, putting her hand out and resting it on my arm. In a low voice she said; "Mr. Carter…please…I understand what you have just said but…."

I lifted her hand from my arm gently.

"No..," I said, calmly but forcefully." I've told you that from two o'clock this afternoon I will give the whole of my no doubt still hazy attention to the task ahead but for now, that's it. I'm done: Finished. I was pretty well done when I walked in and I'm doubly done now. I am going to bed, or at least over there to my couch. Thank you for a very pleasant evening. I have enjoyed meeting you, but regretfully it is time for you to leave. I'm sorry you have to walk down the stairs on your own but a) there is no lift as you discovered on the way up and b) if I accompanied you as I know I should, I would end up in a broken heap after falling off the first step."

Her high cheeks flushed and her head dropped. Sighing, she pulled her over-sized handbag closer into her side, walked past me, opened the door into the hallway, turned once to give me a last plaintive look, half-smiled then walked out, closing the door behind her.

I stood leaning against the frame, listening to the sound of her heels tapping down the corridor then closed the door to my office and returned to my chair, reaching out and grabbing the bottle of whiskey which I could tell had been feeling neglected because it tasted a little bitter.

Leaning back on the creaking hinges I looked out of the grimy window down into the street below. The depressed lamps were dropping weak spots of jaundice-yellow light onto the wet surface like watery spit. After a minute she came out of the street door and walked towards the shiny coupe: I was correct in my guess. It was hers: 'Had to have been.

She unlocked the driver's door, slid inside, made a graceful U-turn and drove off in the direction of the nice side of town. I watched the car until it turned out of sight and leaned back onto the desk, thinking.

She was a very nice lady.

Nice to look at: Nicely dressed: Nice to listen to: Nice to smell and nicely rich, but something in the still awake part of my brain was trying to tell me that she probably wasn't very nice at all. There was something about her that didn't smell as good as her perfume. Something that made the suspicious part of my normally deeply trusting character suspect that she might be trying to use me: Trying to make me make the fall guy in a bigger game she wasn't letting me in on. I needed to sleep on it.

The big, brown, broken-faced clock on the filing cabinet told me with a soft, gentle, apologetic chime that it was one o'clock. I never could quite understand why such a big, ugly clock had such a tiny chime. It was like a bruised, broken nosed heavyweight boxer opening his mouth and the voice of a Mamma doll coming out.

I raised the empty bottle to my mouth, placed the neck against my lips, more in hope than expectation, and to my pathetic delight felt and tasted a final dribble of dregs coat my furry tongue and soak into my throat.

Seconds later, the empty bottle fell from my baby-strength fingers onto the floor and rolled towards the door, but I didn't hear it.

I was asleep.

TWO

The insistent chiming of the four-faced clock on the print works tower finally broke through my mashed and whirling dreams, and with a sudden gasp I snapped my three ton head up off the desk top, throwing myself back into the real world.

I groaned long and low, realising where I was and slowly lowered my right cheek back onto the wood, wishing I was back in my dream, confusing though it had been. Anything was preferable to the aching reality of my nasty little office.

Through one blood-shot eye, I looked blearily over at the big, brown broken-faced clock on the filing cabinet and saw that it was ten o'clock: Heard it actually because the clock was about twenty seconds slower than its big cousin outside and the last of its tinny chimes were sounding faintly in the dust-filled air.

The second thing that came to my foggy mind, after the need for strong coffee, was Leonora Fitzpatrick and I began to reassemble the events and conversations of the night before, going over in my cotton wool head what I remembered of her story.

It sounded plausible enough. There were certainly plenty of good looking low-life shits like the Marcus guy she's been talking about out there, living off impressionable rich women, turning them into willing cash-slaves. I'd come across a few over the years. I even worked for one a couple of years back. No: That wasn't what was making me a little cagey about what she'd told me. It was the speed she'd wanted the thing done. She was pushing too hard: Trying to get me to visit this bum too fast. Midnight for Christ's sake..! Then there was the fact that Cleaver had sent her to me. Why would he do that? She'd said Cleaver hadn't wanted anything to do with it when she'd told him what she wanted doing. That was bullshit: Cleaver had an army of guys that were highly experienced in leaning on sleaze bags like Dexter: They did it all the time. Fat Danny; 'Technical' Jones; 'Fancy' Dave, to name just three…I'd worked with most of them and a man like Marcus Dexter was their bread and butter. They enjoyed it: Frightening off ponces like him was well within their capabilities, so why would Cleaver send her around to me? Was there something deeper going on than I was being made aware of and if there were just how deep was it? Was I being set up? Who by..? Leonora Fitzpatrick or Cleaver: Maybe it was both of them...? Maybe it was none of them and it really was as easy as she had made it sound?

No: Nothing was ever that easy, especially as far as jobs that came my way via Cleaver were concerned.

To prove to myself that it had all been real and not some drunken illusion, I unlocked the drawer, half-hoping I was going to see just bare wood, but the thick brown envelope was definitely there, like a freshly landed, fat trout.

I smiled, reached down, took it out, lay it on the desk, closed the drawer and locked it again, even though it was empty. I'm a very security conscious man.

The thought of a steaming mug of coffee came into my head so strongly I could smell it so I stood up, stretched like an aching alley cat, shrugged on my shabby old rain coat and stuffed the money into an inside pocket. Taking a look out of the window I could see the day was bored with itself already: Grey, overcast and slow looking.

I went out into the corridor, locked up behind me and walked towards the top of the stairs, my shoes echoing on the bare wooden floorboards.

THREE

Ten minutes of sluggish walking and at least a hundred deep breaths later, I arrived at the steps leading down to Ronnie Miller's place – The Blue Oasis: My home from home, not that I liked to call my office 'home' but I had to suppose it was.

Inside the club, Ronnie was sitting at his usual table in the corner, dressed in a bright suit and tie, freshly shaved and over-scented, while the staff cleaned the place up around him.

He looked and smelt like he always did. Prosperous, in his early sixties, silver-haired and wearing his gold rings like symbols of authority.

He smiled when he saw me enter and raised a pink hand for me to come over.

I liked Ronnie and he liked me. I'd known him since I was a young boy when he and my father, God preserve his Rolex, had been partners in a then struggling club called 'The

Green Dog' that they'd poured all of their demob' money into after the army, and as far as I had any at all, he was a friend.

The 'Green Dog" hadn't succeeded, mainly due to the already established clubs taking a dislike to the new kids on the block and the heavy presence of the Macklin brothers who had offered to protect their interests for a large percentage of the profits, but which my father and Ronnie had foolishly declined to pay.

Two clubs later and a move to the other side of town, they did succeed and it was in the Blue Oasis that I'd spent most of my adolescent and teenage years, before joining the army.

After my father died suddenly of a heart attack one Saturday night on his way home from the club, a year after my blessed mum had died of cancer, Ronnie, who had no kids of his own, had become Dad number two.

Like I said, I liked Ronnie. He was a good man: A bit heavy on the aftershave but a good man.

I left my coat with the girl at reception and wove around the stacked chairs towards his table.

"Good morning..," he said, taking a sip of his tea, grinning up at me as I came closer:" Looking a little harsh this morning: A tad hard on the eyes if you don't mind my saying so young man..."

At a silent signal, one of the bar staff broke off from cleaning the glasses and brought over a bottle of whiskey, a soda siphon and some glasses.

I grimaced but said nothing as Ronnie poured out two small shots, pushing one across the table at me. He added a burst of soda to his but left mine neat.

"Get it down son..," Ronnie smiled, tossing back his own glass. "You know it always settles your head."

Reluctantly, even though I knew he was right, I threw the amber liquid onto my tongue and let it grip my throat, wincing as it rippled through me.

"Another hard night..?" he said.

It was a statement of fact, not a question and I nodded.

"Yeah.., "I groaned. "Another."

He poured himself a second shot but left my glass empty.

"They're becoming too much of a habit lately..," "he mused, studying the contents; swirling them around the tumbler:" You need to watch that. It's not good for your health: Everything in moderation son."

"I'm not good at moderation..," I said, shaking away the effects of the whiskey.

"That's the truth..," he mumbled, nodding in silent agreement, lifting his tumbler to his lips and swallowing the whiskey down in one go.

Idly, I looked around at the club, taking it in by the cold light of day.

It wasn't called the Blue Oasis for nothing. The walls and even the ceilings were painted in big murals showing a white-beached lagoon surrounded by palm trees with dolphins, mermaids, exotic fish and birds everywhere. All very cheesy and a bit too bright for my seriously sensitive eyes that morning but at night, under subdued light with half a bottle of something mind-dulling inside you, oddly effective. It encouraged you not to take life too seriously: To just drink and have a laugh. I liked it. It was just like Ronnie himself: Bold, brash and a bit blousy but comforting. You knew where you were with both him and the club: The only thing Ronnie ever took seriously was money, mainly because making it over the years had been no joke.

"You look tired..," he said, caringly, placing his empty tumbler beside the bottle. "In my opinion you could do with a nice long holiday."

It was my turn to nod understandingly.

"I don't disagree with you..," I said, casually." Perhaps I'll go book one this afternoon."

He gave me one of his despairing looks that meant he knew I was telling him to mind his own business.

"Good idea. Why don't you do that..?" he scoffed, knowing full well I had no intention of booking a holiday today, tomorrow or any time in the foreseeable future. I didn't do 'holidays'. I wasn't built for them. My mind was too restless.

"Where did you go last night..?" he asked after a minute's silence.

I shrugged and feigned disinterest.

"A few of the usual places..," I ventured, knowing full well he probably knew exactly where I had been, because the network would have told him where I was, what I was up to and who I was with drink by drink I should imagine:" Marty's, 'The Pacific', 'Furious Freddie's: I finished off at Boston Mikes'."

He sighed.

"Why didn't you come here..?" he said.

"You know why I didn't come here.., "I snorted, smiling:" Because you wouldn't have served me that's why."

"You're damned right I wouldn't..," he said and I could hear the concern in his voice." I would have had you filled with coffee and put you to bed."

I gave him a sideways look.

"Exactly why I didn't darken your bar stools..," I said, accusingly." I needed to drink last night: A lot. I have some things that need drowning."

"Woman shaped things…?" he asked, taking a slow drink of his still hot tea this time.

My head was beginning to throb again, mainly because I knew what was coming.

"Mostly…"I said, closing my eyes and rubbing the bridge of my nose.

"Ilsa…?" he went on. I gave him a look.

"Who..?" I said, sarcastically.

He put down his cup and shook his head wearily.

"That has to stop you know..," he said." That girl is killing you by the bottle and you are letting her. How much have you given her this week?"

I sat forward. Nothing of what went on between myself and Ilsa had anything to do with him, which he knew but I could tell by the look of concern in his eyes he was worried and if I was being honest with myself, I was worried too but not about the booze she was forcing me into drinking: It was more the money I kept giving her, each time telling her it was the last but each time knowing she'd be back for more.

"Nothing I can't afford..," I said firmly, setting my jaw and my voice into a hard, straight line.

He shrugged and examined the nails on his right hand.

"It's your money..," he said dismissively." How you decide to burn it is up to you son, but there are better people to chuck it at than that grubber."

I curled the fingers of my right hand into a fist beneath the table in frustrated anger, the muscles in my clenched jaw twitching at the sadness and surrender in his words. I knew he was right and it angered me that he could see the damage my ex-wife was doing to me. It had been a mistake marrying her: I knew that when I'd walked into the bloody registry office but she, of all the women I had known, had been the only one to grip my brain by the balls and twist my rationality into a sheepshank. She was still doing it but at least we were divorced now, not that you'd know it. She'd been high maintenance then and she still was, five years later, but this time it wasn't her I was bothered about maintaining. It was Frieda: My beautiful little Frieda; five years old and the only living creature on this crappy planet that could reduce me to tears.

She was gorgeous: Had the hair of a goddess and the laugh of an angel. She also had a bad heart and had to live her little life at half the pace she wanted to. It was for her that I gave Ilsa money but I knew, and everyone else that cared about Frieda knew, that it didn't all go into keeping her alive. A good percentage of it went into the tills of designer shops and beauty parlours. I'd made her well aware on many occasions that I knew what was happening and that it had to stop, but she just twisted my brains a little harder and gave me the look that had kept me coming back for more again and again and I knew the words I was aiming at her were just bouncing off like rounds on armour plate. She had me exactly where she needed me and so I kept on funding Frieda's life and Ilsa's lifestyle to the detriment of my own, which is why I had a crappy office in a crappy part of town and took on crappy work for crappy people but every time I got to hear the laugh of my little angel and see the hair of my baby goddess shining in the sun I understood yet again why I did it.

I wanted to stop talking about her and stood up, pushing my chair away from behind me.

"You mentioned coffee..." I said. "If you don't mind, I think I might take you up on the advice."

He pouted his lips, smiled up at me and nodded, fishing around in the left hand breast pocket of his fancy, some might say vulgar, waistcoat.

"Be my guest..," he said, handing the key to his office up to me. I thanked him, walked across the dance floor now being mopped clean in long slow strokes by two older men, and up the steep flight of stairs on the other side of the room, disguised by part of a large mural, holding onto the banister to help keep me steady as I climbed.

I let myself in, switched on the light and slipped the catch on the door. I needed a bit of peace and undisturbed quiet for a while.

The coffee maker was over in the corner as usual, turned on and gently bubbling, the strong smell of freshly ground beans filling the air. I began to feel good already and there was a smile on my face as I made myself a deep mug full of thick black, Jamaican Blue Mountain. It tasted even better than I'd wanted it to and for a few minutes I sat with my feet up on Ronnie's big, tidy desk luxuriating in the moment, eyes closed, thinking of nothing or trying to. My head felt like it was being rubbed with warm silk towels and I knew I was going to feel a lot better soon.

I did and reluctantly, finishing the coffee, I turned my soothed mind to the matter of Leonora Fitzpatrick. I didn't like to admit it but she'd been sitting at the back of my mind almost the moment I'd woken up. What she'd said and how she'd said it had been going round around in my head all the way over to the club and now that I had time to think about it, nothing I recalled made me feel any less uneasy about what she'd asked me to do. I still felt there was something not quite straight about it.

I ran through my reasons again, came up with the same misgivings and decided that before I started walking into another of the many ambushes I'd let myself be led into, I'd try scratching a small itch that was niggling at the back of my skull.

I picked up the 'phone and dialled a number I knew by heart, and as I waited for the call to be answered I looked at my watch.

It was almost twelve.

A gruff, suspicious male voice with a distinctly threatening tone to it spoke into my ear.

"Who is this..?" it said.

He sounded annoyed: Irritated: Had I woken him up? Like me, he was a night bird.

"Mr. Cleaver? It's Matt Carter. I need to see you: Now."

There was a short hesitation which I noted then..;" I'm still in bed Carter, I'm tired and I've got a busy day ahead of me, so 'Now' is not good for me. Make another call tomorrow. Maybe I can see you then."

I sucked my teeth.

"Tomorrow's not convenient..," I said." Now is: I too have a busy day ahead of me but before I start getting on with it, I need to ask you a few questions: Now, like I mentioned."

I heard a yawn then;" Listen Carter. I'm pleased for you that your day is going to be busy. I assume that means you are making some kind of money but I'm telling you, 'Now' is not convenient for me. Do yourself a favour and call me again tomorrow. I might feel a bit happier about things then: More inclined to listen favourably to your questions if you get my meaning."

"I do Mr. Cleaver, but whether or not I survive my day might depend upon the answers you give me to my questions, if you get my meaning..," I replied.

Cleaver sounded curious and annoyed at the same time.

"You push your luck sometimes you know that, don't you Carter?"

"I do, I do..," I said, cheekily because I knew Cleaver liked a man to have his balls on display at all times:"...but that's why you use me as often as you do: Because I push a little harder than most of the goons you keep in your silk-lined pockets. Thirty minutes then?"

There was a slow growl from the other end.

"Make it an hour. If you turn up one minute before I'll push that luck of yours right back up where it comes out: Understand?"

I told him I understood and ended the call. I wasn't afraid of Cleaver, but I respected his capabilities and he knew that. One hour it would be.

I took my feet off Ronnie's desk, went into his chrome and black en-suite wash-room, stripped off my shoes, suit, shirt and tie and underwear, had a hot shower, shaved, stepped back into the office wrapped in a large white towel, walked over to the long, well-stocked wardrobe Ronnie had hidden behind wooden panelling, chose a good, grey single breasted suit from the assortment I kept there, a pair of highly polished black Oxfords, a simple blue cotton button-down shirt and a slim green woollen tie, dressed, checked myself in the full length door mirror, left the office, locked the door, went back down the stairs and returned to Ronnie who was still sitting at his table, talking to one of the waiters.

I gave him the key and he put it back in his pocket.

He looked me up and down and grinned.

"That's better..," he chuckled." Nothing like a good shave, a shower and good suit to make a man fit to be seen again."

"Thanks..," I said, straightening my tie." I'm off to see Danny Cleaver now. We need to have a talk, or at least I need to hear his answers to a few questions that have been chipping away at my brain since I woke up."

Ronnie pouted.

"Danny Cleaver..? I know I always say it son, but just be careful with that slimy son of a bugger..," he said, frowning." He's dangerous and he's clever. Just because you're one of his favourites right now doesn't mean he won't feed you to the pigs if he thinks you're not useful anymore."

I nodded, unsmiling. I knew Ronnie was right. I was one of Cleaver's 'go to' boys at the moment and because of that he gave me more rope than most, but I was more than aware he could very quickly use that rope to garrotte me in an instant if he suddenly changed his mind, which is why I kept my wits very firmly about me when I was in his presence.

"I will Ronnie..," I said." Trust me; I know to keep one eye on my back when I'm around him but he put some work my way last night and there's a bit of a whiff about it. I just want to find out if it's my cautious imagination or I really have been set up for a fall. If I'm happy enough with what he says, I'm going to be down on the South Coast for the rest of the day: Close to Brighton."

Ronnie smiled.

"Very nice..," he said." I like Brighton; Your Dad and I had a lot of good times there. It holds a lot of memories for me."

He leaned forward and patted my forearm.

"I'll see you later son. You have a good day, but be careful."

It took me exactly fourteen minutes to walk to Danny Cleaver's apartment in Mayfair, which made me two minutes early. Bearing in mind his last words to me, I bought a newspaper and waited before crossing the street and entering the red-brick mansion block, rolling the paper into a tight tube, hoping I would not have to use it as the weapon I had just turned it into.

You never knew with Cleaver: You just never knew.

FOUR

I took the shiny chromed and mirrored lift up to the third floor, walked along a soft blue carpet that absorbed the noise of my footsteps, came to Cleaver's flat and rang the bell.

A tall, brutal looking guy in a tight fitting black suit, six foot three or four, with a chest and shoulders that two men and their mothers could hide behind, opened the door and stood staring down at me, his eyes defying me to be someone important. Whoever he was he didn't look very happy. I didn't recognise him: He must be new: Probably still had the prison tags on his underpants.

I said: "I'm Carter. Mr. Cleaver is expecting me."

He looked at his big, heavy wristwatch and snorted, obviously disappointed that I was exactly on time which meant he couldn't beat the living crap out of me, or at least try to. Taking one last tour of my face and body with his dead eyes, he stood to one side, allowed me to enter, signalled me to stand by an ornate side table, closed the door then ushered me down a long hallway past large, expensively furnished rooms. There were some nice pieces in them and I commended Cleaver on his taste or at least the taste of whoever he gave a few hundred grand to for decorating the place. It was old English aristocracy with a touch of Chelsea here and there: Very nice.

When we got to a door at the end of the hallway, the dead-pan giant put a hand the size of a small dog on my shoulder, grunted for me to wait, opened the door and went inside, closing it behind him. After a few seconds he opened it again and with a flick of his wide head he summoned me into the room.

Cleaver, wearing a dark blue, silk dressing gown over a fine white shirt, holding a long, thick green cigar that cost a lot of money and slowly swirling the rich brown contents of a brandy bowl in his right hand, was sitting facing me on the other side of his much too fancy desk.

It was a classy room with high walls, leather chairs, bookcases, oil paintings and statues on tables, and from a central plaster boss on the ornate, white ceiling hung a five tier chandelier, the facets glittering with rainbow sparks of light. It was all meant to impress, probably intimidate, and it did. It told you the piece of East London gutter garbage sitting opposite me had done a lot of bad things over the years to be able to afford all of this and would do very bad things to anyone that upset him.

Cleaver was fat, but it was the kind of fat that used to be muscle. The kind of fat that said 'I was very handy once and could have crushed your fucking head with one hand but now I don't need to because I have lots of other handy guys who will crush it for me': Hard fat: Earned fat. He was almost bald but not quite and what hair he had left was grey and cut close to his thick head. His mouth fell off a cliff at the corners and his lips were thin: The sort of mouth that didn't laugh much unless it was for chilling effect. He had long, chubby fingers, each one adorned with big rings, and the story it told was of a very successful, very clever, very slippery and very, very dangerous man.

There was a third person in the room, sitting in one of the tall leather wing-back chairs on the right of Cleaver's desk, his bulk making it look small: Another very big man and I knew him. His name was Micky Royal: 'Clubber' as his friends called him, not because of any liking for Drum and Bass sweat-holes but for his penchant for literally clubbing people to a pulp with whatever came to hand, usually his huge hands but sometimes an ashtray, a book, a fire extinguisher, or on one infamous occasion the shiny gold award some unfortunate young man had been presented with two nights before. A young man who had run up a very large bill for Colombia's best with Mr. Cleaver and who had fancied himself untouchable because of who he thought he was. 'Clubber' had demonstrated that he was indeed very touchable to the point where he had needed extensive plastic surgery and a new Bentley due to his pulped body being found in its wrecked remains, down an embankment just off the M25. The world believed he had crashed it whilst driving at excessive speed under the influence of all the cocaine found in his system and that was the story he and his studio continue to let the world believe. The guy is now what I believe they call a 'character' actor and a very successful one too, specialising ironically because of his new look, in gangster parts. Only the man sitting a few feet away smoking another long green cigar, staring at me as though I were a target, knew the truth: And Mr. Cleaver of course; Oh yes: And me.

The door was closed behind me, Cleaver motioned for me to approach, I stepped forward and stopped four feet from the front of the fancy desk.

"Good morning Carter..," Cleaver said. "I'm glad to see you are as punctual as ever."

I smiled back.

"That's the army for you..," I said." All that strict timekeeping: Turns you into a walking clock."

Cleaver took a sip of his brandy.

"I wouldn't know..," he said, icily. "I was never in the bloody army. I preferred giving the orders, not taking them."

He saw me glancing at 'Clubber' and grinned, obviously seeing that his presence was achieving its aim, at least as far as he was concerned. He waved his cigar-hand nonchalantly.

"Don't worry about Micky..," he said. "He just happened to be here on business. He and I were just sharing a good cigar, isn't that right Micky?"

Royal said nothing, just took another long pull on his smoke and continued staring at me.

"I'm not worried about him..," I said looking Cleaver straight in the eye." I'm just wondering why you think he and the Hulk behind me are necessary. I came here to talk, not chuck the furniture around."

Cleaver shrugged his shoulders.

"Look Carter. You know me. I'm a cautious man. I got to the position I enjoy now by being careful. I also got to the position I enjoy now by never trusting people who say they just want to talk. Nobody just wants to talk. What they want is for me to listen to them as they mouth on about something that they feel aggrieved over and in my experience if they don't think you're listening or you don't say what they want to hear that's when they, as you put it, start chucking the furniture around. Now, I don't know what it is you want to talk to me so urgently about but I get the feeling it's not to show me pictures of your little girls' first shit so, as an insurance policy I thought it might be better for all parties if Micky were here. He's very fond of my furniture. Kenny..." and he nodded towards the lump of prime beef standing just behind my left shoulder,"...is always here. He's what you might call my 'housekeeper'. He keeps people from breaking my house."

Only Cleaver laughed.

I looked from one of the two hired hands to the other and they looked at me. The feelings of dislike were mutual.

"You two ought to introduce yourselves..," Cleaver went on." All being good you might be seeing a lot of each other. Kenny's just come out of a three year stretch in Parkhurst."

I was right about the underpants.

"They have to go..," I said, firmly.

'Clubber' made a sound like an echoing drain which I took to be a laugh. I turned to look at him and I could see him measuring me up mentally in the same way a funeral director might measure up a corpse.

"Something funny 'Clubber'..?" I said, returning his cold stare with one of my own.

Out of the corner of my eye I could see Cleaver shake his head.

"Calm down Carter..," he said in what he must have thought was a soothing voice. "No-one needs to leave. Just relax and tell me what's on your mind. Whatever it is you can speak freely in front of these two, all right?"

I broke off my staring contest with Royal and looked over my shoulder at Kenny, turning slightly sideways on to him.

"No," I said. "It's not all right. I came here to talk about a private matter, not to be the filling in a knuckle-drag sandwich. If you want to hear what I have to say, and I think you will, these two primates are going to have to go."

Royal put his cigar down on the edge of Cleaver's desk and pushed himself up onto his gorilla-sized feet with hands that were like sledgehammers. Kenny took a half step closer to me. I held 'Clubbers' stone-carved eyes with a long look that reflected his own contempt right back at him.

"Go away, stupid..," I said, quietly. "Go and beat up a traffic warden or something. I don't want you here."

He pulled his wardrobe sized shoulders back, increasing his height by what seemed like a yard and his threat level to 'Highly intimidating'. He took two steps towards me, flexing his girder-like fingers deliberately slowly.

"What did you say to me Carter..?" he said his voice low and growling like a snarling lion.

I let him come close, keeping a discreet eye on Cell-Block-Kenny over my shoulder.

"I said…"

My right foot smashed into his left shin: He let out a bellow of pain; fell back in surprise: Right foot again, this time hard into his left knee: Another yell: He tumbled forward, head down: Two swift blows into the side of his neck: His head rocks sideways:

Kenny, who had initially hesitated, sprung at me, bellowing like a bull, but a backward kick to his balls staggered him and put him onto his knees, clutching his crotch, his melon-sized head lolling forward onto his shirt front.

I turned back to Royal who was trying to stand but failing, and slapped him hard across the right cheek: His head rocked sideways again exposing his throat: Stiff fingers hit him hard in the trachea, sending him crashing back into the chair clutching at his windpipe, trying to breath through his heavily bruised throat, wheezing like a leaking cat between coughs.

Both men lay sprawled across the floor and the chair, groaning and moaning, nursing their separate injuries, Kenny doubled up in bug-eyed pain, eyes bulging, and 'Clubber' making wheezing noises, blood running down his cheek.

I stood watching them, breathing a little fast but otherwise undisturbed. Neither of them was going to be fighting back anytime within the next half an hour: I could afford to relax.

I turned to Cleaver and smiled, lifting a sarcastic eyebrow.

"That's something else the Army teaches you..," I said. "Not to take shit from gym-bunny bully boys: The bigger they are the easier they fall."

Cleaver finished off his brandy.

"Very nice Carter..," he said, leaning back into his big leather armchair. "The others have told me you're a very handy man to have on the books and now I've seen it for myself: Very nice indeed."

He sounded impressed.

"Get up..!" he snarled at the two men but neither could manage more than a few grunted stumbles.

I held my hand out to Kenny.

"Come on big fella'..," I said. "Looks like all that sitting around in prison has made you flabby."

He took my offered hand and held it tight, using me to pull himself to his unsteady feet. For a second he stared at me, gasping and rubbing his crotch, his grip on my hand still tight. I tensed myself, ready to slap him around a bit more if he decided to try and save a little face in front of Cleaver, but I could tell he was wary of pushing his luck. He nodded, released my fingers and stumbled back a few steps, steadying himself against one of the ornate tables, before leaving the room.

Royal was trying to stand, his right hand still around his injured throat, his left gripping the arm of the chair, supporting his weight on it.

He gasped a couple more times, his eyes fixed on my face and a look of hatred across his features that made angry shapes out of his mouth and eyebrows. His right cheek was livid red where I'd smacked him and the blood had run down onto his shirt collar. 'Clubber' really didn't like me very much right at that moment: I could sense it.

"Take your cigar and wait outside..," Cleaver said, coldly." I'll talk with you later."

Royal shuffled past me headed for the door, with the exact same look of simmering hatred in his eyes that Kenny had given me. I think I might have made two new enemies but they would have to wait in a long line for their chance to even the score. There were a lot more before them.

The door closed. I turned back to Cleaver.

"I like you Carter..," he grinned, getting up and walking over to a table laden with bottles. "I like your style."

He refilled his glass and asked me if I cared to join him in a brandy.

I declined: Everything in moderation.

He pouted, nodding his head in surprise.

"Take a seat..," he said, indicating the chair in front of his desk with his left hand.

I sat in it and he returned to his place behind the desk. He relit his cigar, took a long draw on it, and blew out a stream of blue smoke slowly, the whole time looking at me with a calculating expression.

"Okay..," he said. "Go ahead: talk to me. What's troubling you?"

I took a moment, returning his long stare.

"Last night I had a visitor to my office..," I said.

Cleaver raised an eyebrow.

"Glad to hear you're getting business..," he said.

"It was a woman…"

He smiled slowly.

"Even better: A nice kind of visitor to receive."

"Her name was Leonora Fitzpatrick: A very striking lady."

Cleaver made no reply.

"I believe you may know her..?" I said.

He nodded, tapping ash into a crystal ashtray.

"I know her..," he said, cautiously. " As you say, a striking lady. So: She took my advice and went to see you? Good for her. What did she want?"

"You know what she wanted..," I said:" She wanted me to lean on some punk gigolo that was messing with a friend of hers: Getting her into drugs: Taking her money: The usual thing. She'd already been to see you about it but apparently you'd told her you weren't interested: You recommended me instead."

Cleaver grinned.

"I couldn't think of anyone better qualified..," he said.

I shook my head.

"Don't give me that bullshit..," I said. "Any one of your other goons…," and I flicked my thumb back in the direction of the door,"…could handle that. Most of them wouldn't even have to do anything: Just turn up on the doorstep. That'd be enough to put the fear of God into most people: Easy money for even the most stupid of them: So why me?"

Cleaver looked relaxed, even nonchalant, but my instincts for self-preservation detected a trace of discomfort around the corner of his thin mouth and a flicker in his eye. Just as I thought: There was more to Leonora Fitzpatrick's visit last night than it seemed.

"You're right Carter..," he conceded, spreading his hands in a gesture of 'you-got-me'. "Most of the others could handle a creep like this Dexter with one hand behind their big backs but they wouldn't be subtle about it. They're cannons: Battering rams. No finesse. They'd muss him up, probably even break a few fingers because that's the only way they think, but she didn't want him harmed. Shaken but not stirred to use a well-worn expression."

He grinned again but I stayed stony. He still wasn't telling me the truth.

"You've got guys that do finesse..," I said. "Three or four that I can think of straight away. 'Piccadilly' for instance: Very subtle: Charming even. He specialises in schmooze. The killer in pin stripes they call him. It sounds like he'd be the perfect man for the job. No: I thank you for the compliment but somehow it doesn't wash. I can do 'finesse' if it's needed, but I'm no Cary Grant. Subtlety only goes so far with me then I turn nasty. For some reason you wanted me to be the upfront guy for this job and I want to know why."

Cleaver stubbed out his cigar butt and finished his brandy, obviously stalling for time. When he did speak he looked at me through hooded eyes. There was a lot going on in Cleavers head and it was always cold, calculating and brutal. We were all expendable pieces of meat to him. I was one that asked questions and thought too much, but was tolerated because I was better than most of the morons he kept in his pocket, but even the best of meat can go off and I had a feeling I was getting close to my sell-by date.

"Ok Carter..," he said." I'll tell you why I sent her to you and it's really very simple. She came to see me at my office without an appointment, which I don't appreciate as you know, but when I saw how 'striking' she looked I was prepared to give her a few moments of my time. I'm only a man after all and it was a nice way to pass a few minutes I figured: 'Easy on the eye' kinda' thing. I was also a little curious so, anyway, while she was talking, giving me all her bullshit about this gigolo punk guy, I was looking at her thinking; "Why is this lady here really? Who sent her to me with this cock' story about a drug pushing Yank? How did she get my name and what made her think I could help her in the way she seems to wanting me to help? Is this a set up? She doesn't look like 'police' and she certainly doesn't smell like 'police', but, who knows, she could be." All these thoughts, and a few more that aren't very gentlemanly I'm thinking as she is droning on in the background, giving me the eyes and crossing those nice looking legs of hers, and before she had finished I'd made up my mind that firstly, if what she was spouting was true I wasn't going to get involved in any rich woman's sex and drugs shit, and if what she was spouting wasn't true I wasn't going to fall into whatever trap someone was using her as bait for."

"So you sent her to me so that I could fall into it instead..," I said, with a cold curl to my top lip.

Cleaver shuffled in his seat.

"Yes..," he said with a grin on his well-fed face that needed slapping;" That's pretty much it, but don't go getting all hot under that clean blue collar of yours. I sent her to you because I know you are a smart man Carter. A lot smarter than most of the monkeys I keep around me. You're like me in lots of ways but not as ambitious, which is a good thing for you because if you were I'd have been concerned about my well-being a long time ago and had you removed from my worry list."

He paused and allowed his words to filter into my brain so that I could digest them over a period of weeks at my leisure, pushing them deep into my sub-conscious with a look of cool condescension. I raised an eyebrow in thanks for the compliment and in recognition of the threat.

"So, I said I was sorry to hear about her problems, etcetera, etcetera, but that, contrary to what she may have been told, I couldn't help her as I don't get involved in such things but there might be someone who could and gave her your name and address: For two reasons. One: As a way of getting her out of my office because I was tired of listening to her, and two; as a way of getting the opinion of someone who, like me, was a cynical, intelligent bastard that trusted no-one and could smell bull shit six fields away: You in other words. I put her your way because I figured that if she was part of some attempt to frame me or set me up by either the police or someone I've pissed off mightily at some point, you'd work it out and come stomping back like a bull that just realised it's been marked for slaughter to tell me in no uncertain terms that you didn't appreciate being thrown to the wolves, like you just have. Reason number three as well: I figured that if by some chance she really was telling the truth and actually was looking for someone to lay his experienced hands on her old boy-friend, than you would be just the man she was looking for because it would reflect well on me by my recommending you: Good for future business you see. If you did a good job for her, she would recommend me to all of her equally wealthy acquaintances, all of whom have the sort of embarrassing problems too much money and not enough brains need covering up or 'sending away'. Either way, I win, and, if the third option turns out to be correct, so do you my friend."

He sat back, savouring another long drag on his cigar, his eye still on me, waiting for my reaction. When it didn't come straight off the bat he grinned, nastily.

"Well..?" he asked: "Which option is it: Two or three? Two; She's' full of bullshit and it's a trap waiting for someone to fall into it, or number three: She's a rich woman with very poor, embarrassing taste in men?"

It was my turn to shuffle in my seat and I did so, holding his eyes with my own, sizing the fat bastard up a little longer.

Cleaver was sleazy and heartless and it paid a person in terms of survival to not trust him one slimy inch. Over the past few years of working for him, I'd learnt that particular lesson very well and I intended to maintain my so far unblemished record of staying alive. A consequence of learning that lesson was that, as far as options went with Cleaver, there was always another and right at that moment I was thinking there might well be a fourth: The one I had suspected might be the case all through the conversation with Mrs. Fitzpatrick last night, and that was that Cleaver had been setting me up: Shifting the spotlight away from him and his other activities by feeding the dangerous loner of his pack to the police in exchange for a 'blind eye' or another 'Get out of Jail free' card to add to his pile. I decided to play his game for a while and, if there was a string attached, by pulling on it, see who it led back to.

"Number three..," I said, carefully." There's something about her that makes me think she might have a genuine problem."

Cleaver grinned.

"Oh yeah..? Which part of her was it that convinced you: The eyes, the legs or was it the whole package? None of it worked on me of course because I'm older and wiser but I can see how a young stallion like you might have a few very sensitive buttons that could be pressed by a woman like that."

I brushed aside the patronising bull crap and fixed him with an icy stare that did nothing to remove the big grin that was keeping his heavy cheeks from smothering his mouth but made him realise I wasn't a happy man.

"She said some things that made me think she might be telling the truth."

Cleaver pouted and raised an eyebrow.

"Oh..? Care to share what those things might be..?" he said, rolling the fat cigar between his equally fat fingers.

I shook my head.

"No, not really..," I replied: "It wasn't so much what she said but the way she said it, and the way she seemed to be affected by what she was telling me. Also by the fact that she came to see me so quickly after you'd given her my name. If she'd been 'police' or working with them, she would probably have waited a day or so in order for me to be checked out and see whether or not I'm worth wasting time on, but she didn't. She walked up my broken old stairs in the middle of the night and waited for me to stumble back to the office, when she could have just waited until the morning. That told me she must have been pretty desperate to have someone listen to her and hopefully help her out."

Cleaver nodded, bringing the cigar to his lips but not smoking it.

"Good point..," he said, rolling the thought around in his ice-box of a head just like he'd done with the cigar, probably working out whether or not I was taking the bait. "And what's your conclusion then: Is she worth taking a punt on? Is she worth the risk?"

"What risk: That she's a copper or that someone is setting me up?"

Again Cleaver pouted.

"Or... that this nasty piece of Yank shit doesn't turn out to be a bit handy himself and gives as good as you're prepared to try and make him take?"

"Perhaps all three, but I needed to try and eliminate one of the possibilities which is why I came to see you this morning."

He kept his expression low key.

"Oh yes? And which of those possibilities might you have been hoping to eliminate? Which one is it you think I might be linked to: The 'someone-setting-you-up' option?"

I pouted and spread my hands.

"We all play our parts in a very funny game..," I said, non committaly, trying to give an impression of nonchalance:" Some of us last a bit longer in it if we think a few moves ahead so you'll forgive me if I weigh up my options."

He nodded but I could tell there was anger in his eyes.

"You didn't answer my question..," he said slowly: "So I'll make it easier to understand. Do you think I might have sent her to you to set you up?"

I shrugged.

"I like to think not. I like to think that I have been, and still am, of use to you and that to have me banged up and my skills put out of your reach would be a very unwise and stupid thing to do and as I don't believe you are either of those things it is unlikely that you would be foolish enough to contemplate that path but, like I said, it pays to think a few steps ahead and I just wanted to assure myself that, should I decide to come to the lovely ladies rescue, I wasn't walking into a carefully laid ambush."

Cleaver said nothing: he just stared at me in that hard, cold, disconcerting way we who worked for him had come to know and love, deciding whether or not to smile at my cheeky impertinence or have me sliced into six pieces and dropped in the river off the back of a sewage barge.

My luck held and a reluctant smile crept slowly onto his lips but stopped short of an actual grin.

"You are a very lucky little bastard..," he said, pointing a finger at me in time with his words, all the while his gimlet eyes boring into me. "Consider yourself fortunate that I still have a need for your talents, otherwise I might have fed you to the fishes a long while back. There's not many people I'd let get away with what you have just implied, but for the moment you are one of them. Believe me though, that can change very quickly so watch what you say to me in the future. I like you Carter. You're different. You have class and I like class but it don't mean you're immune from my wrath: Believe me or believe me not: If I had wanted you fitted up and handed over to the thin blue line, you'd have been wearing one of Her Majesty's t-shirts and staring out of a stripy window long before now, got that? The reason you are not is that right at this moment in time you are an asset to me in my enterprises, but, like I said, things can change as quick as you can throw a punch so don't come it, understand?"

He took a pull on his cigar and I took the opportunity to apologise, opening my hands in a conciliatory gesture.

"Like I said Mr. Cleaver: You stay alive in this game by thinking a few steps ahead but you also stay breathing by watching your back and that's all I'm doing: Checking the clearing before I cross it. I hope I haven't caused you any undue offence."

I could be a silver-tongued charmer when the occasion called for it and sitting opposite a snarling grizzly you've just prodded with a stick was one of those times. There are times you run forward and there are times you take a tactical step back and I decided that dropping the stick and stepping back was probably the best idea right now.

He seemed placated but there was a simmering look in his eye that said that he trusted me about as much as I trusted him which was as far as my little girl could throw a steam train.

"Well..?" he asked, puffing on his Havana and looking at me with disdainful curiosity:" Are you going to help her out or not: What's the decision?"

I pouted, rubbing my bruised chin carefully.

"I'm still not sure..," I replied." Now I know we're still buddies, the chances are I probably will but there's still a smell about it that's making my nose wrinkle. Something's not right and I need to think about it."

Cleaver stubbed out the cigar in a big crystal ashtray and leaned back again into his chair.

"Your choice..," he said, shrugging his big shoulders." If it was me I'd take a chance but you're the guy that has to face the heat."

I smiled and nodded at his wise words. That was about as close as he would ever come to friendly advice but I appreciated his attempt at democracy. He got out another cigar and reached for the clippers.

"Now: Are you finished crippling my men and insulting my character, or was there something else?"

I cleared my throat, not because I was nervous but because the smoke from the first cigar was settling around the level of my nose by now.

"Well, now that you've told me how much you love me..," I said, with a lop-sided smile on my face to show I was being humorous:" Perhaps you can pay me the money you owe me from that last little problem I sorted out for you?"

He didn't pause from sucking on his new cigar, sending puffs of fresh, blue smoke up into the air, looking at me through the haze, frowning.

"What 'problem' was that then..?" he said between puffs.

"The politician's son that used his Daddy's credit to play on your tables: You asked me to bring his debt level down dramatically."

He smiled and looked at the glowing end of his second Havana.

"Oh yes: Young Hubert. A nice lad: His dad doe's me a few favours every now and again, because of which I allow the pretty little shit a little slack when he brings his floppy-haired friends to the club, but he took a liberty with my generosity and played on his daddy's position in the Cabinet to run up a bill he couldn't, or wouldn't pay. He needed a lesson in the realities of the world…"

"Well he got one and you got your bills paid, so now, in the spirit of our new found respect and friendship, I'm asking that I get my own bill paid."

Cleaver took a long, thoughtful drag, blew a column of smoke towards the ceiling and chuckled, looking at me sideways.

"You've got balls Carter. I'll give you that."

"I've also got bills..," I replied:"...and they need paying."

He nodded, sagely.

"Ok..." he said, slowly, savouring his smoke:" I understand. A man of your sartorial elegance and capacity for drink: You have tailors to pay and bar tabs to level. Come and see me in the morning and I'll have it ready for you."

"No..," I said, putting a hint of menace into the word but not enough to introduce me to a bullet in the skull. "The money was due a week ago. I'd like it now if you don't mind."

Cleaver stopped halfway through taking another pull on his cigar and looked at me with a lingering expression of..." I beg your fucking pardon..?" written all over his fat face.

"What if I do mind..?" he breathed, his head turned slightly towards me, the cigar held a few inches from his shiny lips. His eyes were narrow and reminded me, as they always did, of the crocodiles I used to come across in Belize: Full of primeval menace and cunning: Looking for a weakness: A moment of hesitation, assessing what might happen if and when they suddenly lunged.

I said nothing, just returned his glare, keeping my expression as neutral as I could; staring down the tiger, or crocodile if I was still going with that analogy.

There was a long moment of mutual psyching out before Cleaver grinned and swivelled back around towards me, placing both hands on the edge of the desk.

"You like to push it don't you Carter and I admire that. As I said, you have balls and that's what a man needs to get by in this world but don't forget, balls are no good to you if they're cut off and hanging around my neck with all the others I've accumulated over the years, are they..?" he said, half-joking, half threatening. In my experience his jokes could be funny but his threats never were.

"Not a sight I'd like to see Mr. Cleaver..." I said with a placating smile on my face: "...and I'll keep that image in my mind at all times but I would still like to have my money now...if you please."

His right hand disappeared beneath the edge of the desk and I heard a drawer open. His eyes never left mine as he reached inside and in the few seconds he took to locate whatever it was his fingers were searching for, my heart danced a silent tango in my tightening chest but I kept my face still and returned the stare, half expecting his hand to reappear with a big shiny pistol clenched in it, but instead he produced a large brown, bulging envelope, dropping it heavily onto the desktop.

He opened one end and pulled three wads of cash out, laying them in a line in front of him.

"You can keep those fucking big balls for another few days Carter..," he said, a laugh in his voice." You might need them if you decide to be Mrs. Fitzpatrick's knight in shining bloody armour."

He pushed one of the paper bound wads towards me.

"There's a grand more than I owe you there. Take it: You did a nice, discreet job. Everyone was mutually happy with the result, especially Hubert who assures me the week he spent in hospital gave him time to contemplate the errors of his somewhat spoilt thinking. Nasty things skiing accidents, wouldn't you say Carter?"

I reached forward and pulled the bundle of crisp new notes towards me.

"Very nasty..." I said:"...but quite common at this time of year amongst a certain set Mr. Cleaver. Luckily for him it was a clean break. He's young. He'll heal quickly."

"Just what his father said..." Cleaver smiled, returning his attention to smoking his cigar.

I put the money into an inside pocket and stood up.

"Thank you..," I said." I'll send you a receipt in the morning."

Cleaver chuckled.

"Fuck off Carter before I decide a pair of silver balls would go well with my tie pin..," he said.

I left, nodding to the two broken giants, half sitting, half crouching in corridor chairs, nursing their wounds. They didn't smile back but I didn't care. Those wounds were self-inflicted as far as I was concerned.

Outside, away from the over-warm heat of Carter's luxury slaughter house, the air was cold and I pulled my coat tighter around me as I walked, headed back towards Soho.

I walked slowly and took the long way because I needed to think. Firstly about Cleaver: I still wasn't totally convinced he hadn't actually set me up for a deliberate fall. Despite what he said, he wasn't above that kind of thing as a few of his previous associates had found out, so that meant I had to keep one eye on anything coming from that direction. I was touched though by the way he felt about me: Touched in the same way it feels when you're touched by a scorpion.

Secondly about Mrs. Fitzpatrick: Where had she gone after leaving me? Not the hotel obviously. Why, if she even half believed I might get in touch with her, would she give me a false address? It didn't make immediate sense. Maybe if I'd said straight out that I'd help her she would have gone there to wait for my call but that didn't work because according to the receptionist she hadn't even made a reservation. Ok, the prices that place charged probably meant there would always be a room or two available at short notice but why not just make one in the first place, even if you were never going to use it? I turned it over in my mind: Perhaps she had never intended to go there. Perhaps she had hoped that I would wake up, decide to just go straight to Sussex and have a quiet word or two with the creepy gigolo for a few hours first and then come back to tell her what the conclusion was, but by the time I'd done so she'd have vanished, never to be found by me. That began to make a kind of twisted sense. By coming to see me so late, it would have been almost certain that no-one would had seen her arrive and the only person that would have known about her visit at all would have been Cleaver. So, if it had all gone wrong and I or Rasputin had ended up dead it was a pretty sure thing that he wasn't going to connect himself with her so he'd deny he had ever seen her, and she could say the same about me. She could say she had never met me and would have no idea what the police were talking about. Even if I'd survived and come looking for her she wouldn't have been there at the hotel so I would have been left hanging in the breeze, way out on a limb, with no-one to point a finger at, the blood of an American drug dealer, if that's what he was, on my knuckles. Did she even exist; was she really called Mrs. Fitzpatrick?

As I reached the corner of Piccadilly and Regent Street, I smiled despite the chill wind in my face. This lady was potentially a real piece of work. Not only was she a picture to behold she was a lot more cunning than I had thought. It began to look like she had she come up with the perfect way to get her revenge on whoever this Dexter guy was and have no connection with it at all as far as the world was concerned.

This was quite a dance I might be getting myself involved in: A deadly dance that might end with me left standing alone in the spotlight, blood all over my tuxedo, my partner waltzed off into the shadows.

I had to be careful. I don't like dancing, especially to music I can't hear.

FIVE

'Tug' Bateman was sitting in his little glass office, tucked away at the rear of his back street garage.

He had a broad face, sandy hair and the build of a man used to throwing engines around.

I'd known 'Tug' for a long time: ever since my army days. He'd been a Mechanic in the R.E.M.E and knew everything about every kind of engine but absolutely nothing about people. Consequently he'd had a lot of problems in his life and had hidden himself away in the shadows of the city in a small garage where he could fix cars and meet as few of them as possible. Anyone that came in through his sliding doors just wanted their cars fixed: Nothing else. They paid and left: simple as that.

He was wearing his usual filthy old boiler suit and reading a well-thumbed auto' magazine when I walked in and looked up, a frown on his big face, wondering who had come to disturb his peace, but when he saw it was me he grinned.

"Hello Carter..," he said, putting the magazine down and rising to his feet.

As I got closer he frowned again but kept the grin.

"Been in the wars again, I see..," he said, indicating my damaged face with a nod of his tousled head.

I rubbed my cheek and jaw subconsciously.

"Not really a war 'Tug'..," I said." More of a minor skirmish really."

He snorted, both hands deep in the pockets of his overalls.

"Nothing changes with you SF boys, eh..?" he said. "Always walking into trouble..."

"I must have 'punch me' tattooed on my forehead I suppose..," I chuckled back at him.

He laughed and there was a seconds silence before he asked what is was he could do for me. I asked if he had any cars for sale.

He pouted his lips and thought for a moment.

"For your-self..?" he asked.

I nodded.

"Broken the last one I sold you then, I take it..?" he asked, wearily.

I nodded again. He'd sold me three cars over the past year and each one had ended up U.S. or 'Un-serviceable' to use the army jargon, which considering that 'Tug' was probably the best mechanic in the city and even he couldn't put them back together, meant that they were definitely broken.

He sighed, a pained look on his face. 'Tug' loved cars and it was a genuine sorrow for him to see them ill-used but he knew what I did for a living and he knew the way I sometimes needed to operate so had come to accept, reluctantly, that anything I took from him was either going to come back in pieces or not come back at all.

"I've got something..," he said, warily as though uncertain he should be telling me about it because he knew he would probably be sentencing it to death. "Ten years old but virtually new: The owner needed money fast and sold it to me for half of what it should have been just to get some cash in his pocket. It's a coupe: Fast, only eight thousand miles on the clock. I've had a good look at it and made a few adjustments so that it runs even better than it should."

I didn't doubt it but what it was made no odds to me. I just needed a car. How fast it went was irrelevant.

"Is it ready to go..?" I asked.

He nodded.

"Licensed for another three months: MOT'd for another six: The log book is solid and the tyres are good. 'Just needs fuel."

"How much...?"

"Cash I assume..," he said.

I took Cleaver's envelope from my coat pocket and he saw the bulging sides.

"Nineteen hundred...," he said after a moments' thought.

I smiled. 'Tug' and I went back a long way and I knew he wasn't a greedy man. I trusted him to ask for a fair price and I also trusted him when he said he'd made sure it was working well. If that's what he said he wanted then it was worth it and was probably not far off what he'd paid for it originally. Like I said, he wasn't a greedy man.

I counted out his money and handed him the notes.

"I'll need a receipt..," "I said.

"Of course..," he replied, reaching into the drawer of his battered, oil-stained old desk to put the money away. "I'll stick a few gallons in the tank for you too. Are you going far?"

I put the still bulging envelope back inside my coat.

"Not sure..," I said, casually." I haven't decided."

He knew not to ask too many questions and, after he'd written the receipt and given it to me, told me to wait out the front and he'd bring the car around.

Minutes later he drove around the corner in a gleaming black Ford Puma: A nice little car that looked like it wanted to race. I smiled a little as he pulled up a few feet from me and clambered out. It shone nicely which was a pity: Most of the cars I drove ended up dirty and bent if not actually folded in half. This one was pretty. It would have been like taking a puppy and throwing it into a bear pit but then a car was a car as far as I was concerned: There and back: That was all I wanted it to get me, and out of trouble if that was needed.

I watched him fill the tank with fuel from a dented jerry can and took the keys from him when he'd finished.

"There you go..." he said. "Try not to break this one, eh? She's a sweet little thing...If you do bring her back, it'd be nice if it was in one piece and in a condition I could work with, not in need of a decent burial like the others."

I laughed which made my jaw sting, unaccustomed as it was to such a thing, and slid into the sporty driver's seat, adjusting the leg length to accommodate my long shanks. It was small inside and basic but sporty and had a good feel to it. Everything looked functional and racy: Nice old-fashioned white analogue dials: I liked it.

I started the engine and drove away, the note from the exhaust sounding throaty and eager. The smile stayed on my face as I pulled out into the street and began to weave around the traffic that seemed to tower over me. I wasn't going in any particular direction to begin with so just went with the flow, using the time to not only get used to the car but to think about my next move as far as the Fitzpatrick woman was concerned.

What might have happened if I'd taken the work on face value and just gone straight down to Sussex? Would I have walked straight into something as I suspected? What would have been waiting for me when I got down there? A trap: Set by who: Cleaver: The police: Mrs. Fitzpatrick: Maybe a combination of any or all of them?

It began to rain and I decided to stop driving in circles. I needed somewhere to go: Somewhere to think: Back to my office? It seemed like an idea and I made a right turn at the next lights but changed my mind before I got to the next junction. Images of the fragrant Mrs. Fitzpatrick kept filling my mind. Images of her talking, crossing her legs, smoking; of her walking out of my office but most of all just images of her looking at me, watching me with those clear, intelligent, cunning eyes, assessing my reactions to what she was telling me. I hadn't noticed it all too clearly in the whisky haze of last night but now I had a booze-free head, I could recall a lot more things and the more I went over what she had said and the way she had said it, the more I became convinced there was a lot more to this than meets the eye.

She wasn't telling me the truth, or if she was then it was only half the truth. The whole thing was very probably an act and she was a very good actress, but why and on whose behalf?

Suddenly, like a lightning bolt from the dark clouds above the roof of the car, something else occurred to me and I pulled over into a space between two vans and turned off the engine, wanting to give myself time to decide what I wanted to do about it.

What had just occurred to me, and I didn't like myself for admitting to it, was that I was curious. I was actually intrigued and I hadn't been either of those damned things for years.

I knew I was stupid to even think of acting upon such feelings: Stupid for contemplating for one second walking into a trap that all my instincts were screaming at me not to set off, but a stronger feeling was at play in my head now and it was telling me that if I didn't at least take a peek at what this might be all about I'd be turning it over in my mind for ever, letting it eat into my brain like some parasite until it drove me mad. It was like all the times in the past when I'd stood in front of a building that everyone knew was booby-trapped and could bring only death, but I still went into: Something takes over your mind and makes you enter; makes you creep up to that door at the end of the spooky corridor and open it up, knowing full well that something very bad could happen if you do.

I was beginning to feel angry now. I was almost all the way sure I was being set up: I could feel it in my aching, cynical bones and a disbelieving voice was yelling at me that there was a very big chance what I was about to do could blow up in my face, leaving me high, dry and suckered but I knew why I was doing it.

I was doing it because I didn't like that someone had decided that I was expendable: That I was stupid enough to fall like a heap of bricks for a beautiful woman who fluttered her eye lashes at me as she wove some lolly-tongued story designed to make me dance like a love sick puppet on the end of her strings. I was doing it because I wanted to find out if she was the one pulling those strings or if it was someone else doing it and, if it was, who that someone else was and why they wanted me to take the punch.

I started the car up again and pulled out into the heavy traffic, turning left again at the junction, nosing the car in the direction of Sussex.

SIX

A few hours later I stopped the car at the start of a single track, gravel road that led about thirty yards up to a set of high iron gates, behind which was a drive that curved to the right around a copse of mature trees to a house I couldn't see.

I walked carefully up to the gates, looking around for any cameras that might be watching me, but saw none and pushed on the ironwork, the gates swinging apart soundlessly on well-oiled hinges.

I pushed them open enough for me to drive through, parked the car beneath the thick, heavy branches of an old oak tree a few yards further on, tucking it off the drive itself so it couldn't be seen too easily, closed the gates and walked cautiously up the gravel, staying alert.

I saw the house when I rounded the trees: A large, elegant Georgian affair: Five windows at the top, four on the bottom with a columned door in the middle, sitting on a slight rise about two hundred yards ahead. It was a nice house: Very English and quietly self-assured, no doubt just like whoever owned it no doubt.

To my right were thick rhododendron bushes, rain-loaded cedars and oaks dotted casually around. It was all a very pretty picture but the only thing I was looking out for was the first signs of a steel trap slamming down on me so it was lost on me.

A small path ran off the driveway into the trees a few yards ahead, and I decided to walk along it, keeping just inside the tree-line, hoping it might lead to a side door or a back way into the house, but instead it led me to a small clearing were the un-cut grass was thick and glistened with the recent rain. It also led me to a sight that made me step back into the bushes and lean against a tree, watching.

A young woman, about twenty five, maybe older, but definitely in her mid-twenties, wearing a silky, pale grey, full length evening dress that clung to her very nicely, was dancing beneath one of the larger trees, slowly turning and gliding around, arms spread out, eyes closed, moving in time to some tune in her head. She looked a bit unsteady in her high heels but it didn't seem to be worrying her as she twirled about, her eyes closed, oblivious of the world, stumbling every now and then but recovering without any change of expression.

Her hair was short-blonde and had been well cut by someone who knew what they were doing and probably charged accordingly, but now the rain had hit it and it was wet and stringy, clinging to her neck and cheeks. She had a long, dark grey evening coat over her dress and a small, pale grey clutch bag hanging from her left wrist which swung from side to side as she flung her thin arms out and around like the thin branches of a young sapling. A string of pearls circled her throat and there was a diamond bracelet dangling and sparkling arrogantly from her right wrist. She looked what she obviously was: A delicate, spoiled, drunk, rich girl.

For another minute I carried on watching her from the shadow of the tree, then stepped into the clearing, picking up a twig and deliberately snapping it as I moved forward.

Instantly, her eyes flew open and she stopped in mid-swirl, her arms falling limply to her sides; her bag slipping off her wrist and into the grass, staring at me with a bemused expression on her face as I came closer, as if not too sure of what to make of me or my sudden appearance, then her features relaxed and she leaned back against the trunk of the tree she'd been dancing beneath and regarded me with dull, drunk, bored eyes.

"Hallo..," she said in a reedy, tired, emotionless voice. "Who are you: One of Marcus's friends?"

I didn't tell her my name.

"Do you like dancing under trees in the rain…?" I asked.

She laughed, shrilly.

"Yes…" she shrieked, flinging her arms out. "I love it! I love dancing in the rain. It's so nice…!"

She hugged herself and rocked from side to side, biting her bottom lip at the thought of how much fun it was.

"I used to dance in the rain a lot..," she went on, her voice a little more melancholy suddenly, as if my question had awoken a memory;" We used to dance out here in the grass without any music. We liked dancing without music. We made our own music, in our heads. It was fun!"

"We..? Whose 'we,'" I asked.

She stopped rocking and looked at me from under her lashes, the smile wiped from her face. I was surprised by the sudden turn of mood but kept the casual smile on my lips.

"All of us..," she hissed through gritted teeth. "Everyone that used to love me…"

She sounded like she was talking about people from a long time ago.

"Who would that be then: Brothers: Sisters?"

She shook her head.

"I don't have any brothers or sisters."

"Parents..?"

She stared at me.

"You're very nosey..," she said, haughtily, changing the subject. "It's none of your business who used to love me."

I shrugged.

"Maybe…," I said, casually:" I was just curious, that's all."

She took a deep breath as if trying to clear her head and continued staring at me as if just realising for the first time that I was really there.

"Curious? What about..?"

"About why you're not happy…"

She frowned and I could see I was lowering her mood.

"What makes you think I'm not happy?"

I shrugged again.

"Just a feeling..," I said. "Forget it. It's not important. You keep dancing. It looks good."

She stared into my face for a few more seconds, taking me in: Assessing what I'd just said through the filter of drink, then smiled, awkwardly.

"Who are you..?" she asked again. "You never told me. Are you the man I'm supposed to meet? Are you one of..?"

"Marcus's friends..? You could say that. I was told he might be here today."

She pushed herself away from her the tree trunk.

"Well: Whoever you are, you have a lot of cheek sneaking up on me like that and asking me if I'm happy. That's no-body's business but mine..," she repeated, petulantly.

Her voice had become thick, her enunciation was difficult to understand and I could see she was finding it hard to stay awake. Whatever energy she'd had was used up by the dancing and now that she'd stopped, the drink was settling back around her brain like a heavy blanket. Her head sank onto her chest and she yanked it up with a jerk.

"I'm tired..," she said, weakly." I think I need to sleep."

"I can see that..," I said as charmingly as I could, walking a few steps through the long grass towards her. I wanted to keep her talking a while longer because I had a pretty good idea of who she was. I also had a pretty good idea that if I didn't keep her talking she'd probably just curl up in the grass and start snoring:" Let me take you up to the house. You can sleep there."

She nodded.

As I came closer to her I stepped on the bag that had been lost in the tall grass, stooped down and picked it up. There were a set of initials set into one of the corners that confirmed to me who she was: C.D.

"My names' Carter by the way..," I said, handing her the slightly damp bag, noticing that it seemed a little heavy. In my experience, women's evening bags were usually pretty light. They never seemed to have much in them to make them heavy, but hers did.

She snatched it impatiently from me before I had a chance to try and feel what might be weighing it down and looked at me, jerking her head up for the second time. I was losing her.

"Well Mr. Carter..," she sniffed; the ghost of a smile on her lips:" I have to suppose that it is nice to meet you but that will have to remain to be seen."

I gave her one of my most disarming grins.

"It is nice to meet me..," I assured her. "I'm a very nice man. You'll like me. I take it you are Charlotte Dexter?"

She frowned and tilted her head to one side as she looked at me.

"Yes..," she said, uncertainly. "I am. How did you know that?"

I pointed to the initials on the bag she was clutching.

"Your initials, the fact that you asked if I was one of Marcus's friends and the fact that you are dancing in the garden of Marcus Dexter's house. I put all the clues together and came up with what appears to be the right answer."

"Very clever..," she said, vacantly, her head wobbling slightly. She waved her free hand, the one with the diamond bracelet decorating it, pointing a finger roughly in my direction. "You...are a very clever man Mr. Carver."

"Carter..," I corrected, nicely:"...and thank you," I said, giving a modest pout as if humbly acknowledging the truth. "Some might say that."

She brushed the sleeves of her coat distractedly as if trying to remove imaginary dirt.

"Did you come here to find my husband..?" she said.

I nodded.

"Yes. Like I said, someone asked me to come here and meet Mister Dexter, but ringing the door-bell didn't work so I was coming around the side to see if there was anyone in the back and came across you dancing."

"There is no-one in..," she said, thickly.

"Ok..," I replied. "So when do you think Marcus is going to come home?"

She shrugged.

"I have no idea..," she said and she sounded as though she really didn't care:" He comes and goes as he pleases."

She lapsed back into silence and her head drooped. I could see she was about to fall over.

"I have an idea..," I said quickly. "How about we get you inside the house like we originally said?"

She looked up, her eyes blank, and smiled stupidly.

"I think that's a very, very good idea. Let's go inside and have a drink."

I wasn't too sure about the 'drink' part of the idea but if it got me invited inside the house instead of the other way, it was worth agreeing to.

"Ok: sure..," I grinned. "My car is down by the gate though. Shall I go and get it first?"

I didn't want her falling down or falling asleep on me but I also didn't want Dexter being forewarned about me being here so I needed to get the car hidden away somewhere.

She frowned slightly then waved a hand magisterially around, indicating the house in a vague kind of gesture.

"If you want to..," she said. "Bring it up to the house and leave it at the back. I'll wait for you there."

I wasn't sure about her walking up to the house on her own without support of some kind so suggested it might be better if she waited where she was until I came back for her. Thankfully she agreed and leaned back against the tree she'd been dancing around, her eyes closing. I hurried back down the path, jumped into the car and drove it up to the house, parking it at the back beside what had been, or maybe still were, the stables.

When I got back to the clearing Charlotte was still there, leaning against the tree as before and singing softly to herself. She stopped as I appeared and watched me through bleary eyes as I approached. Her bag had fallen off her wrist again and lay at her feet. I picked it up and handed it back, noticing again how heavy it was, taking the opportunity provided to me by Mr. Martini and his friend Olive to have a little fondle of the silk and raised my eyebrow a little at the outline of what felt like a small handgun. Could this be the gun Mrs. Fitzpatrick had told me she carried for protection against Dexter? More than likely but I didn't have the chance to check it out because she snatched the bag away from me again and tucked it under her arm, a haughty look on her face. I smiled back at her, graciously, and stepped back, suddenly very interested in finding out more.

My experience was telling me it had almost definitely been a gun, but my instincts were telling me to be very cautious. A loaded weapon in the unsteady hands of an unsteady woman could be a lethal combination and I needed it to stay in the bag, not be pointed at my face.

I indicated the house through the trees.

"Shall we..?" I said.

We began to walk, with me clearing any branches and obstacles from her path as she stumbled towards the back of the building. She was wearing a rich, heavy perfume that probably cost more than it should but I didn't like it. It was too heavy for my taste but, because I was so close that I could catch her just in case she fell over, there was a lot of it and I was forced to breathe it in.

It took longer than I wanted to get to the back of the house and I was getting a little impatient with her, not to mention a little anxious in case Dexter came back during the stumble-walk and found me with his wife. I wanted our meeting to be on my terms not his.

When we finally reached one of the three doors at the rear she fumbled around in her bag and brought out a small bunch of keys, took too long trying to figure out which was the right one, eventually found it, missed the keyhole a couple of times, discovered it by luck more than application, threw the door open and then we were inside, standing in a long, dark passage that obviously connected all of the working rooms at the back of the house.

"There should be a light switch somewhere on this side of the wall..," she mumbled. "Find it will you?"

I left her leaning against the door, found the switch, clicked it on, and a row of lamps on cold, undecorated white walls flooded the stone-floored hallway with light, showing that it led off to our left and right in a straight line to both wings of the house. We went right, past a scullery and a utility room, then took a left into another corridor that led through to what I assumed was the front reception hall: A big, well-furnished space with a large chandelier hanging from a tall ceiling, good oil-paintings on all the walls and a black and white tiled floor. Stairs led up to the next floor but Charlotte walked straight across the hall, through a half-opened set of double doors to the right and into a comfortable, good-sized room with high ceilings, more paintings, expensive old furniture, lots of books and a huge fireplace. I was impressed.

Moving across the carpet with the ease of a woman born to such things, she made straight for a tall cabinet filled with bottles of drink, stopping just before she reached it and flopped down carelessly into a silk-faced wing-back chair.

"Fix us both a drink would you Mr. Clever..?" she said, dreamily, gesturing loosely at the drinks cabinet.

"Carter..," I reminded her, crossing the room.

She smiled.

"Of course: Mr. Clever-Carter..," she giggled.

I put together a nice looking 12 year old single malt whiskey and soda for myself, poured a half tumbler full of ginger ale for her, smeared the rim with whiskey so that she'd smell it and think she was drinking alcohol, and carried it to her. I needed her as compos mentis as I could if I was going to get any pre-meeting intelligence from her on Marcus Dexter.

She took it from me without any thanks and threw half of the drink straight down her throat, instantly frowned and looked into the glass quizzically.

"This tastes odd..," she said, turning her puzzled gaze up to me.

I grinned, apologetically.

"Sorry: 'Probably put a bit too much ginger ale in it. I'm not a ginger ale man myself so I never know how much is too much."

She looked pained and took another sip.

"Well this is too much..," she huffed, but kept sipping:" Light me a cigarette...," she snapped, contemplating her wet shoes.

"I could..," I said, evenly:"...but don't you think you ought to be getting out of those wet clothes? You'll catch a cold sitting around in..."

"It doesn't matter..," she said, airily." I couldn't care less what I catch. A cold or anything else: I don't care about being wet. What I do care about is having a cigarette."

I took a long, French looking cigarette from a silver box that was beside the drinks cabinet and gave it to her, lighting it with a heavy glass lighter that stood beside the box.

"All right now..?" I asked.

She took a long drag on the gold-banded cigarette but said nothing, just slumped further down in her chair and sighed heavily.

"Would you like another drink..?" I asked.

She nodded and held up the empty tumbler. This time I put in a small measure of the mildest whiskey I could find and then the ginger ale. I needed her awake but I also needed her talking and she looked as though she might be about to start falling asleep. I gave her the drink, taking a small sip of my own.

"There's less ginger in it this time..," I said.

She snorted.

"It still tastes strange but that's all right. It doesn't matter. Nothing matters. Nothing at all...Nothing matters one little bit."

She sounded tired and angry. I pulled a big chair closer and sat in it, facing her. I could see her eyes were drooping and I knew I didn't have long to question her before she melted away.

"Tell me something Mrs. Dexter..."

"Charlotte..," she sighed, a thin smile on her face. "Call me Charlotte. I don't like being called 'Mrs. Dexter'."

"Ok Charlotte...'" I continued. "Why do you have a gun in your bag?"

She looked at me.

"I beg your pardon..?" she said, suspiciously.

"I asked you why you have a gun in your bag."

For a moment she made no reply, just stared at me with half-closed, calculating eyes, her expression blank then she took a deep breath inwards.

"What makes you think I have a gun in my bag..?" she drawled.

"I felt it when I picked up back in the clearing..," I said as casually as I could.

Again she didn't reply straight away.

"What kind of question is that to ask a lady..?" she said.

"The kind of question you ask when you find a gun in her bag..," I replied keeping my eyes fixed on hers.

She took another drink of her ginger ale, stalling for time.

"Do you have to have a gun in your bag Charlotte..?" I asked, breaking the silence and forcing the issue. "Are you frightened of something, or should I say 'someone'?"

She smiled slowly as if realising something for the first time, and her eyes took on a glint of understanding.

"You are a very strange man Mr. Clever-Carter..," she began to say, getting my name wrong again, but I didn't bother correcting her, deciding instead to cut across her.

"Is it a person you're afraid of or an occasion..?" I said:" Maybe both: Maybe someone doing something to you on an occasion?"

She kept smiling but it was a cunning smile: a smile of dawning perception.

"I don't think you're a friend of Marcus at all Mr. Carter..," she said, contemplating me over the rim of her almost empty tumbler.

I ignored her.

"Is that why you keep a gun with you Charlotte: In case an occasion arises where someone might try to harm you..?" I continued.

"None of Marcus's friends are like you..," she said, as though I hadn't spoken. "You are different. You have..."

She hesitated.

"...balls!" she finished, happy with her choice of word, almost launching it at me. "My husband's friends are tough, or like to think they are, but none of them have any balls. They just roll over and do whatever it is he tells them to do: They never ask any questions. You ask questions and very straight ones too. That's interesting."

She emptied her glass and dropped it onto the carpet, nodding approvingly at what she had just said.

"I think I might like you Mr. Clever-Carter..," she went on, her smile wider now, her eyes sparkling: Still vacant but sparkling. I smiled back.

"I'm glad you do..," I said.

"Why are you glad I might like you..?" she asked. "You don't know me."

"Because right now you are the one with the gun in your bag and if you didn't like me you might just decide to point it at me."

She laughed, awkwardly, pointing a limp finger in my direction.

"That's another clever answer Mr. Carter. You make me laugh: None of Marcus's 'friends' make me laugh at all. In fact they make me angry..," she said.

"And just a little bit frightened..?" I pushed.

She pouted and sat up clumsily, one shoe slipping off her heel in the process and dangling in mid-air.

"Just a little bit..," she agreed. "But not as much as..."

Her voice trailed away and her head slumped back into the chair. I sighed. She was on the wobbly edge of passing out now. Was it worth pursuing with the questions: Would her answers make any sense? I decided they might or at the very least whatever she said would be based on truth.

"So would I be right in saying you carry the gun for your own protection or would it also be because you might decide to use it for a specific reason one day?"

It took a moment but she answered, albeit with her eyes closed.

"You are a very percefftive..," she slurred. "PerCEPtive... man Mr. Clever-Carter...," she corrected. "You obviously do a lot of thinking, which is something none of my husband's friends do: Ever. They never think. They just let him do all the thinking then..."

She stopped in mid-sentence.

"'Then' what Charlotte: What do they do?"

"They go off and do whatever it is they think he wants them to do..," she breathed. I was losing her. Her brain was closing down but in that limbo state there still might be the chance of getting a revealing, unguarded answer to a direct question.

"Charlotte? Listen to me: Do you keep the gun to protect yourself or because you want to use it to shoot someone?"

She smiled again and I could tell the part of her brain that was still working was cogitating on the question, forming an answer to it with whatever it had left to work with. It was a peculiar smile as though what she was thinking about wasn't a nice thing to think about but had been thought about before. I leant forward, moving closer because her voice was losing its edge and I could tell that her answer, if it came at all, would be at half volume. Close up she looked older. Back in the clearing, in the speckling light that came through the trees, she looked young, fresh-faced, even beautiful but here in the under-lit gloom of the big drawing room with only a lamp light falling across her face, she looked older: Ravaged. Her skin was lined and there were tiny pock marks on her cheeks and dark rings around her eyes. Not heavy ones but they were getting that way. There was an unhappiness about her features that was beginning to eat away at her beauty.

She said something but it was not much more than a whisper and I missed it.

"Sorry Charlotte..," I said, coming even closer and twisting my head to hear her words if they were repeated. "You said something then but it was too quiet. Did you say you wanted to shoot someone? Who: Who do you want to shoot Charlotte..?"

She frowned suddenly and scrunched up her eyes as if she was replaying a scene in her head that wasn't pleasant.

"I was at a party..," she said, suddenly. "It was a stupid party: Very boring."

She opened her eyes for a moment, didn't really register me at all, and closed them again, her next words coming out like mist.

"Most parties are stupid..," she said. "I hate going to parties."

"Was the party last night stupid..?" I asked. She nodded.

"Yes: One of the worst. I hated it."

"Is that why you drank so much: To make it less boring?"

"Yes…I wanted to have fun for once: I wanted to be happy but they wouldn't let me: HE wouldn't let me..!"

"Who wouldn't let you be happy..?" I asked but she wasn't listening: Her mind was back at the party.

"He always makes me go to his parties but I'm never allowed to be happy. I always have to be serious and…and…"

She trailed off again.

"And what Charlotte: What is it you always have to do..?"

"Entertain his friends, but they're not his friends. They're his business pals. They hate him as much as everyone does but they are afraid of him so they pretend to be his friends. They don't want to...They..."

"Why are they afraid of him Charlotte..?" I said, straight into her collapsing face. This was getting interesting. Was she talking about Dexter?

"I like parties when they begin..," she continued, wriggling her shoulders a little deeper into the chair. "Each time I go to one I like to think this one might be good this time but they never are so I start drinking lots and lots of lovely brandy and whisky to make them seem happy. I like brandy. I like whisky..."

She licked her lips.

"I like any drink..," she finished, a peculiar, strangled laugh scuttling up from her throat. "But it doesn't work. Instead of feeling happy I start to think and then I feel sad: I start to think about him and what he wants and when I think about that I drink more brandy to try and stop thinking but it only makes me think about him even more and then I start to think about him in a bad way."

"What kind of 'bad way' Charlotte: What kind of 'bad way' do you begin to feel about 'him'?"

She suddenly opened her eyes.

"Who are you..?" she said, a look of confusion on her half-shadowed face. There was also a hint of fear.

"I'm Mr. Carter Charlotte: You remember me? We were dancing outside, under the trees. I brought you home from the party."

"You're one of Dexter's friends..," she said, quickly, struggling to get up. She was definitely frightened suddenly, I could tell. I put my hands on her shoulders and tried to keep her still, speaking in a calm, open tone: Smiling into her face.

"No Charlotte..," I said. "I'm not one of Dexter's friends. I just wanted to talk to him, and you said if I brought you home I could meet him. I'm just a businessman: I want to ask him a few questions: Get his advice on something. That's all."

She shook her head, but didn't struggle too hard against my hands.

"No..," she whispered, her eyes searching mine for the truth. They were wide now and filling with concern. "He sent you here to kill me didn't he? He sent you here to make sure I didn't say too much..."

I put my finger on her lips and shushed her into silence, smiling: Smiling all the time.

"I promise you I'm not here to hurt you Charlotte..," I grinned. "I'm only here to talk with Dexter. He has no idea I have come to the house."

She seemed to calm down slightly and I could feel the tension leaving her shoulders, but still she held my eyes with a look of distrust, hunting for the lie.

I leaned back and let go of her, smiling: Still smiling. It was making my jaw ache keeping the damned smile going but I knew it had to stay there for a bit longer.

"Would you like another drink..?" I said, soothingly. "How about a brandy: You like brandy don't you?"

She nodded, uncertainly, and I walked over to the drinks cabinet again, this time to give her a real drink: She needed it and this time I didn't think it would put her to sleep. The shot of adrenalin that had just pumped around her body had shoved her few steps back from the edge of oblivion: She'd be good for a while yet. I wanted her to talk more but she had to be a bit more in control. Not too much or she might realise what she was saying and clam up. I reckoned it would be a risk worth taking to give her one last brandy. I made it a big one, handed it to her and watched as she sipped at it greedily.

"Were you talking about Dexter just now..?" I asked, watching the Courvoisier lessen. "Is it Dexter you think wants to kill you?"

She took a deep breath and nodded her head, unsteadily.

"Yes..," she whispered. "I think he does. He doesn't love me anymore, I can tell. He just wants my money. That's all he ever wanted."

I could see her eyes beginning to tear up and I leant forward again, stroking her chin with my finger, reassuringly.

"Hey now: Come on Charlotte. Don't cry. I'm sure that's not true..," I said, as convincingly as I could.

She took another swig of the brandy. It was a good job I'd made it a treble.

"It is..," she trembled, her voice high and beginning to whimper. "He's a bastard and I hate him. I hate what he's done to me and what he's done to my friends."

"Is that why you want to kill him?"

She nodded, her eyes fixed on a point under the carpet, a few miles down.

"Yes..," she breathed, sounding relieved to be able to say it almost out loud. "Yes, it is. I think about killing him more and more lately. I think about..."

She hesitated, a break in her voice.

"I think about shooting him in his lying face. I want to see him beg me for mercy. I want to hear him say he loves me just one more time before I kill him. That's why I have the gun so that one day, when I get the courage to do it...When I feel the rage in me grow strong enough for me to pull the trigger...I will shoot him. I will kill him! That's what I want to do now..!" she squealed, her eyes filled with water suddenly and a look of angry despair on her care-worn face.

"Now, now Charlotte..," I said quietly, keeping my voice low and even the way you would to a puppy that was about to tear your favourite shirt to pieces unless you could persuade it to let it out of its mouth. "Take it easy. Calm yourself and take a few breaths. You are getting..."

"What..?" she blurted. "What am I getting: Silly? Hysterical: Emotional?"

She turned her wild eyes on me and pinned me with them. They were dangerous and if I'd been Marcus Dexter right then I'd have been dead: No doubt about it.

"No..," I said. "You're getting brandy on my trousers."

I took the tumbler from her fingers that had loosened their grip anyway and pushed her gently back into the chair from which she had begun to rise. She settled back, still angry but smoothing out slowly. I leaned away.

"That's better..," I said. "No need to worry now. There's no-one here to kill you. Just me and I am a nice guy, remember? I told you that while we were dancing. I'm a nice guy, ok?"

She looked up from the hell she'd been staring at and smiled as if noticing me for the first time; almost as though she were glad to see me.

"How did I get here..?" she asked, looking around the room in curiosity. "Did you bring me?"

I looked into her face, more specifically her eyes. She was drunk: there was no doubt about that but there was something else in there.

"No..," I said quietly, pushing a few strays strands of hair away from her eyes. "I didn't. Somebody else must have brought you. Can you remember who?"

"A party..."she mumbled. "I was at a party in London. It was a nice party. My friend was there. She told me..."

"She..?" I said, suddenly curious.

She frowned, trying to focus on me.

"Who...?" she mumbled.

"You said "she" told you...Who is "she" and what did she tell you to do..?"

"She told me I needed to go home...That's it! She told me I needed to go home and that he would be coming home soon."

"And who is "he"..? Your husband?"

She smiled widely and nodded heavily, her eyes glazed and closing.

"Yes..," she burbled:" My loving, lovely, awful husband. She said he would be coming home soon and that if I wanted to see him I had better be leaving."

I looked at my watch. How soon I wondered? How long had she been here before I'd found her? It couldn't have been that long. Nobody, not even the fairies, dance under trees in the rain for hours. He could be here any minute or he could be home in a few hours. It was hard to tell but whichever it was I needed to be ready for him, not be caught nursing his boozed up wife.

I waited for a few seconds before trying again with the same question.

"Can you remember who brought you back from the party Charlotte: Who drove you here?"

She looked at me again with a stupid expression on her face.

"I don't know..," she said, hazily:" One of her friends I think. You wouldn't know him: Just a man. A boring man. You said you weren't his friend, so you wouldn't know would you? Would you Mr. Butcher...Is that right? No...It's not that is it? It's...Carol. Yes Carol. Mr. Carol: Mr. Christmas Carol..!"

She began to giggle.

"I like Christmas Carols Mr. Carol, do you? You must do...Which one do you like? 'Oh little town of Bethlehem..?' I like that one: sing it for me Mr. Carol..!"

She began singing the carol in a high, thin, reedy voice that was flat in all the wrong places, giggling as she sang.

I picked up a table lamp from a table and brought it close to her face, clicking it on, flooding her with light.

"Put that out..!" she hissed, throwing her arms up to block the light, but I grabbed her wrists as lightly as I could and dragged them down into her lap. "Put that out..! I can't stand it! It hurts! PUT IT OUT..!"

I switched off the lamp and put it back onto the table: I'd seen what I needed to see.

"What is it..?" I asked her. "What did you take tonight? Coke: Heroin? I can hardly see your pupils. You've been shooting something haven't you, on top of the drink?"

She laughed up at me like a peevish hyena.

"Why not..?" she tittered: "Why not take some of his drugs? He gives them to everybody...Everybody... especially me. He keeps me happy with them...He's a very thoughtful..."

"When did you take whatever it was..?" I demanded, seeing that she was sliding away fast. The combination of the booze and the drugs was boiling up inside her brain and it looked like the lid might be about to blow. "When did you take the drugs Charlotte?"

She sucked a lungful of air into her lungs through her nose, held it for a few seconds then let it out again in a long rushing stream.

"In the car after the party: You gave them to me, remember...You gave me drugs when you brought me home. Thank you Mr. Christmas: You are such a nice man...Such a nice man."

She began to sing the carol again.

"I didn't bring you here Charlotte..," I said firmly but she wasn't listening." Someone else did. Someone else gave you the drugs. Can you remember what drugs they were? Was it coke Charlotte..? Come on…Tell me. I'm you're nice friend. We dance together don't we? Tell me what drugs you took in the car…"

She stopped her pitiful rendition of whatever carol it was she couldn't sing and looked at me seriously.

"Are you my friend..?" she said. "Are you my best, dancing friend? Are you the friend I found under a tree? I found you under the tree just like a nut…"

She giggled again suddenly.

"You…," and she pointed at one of the three 'me's' she must have been seeing; "You are a dancing nut…"

Her giggling gave way to a full blown guffaw and her head rocked from side to side. She was getting to the point of implosion and I needed her not to be here.

She banged her fists on the arms of the chair and burbled something about shooting nuts but I didn't have time to listen. I tried a different approach. There was still an answer in her head yet and I wanted to get it before that head cracked wide open.

"When do you think Dexter is coming here Charlotte..?" I asked, gripping her pretty jaw in my left hand and stilling her head, forcing her to look at me. "Did your friend say when he might get here? He isn't here yet I know but he's coming isn't he?"

She looked at me with an expression of total incomprehension on her face.

"He's coming..," she said from far away. "He's on his way and when he gets here…"

She put two fingers together like a gun and pointed them between my eyes.

"BAMM..!" she said, grinning widely. "He's going to get it right between his beautiful eyes… He's going to get my eyes between his big, beautiful…"

She drooped her head onto her chest and her voice sank into the back of nowhere. Her shoulders and legs relaxed and one thin, wet-sleeved arm fell off the chair and swung down over the carpet, her long nails rasping across the pile. She'd passed out.

I stared down at her angrily but there was a shot of pity in with it too. What a waste… She was a nice girl…probably: Or rather, she had been. Sometime back when she was a sweet Charlotte Richie-Rich and just a companion to Mrs. Fitzpatrick, she was more than likely just a sweet, naïve kid that liked dancing in the rain and cute stuff like that: straight out of finishing school if those places still existed. The pathetic, crushed, scared woman I was looking at now was the result of someone's corrupting handy work: the kind of person that takes advantage of wealthy, innocent girls that like ponies and dancing in the rain, makes them fall in love with them and then turns them into junkies; dependant upon them for their next fix and willing to 'entertain' their friends in return for nothing and all of their families money as an aside: Someone like Marcus. Maybe the Fitzpatrick woman was right about this Dexter. Maybe this wasn't a trap and she really did want to rescue her friend from the big bad Marcus: Then again, thinking with my cynical hat on not my floppy, sentimental hat, she could still be using me to put something over on him: something to her advantage but not to mine. I had to admit this was turning out to be more interesting than I'd first thought: More interesting but also more dangerous. There were guns and drugs involved now and that usually meant trouble and I got the feeling that when in this particular case, when it came, it would arrive in big portions, the kind it would be hard to swallow. I knew I had to be a lot more careful than I'd planned to be. A beating I could take: A bullet in the wrong place I couldn't.

I picked Charlotte's limp, damp body up out of the chair and carried her over to the long sofa on the other side of the fireplace, then went out of the room, looking for a wrap or a warm coat to put around her.

The rooms on the ground floor were big and equally well-furnished, which meant that whoever actually owned the place had natural taste and old-money sophistication, which more than likely counted Marcus out. He was only renting it because it probably gave him an 'in' to the kind of people he needed to get to know over here. The sort with lots of money and secrets they needed to keep. He sounded pretty cheap himself...A money-grabbing, drug-pushing gigolo from California: A wise-ass American wolf in a field full of fat, rich, stupid English sheep. I knew the sort and I hated him already.

Eventually I found a big woollen coat on a hook in a back room and brought it back to front room. Charlotte was still lying where I'd put her...asleep on the sofa. Her face was very pale and her mascara looked like rivers of black blood running down a snow bank where her wet hair had fallen across her 'lashes.

I raised her up, slipped the coat around her shoulders, slotted a wilted arm into each of the sleeves and did up the buttons on the front. Laying her carefully back down again, I looked for her bag, found it by the drinks cabinet and looked through the contents.

Besides the neat looking Smith and Wesson snub nose pistol there were the usual things a woman carries around with her in a hand bag: Keys, a pencil, a small note pad, lipstick, make-up, a powder compact with her initials on the front, a couple of high-limit credit cards, some loose change and folding notes and, at the bottom, two small bottles with what looked like Chinese writing on them. They were both empty. I unscrewed the lid on one of them and took a sniff: Opium. I'd smelt it before, pretty much everywhere I'd been but in Hong Kong firstly. Was that what she was on tonight? I doubted it. Opium puts you into a deep sleep pretty much instantly. You didn't go dancing around trees after taking opium unless you were being chased by a dragon in the weird dream you were having.

There was one more thing at the bottom of the bag and I almost missed it. It was a creased-up business card and the name on it made me raise an eyebrow: "Micheal J. Carrington: MD" with an address in Belgravia: An address and a name I knew, except I, and a lot of other people like me, only knew him as "The Doctor".

I returned the card, and all the other items, into the bag. Not the gun though. I put that into the inside pocket of my coat: Finders keepers with that thing. It was too dangerous an item to be left in the possession of a drunken junkie with a burning desire to shoot her husband. Safer with me: Well, safer *for* me anyway.

I decided to take her back to London with me. She couldn't be left on her own in the state she was in and even if Marcus came home she'd still be pretty much alone. From everything I'd heard, I doubted he would be the caring, concerned kind somehow: If she dies, she dies was probably one of his mottos for a full and happy life.

No: She needed medical attention or at least somewhere safe to sleep it off. I thought about taking her to the doctor on the card but scrubbed that idea, for the time being at least. In the kind of corrupt, debauched world these people squirmed around in, he was probably the one supplying the drug of choice to his rich clients. Where I could take her would need some thinking about but that would have to come later. First I had to meet the lovely Mr. Marcus DExter for myself and see if he lived up to the reputation he'd been given.

I shoved the bag into one of the big outside pockets of her coat and lifted her off the sofa, half-walking, half dragging her to the back of the house and through the trees to my car. She wasn't heavy but the fact she was out cold meant she couldn't help me and that made her more awkward than heavy.

I leant her against the side of the car, held her up with one hand, opened the small passenger door and man-handled her into the left hand seat, propping her upright with the seat belt. With a bit of an effort I managed to wind the angle of the seat backwards until she was in an almost supine position and then positioned her head so that if she threw up, heaven bloody forbid, she wouldn't choke. There was a thin coating of sweat on her forehead and I did a quick check of her temperature and breathing but she seemed peaceful enough so I left her sleeping. I locked the car doors and went back to the house, turning off all the lights I'd turned on as I'd come out.

Back in the drawing room I mixed myself another good whiskey and soda and sat down in the big armchair that Charlotte had been sitting in before, and as I sat drinking it, I thought and as I thought an idea began forming: An idea that grew out of my suspicions and some of what Charlotte had said, and the more it grew the less I liked the shape it was taking.

SEVEN

I'd finished the drink and was just about to mix myself another when I heard the noise of a door slamming.

It sounded like it came from the front of the house but I couldn't be certain.

There was a slight pause, during which I put my empty glass down on a side table, then I heard footsteps, coming closer: Confident sounding footsteps, made by someone who had a purpose: Heavy treaded, sure of their destination and of what they were going to do when they got there.

They stopped just outside the door to the drawing room and I watched as the handle moved downwards, one half of the double doors opened and the man I assumed had to be Marcus Dexter entered. I assumed it was because he fitted the mental picture I had put together of him in my head almost to the tee.

The first thing that struck me as we stared at each other in those first two seconds was that whatever else he might have been, Marcus Dexter was impressive.

He stood in the door frame still gripping the handle, looking at me with piercing blue eyes that were over six foot from the floor, meaning that in total he was about six foot four inches tall. He had the width of shoulder to go with his height, a narrow no doubt ab-filled waist, and the relaxed stance of a man who knew his capabilities and felt confident they were far superior to everyone else's.

He was dressed in a perfectly-cut black tuxedo that only emphasised his physique, slim black trousers and highly polished evening shoes that glinted in the light from the windows. His white shirt, open at the wide neck, was spotless, the un-knotted black silk tie loose around the collar. Everything about the man was almost perfect but not completely.

His face let him down slightly: Not much, but it was the one place where the perfection he was striving for was smudged a little. It was what you might call 'interesting'.

It was square with a chiselled nose that was a couple degrees off skew but not badly: A jaw that looked as though it had been re-built by a very expensive plastic surgeon: lips that should have been fuller but were a touch too thin and un-naturally blonde hair, greying slightly at the temples, sweeping back from a forehead trying to give the impression of being intellectual but that had a touch of the Neandatharl about it. To sum him up, he looked false: Constructed: As false and constructed as the perfect white teeth he was displaying to me behind his amused, slightly predatory smile. He looked like a man that had spent a lot of gullible women's money on creating a means of cheating more money from even more gullible women.

The other impression he gave was of a man who knew exactly what he wanted, from whom he wanted it and would stop at absolutely nothing to get it. Prepossessing was a word that came to my mind amongst a lot of others, some less flattering. There was something 'wrong' about him but then again that could just have been me and my in-built cynicism filter. I knew within half a second that I didn't like him.

He closed the door behind him and stepped into the room.

"Good morning..," he said, pleasantly, his deliberately cultivated accent still carrying a slight Californian twang, some of the original seeds of his back street origins obviously stubbornly refusing to die, his smile dazzling and like the rest of him, almost perfect:" I'm delighted to meet you."

He glanced at the empty tumbler a few inches from my hand and the bottle of good whiskey standing outside of the drinks cabinet.

"I'm very pleased to see you've made yourself comfortable."

I rose to my feet to meet him just in case he intended coming straight at me but he stopped a couple of well-shod paces away and looked me up and down for a second, sizing me up, probably finding me wanting.

"How did you get into my house....?" he asked politely but there was an edge to the question.

"I rang the bell when I arrived..," I said:"...but no-one answered, so I went around the side and found a door that had been left unlocked."

He raised an eye brow.

"You must have wanted to see me quite urgently..," he said, the smile fixed in place by the glue of insincerity. "Most people, if they find there is no-one at home, leave and come back later. Only the really determined walk around the house looking for open doors they can slip through like a curious rat."

He dwelt on the last word, rolling it around behind his dazzling teeth for a few moments before allowing it out. I got the idea but kept my smile, which was not quite as dazzling but equally insincere.

He walked past me to the booze cabinet and poured himself a large drink then turned, glass in tanned hand, appraising me again, the glowing smile only on his lips. His eyes were not happy, I could tell.

"Have I kept you waiting long Mr....?" he said, taking a sip of his drink.

I pursed my lips and tried to sound casual: Nonchalant.

"Oh, only about an hour or so..," I told him.

"An hour..?" he said, both eye brows lifting now. He took another drink. "My, my: I must apologise. If I'd known you were coming I would have hurried home sooner. Keeping you waiting so long, uninvited and unattended in my empty house is unforgivable of me. Please accept my regrets."

I nodded my acceptance of his 'regrets'.

"Excellent. So: Here you are Mr...? I'm sorry but I'm afraid I still don't know your name despite my asking several times..." he said, regarding me with over-mannered courtesy.

"My name is Carter..," I said.

He took another sip of his drink.

"I'm very pleased to meet you Mr. Carter..," he said. "Forgive me but have we met? Your face isn't at all familiar."

I shook my head.

"No: We haven't met until now...," I said.

He looked puzzled and amused at the same time.

"I thought not..," he mused, taking another sip. "My next question then has to be, why are you here? What is so urgent that you felt compelled to find a way into my home and help yourself to my drinks: Do have another by the way..," he finished, pleasantly.

"Thank you..," I said. "That's a very nice idea. I will."

I went over the cabinet and mixed myself another whisky and soda, noting that the bottle was now almost half empty, or half full depending on how you looked at things. I'm an eternal pessimist and a drinker so it was half empty as far as I'm concerned. I wasn't worried though: I could see another bottle tucked away on the second shelf so maybe there was a hint of optimism built in there.

All the time I was making the drink Marcus was watching, his eyes running over me, obviously sizing me up and assessing the threat level I might be to him if he decided to stop being so affable and revert to type which I felt pretty sure wouldn't be too long now once he found out who I was and why I was there.

The drink fixed and in my hand, Marcus opened the conversation again, still warm-worded and friendly but with a sharpening edge to his tone.

"Now that you have yet another drink from my cabinet Mr. Carter, might I ask that you answer my question?"

I took a good swallow of the excellent whiskey, savoured it for a few seconds then replied.

"I'm sorry..," I said. "Remind me what it was again."

His smile didn't slip but his eyes hardened.

"Of course: Your powers of concentration must be a little reduced if the level of the bottle from which you have been helping yourself is anything to go by. I asked what was so urgent that you felt compelled to wait an hour in my chair, in a house into which you weren't invited, to ask me a question or perhaps 'questions' which you did not think it polite to call up in advance and ask if I would be interested in hearing."

"Well are you..?" I asked.

"Am I what Mr. Carter..," he said, a little impatiently I felt.

"Interested in hearing my questions?"

Marcus inhaled through his off-line nose audibly, took another sip of his drink and looked long and hard into my eyes. I was getting to him at last which is what I wanted. I needed him in the mood to make a slip up and let a sliver of truth out from behind the almost perfect plaster cast mould he was working behind.

"I might be if I knew more about you Mr. Carter..," he said carefully. "Shall we start with my asking what you do? Are you a lawyer perhaps: A solicitor: Maybe a policeman?"

I shook my head and laughed gently.

"No..," I said. "None of those things, but it's interesting that you thought I might be from one of those particular professions, all to do with the law? Do you have many dealings with the law: Are you often visited by such people?"

He snorted, his smile now lop-sided. He was entertained by my reply I could tell but growing ever so slightly annoyed now.

"You are a clever man Mr. Carter..," he said slowly.

"You're the second person that's told me that this morning..," I said disarmingly.

"But you are also becoming a little irritating if you'll forgive me for saying so..," he went on, ignoring my remark. "Now, if you would be so kind as to answer my question? What is it that you do and what is it that you wish to ask me?"

"That's two questions..," I smiled: "...but I'll be happy to answer them both."

"Thank you so much..," he smarmed, raising his glass to me in a salute. The dislike was now mutual.

"My pleasure: I am…"

I hesitated for a second trying to find a title that would cover what I did without making him call for the police.

"…an adjustment broker..," I said, pleased with the title.

He arched one of his well-defined eye brows and looked at me with an expression of bafflement mixed with doubt on his face.

"An 'adjustment broker'..?" he said, turning the words around carefully in his mouth. "Very interesting: You'll have to forgive my ignorance Mr. Carter but that is a profession I don't believe I've ever come across before. Would you care to explain what it is an 'adjustment broker' actually does and how that might be of any interest to my-self?"

"Certainly..," I said, thinking of a way to describe what I did, again without him calling the police. "I 'adjust' circumstances and their potential consequences or outcomes should they remain un-adjusted."

My answer made no sense to me so it wasn't surprising that his puzzled expression remained unchanged.

"I'm sorry but I still don't understand what it is you do..," he said, slipping a well-manicured hand into one of his trouser pockets and waving his almost empty tumbler about to emphasise his bafflement. "Please try to explain it to me once again but in less obtuse terms."

"My apologies," I said, placatingly. "It is a difficult concept to be specific about. In plain words, what I do is intervene in situations and try to either negotiate a change in the outcome or suggest alternatives that may bring a more mutually agreeable solution to what might have become an implacable stalemate."

Marcus shook his head.

"That is a little clearer," he said:"...but I still don't quite understand. What kind of 'situations' do you intervene in and in what way do you offer 'alternatives': Alternatives' to what?"

"Alternatives to what otherwise might be a disadvantageous outcome. I offer to put forward my client's offers or solutions in an attempt to prevent an unfortunate conclusion or aftermath."

Marcus shook his head as though flicking away a troublesome fly.

"I'm sorry Mr. Carter. Either I am being particularly dull minded which I do not think I am, or you are being deliberately opaque, which I suspect you might be: Solutions to what? "

"Very well..," I smiled in what I hoped was an annoyingly patronising way: "Very simply: I act as either a mediator or an enforcer of intent between opposing parties when the point of no return appears to have been reached in a dispute or a matter of immutable conflict or difference."

I was impressing myself with all of this. Maybe I should write it all down and turn it into a piece of paper I could hand around to potential clients, but it was probably just the drink giving my brain a kick. I'd forget it all in the morning.

His face lit up as a moment of clarity dawned.

"Ah: I think I understand..," he smiled. "You are a negotiator: You bring about what you call 'adjustments' in peoples or companies attitudes or requirements."

"Very well put..," I said: "And quite correct. I try to persuade the opponents or conflicting parties to be more pliant or sympathetic to my client's situation or wishes. I am a 'persuader'."

"Are you indeed Mr. Carter..?" Macro beamed, delighted it seemed with my title. "That sounds very interesting and, if I may say so, not a little sinister. How very 'gangster-like'..," he chuckled, emptying his glass in one last swallow:" Is that what you are Mr. Carter: A gangster..?" he said in a slow, slightly menacing voice.

I shook my head.

"No..," I said calmly, reaching around for the half empty bottle. "I'm not a gangster. I'm more a..."

"Messenger boy..?" Marcus ventured, sarcastically:" You were sent here by someone to pass on a message perhaps: an offer maybe: Possibly a warning of some kind?"

I mixed myself another whisky, adding more soda than before. The whisky was very smooth but it was beginning to have its effect on me and I knew I needed to stay as clear headed as my taste buds would allow me to.

"Not quite..," I corrected as I swooshed in the soda: "I was asked to come here in order..."

"Who by..?"

I raised the tumbler to my lips but didn't drink.

"Someone I am very curious about..," I said meeting his eye.

"Now we both are..," he grinned. He began to make himself a drink. "Suddenly I am no longer a little annoyed by you Mr. Carter..," he continued:" Suddenly I am intrigued: Not only about you and your strangely exciting profession but by the identity of your client: the one that you too are intrigued by."

"I didn't say 'intrigued'..," I chided: "I said 'curious': There's a difference."

He laughed.

"Not really..," he said: "both words mean essentially the same thing: We are both wanting to know more about the person who has employed you to run this errand. I take it you represent a person not a company?"

I nodded.

"How interesting..," he said, stroking his wide chin:" Now who can it be I wonder: Which one of my many acquaintances would employ a man with a note to come running up my path instead of asking me directly to my face whatever it is they want to ask? Let me see: someone with very little back bone: someone with a lack of confidence in their ability to face me and ask or demand whatever it is you are about to impart without being intimidated by my sheer presence? Hmmm...That could be so many of them."

I said nothing: Just stood on the carpet drinking his very nice whisky listening to him feel good about himself, waiting for him to stop preening his ego.

"No..," he finally said after a melodramatic show of pondering designed, no doubt, to show how little he cared or was worried about me and whatever it was he believed I was there to tell him. "...No; I cannot think. You will have to tell me."

He threw back his drink.

"Please Mr. Carter. Fulfil your task: Earn your fee and reveal whatever mysterious offer, suggestion or demand it is that you have sent to present to me. Begin your 'adjustments'. Commence with your 'persuading'."

I smiled patiently and waited until he had stopped giggling like a schoolboy.

"Very well Mr. Marcus..," I began.

"One moment..," he said raising a long, bejewelled finger. "What makes you think I am Marcus? I could be one of his friends staying at his home for a while: I could be his brother."

I shook my head.

"I doubt that Mr. Dexter. To begin with I was told what you were like: That you were from California and still had an accent despite your attempts at cultivating an air of European sophistication: That you were renting this house for the season and that you would be here this morning at about this time: The fact that you came straight through the front door and into this room without breaking pace gave me another fairly strong clue but the clincher was your initials: 'M.D.', cut into your signet ring. Unless all of those things are wrong, which I know they're not, you are Marcus Dexter."

He shrugged his large shoulders, playfully.

"Very good Mr. Carter: I can see you are quite a professional 'persuader'. You do your research. Please…Carry on with your business here."

"It's not exactly 'business'..," I said. "It might turn out to be but at this stage it is more of a demand."

"A demand..!" Marcus breathed in mock alarm. "How very dramatic: I am very rarely faced with a 'demand'. Do continue."

I took a few steps away from the cabinet, putting some room between myself and Marcus just in case he didn't take kindly to what I was about to say. I hadn't intended to come this far when I'd set out from London all those hours ago. All I had told myself I was going to do was take a look around: Size up the situation: Have a think about whether or not I was going to actually do as the Fitzpatrick woman wanted me to; earn the money that was nestled in my pocket. Somehow without realising it I had gone three steps instead of one and now not only did I have Marcus's drug-addled wife hidden in my car but I was standing right in front of the man himself risking my whisky-filled neck by delivering an ultimatum that I had a pretty fair idea he wouldn't take very well: Before I could begin though he raised a finger again.

"Let me ask you first if your client is a man or a woman Mr. Carter. I would hazard a guess that it is a woman..," he said.

"Why is it more likely to be a woman..?" I said. "Do you have a lot of trouble with women?"

He smiled.

"Not at all, or at least I personally don't have any trouble at all with women. It does seems however that women have trouble with me, so I would have to guess that you may be here representing an irate woman. Am I correct?"

"Correct, but what makes you think it might be trouble..?"

He laughed, mockingly.

"I doubt you'd be here to 'persuade' or 'negotiate' if there were no trouble involved, do you?"

He dropped the grin and turned it into a polite smile.

"Now Mr. Carter: If you wouldn't mind getting on with whatever it is you are here to do? I have rather a busy morning and this unexpected interlude, interesting though it is, is eating into my valuable time."

I put the remains of the drink on top of the fireplace.

"I understand..," I said: "So I'll keep it brief."

"Excellent..," Marcus said, nodding his head in sarcastic approval.

"I am here on behalf of a Mrs. Fitzpatrick..," I began.

"A married lady..? That is indeed intriguing. I don't believe I have had problems with a married lady for quite some time. Do continue."

I gave him a 'Yeah, right' look and carried on.

"Mrs. Fitzpatrick came to see me in my office last night…"

"You have an office..?" he interrupted. "I thought perhaps you met your clients in cheap cafes or alley ways. An office..? You must be fairly good at your 'job' then to afford an 'office': Very impressive."

I gave him a few seconds to get his sneer over with then carried on, all the time thinking how much of a pleasure it would be to be able to wipe the slimy smile off of his plastic face with the back of my hand at some point, hopefully soon. The man was too full of his own crap to notice the smell of self-satisfaction he was giving out but maybe what I was about to say would do it for me, although I doubted it.

"As I was saying..," I went on:" Mrs. Fitzpatrick came to see me last night."

"I take it I am supposed to know who this 'Mrs. Fitzpatrick' is..?"

"I think you'll find you do..," I said.

He pouted and held his chin, looking down at the carpet in thought.

"Hmmm…A married lady: Mrs. Fitzpatrick…"

He looked up and waggled his fingers.

"Indulge me: Is she attractive? I pride myself on only having problems with attractive women."

"I thought so. She's a very beautiful lady..," I found myself saying without knowing why. "She's also very rich."

He grinned widely.

"That goes without saying Mr. Carter..," he preened. "I would not involve myself with a married woman unless she was at least one of those two things and it would seem that in this case your Mrs. Fitzpatrick appears to be both: Odd that I cannot recall her. I rather think I should."

"If what she told me was true then you definitely do..," I said, "...but I don't care whether you do or you don't. All I know is that she paid me a nice sum of money to come down here and talk to you."

He smiled happily to himself, relishing the idea it seemed.

"How very intriguing: I wonder why she wanted to do that?"

"If you'd stop interrupting you might find out..," I said, this time without the smile.

He laughed and put his hands up in pretend alarm.

"Forgive me..," he said. "This is all very amusing. Do carry on."

"Thank you Marcus..," I said, my thinly spread patience with him wearing through now.

"People I don't know usually call me Mr. Marcus," he said disapprovingly.

"That's very respectful of them..," I said: "Now may I continue *Marcus*?"

He shrugged his shoulders.

"As you wish, *Mister* Carter ..." he said, casually.

"Good. As I was saying..."

"Tell me something *Mister* Carter...," he said, looking down at his immaculate tuxedo and flicking non-existent lint from the sleeves. "What would happen if I suddenly decided not to listen to your clients 'demands' at all or allow you to remain in this house another minute? What would happen if I were to issue you with my own demand that you leave without saying another word?"

I finished off my whiskey.

"To be honest, I hadn't thought about that..," I said. "Well: I suppose one of two things. I could accept your refusal to enter into the negotiations, walk out of that door and go back to London to tell my client I tried but got nowhere."

"Or..?"

"I could try and persuade you to listen."

"Ah: Of course. That's what you do isn't it? You persuade people to do what they are asked to do, in my case listen to whatever it is your 'client', the beautiful Mrs. Fitzpatrick, feels I should hear."

He pretended to mull over the two options.

"If I were to choose the second option: To force you to 'persuade' me: What would that entail?"

"I would point out to you that by refusing to listen to my client's requests…"

"Requests..? I thought they were 'demands'? 'Requests' sounds less weighty: Less dramatic."

"..By refusing to listen to my clients requests, I would become personally more curious as to your reasons why not."

He looked surprised at that last answer.

"Personally curious..?" he repeated. "Well that is interesting. Why would you have a personal curiosity in my not responding to Mrs. Fitzpatrick's 'requests'? Surely your job is purely to deliver the message and report on the outcome, not to become intrigued or affronted if I chose not to play her game, whatever it is?"

"Normally maybe, but in this case the strong impression that my client gave was that refusal by yourself to even listen to her demands, let alone refuse to comply, would be unacceptable and that my skills were to be used to the full in order to bring about a satisfactory conclusion."

Marcus folded his arms and considered me and my words with a titillated expression on his grinning face. He was genuinely amused by what I'd just said and I had to admit it did sound a bit pompous. I knew what I wanted to say but using expressions like…'beat the smile off of your condescending face and force you to take me seriously..' or simply…'knock some of the arrogance out of you…'wouldn't go down well and might just have the opposite effect so I had decided to try and sound business-like and pretentious just like him.

"Your skills..?" he chuckled.

I knew he'd pick up on that.

"What 'skills' might those be Mr. Carter: What particular set of abilities do you possess that would persuade a reluctant participant like my-self to acquiesce to your ultimatums? Surely you don't mean physical persuasion? That would be most disturbing, not to mention illegal."

I returned his stare with one of my own that wasn't so amiable. He knew perfectly well what I meant but he knew I couldn't actually say the words because the stage hadn't been reached yet where I might have to demonstrate my skills to him. All I could do at this particular moment in the process was lay down the implications of his refusal to take my mission seriously which, in most cases was usually sufficient to bring the whole thing to a satisfactory conclusion, pretty much in accordance with my clients wishes, but I knew with a man like him that would only be seen as a challenge: an invitation to take it to the next level.

He saved me the awkwardness of trying to expand on my potential modus by slipping both hands into his pockets and rocking back and forward slightly on his heels, all the time smiling at me with a knowing look in his eyes.

"I'll tell you what I think I might do Mr. Carter..," he said: "I think I might actually satisfy your curiosity but not because your beautiful client's demands mean anything to me. I will satisfy your curiosity simply because it will amuse me to do so."

"I don't give a monkey's about your reason..," I told him. "What I want is for you to listen to her demands and give me your answer."

"And if I don't..?"

"Don't what..?"

"If I don't give you an answer: If I didn't satisfy this 'personal curiosity' of yours: What would you do?"

"I'd consider the job only half done..."

"Meaning..?"

"Meaning I would endeavour to complete it."

He smiled a half-smile that lifted up one side of his mouth.

"You continue to interest me..," he said: "How would you 'endeavour to complete it'? What would you actually do to gain the answer I am so obviously reluctant to give?"

I picked up the empty tumbler, looked into it and shrugged.

"I suppose I'd just have to hang around here until you got sick of the sight and sound of me and decided to give me some sort of reply. That's all I want you know: A response I can give her."

"So that she can what..? Pay you more to return and be a little more forceful in your techniques of persuasion?"

He nursed his glass between his fingers, contemplating the floor. His smile was only vague now: A dim shadow of what it had been before its battery had run down. I could see he was thinking and was coming to a conclusion which I doubted I was going to like. After a few seconds, he looked up from his musings on the pattern of the carpet and I could see that the batteries had finally died: his smile was gone and his lips had settled into their default position of cold neutrality that matched the steel in his eyes.

"All right..," he said, flatly. "I'm going to tell you where I'm at Mr. Carter."

I gave him a cheeky grin back.

"About time..," I said.

"I've decided I am bored with this conversation: I have also decided that I don't like you and because of both of those things I'm going to ask you to leave with your demands or requests unanswered."

He sounded impatient now, as though the playing was over. It was 'serious' time now and he wanted to get on with his day.

I rubbed the back of my neck.

"That's ok..," I said: "I'm getting bored with this conversation myself and I don't like you either. From what I've heard I expected you to not be a very nice man and from what I've seen you're a pretentious twat, so the feeling is mutual, but I'm afraid, professionally speaking, I can't leave without an answer to my clients demands. She paid me to do a job and so far I've not done it. So: whether you like me or not, I'm going to have to fulfil my task."

For the merest moment I thought I saw him flinch but if he had done it was over in a half second.

"Is that so..?" he said coldly. I nodded.

"I'm afraid so."

Suddenly there was a small lift to the corners of his mouth and a crinkle to the edges of his eyes.

"Let's look at this impasse from another direction shall we..?" he said slowly: "Someone has been saying bad things about me haven't they Mr. Carter. Someone who is not well disposed towards me: Your mysterious client, the apparently beautiful Mrs. Fitzpatrick, who I still cannot recall meeting, I assume: If it is her then I can only believe she feels she has good reason to do so, but because she knows that until this morning you would not have met me, when she came to see you last night she knew she needed you to feel hostile about me in order for you to sympathise with her demands and to strengthen your will and sense of purpose: To put you firmly on her side in our 'negotiations': Therefore I would assume that you came here with a lot of odd ideas that she put in your head about me: Ideas that prepared you to meet someone you would dislike."

I made no comment, just watched his mind working. I got the feeling he was becoming as curious about my client as I was. I also got the feeling he was preparing the ground for something and I sharpened myself to be ready for whatever it might be.

"If that's correct then it is unfortunate..," he continued: "Because Mr. Carter I think that you and I might share several similar characteristics. I believe we are the same in some ways."

He waited for a reaction but I remained silent. I wanted to see how this would unfold.

He smiled knowingly at my lack of response.

"I think, truly, that if we had met under other circumstances you might very well have liked me. We have certain 'traits' in common."

He nodded to himself, warming to his theory.

"But..," he conceded: "You haven't met me under normal circumstances, which is a pity, because I feel strongly that had we done so I may have liked you too."

I doubted that.

"So…" he sighed. "As I said before, we have reached an impasse. I am not inclined to answer or listen to the demands of your unknown client, the fragrant Mrs. Fitzpatrick, and you say you will not leave until I have done so. Where do we go from here? What could the solution be?"

He did a little thinking and I began to think he might be coming around to my way.

"Very well..," he said eventually. "I realise suddenly that I am as curious about her and her demands as you are so I will concede you a few moments within which to try and 'persuade' me to take them seriously. Firstly, please tell me about who she is and what connection there may be to me. If I can be convinced that the connection is genuine and in any way ought to be considered then I will respond but I warn you: If I think this is an attempt to shake me down or attempt to con' me out of money, my response will be frank and possibly brutal. Do you understand?"

I grinned at him. I'd worn away at his resolve and opened up a gap in his unexpectedly tough armour. I just needed to plant a few small grenades in there that might blow his façade of affable intellectuality apart and expose him as the money grubbing, drug pushing gigolo he really was.

"All right..," I said. "Here it is. Mrs. Fitzpatrick came to see me last night and offered me a tidy chunk of cash to come down here and scare you into accepting her demands."

He looked at me, still smiling, evidently pleased with the thought that someone hated him enough to pay a guy like me to try and scare him. He seemed to be relishing the idea.

"I wasn't too sure about the idea at first..," I went on. "I don't usually take work from people that just turn up at my door, unannounced, especially late at night. I prefer them to be recommended to me by people I know and for those people to warn me they were coming. In my business you can't be too careful."

"Of course..," Marcus said:" The persuasion business can be precarious I would imagine: The line between legality and illegality must be quite thin at times."

I ignored his insinuation, even though I knew he was right and crossed in front of him, walking back to the cabinet.

"May I..?" I said, picking up the much loved bottle again.

"Be my guest..," he said and I could sense his eyes on me as I mixed up another whisky-soda this time a little heavier on the whisky. I took a good sized sip then returned to my story.

"She was disappointed with my initial reluctance..," I said; "...and told me a few stories about herself and about you. As you say; probably to try and pluck at my non-existent heart strings and get the old eye-juice flowing but I wasn't buying it. She tried hard though. She let a little of the juice flow herself but I'm not the sympathetic kind and told her I wasn't falling for any of that. She left eventually, still not sure I was going to do what she'd asked which obviously annoyed her but like I said, I don't put a lot of trust in people that walk straight through my door without an invitation. She could have been anyone..."

"Quite so..," Marcus said. "She could have been sent by the police could she not? You agreed that the nature of your profession carries with it a whiff of illegality. You might have been being set up."

That rocked me but I gave nothing away. I'd already been thinking that but not too seriously. It was true. I could have been. I knew nothing about her: Only what she had told me, and the call to the hotel earlier had already shown me she was a liar. This whole thing could be a very elaborate, carefully constructed plot of some kind that needed an unsuspecting guff like me either to provide the alibi or be a victim, depending on what it was all about. I could be playing right along with a plan that I couldn't even begin to understand, but I put the thought to one side for the moment and concentrated on what I did know, adjusting my thinking a little to take the possibility into account, part of my brain pondering in a corner about why he had thrown that into the soup: To spice it up or to poison it?

"What stories did she tell you Mr. Carter...?" Marcus continued; "...and what was, or perhaps still is, the connection between her and me? The name continues to rings no bells I'm afraid."

I took another sip then told him what the Fitzpatrick woman had told me: All about her having gone to California to help get over her depression and meeting him: About how charming and friendly he'd seemed: How he had introduced her to a lot of people: How she had relaxed: How they had become lovers.

Dexter's eyebrow rose at the 'lover' part but he said nothing and allowed me to carry on. I could tell behind the glittering eyes he was trying to work out which one of his no doubt many 'lovers' Mrs Fitzpatrick might be but his expression gave nothing away and I continued.

When I told him that they had been married, he knotted his eyebrows, still smiling, but a little less cocky suddenly.

"Married..?" he said in a surprised voice and I saw the look of sudden recognition in his eyes. I was also pretty certain I saw concern as well but he stifled any emotion that he might have suddenly been feeling and made no further comment.

"Yes: Married, and that's when things began to change. She found out you had a history…" I went on:"…A very bad history and that from all accounts you aren't a very nice man."

He smiled wickedly.

"I'm sorry to hear that..," he said." I've always prided myself on being a very nice man, at least to begin with…"

I really wanted to slap his self-satisfied face around a couple of times but held myself in check, taking another sip of whisky instead. With any luck, the face slapping part might come later.

"She found out that you made your money mostly through blackmailing rich women: That you were violent."

He pouted as if pondering the point, tilting his head to one side.

"Perhaps, but no more so than necessary…" he said in an innocent, mock hurt voice.

Again, the need to give the man a whack on the nose almost won out but I knew that would put the ball in his court and I needed it to stay firmly in mine so I carried on, fixing him with a hard look that I hoped would make him realise I was being serious but he just smiled back at me, slyly.

"Continue with my character assassination, please..," he said, raising his tumbler to his thin lips:" It's fascinating."

"She filed for divorce despite your threats and violence against her…"

"Really: I was violent again? My: I was a bad man wasn't I?"

"You made her life pretty unbearable by all accounts…" I went on: "…but she wouldn't be intimidated and got the best lawyers money could buy over there to keep you under control. It seems the police became involved at one point as well."

Dexter smiled broadly.

"Well, well…" he said, reflectively; "I am beginning to remember things now Mr. Carter but not quite in the same way you are putting it. However: Please do carry on. I am enjoying listening to you reeling out the rope with which you will very soon hang yourself, metaphorically speaking of course."

I drained my glass and put it on the arm of one of the big, leather club chairs that dotted the room.

"Eventually the divorce went through but not without you threatening her with retribution. Apparently you're a real sore loser. Like most bullies you don't like being told what to do, especially by a woman. You didn't back down so my client started to become worried. She feared for her safety and flew back to London, taking with her the young companion she had come to the States with. A girl called Charlotte. A nice, sweet girl according to Mrs. Fitzpatrick. Naïve and gullible: Very rich: The kind you seem to go for. Strangely Charlotte wasn't very keen on leaving and told Mrs. Fitzpatrick that she wanted to go back, which made my client not only very curious but very worried. Why would she want to do that? She had a loving family back here. All of her friends were in London. What would make her want to hurry back to L.A.: What could possibly be so appealing about a city with you in it? It turns out that was the reason. It was you she wanted to run back to like a love-sick kitten. It seems you had been having an affair with young Charlotte all the while you were married to Mrs. Fitzpatrick which wasn't very nice was it?"

Marcus shook his head and shrugged, finishing his own glass.

"You know, I'm actually very glad I met you Mr. Carter..," he said, laughing softly:" If I hadn't I wouldn't have been so amused and believe me, after the crushingly dull night I've had, I could do with being amused. Do go on. No doubt you have more?"

I walked over to the window and looked out across the drive. It had started to rain.

"A lot..," I said. "While you were playing around behind the scenes, you worked on her, convincing the trusting girl that it was Mrs. Fitzpatrick that had made your life a misery. You turned the love-sick little lamb against her, making her think you were the wounded party, getting her to lick your wounds and anything else you told her to lick. She was obsessed with you and believed every word you screwed into her. She was like putty in your experienced hands."

"What can I say Mr. Carter? Women like me."

I balled my fist but kept cool. Later, I told myself: Hopefully he'd do something stupid to make me knock the smugness out of him. I continued:

"So, as soon as the divorce was finalised, she flew back to you expecting everything to be all sugar and roses, but to everyone's surprise, within a couple of weeks she came back with you in tow. Mrs. Fitzpatrick says it was because you were bored with LA. You wanted to spread your wings: Break into a new area of opportunity so you used her and her rich connections to begin making yourself known to the London crowd. They of course, lapped you up because you were something new in their dull, spoilt lives: A smarmy American let loose amongst London's bored, rich, unsuspecting sheep. Easy pickings for a hungry predator like you."

Dexter chuckled to himself but let me carry on, an arrogant smile lifting one cheek. I was getting into a stride now.

"According to her, it didn't take you long to work your spell on the poor little lambs; charming them; schmoosing them; amusing them but also making them dependant on you in the only way guys like you can."

He looked up at me from the corner of his eye, the smile still in place.

"And that way is..?" he said.

I stared at him knowingly which is a skill I've learnt over the years.

"You quickly made yourself into the go-to guy when they wanted to satisfy their selfish de-generate needs. You get them all the sex and drugs they want..," I said, casually:" You supply those poor, wealthy suckers with the 'distractions' they need to keep them from realising what a waste of time, space and oxygen they all are, but you don't just do it for the money you make from it, and this is me talking now, based upon my experience of working for men like yourself. You collect them like 'Get out of jail cards' for the future because those sort of people have a lot of connections: These are the top layer. Most of them are untouchable and that's what men like you need: Untouchability, so you build a wall of dependent, blackmailed people around you behind which you manipulate them for your own twisted pleasure, keeping them addicted and tucked away neatly in your pocket for future use."

He gave a quick, accepting laugh then looked up: Not at me but at the ceiling and scratched his throat, obviously thinking over what I'd just said.

"My, my..," he grinned, eventually, slipping both hands into his pockets:" I am a very bad man aren't I?"

He looked around at me, his grin fallen away, but there was still a hint of amusement in his eyes and he smiled slowly. If the man was rattled, which I got the feeling he was beginning to be, he wasn't going to let it show: Not to me anyway.

"If your client is correct in her rather dramatic allegations of course…"he finished.

An edge had returned to his voice now and I could tell a nerve had been tickled.

"There's more…" I said.

"Of course there is…" he oozed:" Do please continue. We haven't reached the denouement yet have we? The reason you are here: Her demand."

The last two words were soaked in bitterness and spoken with a shark-like smile through which they slipped like poisoned knives obviously aimed straight at my fear button, but they missed. I continued:

"As soon as you could you married the pitiful girl and began spending her money in giant handfuls, scattering it around like rice at a wedding on parties, cars, a yacht and houses in France and Italy. After a few months, when you felt you were in enough control, just as you'd planned you brought a lot of your old cronies over from the States and, with them in the background, you were really able to run through the innocent things like a disease. You turned the yacht and the house in France into brothels and got even more influential people hooked onto your ever widening Gucci belt. In very little time you became the number one guy to go to for whatever it was the rich and stupid of this town wanted."

Marcus poured himself a small brandy as I was talking, but didn't invite me to do the same so I carried on, watching his face for a sign that I was hitting home but he just kept on smiling that irritatingly superior smile that I had come to hate, sipping on his drink as I went on.

"You didn't even try hiding anything of this stuff from your lovely wife though…"I went on: "No: You didn't give what we over here call 'a monkey's toss' about her…You raided her piggy bank openly because you knew she was an addict and you were her supplier, so she wouldn't and couldn't do anything about it. You kept her almost permanently high on drugs so that most of the time she didn't even know how much you were stripping her account clean, but sometimes she came down enough to realise what was going on and started questioning things which caused problems. Twice she took the advice of her parents and friends and threatened to divorce you but no doubt in your own subtle way, you made her change her mind and she dropped the idea."

Dexter spread his hands, lifting his waxed eyebrows.

"And the evidence for all of this..?"

"My client has copies of letters she wrote to your wife telling her all the gory details about your history of violence towards her and other women and your police record, but, as you knew she would because she had to, Charlotte ignored them. She even wrote back saying that if my client continued trying to break up her marriage she would take her to court for slander. She locked herself away, stopped taking any calls and when it all got too much for her rotting little brain to cope with, she ran off to the house you bought in Italy so that none of her friends or relations could get anywhere near her. She is completely in your power."

I stopped talking and there was silence in the room.

"That's quite a story," Marcus said, staring into the space between us, going over what I'd just told him, a smug smile cosying onto his lips, almost as though he were congratulating himself on what a smooth bastard he was. After a few seconds he re-focused on me, his smile turned up to include me in its self-satisfied warmth. If eyes actually could sparkle, his would have been. He nodded wisely and frowned in recognition of having come to a profound conclusion.

"Mr. Carter..," he said:" I am a man who, for some reason which modesty forbids me exploring too far, seems to instantly attract women."

He shrugged in a 'What's a guy to do' kind of a way.

"Invariably they fall in deeply in love with me, some of them to the point of obsession..."

I returned his supercilious, patronising grin with a cold, hard stare. God he was an arrogant, self-satisfied piece of shit, I thought but said nothing: Just let him carry on masturbating.

"When I lose interest in them or show none at all..," he went on,"...quite a few of them have become stupidly jealous, rather, it would seem, like your Mrs. Fitzpatrick."

He held his chin and knitted his brow in a mock serious pose, nodding his head for a few irritating seconds then pointed a finger at me.

"You know, now that I have had time to think about it, I do remember this lady of yours and you are right. She was, probably still is, a very handsome woman. As I recall I allowed her to become attached to me purely for the novelty of bedding an English woman and I was very happily surprised to quite quickly discover that she was actually very passionate: Not at all a cold, stuck up, frigid bitch as I had always assumed your British women would be, at least not in bed. Quite the opposite in fact."

He took in a deep breath, holding my stare with an amused one of his own.

"We had a deeply sexual relationship for a few months and, I think it would be fair to say, I taught her more than a few 'tricks', for want of a nicer word, that she would certainly never have learned from her fellow Englishmen, no offence intended Mr. Carter, " he grinned.

I gave him a "…Go fuck yourself…" look.

"We married. That is true..," he continued:"…but if I am being truthful, and I feel you would like me to be, for my part, it was purely for financial reasons. She had a lot of money and I wanted all of it or at least as much as I could screw out of her. It did not take her long to realise that I held no feelings for her whatsoever apart from the occasional moments of lust but even they dwindled as I found a myriad of renewed pleasures elsewhere. When she became angry at my lack of interest in her, even as a woman, she became 'harpy-like'. She went mad, threatening me with all sorts of dire consequences if I didn't return to her bed or respect her in the way she felt entitled to be. I have to admit my own frustrations at her jealousy came out in physical form on more than several occasions, but…"

He shrugged.

"…she became jealous to the point where, and you may find this difficult to believe, I feared for my own safety. Beneath that very English, cool exterior, I'm afraid your Mrs. Fitzpatrick has a very nasty temper and I became tired of her petty jealousies: Her tantrums: Her piques of temper, and so, as she rightly says, I found 'succour' shall we say in her delightful young companion: Charlotte. A quite delicious specimen of the 'English Rose' I had developed a real taste for. You can understand Mrs. Fitzpatrick's attitude. She was, perhaps rightly, furious. Her spats became full blown hurricanes of fury: quite terrifying to behold so, in order to smooth the by now highly turbulent and quite tedious waters we were being tossed around in, having something of a reputation for sudden and occasionally violent tempers myself, I gave her a taste of what she had been giving me which did not go down well with her. As I recall, she chose to have the police involved in an effort to blacken my character, resulting in my threatening her with counter actions unless she withdrew her complaints which she finally did, choosing instead to return to London from where she continued her divorce proceedings."

For someone who had just basically admitted to drug-dealing and violence towards women, he was looking and sounding remarkably cool and carefree about it: Almost as if it were a skill he was proud of: One he had honed to perfection over the years. If it were possible, I disliked him even more now than I did five minutes before, and the more he spoke the more that dislike was growing.

Dexter flicked his wrist over, looked at his stupidly expensive watch, and gave a dramatic sigh.

"Forgive me Mister Carter..," he said, boredom in his now irritating voice:"...but suddenly I've grown rather tired of this, up until now, quite amusing and not entirely uninteresting little interval in my plans for the rest of the day."

He crossed back to the drinks cabinet and re-filled his tumbler, continuing to talk as he did so:

" I was going to continue with the rather awful and drearily dull history of my fateful dalliance with your client, but I see that I have wasted rather more time than I initially intended by listening to you and your explanation for being in my house un-invited, and I don't intend to waste any more of it."

He took a small sip of the brandy and smiled.

"I'm tired: Very tired as a matter of fact. It's been a long night, although highly profitable as always, and...I have neither the energy nor the inclination to indulge you or the once delicious but sadly now merely bitter and sour-tasting Mrs. Fitzpatrick any further. Please do me the favour..."

He took another, longer swallow of his brandy:

"...of stating what it is your petulant client has paid you to come and demand. In all honesty, I would prefer it if you'd simply finish your drink, button up your cheap suit and leave, but because I know you won't and I don't want to waste anymore of my increasingly bored time trying to make you do so, I think allowing you to tell me what I don't really want to hear would give you the ability to return to her, albeit with your mission only half accomplished because you will not have any kind of an answer from me to give her, and then continue with your exciting life and profession, using your undoubted skills to continue attempting, possibly even succeeding, to intimidate or, as you choose to put it, "persuading" others to accept your future clients terms, content in the knowledge that our paths will never have to cross again and that Mrs. Fitzpatrick will not be asking you to help her any further, which I think would be a win for both of us, don't you agree?"

I stared at him long and hard, allowing the silence between us to tighten.

"You like talking, don't you..?" I said, slowly, my eyes telling him I wasn't impressed by his monologue and didn't give a damn about his kind, patronising offer.

"Not any more, at least to you..," he grinned:" Now are you going to give me the ultimatum or 'demand' and leave or…"

He finished his drink and placed the tumbler down.

"…am I going to have to make you leave?"

"And how would you do that..?" I said, my words even and heavy with menace, like the blade of a long knife glinting in the dark. I wasn't worried by this man and I wanted him to know it.

"One of two ways..," he nodded, pursing his lips and considering his next words:" I could call the police, tell them you broke into my house and are demanding money from me, threatening me with violence, give them the name of your client and set in motion a world of investigation, prosecution and jail I would imagine a man of your type attempts almost daily to avoid, or…?"

He grinned, impishly:" Or, I could make you leave myself."

I kept my eyes hooded, my voice level and my words hard.

"I'll repeat the question. And how would you do that exactly?"

Marcus added another inch to the width of his grin and chuckled, meeting the steel of my eyes with the twinkling blue diamonds of his own.

"By fucking you up Mr. Carter…," he winked: He actually winked:" How badly..? Well…That depends entirely upon my self-control which I have a feeling I may lose quite quickly. Not too badly though. Just enough to make me feel happy and for you to definitely reconsider carrying on with this mission you've been foolish enough to take on. When I've done that, I'll leave you on your own to recover and make your way back to your seedy little office, bleeding quite badly, trying to breathe through the nose I will break and somehow manage to drive with the fingers I will snap, and then continue with my day as I had intended to when I first came back: A quite important phone call, a hot bath, some breakfast and then what I believe you English like to call a "nap".

He dropped his smile and looked me right in the eye.

"Which of those options would you like to choose Mr. Carter? Personally I'd go for the first. The other one would lead to complications. Certainly a lot of pain."

"What if there's another option..?" I said, coldly.

He raised an eyebrow.

"And what would that be..?" he said, courteously.

"That I fuck you up instead, still tell you my clients demands, sit back in that chair drinking more of your expensive whisky while I wait for you to recover, listen to your answer then deliver it back, "mission fully accomplished", leaving you to look for your teeth and reset your arm, ribs and knee-caps?"

Marcus pouted and rubbed his smooth, square chin as if seriously considering the offer.

"Do you know I hadn't considered that option..," he mused, mockingly, then he looked up at me, decision made:" I think I'll decline it however. Thank you for offering it though. Now, please: Have you made your decision..?"

"I've made it..," I muttered, taking two steps nearer, never letting my eyes leave his, my intention obvious in my face.

Instantly, his expression changed and his balled-up right hand came flying at me, fast.

Just as fast I blocked it with an arm lock and made a grab for his throat, but in a blur that I hadn't expected he put a wrist-crush on my right hand, dropped suddenly, smashed me hard in the stomach with two swift, well-placed kicks with the heel of his shoe, brought the edge of his right hand down on my cheek and jaw in a series of rapid, brutal blows, twisted my right arm behind my back and kicked me again, this time just behind the left knee, sending me crashing to the floor, where I lay, face down, shocked, badly winded, fighting to breathe and half-paralysed.

His voice came down to my ringing ears from a long way off.

"It seems you chose badly Mr. Carter..."

He bent down, slipped his fingers in my shirt collar, gripped it and yanked my stinging, bleeding head up from the carpet, lowering his face to mine, a sadistic, highly satisfied grin on his bright-eyed face.

"I'm sorry not to be able to continue hurting you Mr. Carter..," he breathed, obviously enjoying my pained attempts at breathing:"...Believe me: I really am, but unfortunately I do have that phone call to make and the people I will be talking to don't like to be kept waiting, so I'll leave you here and make you a large drink which I'll leave on the table for when you feel able to get up onto your feet. That should numb the pain enough to enable you to stumble back to your car and somehow drive carefully back to wherever it is you exist, with my promise to you of a far worse beating if I have the misfortune to see you again ringing in your bruised head."

Two sudden hard and fast back-handed slaps across my cheeks rocked my brain, opening the skin.

"Oh, one more thing…"

He let go of my collar, stood over me as I dropped to the floor again, drew back his foot and gave me a nice, solid kick in the stomach again. The sort of kick I'd have been proud to have given someone else. The sort of kick designed to double a man up and send waves of searing pain right through his body, which is exactly what his kick did to me.

I had time for just one long, vomiting groan before thick black curtains wrapped themselves around my mind and I went out.

EIGHT

The long, all-too familiar and all too painful process of coming back from the dead was never pleasant and this time was no exception.

What with the tender, egg-sized lump on the back of my head from hitting the floor, my body aching all over, my face stinging like I'd washed it in acid, and a dull, deep throbbing pain in my stomach that I wouldn't have wished on anyone apart from the guy that gave it to me, I knew had to just lie on the floor in the semi-darkness for a while, groaning and holding my stomach, and while I did that, I kept trying to get my thoughts in a straight line again, telling myself that all in all, the meeting could have gone a lot better.

Eventually I managed to move a little; started to work my legs about, took a deep, agonising breath and rolled onto my back, groaning and gasping, attempting to sit up, thinking very bad thoughts about the man that put me down here in the first place.

Dexter was a nasty, self-satisfied, arrogant, over-confident, ruthless ego-maniac, but, as I'd just discovered, he was also very good at looking after himself, probably because, doing what he did for a living, he couldn't help but make a lot of enemies and there would be guys like me out there every day wanting to harm him or have harm done to him. Of course, it could also be that he just got a big kick out of stomping the living crap out of people, which I didn't doubt for one second, having been on the receiving end of his well-placed feet, but whatever the reason was, he was fast; Faster than I expected, and I was going to have to bear that in mind the next time we met, which, as I'd lain on his carpet, groaning and coughing up bile, I'd decided we most definitely were and as soon as possible because, if the main reason for coming here initially had been simple, stupid curiosity, then that curiosity had now been replaced by something far stronger and far purer.

Good, old-fashioned, hard-eyed, ice cold hatred.

Finally, after a couple of painful and clumsy attempts that felt like I was about to split in half, I managed to get up onto my feet and stand upright, walking around in slow, unsteady, stumbling circles, one hand clutching my side, the other holding onto the back of a chair for support. It wasn't nice but, with heavy breathing and through gritted teeth, it gradually became bearable and I made my way carefully over to the light switch, flicking it on when I got there and looking around me. The room was as I'd remembered it being, except that now the drinks cabinet was empty of bottles and there was just one small, lonely glass on the flap, placed on top of a sheet of writing paper and half-filled with whisky.

Taking a long, deep, pain-killing breath, I walked carefully over to it, snatched up the drink, threw it straight down my throat in one biting swallow, shuddered as the golden liquid burned into my soul and read the words on the paper:

"Enjoy you're drink mister Carter. As you can see, I keep my promises and I promise that if I see you again, I will enjoy making you feel a lot worse than you do now. Please do give my regards to Mrs. Fitzgerald.   M.D."

I put down the glass, shook my head and walked, painfully, over to the door, peering around it cautiously when I got there.

The hall and the corridor were empty and the house was quiet. Dexter was either having the hot, soothing bath he'd mentioned or was upstairs napping, bless him. The thought did cross my mind to find him and beat his sleeping face to a bloody pulp, but decided I probably wouldn't make it even halfway up the stairs, so instead, hissing at a sudden explosion of fireworks at the top of my hip, found my way to the front door, slipped out of the house and went looking for my car.

I found it, untouched, with Charlotte curled up just where I'd left her, still asleep, deep in whatever kind of drug enhanced dream she was flying through.

As quietly as I could so as not to wake her, trying to stifle the groans and grunts of searing agony as I very slowly and very carefully folded myself behind the wheel, I started up the car, backed out onto the gravel drive, drove through the iron gates and headed back towards London, focusing hard on staying on the road, biting my lip against the pain.

NINE

The drive into London took more than an hour and was almost unbearable but somehow I managed to make it and, pulling up in a quiet Mews just off Sloane Street, made a wheezy call on my mobile.

After a long time, a sleepy Scotsman's voice said; "Hello..?"

"Jock..," I said, clutching my side as another spasm ripped through me:" It's Matt: Matt Carter. I need your help."

'Jock' McManners, another old army pal of my fathers, six foot four; red-haired; heavily moustached; fiery-eyed and still with the hardened body of the boxer he used to be despite being in his late fifties, sighed heavily.

"Again..?" he said, sardonically:" What is it this time? You needing somewhere to hide for a while: Wounds dressing..? What?"

"I've got a woman in the car. She's in a bad way. Drugs and drink. Too much of both."

Another heavy sigh.

"You don't say. Anyone I know..?"

"I very much doubt it..," I breathed, trying to stifle another gasp:" I didn't know her until this morning. She's in a spot of trouble so I need a place for her to stay for a while. Somewhere safe where she can be put to bed and sleep off whatever she's full of. I thought maybe you and Carol could help me out?"

There was a yawn and I could sense he was thinking it over. The last time I asked for his help the guy died on his carpet which didn't please him much because he'd only just had it laid.

"Okay..," he grunted, ill-naturedly:" Bring her around the back, but I don't care if she is one of your bloody girlfriends, okay? If she bleeds on anything or starts dying she goes and you still pay the usual fee: Understand..?"

"Don't worry Jock..," I said, smiling:" She's not a bleeder and she's not one of my girlfriends. Usual fee. I'll be at the back entrance in five minutes."

I drove around the back of the building, parked up nice and discreet behind the dumpers and waited for Jock to stick his head around the side door. When he did he was in his dressing gown: The one with his initials on the front pocket. I got out of the car slowly and came around to his side, needing a hand on the bonnet to help get me there.

"She's a pretty one...I'll gi' you that..," he said, peering in through the passenger window at the still unconscious Charlotte:" Why is it always the good-lookers who get themselves in this state?"

"Sometimes they don't know they're getting into this state..," I said, dealing with the lancing pain in my side:"...and by then it's usually too late. This one's lucky. I found her dancing in the rain."

He looked at me curiously.

"What the fuck was she doing dancing in the rain..?" he gruffed.

"Getting wet..," I said, opening the passenger door. It was none of his business and my tone told him that.

"Makes sense..," he muttered, knowing that was the best answer he was going to get:" Okay; Lets' get her up the stairs then."

Charlotte wasn't a big girl by any means: Slender in fact: Maybe even a little skinny, but it wasn't easy trying to get her dead-weighted body up two flights of stairs and along a hallway. A few times I thought I was going to pass out with the pain and strain, but after a lot of hauling around, we managed to get her into Jock's flat and lay her on the bed in one of his three bedrooms. I know what you're thinking and you'd be right thinking it: A flat with three bedrooms just off Sloane Street? Jock must be loaded and he was, none of it earned legitimately, but that's another story for another time and was also the reason he knew not to ask questions. Jock had earned most of his money working for some very dishonest, often very brutal people and was one of the very few that were able to get to a ripe old age and enjoy the money they'd been paid. A lot of guys never lasted more than a few years, but Jock was naturally good at what he did and I was more than happy he was a friend and not an enemy.

In the large and expensively furnished sitting room, while Jock's wife, Carol, began fussing around, undressing Charlotte, making her comfortable, boiling water for two hot water bottles and finding the smelling salts, Jock made a pot of black coffee for me and a decent sized brandy and soda for himself, then sat like a ginger giant watching me wince my way through two cups of hot, thick Java, swallowing handfuls of assorted pills.

"Yon' girlie in there doesn't look good…"he said, watching me move my jaw cautiously and flinch when it punished me for not being cautious enough:"…and neither do you. Looks like a hell of a night you'se two had."

"It was Jock..," I groaned, adjusting my position in the big armchair for the fifth or sixth time, beginning to feel a little less like a split punch bag and a bit more human:" For both of us, but I think I came off worse."

"Aye, I can see that..," he grinned:" A friend of yours..?" he asked, slyly.

I shook my head, carefully.

"No…Not a friend..," I moaned:" Let's just say "a damsel in distress".

I got one of Jock's famous snorts.

"Another one..?" he grinned, shaking his big head:" What is it with you and damsels in bloody distress? You're just like your fucking dad: Gallant and stupid. The times I've had to pull him out of the fucking fire and put him back together again after he'd gone to a poor wee girl's aid."

He snorted again, but this time there was a grin of fond remembrance behind it.

"What's she full of by the way..?" he went on:" Booze or drugs?"

"Mostly drugs..," I said:" Coke is my main guess but there might be a few Blue Angels in the mix from the way her eyes are. I looked at her arms and I can't see any needle marks."

"There wouldn't be..," Jock said:" She's a cocktail dress kinda' girl. I can tell looking at her. Swanky fucking parties and private yachts. Can't have any needle marks showing in her Givenchy can we..?"

He poured himself another brandy while I poured myself another coffee.

"How about you? You don't look too good yourself? You okay?"

I nodded.

"I've been better..," I said, draining the third cup dry:" Nothing worse than I've had before though."

"Well that's saying something. I've seen you looking pretty bad son. You know, you ought to think seriously about doing something a little less dangerous for a profession."

I smiled at him, trying not to pull the muscles on my jaw too tight.

"I'm good at 'dangerous' Jock. You know that. You taught me how to be. I'll be fine. Just a few more pills, a couple of brandies and…"

"You'll be asleep..," he grinned, widely:"…and then I'll have to charge double for looking after you'se as well."

"Don't worry..," I said, sitting back and folding my hands together across my chest, closing my eyes, letting the warmth of the flat and the softness of the cushions comfort me:" I'm not planning on sleeping. I have bad dreams if I sleep too long. Besides, I can't afford your rates. I haven't been paid enough on this job."

"So it's a job then is it, not just another club-crawl gone bad..?"

"No..," I sighed:" Its business…"

"Business that went bad..?"

I opened one eye and looked at him, a small, reassuring smile on my face.

"A little..," I said:"…but I'll make it better."

Jock grinned back at me and winked.

"I'm sure you will sonny. I'm sure you will."

He stood up and pointed at the almost empty pot.

"You okay for coffee..?" he said:" I can make another one if you still feel shaky, and don't worry if you do want to crash out by the way. You've put a lot of work our way. Paid for a few nice cruises. This one will be on the house. Call it a favour to your dad, eh?"

I was about to tell him, in a mocking voice, how touched I was at the sentiment when the door opened and Carol looked in.

"She's waking up..," she said, her strong Cockney accent an attractive contrast to her fine, high-cheeked looks.

When I got to the bedroom, Charlotte was propped up on four big pillows like something from an old black and white movie, her diamonds and jewellery on the bedside cabinet.

"Where am I..?" she breathed, her blood-pink eyes wide, staring at us with a fearful, confused look on her grey-pale, sweat-slicked face:" Who are you..?"

She looked bad and probably felt worse.

I stepped forward towards the bed, slowly, the way you'd approach a scared bunny rabbit, while Jock and Carol stayed by the door, not wanting to overwhelm her.

"Don't you remember me..?" I said, calmly, not getting too close:" Matt Carter. We met this morning at "Devil's View"."

She continued staring up at me, her eyes searching my face, trying to put me together like a jigsaw without a picture, then;

"I remember..," she said, sounding relieved but also amused at the same time:" You're "Clever Carter"…No, no…Wait…Carol: Christmas Carol. That's it..! You're Christmas Carol..!"

There was a suppressed snort from behind me and the sound of Carol shushing it away.

"It's all coming back to me..," Charlotte continued, staring at me as though I were appearing an inch at time through a mist:" We danced beneath the trees didn't we? Yes, yes…We did, and you made me a drink? In the house. You made me a drink in the house and…and…asked me questions about…"

Her face froze:

"What happened to you..?" she said, half-whispering, pointing at my face, noticing the bruises for the first time.

I rubbed my chin and cheeks self-consciously.

"Your husband and I finally met..," I said, trying to make light of the fact I'd had my face slapped around like a beach ball:"…and you were right. He's not a very nice man, is he?"

"No he's not..," she whispered, shaking her head slowly, staring into the distance, her eyes filled with what I assumed were bad memories:" He's not…"

Suddenly a flush of fear washed over her tired, pinched looking face and she sat up, snapping her head forward, dread in her voice.

"Oh God..! You didn't try to do anything stupid to him did you..?" she gasped, panic-stricken:" No, No..! Don't say you did..! He'll blame me. He'll say I sent you..! He'll…He'll…!"

"Relax…," I said, stepping forward quickly, the sudden lightning bolt of pain in my ribs telling me it was too quickly, and placed my hand on her shoulders, gently easing her back into the pillows:" Don't worry. He won't think that at all. Nothing I said to him had anything to do with you and I never mentioned you once. I promise you he didn't know you were there."

She lay back, looking up at me from the pillows, eyes wide with fear and doubt like a whipped dog, terrified; wanting to believe me but uncertain. Dexter had obviously done a real job on her: Turned her into an addict, made her totally dependent then made her terrified of upsetting him.

After a few seconds, she seemed to calm down and I saw the tension fall away from her shoulders but she still looked suspicious.

"Where am I..?" she said, looking nervously around the room, noticing Jock and Carol for the first time:" Who are those people..?"

"We're back in London..," I said, reassuringly:"…at the flat of some good friends of mine."

I turned and indicated the two in the doorway.

"This is Jock and his wife, Carol. They are going to be looking after you for a while: You'll be okay with them, trust me. They're very nice people. You're perfectly safe, or at least you are as long as you stay here for a while."

"What do you mean "perfectly safe"…?" she said, frowning, shifting her gaze from me to them continuously, her eyes confused:" "Why am I here? What am I doing in this bed?"

She was starting to panic again.

"Please: Calm down..," I said:" You collapsed, okay: Back at the house, remember? Just after our little dance? You passed out after drinking all night at your husbands' party.

'Must have had a bit too much of something so, I brought you here to sleep it off. That's all. Like I said, you're safe. They'll look after you."

She looked at me as if not understanding what I was saying.

"What do you mean they'll look after me..?"

Her voice started to rise and she sat upright again, teeth clenched in fury, her eyes burning into mine.

"There's nothing wrong with me..!" she began screaming:" I don't need looking after..! I'm perfectly fine..! Take me home..! TAKE-ME-HOME..!! You have no right to keep me here in this…this…place! I insist you…" But she didn't finish the sentence because suddenly she fell back into the pillows, her eyes rolling back into her head; her mouth gaping open.

Carol pushed past me and took her face in her hands.

"She's passed out. Some kind of seizure..," she said, coolly:" it'll be all the drugs and drink she's 'ad."

"Will she be all right..?" I said, concerned. She didn't look all right.

"She'll be okay..," Carol nodded, reassuringly, staring into Charlottes' eyes as if she was studying a diamond:" I've seen it a lot in the clubs. 'Appens to posh girls all the time. Too much money: Too much drink: Too many drugs: Not enough brains."

She turned to us and told us to go, shushing us away with an impatient wave of her hand.

"Don't worry: I'll 'andle 'er..," she said:" She'll be right. Just go and 'ave another drink or something."

So we did.

Back in the sitting room, with another coffee in my hand and another brandy in Jocks fist, I told him about Mrs. Fitzpatrick, the trip to the big house, finding Charlotte dancing under the trees, my conversation with Marcus and about how he managed to knock the crap out of me without even messing up his hair. I also told him about the gun I found in Charlottes purse, which made him raise an eyebrow.

"Has she still got it?"

"It's in the car. I didn't think it was a good idea to keep it within her reach, the state she's in."

"Very wise. A drunk woman with a big shiny gun is not the best combination. Do you reckon she was going to shoot her husband wi'it?"

I nodded.

"I think that thought might have been on her confused mind to begin with: She certainly hates him enough, but as the night went on and her mind turned to mush, I reckon she wouldn't have been capable of it anyway. I doubt she could have even taken it out of her bag, the state she was in."

We stopped talking for a moment, each thinking their own thoughts, mine mostly about what had happened earlier and what I was going to do about it. What was I going to do? What could I do, and, more importantly, why would I want to? I'd made some money, met some interesting people; had a nice drive down to Brighton: Why not just leave it there? Let the mean rich people carry on being mean to each other: Not really my problem. I'd done what I'd been paid to do and it hadn't worked. I'd never given a guarantee that it would so no promises broken. I should buy another couple of bottles of Scotland's finest, go hide in my loft like I usually do, lick my wounds and wait for some other kind of trouble to come creaking up my stairs. That's what I should do, I knew that, but the trouble was I'm a stubborn man who doesn't like being beaten by another man, especially a man like Marcus. I'm too much of a gentleman. I take after my father that way. I like women in all the ways a man should, including being nice to them. A man that beats up women or terrifies them for his own, twisted pleasure isn't a man in my eyes and they deserve to be terrified back. Besides, it hurt my pride to be floored by a sleazy pimp like Dexter. I wanted to go back there and...And what..? Get myself killed next time?

I'd just finished my coffee, when Carol's voice from the doorway made me lift my head up from staring at the carpet.

"She's awake again..," she said:"...and she's asking for you."

Charlotte was sitting up again, looking better but not a lot.

"How are you feeling..?" I asked, genuinely concerned, too much of a gentleman to tell her she looked like death's older sister:" You passed out on us a while ago."

"Not sure..," she said in a tired half-whisper:" I think I'm okay but..."

"You'll be fine..," I said:" Carol was a nurse before she met Jock. She's used to people being ill."

"I'm not ill...," she croaked, her thin, blue-grey lips twitching:"...Just hungover."

"That as well..," I grinned, trying to lighten the mood and keep her calm:"...but you were definitely ill. Drink and drugs don't mix well, and you had a lot of both."

She didn't like that and shot me a look like a harpoon out of a gun.

"I don't take drugs..," she began to say, her eyes hard on mine, glittering with anger, but I raised a hand and threw four empty phials onto the bed.

"You do take drugs..," I said, firmly but amiably:" A lot of them. You took these and if I hadn't come along when I did you'd have taken a lot more."

She tore her gaze from the phials and looked up at me, her fingers gripping the sheets.

"Those aren't mine..," she hissed, unconvincingly.

I smiled down at her, an "Oh yeah?" expression on my face.

"They came from your purse..," I said, calmly.

"Those-aren't-mine..," she repeated slowly, watching me like a snake watching a circling mongoose.

For a fleeting second I thought about carrying on sugar-coating it all for her: Telling her it was okay: "I believe you: Just get some rest: You'll be fine." All that stuff, because she was ill and probably felt bad, but then decided not to dance around anymore. I'd danced with her before and look where it got me.

"Well, I think they are..," I said tightly:"...I also think that it's lucky I found you when I did, because if I hadn't, it's my guess you might have been in a lot of trouble."

She threw me a challenging look.

"What do you mean..?" she asked, haughtily:" Why would I have been in trouble..? What kind of trouble..?"

I folded my arms and tilted my head, holding her angry stare with my own calmly indifferent one.

"The kind that comes from drinking too much, taking too many drugs and carrying a loaded gun around in your purse..," I said, impassively.

That knocked her back and she fired me a second harpoon look. A real sharp one.

"A gun..? What are you talking about: I don't have a..?"

"A Smith and Wesson Snub Nose thirty-eight..," I said, matter of factly:" Fancy engraving all over it, with the letters 'MD' monogrammed onto ivory hand grips: I found it in the bottom of your purse, amongst all the drugs and credit cards. You have a lot of both by the way."

For a long moment she didn't speak, just stared at me, a battle about how to react going on behind her eyes, then, realising there was no point in trying to deny it, she shrank slowly back into the pillows.

"It's not my gun..," she half-whispered, almost apologetic.

"I guessed that..," I said:" A bit heavy for those thin little wrists of yours. I see you more with a nice little Beretta to be honest. Much more of a ladies gun. Better for someone of your stature. It's your husbands' isn't it: Marcus Dexter? His initials."

She nodded, dejectedly: Reluctantly.

"I wasn't going to..," she began to say but trailed off.

"Use it…? I'm pretty sure you were..," I smiled knowingly:" Stupidly, but, under the influence of alcohol and your husbands finest Colombian white so it's understandable, you told me you hated your husband and that when he came back, you were going to shoot him."

She looked shocked: Shocked that I knew and shocked that she'd told me.

"I…I…wasn't..," she insisted, but I could tell by the expression on her face she knew I knew she was lying.

"Why did you have it with you then? I doubt you carry one around with you normally. Your husband may look like a pimp and talk like a B movie gangster, but he's not stupid. He knows you probably hate his oily guts and he's not going to let you anywhere near a gun of your own. Looks to me like you had it in there for a reason."

Silence again. She didn't want to talk obviously. I did though.

I unfolded my arms and leant back against one of the chairs.

"You know what I think..? I think you came home early from the party because you were angry with Marcus for making you go, had a few more drinks, sniffed up a few more packets of Colombian for courage, went to wherever he keeps his gun then went spinning out into the garden to wait for him to come back and when he did, I think you were going to put as many drug-fuelled bullets through his black heart as your twitchy little fingers could send his way. I think you were determined you were going to kill him not only because you hate him but because you were terrified that if you didn't manage to pull the gun on him and he found it on you, he would hurt you very badly like he's probably done a few times before. I think you hate him very, very much for what he is and what he's turned you into, and that you've wanted him dead and the misery of your existence to end for quite some time."

"How dare you..!" she snarled, her eyes blazing with indignance, like a naughty little rich girl caught by the housekeeper fucking the chauffeur:" You have no right to talk to me like that..!"

I grinned at her, disrespectfully.

"I have every right..," I said coolly:"...because you owe me: Big time."

Her eyes widened in disbelief then hooded, her mouth tightening into a cat's arse of barely-controlled fury.

"I owe you..?" she breathed, slowly:" I *OWE* you..? What the HELL makes you think I owe you *ANYTHING*..!??"

"Well...How about the fact that I probably saved you from going to prison for thirty years for killing your husband for starters, and then there's the fact that by bringing you here I've increased your chances of not being killed by him instead. I think those two facts give me the right to say you owe me."

Her face tensed but she said nothing, just lay there surrounded by plump, silk cushions trying to burn a hole through my head with her eyes.

"Killed..? What do you mean "killed"..?" she finally said, once she'd accepted that I wasn't going to fall on my knees and beg her forgiveness for daring to talk to her like a spoilt brat:" He wouldn't dare..."

"Oh I think he might..," I said, moving over to the bed and sitting on the end of it, leaning towards her:" He's what we professionals call an absolute bloody bastard, and what he told me while we were still on speaking terms was that you've started to bore him and that he's thinking of making the way clear for him to go find the next Mrs. Marcus Dexter."

"He wouldn't..," she growled through gritted teeth, her eyes still on "stun".

"I beg to bloody differ I'm afraid..," I said:" I got the very strong impression that he would. Like I told you, your husband is a very nasty piece of work, and I'm pretty certain that when he finds his guns gone he's going to put two and two together in that nasty little mind of his and decide that your disappearance and then me turning up at his house threatening him can only mean you intend him harm and, being the bad man that he is, his natural instinct is going to be to find you before you find him, which is why, I thought, just for a couple of days, it'd be safer if you stayed here."

She made no reply for a long few seconds, her cold, focused stare turning from enraged despisation to cold loathing.

"Who the hell do you think you are..?" she rumbled, each word coated with slow-burning acid.

"Doesn't matter who I am. What's important is what's going to happen to you next, and that is, you are going to take the medicine Carol is going to give you, go back to sleep and not wake up until your brain is a lot clearer. When you do wake up, I'll have found somewhere else for you to go. Nowhere salubrious I'm afraid because I can't afford 'salubrious'."

"What happens if I say no..?" she said, petulantly:" What happens if I just get up, walk out of here and…"

"And what? Go back to the man that did this to me…"

I touched my jaw, wincing at the stab of pain that punished me for doing so:

"…and who now believes you may be part of a plan to bring him down? I doubt hubby's going to welcome you back with open arms, do you? He's got a bit of a little bit of a temper on him in case you hadn't noticed, and I get the distinct feeling he holds grudges."

She sat forward.

"You can't keep me here..," she said, defiantly" I want to go…"

"Where: Home..? Which home? You've probably got a few you can run to, but I get the feeling that if you pop your drug-addled head up anywhere during the next few days, especially at one of your 'homes', Marcus is going to find you and within a very short space of time you won't look quite so pretty."

She fell silent which I took as an admission of acceptance, so carried on.

"So: The way I see it is this. You've got three choices. One: I let you go home..."

"*LET* me..?" she snapped.

"Yes..," I snapped back:" Let you..!"

She fell silent again, sulking, and I continued.

"I let you go home and you die tragically of an overdose in the arms of your adoring, grief-stricken husband. Two: I drag you 'round to a police station, say I found you wandering about in front of my house, coked up to the eyeballs and waving a gun around threatening to kill people which means you'll be arrested, locked up, and with the amount of stuff still in your system probably end up on a high security Detox wing somewhere, or three, you stay in that big, comfy bed, sleep off the drink and the drugs, let Carol perform her usual miracle, get well enough to leave and then we use your money to find a hidey hole where lover-boy won't find you, giving me time to go back and have another try at persuading him to be reasonable. If it was me in your shoes, I think I'd be seriously considering going for option number three."

She rolled her eyes and sighed heavily.

"All right. You win. I'll go for option three."

"And you'd be right to..," I smirked:" A very wise choice if I may say so. Now, lie back, close your pretty, pink eyes, go back to whatever crazy dreams you were having and let me think about what to do about that bastard of a husband of yours."

Like a puppet with its strings cut, she slumped back into the pillows, all the fight gone out of her, her grey, drawn face looking even more exhausted than before with the effort of trying to cope with the last few minutes.

"Be careful..," she mumbled, before closing her eyes and slipping rapidly back into what looked like a deep, almost catatonic sleep.

I got up off the bed, asked Carol to keep a close eye on her, looked back at the pathetic looking figure beneath the sheets and, after a short word with Jock, left the flat, driving on auto-pilot back to my office, thinking about Marcus Dexter, Mrs. Fitzpatrick and what the hell I was going to do about both of them.

TEN

After stopping to buy a couple of bottles of whiskey, one very good one and one very cheap one, I climbed the badly lit stairs to my office, the bandages Carol had wrapped around my rib-cage and shoulder feeling tighter with each step, took a few deep breaths at the top to recover, opened the door, threw off my crumpled jacket, lowered myself onto the sofa, opened the good bottle, poured a large tumbler full of the golden cure-all and lay back staring at the cracked ceiling, continuing to try and work out in my pounding head why the hell I was, yet again, sticking my too often broken nose into other people's business.

Another full tumbler later I still didn't have any answers apart from " …because you can't keep your nose out of other people's business…", so, once I'd realised I wasn't going to walk away from this, I put the empty tumbler down, screwed the cap back onto the bottle, stood up, caught my breath as yet another lightning shaft of pain shot up my side, walked over to the desk and began making a series of phone calls to the best hotels in the city: Claridge's: The Connaught: The Savoy: The Ritz: The Dorchester and Browns, and half a dozen others in the same league as the Beaumont Park, trying to find the mysterious Mrs. Leonora Fitzpatrick, but none of them, not one, had heard of her. She wasn't nor ever had been a guest, and at none was she booked in for future arrival.

I closed the line on the last call and leaned back in my chair, trying to make sense of it. Had she changed her name? Was she actually staying in one of them but under another name: Her real name? If so, why had she'd lied?

I couldn't get it out of my mind that this was some kind of set up but no reason why made any sense to me. Maybe it wasn't her: Maybe it was Cleaver, but Cleaver had no reason that I could think of to set me up and Dexter genuinely seemed to have no idea who I was or why I was there, so I doubted very much it was either of them. So, if it was a set-up it had to be her, but why: What was she up to, and why choose me?

I decided I was tired of thinking and needed to freshen up, so I locked the office and drove, very carefully, to the Blue Oasis.

When I got there, Ronnie wasn't in which I was glad of. There'd only be questions and I didn't want questions right now. I had enough of my own with no answers. Accepting a strong coffee from Benny-Jack, the bar manager, I took it upstairs to Ronnie's office, went into the wash-room, stripped out of my clothes, wincing and sucking air through my teeth as I took off my shirt and pants, took a good, long, hot shower which helped soothe my aching ribs and cleared my head nicely, shaved carefully taking care not to nick myself: (I had enough cuts and bruises as it was): Splashed on some good cologne, walked over to the wardrobe, chose some more casual, less-fitted clothes this time, checked myself in the door mirror, saw a beaten but still good looking man looking back at me, a little used and abused maybe but okay now that he was showered and shaved, went back into the office feeling lighter and sharper, pocketed my phone, car keys and wallet, left Ronnie's office, went back down to the bar, said 'hi' to a couple of the staff who said 'hi' back, told Benny-Jack to tell Ronnie I might be back later that evening, went outside and sat in the car for a few minutes, using my clearer head to decide a few things.

By the time I turned the key and nosed out of the car park into the street, I'd decided three things.

One: I didn't like Marcus, because he was a bad man that hurt women and because he'd given me a good hiding.

Two: I didn't like Leonora Fitzpatrick because she'd lied to me and was using me for reasons I couldn't work out and three: That I needed to go and see The Doctor.

The first two things I'd work out how to deal with later.

The third I could do right now and wove my way through the heavy traffic towards Knightsbridge.

ELEVEN

When I finally arrived in Cadogan Square, I found a parking spot close to the particular very expensive looking, cream-fronted, three storey town house I was looking for, paid for two hours by card, mounted the steps, rang the brass doorbell, waited for the buzz and click, pushed open the glossy black door and stepped into the understated but very classy reception.

The equally classy receptionist sitting gracefully behind the antique desk- a smart looking, older woman in four inch heels and very well cut hair- flashed a tight smile at me that meant nothing, asked me my name, looked me up in her appointment book, found me...(I'd called ahead before setting off)...spoke with a very plummy accent into a slim intercom, told 'The Doctor' I was here, asked me to go straight up, flashed me another over-polite smile, returned to her non-existent work and instantly forgot all about me.

One blue-carpeted floor up I knocked on the tall white door I'd walked through several times before, waited for the muffled invitation to enter and stepped into what looked more like the library of a stately home than the consulting room of a doctor: Very fine antique furniture, rows and rows of books, red silk walls, large oil paintings within dark-wood panels and a four-tier chandelier hanging from an ornately plastered ceiling. Everything about the room was designed to show that this was the room of a rich and influential man who was not be fucked with, and it did its job exceptionally well.

The man sitting behind the gilded French ormolu desk on the other side of a large Persian carpet and who watched me walk across it towards him, was well-tailored, fifty years old, lean-faced and grey-haired and was definitely not to be fucked with, not only because of what he did for people but also because of the kind of people he did things for: People that would not take kindly for the man behind the desk to be fucked with, and as it happened, I happened to be one of them. I liked him and smiled as I came closer.

"Ah, Mr. Carter..," the elegant man known simply as 'The Doctor' said, half-rising to his impeccably shod feet and indicating one of the two Georgian chairs in front of him:" Very nice to see you again. Please: Do take a seat."

When I'd sat down he took a long, studying look at me and said:" How is your shoulder now? Still giving you trouble? I know it might be vaguely pointless of me to repeat what I keep telling you but I really would advise you to try and refrain from any sudden or over-violent movement of it. The same advice goes for your lower back, your right knee and, of course, your nose. I doubt further surgery would be of any use if it, or any of those other parts, were to be broken again."

"Advice taken..," I said, crossing my legs and folding my hands in my lap:"...but unfortunately not always able to be acted upon."

He spread his hands apart in gesture of polite acceptance.

"Of course..," he smiled, charmingly:"...All I can offer is advice. The necessities of your reality must take inevitable precedent."

I smiled back and we nodded in mutual understanding. That's one of the reasons I liked the man. He was very polite and very understanding and used big words very well.

The other reason I liked him was because he knew what the patients that paid him a lot of money to patch them up and enabled them to continue making the sort of money it took to afford his level of skill, diplomacy and discretion, did for their often illegal livings. 'The Doctor' repaired, revived and kept alive the sort of people that couldn't take their injuries to a hospital or to a doctor that was burdened by scruples. Scruples and an inquisitive mind were not things "The Doctor" possessed. He didn't ask and you didn't tell: A very simple, and ironically, a very honest arrangement that made him comfortably wealthy and gave him a level of protection the fucking President would be envious of.

"Are you in pain Mr. Carter..?" The Doctor asked, guilelessly:" Your gait, the facial tics you give involuntarily when you move your shoulder, hips and jaw and the bruising around your lower left mandible, zygomatic-maxillary suture and the mental foramen tell me you are."

I smiled, tightly.

"Well observed doctor..," I said, impressed as always by the man's instinctive eye for detail:" I am a little but it's bearable, thank you. That's not what I'm here for today, however."

"Interesting..," he mused, his eyes roaming over my face, diagnosing things no doubt I couldn't even pronounce:"...but, if you don't mind, I will examine you later and perhaps prescribe something that will alleviate your obvious discomfort."

"That would be good, thank you..," I agreed.

We smiled knowingly at each other.

"So what did you come to see me about..?" he asked, charm itself.

"I want your help with a problem that involves someone I know, and possibly you may know as well."

The doctor raised an eyebrow.

"Indeed..? I'm intrigued. Please: Do go on. If I can help then, of course, I will."

"Thank you..," I said, sitting upright and adjusting myself, my ribs starting to hurt:" I appreciate any help you can give me. I've become involved in a situation that concerns a woman who is, I strongly believe, in serious danger, both mentally and physically, of doing herself irreversible harm."

"That's very unfortunate. Can I ask why?"

"I don't want to go into too many details..," I went on:"…because, like yourself, I don't like talking about my personal business and the personal lives of others."

"Commendable and true Mr. Carter, and I wouldn't dream of asking. Please go on, and tell me only what you wish me to hear."

I smiled a tight smile of thanks and continued.

"Because I'm very good at doing what I do, I've been approached by a certain party to keep an eye on a woman. My client believes, and fears, that she has been taking drugs on an increasingly large scale and feels certain that her supplier may well be her husband."

The Doctor raised both eyebrows this time and nodded, sagely.

"A shocking thing to hear Mr. Carter. Truly shocking, but how is it you think I can help, and perhaps more importantly, how is it that you think I may know this woman?"

"Because…"

I hesitated:

"Because I believe she may be a patient of yours or at least she may have been in the past."

He looked at me for a long time, giving nothing away in his expression, then spread his hands in a gesture of possibility.

"Indeed..? Well, I know many people Mr. Carter, from all walks of life. My patient list is large and…"

"Charlotte Dexter…" I interrupted, watching his face for any flicker of recognition but all I got was a controlled silence, during which, once again, he studied my face, as if looking for something, then he nodded, a slow smile lifting the ends of his mouth very slightly.

"You are correct Mr. Carter. Mrs. Dexter is, or rather, 'was' my patient but I'm afraid I haven't seen her for several months now."

I breathed a subtle sigh of relief. My guess, and that's all it was, had been correct. I had no proof that she had ever been a patient of his, but the card in her handbag showed she at least knew about him.

"Might I ask how you knew she is, or was my patient..?" The steely-eyed man across the leather-topped desk said:" The people I treat demand and expect, complete discretion and anonymity when they come to me and, in return for a not inconsiderable fee that is what they can be assured they will get. The thought that Mrs. Dexter would have told you that she…"

"Mrs. Dexter didn't tell me a thing..," I again interrupted, not wanting to tell him I found his card in her bag, a definite no-no as far as patients of his were concerned. If the police ever found out he serviced pretty much the whole of London's underworld and most of the dodgiest characters in British society, the lid would be off a real Pandora's box:" I merely put two and two together, based upon what I've come to learn about her and the world in which she moves, and came up with the very strong probability that you might be the man she turned to in her hour of increasingly great medical need."

I held up my hand and counted my fingers off, making up my explanation as I went along: I'm good like that.

"One: You only see patients who are either very wealthy or who have been sent to you by very wealthy people who need their services, myself falling into that category, and who cannot go to a doctor who would not or could not understand or tolerate the ways in which these people made their money, or the ways in which they gained the problems they find themselves burdened with, most of it either illegal or socially unacceptable. Charlotte Dexter is very wealthy indeed and her drug habit, although known about within her inner circle, would definitely be considered socially unacceptable.

Two: Those people, again myself included, require a high level of discretion and a guarantee that their problems will not be discussed or discovered by anyone outside of this room and that any treatment, surgery or services you offer them will be undertaken with the utmost skill and under the strictest veils of sensitivity. Apart from being more than wealthy and well connected enough to meet all those criteria, Charlotte Dexter has the double problem of being married to a man who, from the little I know of him but the kind of person I fully understand him to be, would demand that you stick to all those guarantees and promises. So, when I discovered that she was in need of medical help beyond that which I am able to provide, I put my thinking head on, tried to imagine who she might have turned to in the past when in need of urgent help and came up with you. A man with a trusted reputation amongst the rich and powerful for total diplomacy and lack of personal judgement, and…"

I gave a cheeky wink:

"…it seems I was right."

The Doctor nodded again in quiet appreciation of my monologue, or maybe it was my gauche naivety. I didn't know and I didn't really care: I just wanted his help with Charlotte.

"Very perceptive and instinctual of you Mr. Carter. I applaud your almost "Holmesian" approach to deduction. I can see why your services are in demand. As you say, you are obviously very good at whatever it is you do."

"I am: Very. I'm also in a hurry because I think Charlotte Dexter is very ill and close to breaking and I need your help to keep her together."

"What kind of help Mr. Carter?"

"Drastic help. Complete detox': Rehabilitation: Forced if necessary: Hiding away from her husband: Somewhere he can't find her."

"All very easily said Mr. Carter, but not so easily done. Mrs Dexter is over twenty one and, as far I recollect from her last visit it to me, although ill, she was not certifiable in anyway. In view of those things, I can only deal with her through her own instructions."

"You mean legally of course, don't you, but we both know what the vast majority of your patients do is very often illegal and the problems that they need attending to were caused in the pursuit of criminal activity. They come to you because you know that and because you know that, you can send them to places set up to deal with them. Places that are below the legal radar and which you can charge a very large amount of money for. That's what I'm asking you to do for Charlotte Dexter. Send her somewhere that can do what's needed for her and at the same time keep her safe."

"Safe..?"

"Yes, safe. I won't go into any details but I saved her from doing something very stupid to her husband under the influence of drink and drugs that she will try and do again unless she can be put away somewhere safe and secure. If you know her husband at all, you will have very quickly realised he's not the forgiving or tolerant sort and he might just decide that you as well as Charlotte tried to cause him pain and embarrassment, two things I would call his "triggers to payback"."

"I'm still not sure I can…"

"Your choice doctor. You don't have to help, and knowing Marcus Dexter as I do, I can't say I blame you for not wanting to pull his triggers, but she needs help and if you can't or won't give it, then I'm going to have to hand her over to the police."

For the first time I saw a serious look enter his eyes.

"I'm very sorry you feel you may have to do that Mr. Carter..," he said:"...I'm afraid that would very possibly be considered a foolish thing for you to contemplate, not just by myself but by others who might see any involvement with the police that may lead them to me and by some means to themselves as wholly unacceptable."

I saw the point he was trying to make and understood the threat he was implying, but I knew the threat to Charlotte's life was more immediate.

"Why do you think it would be necessary to hand her over to the police if I may ask?"

"Because earlier this morning she was about to commit a murder and if I don't get her put somewhere where she can be watched twenty four hours a day and heavily sedated, she is going to get her scrawny little hands on a lot more drugs, find another gun and use it to kill her husband."

"An alarming prospect. Do you think that might be a possibility?"

"I think it would be a certainty. Charlotte Dexter hates her husband. He has used her both physically, socially and financially, filled her with drugs, ostracised her from her family, threatened her friends to keep them from trying to contact her and, from what I have discovered, plans to throw her away for a new body to suck the blood from. I fully believe that if she escapes from where I've put her temporarily she will dose herself to the hilt with drink and drugs, either morphine, cocaine or heroin..."

"Probably heroin. She had always had a heroin addiction but I was keeping it under control until her husband came along and took her away from treatment. I would imagine by now that she has a very serious heroin problem."

"Okay: Heroin. She'll fill herself with heroin, lie in wait for her husband and shoot him dead."

The Doctor shook his head sadly.

"That is a very great shame. She used to be a lovely young girl. Her parents brought her to me as a teenager with issues of self-confidence and then problems with marijuana that had started at boarding school. I did what I could to contain her usage but she was a very gullible and rather wide-eyed girl: She fell in with a rather louche crowd and twice had to be sent to a clinic I help run in France to be de-toxified. I'm afraid Charlotte is not a strong woman, mentally or physically. Added to her other problems, her heart has been weakened by the strain she has put on it. The last time I saw her was six months ago and I got the feeling she was even more unhappy than usual. I'm afraid she just isn't strong enough to cope with that level of despair."

"Six months? That would be about when she married Marcus. I doubt even the strongest minded woman could stand up to Marcus Dexter. I assume you've met him?"

"Only once and found him a very…"

He paused:

"…Difficult man. Arrogant: Self-obsessed and conceited. A text book narcissist, but rather brutal in his manner and attitude. He didn't approve of my treating his wife and told me, rather forcefully, that she wouldn't be requiring my services any further. He settled her account and left with her in very submissive tow. From that day I never saw nor heard from her again."

There was silence for a few moments then I said:

"Look Doctor. This is very serious. I believe that Charlotte is not only very angry with her husband but also very ill. When I found her this morning she was hallucinating and on the verge of collapse. I brought her back to London and just after I got here, she did pass out. She's with a friend of mine at the moment. His wife used to be a nurse and is treating her as best she can with mild stimulants and atropine, but her pulse is very weak, she slips in and out of unconsciousness and when she's awake acts very confused with big mood swings. She's getting beyond the skills of my friends to handle and while she's in that state I can't progress with what my client has tasked me to do. That's why I came here."

"And what do you wish me to do? Without her husband's consent I cannot…"

"Her husband is never going to give his consent. In fact, if her darling husband finds out I've got her he's going to flatten the city looking for her and then make her life even more of a misery than he already has, if he doesn't actually kill her. Forget his consent. You've by-passed the law before. Do it again."

The good "Doctor" sighed heavily, steepled his fingers and sat in thought for a while, looking into middle space then, moving in his chair, he nodded his head slowly.

"Very well Mr. Carter..," he said:" I could put her into a very exclusive and very private clinic I consult at down in Kent. It has a highly confidential patient list and the government pay a lot of money to "look after" those they deem of use or importance to them. Because of that, the level of security is very high. She would be more than safe from her husband."

"Don't worry about her husband..," I said:" He won't be a problem. I'll see to that."

He gave me a look and I gave him a confirming look back. He understood what I was saying and he could see that I understood he understood. He looked reassured and smiled, confidentially.

"Very well Mr. Carter. If you can guarantee that Mrs. Dexter will be left in my care without the possibility of interference from Mr. Dexter, I will enrol her in the clinic this afternoon. If you would leave details as to the address where she is at present, I will arrange for her to be picked up and taken to Kent early this evening."

I stood up.

"Thank you..," I said, extending a hand:" I'm very glad you've agreed to help Doctor. I know she will be in very good hands. Any bills can be sent to her parents of course. I'll let my client know and she will tell them."

"My pleasure Mr. Carter. I'm glad you came to see me. Charlotte was such a lovely girl and a charming young woman before the world began to mistreat her. I will do my very best to ensure she recovers as fully as she will allow."

He took my hand and shook it, a little too hard and I winced.

"As I thought..," he mused, motioning me over to a low, surgical table in the corner of the room beneath a large portrait of a be-wigged man in an seventeenth century frock coat with a familiar looking nose:" You have rotationary problems with your upper right shoulder and what may be ancillary tearing of the latimus dorsi, brachial bicep and the upper deltoid. If you wouldn't mind taking off your shirt and allowing me to examine you..?"

I stripped off my shirt and lay on the bed which he lifted higher, bringing me closer to the big portrait: Close enough to be able to read the name of the man who was standing at a table covered in very learned looking books with his hand resting on a skull. The name meant nothing to me: Nathaniel Carrington: Surgeon, Apothecary and Physician to His Majesty king Charles the Second, but his face did.

It was the spitting image of the man gently examining my right arm and shoulder.

The man known to the underworld of London as "The Doctor", and, knowing the way things worked as well as I did, probably "Surgeon, Apothecary and Physician to King Charles the Third", as well.

TWELVE

I drove back to Jock's apartment feeling a little better after the painful but skilled manipulation "The Doc'" had given me, plus the box of magic pills that were starting to take away the dull ache I'd been putting up with ever since the never-ending drive back from Brighton so, by the time I knocked on Jock's door my mood had lifted and I was feeling more like my old self again.

When the big man finally answered and let me in, I asked how Charlotte was.

"Not great..," Jock said:" She looks like hell and won't eat or drink anything Carol tries to give her. She's been sitting wi' her since you left: Seems to think that if she's left alone for even a moment, she'll try and finish herself off somehow."

I sighed and went down the hallway to the bedroom.

Carol was sitting on a chair at the side of Charlotte's bed, a worried look on her face, and when I entered she gave me a strained smile, got up, whispered in to my ear telling how concerned she was about Charlotte's state of health, told me to be gentle with her and left the room, closing the door quietly behind her.

I could see why she was concerned. Charlotte looked like a dead fish, draped across the pillows, staring at the wall, the straps of her nightdress hanging off her thin, bony shoulders, her hair in unruly strands across her face, and the light from the bedside lamps catching the tears on her pale, grey-skinned, drawn cheeks, making them glitter.

"How are you..?" I asked quietly, genuinely worried. I knew it was a stupid question because she looked bloody terrible and probably felt ten times worse, but I tried not to let on I could see it.

"Bloody awful..," she replied, almost inaudibly, not looking away from the wall, her words muffled by the pillow:" I'd rather like to die now, if that's all right?"

"Not allowed I'm afraid..," I said, cheerfully:" House rules. The last time I brought someone here they actually did die and Jock wasn't happy about it: Ruined his carpet.

I'm still paying the fucking cleaning bill so I'd rather you didn't die, at least not here if that's okay?"

My attempt at lightning the mood obviously didn't work because she began to sob.

I stepped forward and sat on the side of the bed.

"Hey, hey..," I said, resisting the temptation to stroke her hair and make her feel better:" No need for any of that. Every things' going to be all right now, okay? I've found you somewhere you'll be taken care of and where you'll be safe. They'll be coming to get you in a couple of hours and when you get there, they can begin taking all that crap out of you. In a few weeks you won't know yourself."

"I don't know myself now..," she sobbed, her bony fingers clutching the pillow tightly, more tears running down her face:" Who am I: What am I..?"

"You're a very sick woman..," I said:" But I promise you, you won't be soon. The place I've found will make you feel good about yourself again. It better do. It's fucking expensive. I'll want my bloody money back if you still look like this in a few weeks."

"What if I don't want to feel better: What if I like feeling like this? Dead inside… What if..?"

I clenched my teeth and took a deep breath. I'm not good with self-pity: I don't react well to hearing it: It gets you nowhere: Just makes you look and sound pathetic.

"Cut it out..," I said, firmly:" That's the drugs and drink talking, and they're both talking shit. You need to stop feeling sorry for yourself, sit up and get ready to leave. You'll be there a few weeks so you're going to need some clothes and personal stuff. Give Carol and Jock the keys to wherever you live, tell them what you want and they'll go and get it all. I'll stay here with you until they come back."

She looked at me like a child that's just been scolded.

"You remind me of my husband..," she whined petulantly into the pillow, shooting me a look of anger and defiance through her matted strands of hair.

"No I don't..," I said snappily, not liking being compared to a self-obsessed, woman-beating bastard:" I'm nothing like your fucking husband. Your husband is a bloody sadist who would have dragged you out of that bed and thrown you across the room a couple of times by now with a big smile on his face while he was doing it and then given you another armful of drugs to shut you up while he spends more of your money. I'm doing the opposite. I'm putting you in a place where everything he's put into you will be taken out and you'll be given the chance to get clean, so…Stop acting like a sulky kid, sit up, wipe those tears from your face and start behaving like a grown woman."

"No..," she simpered, hugging the tear-soaked pillow to her:" I won't..! I don't want to go to any stupid clinic..," I want to die: Here: In this bed. I want to…"

I leaned forward, my arms straddling her curled up body, frustration and sudden impatience blazing in my eyes.

"I don't care what *you* bloody want..," I snarled, the tone of my voice telling her I was tired of this spoilt little girl routine now:" It's what *I* want right now that counts and right now *I* want you to pull yourself out of whatever snot-filled pit of self-imposed decay you've dug yourself deep into, quit whining like a runny-nosed brat, sit up, hand me the keys to whatever stupidly expensive flat or house it is you live in, tell Carol what it is you need packing and just lie there like an ungrateful rag doll while people who don't even know you run around trying to make your pampered, overindulged little life a bit better for you."

She stared up at me with a mixture of fear, disbelief and respect in her eyes, unsure for a few seconds how to respond, then, like a broken puppet with half its strings cut, she made a half-hearted attempt at sitting up, shaking her head sulkily. I'd guessed right. Being nice didn't work with her. You had to be strong and demanding. She was so used to bastards like Dexter dominating her life that she only reacted to being told very firmly what to do.

"Good..," I said when she'd settled herself back into the pillows, giving me sullen looks:" Now do as your told, stay there and I'll send Carol in for your list of things. When you've done that, give her your keys and address, and she'll get what you need."

She started to say something, but I ignored her and walked out of the room, imagining the glowering, surly looks I was being given as I closed the door behind me.

Five minutes later, after Jock and Carol had left and I'd topped up the drink I'd made for myself, I went back to see her.

When I entered the room she looked up from the nails she was picking and gave me the evil eye.

"Why are you doing all of this..?" she snorted sarcastically, tossing her hair contemptuously in what looked like an attempt to regain some of her poise and dignity but only made her look like a petulant kid:" What's in it for you: Why are you helping me..?"

"Why not..?" I shrugged, taking a sip of the whisky, watching with interest as her eyes followed the tumbler up to my lips and back down again, the expression on her face almost entranced, as though seeing a unicorn for the first time. It was obvious she wanted, no, *needed* a drink very, very badly. I could tell by the way she was looking at the glass and sub-consciously licking her lips that her addiction to alcohol was as strong as her addiction to drugs.

I took a slow, deliberate pull of the whisky and put the half full glass down on a sideboard.

"Could I just...?" she breathed, licking her lips and lifting a hand, her fingers moving towards the glinting glass like a tentative spider.

"No..," I said, curtly, moving the glass out of her reach:" You can't, but you *can* tell me about Leonora Fitzpatrick."

"Who..?" she said, absently, still staring at the glass.

"Leonora Fitzpatrick. She's a friend of yours, and of your husband."

Her eyes narrowed, and I could see her thinking, her gaze flicking from me to the glass, trying to recall the name, then suddenly they widened.

"Leonora..?" she said, smiling widely: Almost manically:" Of course I know Leonora. Why did you mention her? Do you know her as well..?"

"I do..," I said, leaning back against the wall and crossing my arms, watching her watching the glass:"...but not as a friend. More as a client."

She frowned and looked at me.

"A client? What do you mean..? What are you...? What do you do...?"

"I'm..."

I hesitated, not sure of how to describe what I was.

Her frown deepened.

"Yes? You're what: A private detective or something..?"

It was my turn to frown.

"Not exactly a detective..," I said, uncertainly.

"What then..," she said, suspiciously:"...and why would Leonora be your client? What is she paying you to do..?"

There was another silence while she waited to hear my answer and I tried to think of one.

"I fix problems..," I said, guardedly.

She looked at me, sideways.

"Problems? What kind of problems, and what do you mean by 'fix' them?"

What had I got to lose? Tip-toeing around wasn't getting me anywhere.

"I mean I try to smooth out situations that have become messy: Persuade people to change their minds or attitudes: Make them see the error of their ways."

She stared at me for a few moments, trying to compute my cryptic description of what it was I did then nodded in understanding.

"You mean my husband don't you..?" she said, quietly:" Leonora wants you to "fix" my husband."

"Sort of..," I said:" Although not so much him as your situation with him."

She lowered her head and started to cry again, her thin shoulders lifting and falling with her sobs.

"Of course..," she wept, shaking her head, gazing with wet eyes down into the pillows:" My situation. My God awful bloody situation. The one everyone warned me about. The one Leonora warned me about..!"

Suddenly she jerked her head up and looked at me.

"Is she paying you, or are my parents..?" she asked, pearly tears chasing each other down her cheeks.

"Not sure..," I said, my voice soft and sympathetic again. A crying woman makes me go all soft: A crying man just makes me angry:" Just her I think, but it might be both."

"She is, of course she is..," Charlotte cried, her weeping eyes red with what...Anger? Shame?

"...She's such a good friend and such a strong woman..," she went on, her teeth clenching now. Definitely shame:" She's as strong as I'm weak. Weak and stupid!"

Her tears became fatter and rolled from her eyes as though a tap behind them had been opened wider.

"I am stupid..!" she wailed, snatching at the sheets:" I am stupid and pathetic and...and...I should have listened! I should have seen what kind of man he is! Everyone warned me he was evil. They all told me what he did to women: What he made people do for him..!"

Like I said, self-pity did nothing for me and this was getting us nowhere so I picked up the glass and offered it to her. What the hell I figured. She's going to be dried out soon so one last drink isn't going to make a difference and if it distracts her and quietens her down then why not?

Instantly she stopped crying, reaching out for it like a drowning man reaches for a thrown rope, but I pulled it back, just out of the reach of her clutching fingers.

"Ah ahhh..," I said, holding the glass within inches of her grasp:"...Calm down. Lie back, take a few breaths and I'll let you have a drink...but no more crying, okay?"

It worked. Staring at the glowing gold liquid in my hand as though it were the face of God, she lay back into the pillows.

"That's better..," I soothed, keeping my voice level and encouraging:" Now, drink this, close your eyes and try to sleep. Everything's going to be okay: I've got it all straightened out. There's nothing to worry about, anymore. We just need you to get to that clinic. Once you're there you'll be safe from Marcus. He can't reach you where you're going."

As I'd promised, I gave her the drink and stood watching as she gulped it down in two, big, hungry swallows, dropping the empty glass onto the floor like a forgotten lover when she'd finished, a look of almost orgasmic bliss on her face. Christ, she had it bad. Whether it had been Dexter or just her own boredom that had driven her to alcohol, she'd fallen cork, bottle and glass headfirst, straight into the barrel.

I scooped up the tumbler and placed it on a sideboard.

"Another... Please?" she mewed up at me like a starving kitten.

"No..," I said, coldly:" Not now. Now you close your eyes, you think of nothing and you sleep, got that? When Carol comes back she'll get you dressed and give you something to eat. The car from the clinic will be arriving to pick you up in a couple of hours and you need to be ready."

She nodded weakly, took a last, lingering look at the glass in my hand, licked her lips, closed her eyes and within seconds sank into a deep sleep, leaving me standing over her, looking down at her exhausted face and thinking very bad thoughts about Marcus Dexter.

Back in the living room, I'd just poured myself another whiskey to replace the one Charlotte had devoured, when Jock and Carol came through the front door, Jock carrying an expensive suitcase and Carol carrying two small, equally expensive, matching vanity bags. They took them into Charlotte's room.

After they'd taken them to Charlotte's room, Jock returned, accepted the drink I'd poured for him and as we sat drinking, I asked if everything had gone okay and he nodded, saying he'd kept a careful watch on the street outside as Carol had found the things on the list, but hadn't seen anything or anyone suspicious. I then asked what the flat was like and he told me it was large, very nicely furnished, but bloody untidy. The curtains were all drawn, there was a hell of a lot of booze standing or lying around on almost every surface, the beds in each of the three bedrooms were a mess and there were silver trays in every room, including the bathrooms, with what looked like the remnants of cocaine smeared across them. Charlotte, it seemed, was a real party girl. Any messages on the Ansa-Fone or left lying around, I asked..? He shook his head: No; nothing. He'd checked.

For another ten minutes we sat drinking, quietly absorbing the smooth, peaty caramel of the whisky then Carol came in to tell us that Charlotte was dressed and ready, and that she was going to make her a light meal of eggs to give her some energy and line her stomach: Would I like some while she was making them? I said yes I would, thanked her and jokingly told her to put them on the bill, which she laughed at scornfully, told me not to be so soft and went into the kitchen. When she'd gone though, Jock leaned forward conspiratorially and said to ignore her and make bloody sure I did put it on the bill. Eggs is eggs and money is bloody money son, he said raising his glass in a mock salute. I laughed and smiled uncertainly at the big guy, not sure whether he was joking or not. You couldn't always tell with Jock and I had no intention of incurring his wrath over a half dozen eggs. I'd seen him break a man's hand once for drinking his tea.

The eggs were good and so was the coffee and when I'd finished eating, I took the plates and coffee cups into the kitchen, dropped them into the dishwasher, waited whilst Carol went back into Charlotte's room and Jock went down the hall to the toilet, took the key to Charlotte's flat from the table and dropped it into my pocket. I needed to search her flat myself. No offence to Jock, but I knew what I was looking for: He didn't.

Halfway through making myself and Jock another coffee, Carol returned to the living room.

"She wants to talk to you..," she said.

"What about..," I asked but Carol just shrugged.

"I don't know. One minute, she was calm and quiet, letting me get her ready, then suddenly she became agitated: 'Got a wild look in her eyes and said she needed to talk to you: Ask you something important. She wouldn't tell me what it was, just kept saying you would understand."

"Lets' hope I do..," I sighed, putting down the coffee.

When I walked into Charlotte's room, I found her dressed, her hair brushed, standing unsteadily beside the dressing table; one thin hand on the wall to keep her balance, her eyes red from more crying. She looked more presentable than before, but she was still a mess. When she saw me come in she looked up and there was tangible mask of fear clamped tightly around her face.

"Carol said you wanted to talk to me..," I said:" What about? Are you okay?"

"The gun..," she asked in a tight half-whisper:" Where is it?"

I gave her a steady look.

"It's safe. Why..?" I said, coldly.

Her stare faltered and she broke away from me, gazing at the ground for a second, composing herself, then looked up again, straight back into my eyes.

"I need it..," she said, putting as much firmness and bravado into her words as her nervousness allowed her to, but there was a shake to her voice.

"No..," I said, evenly and with a firmness to my words she couldn't match:" You don't need it...Not where you're going. I've told you: You'll be perfectly safe there and anyway, I don't think they like having their badly fucked up clients bringing guns into their clinic. There are house rules about shooting at the staff. Bad form, don't cha' know...?"

I tried to bring levity to the conversation but it didn't work its usual magic.

"Please Carter..," she breathed, real fire and determination in her eyes:" I must have it."

"No..," I repeated:" I plan on seeing your husband again soon. Maybe even tomorrow. If you're afraid he'll see it's gone, I'll return it. Discreetly of course."

She pushed herself away from the wall and sat down on the bed, looking up at me, tears welling in her eyes again.

"I don't want you to give it back to him..," she snarled, angrily:" I want to keep it for myself..!"

I returned her fury with a calm back-stroke.

"Why..? You're never going to see him again after the clinic's cleaned you up. You're going to be free of the bastard."

A big, silver tear spilled onto her cheek.

"That's what worries me..," she trembled:" When I'm not there anymore: When I'm back out. He'll find me. He has a lot of friends: Influential friends: Friends that owe him favours. He will use them to hunt me down. I've gone too far this time. I need to have something to protect myself from whoever he sends to find me."

I could see her point and half agreed with it but she still wasn't getting the gun. Who knew what she might do with it. The way she was right now she'd probably shoot herself with it.

"Still a "no" I'm afraid..," I said, looking down at her, coolly:" A gun is a dangerous thing at the best of times. In the hands of someone full of drugs, drink and fear it's bloody lethal. I keep the gun. By the time you come out of where you're going you'll be clean and you'll be safe: I'll make sure of that: I promise."

"You can't promise that..," she snapped, her eyes wide and wild:" You know you can't. You've met him. You know what he's like. He's ruthless. He'll do anything to keep himself…"

"No..," I said, coldly:" He won't because I won't let him. I've told you and I'm telling you again. By the time you come out of that clinic he won't be a threat to you and he won't be a part of your life, anymore. I'm going to make it my personal goal to…"

"To what..?" she spat:" Kill him? Is that what you're going to do, because that's the only way you'll be able to keep that promise: Put a bullet through his head: Anything else is just words: Useless words..!"

"You - don't – get – the - gun..," I said, slowly and steadily, locking my eyes with hers, showing her I meant what I said.

She returned my stare with a long one of her own.

"Then I don't go to the clinic..," she said petulantly:" I stay here, throw a chair or something through that window, then scream as loud and as long as I can until someone calls the police and I start telling them lies about you and my husband, telling them he paid you to kidnap me and keep me here. My guess is you're a bad man mister Carter. You must be if you were paid you to try and threaten Marcus. People who get paid money to do that kind of thing are usually just as bad, if not worse, than the people they've been paid to threaten and if you are a bad man then the police will probably know about you and they will believe me when I make up a story to make you look even badder..."

I winced at that: "Badder" is not a real word. It offended my love of the English language.

"That's not nice..," I said, a pained expression on my face, meaning her using an ungrammatical word but she took it to mean all the crap she was coming out with about the chair and kidnapping.

"I don't care. If you don't give me that gun I'll..."

"I know what you'll do...You'll stamp and shout like a spoilt little brat and do your best to get me a twenty year stretch for kidnapping. Not very nice after all I've done for you..," I said.

Her stare hardened into a stubborn glare.

"Yes..," she hissed:" I will. I will..."

"All right, all right..," I said, holding my hand up and stepping away from the wall I'd been leaning back against, smiling when I said it, but not because I was amused about what she'd said, but because I'd already decided she could have the bloody gun if it would shut her up and stop her crying. I could do without all the noise and chaos I didn't doubt for one minute she'd create if I didn't do what she'd asked. She could have the damned gun if it made her feel happy and safe:" I'll get the bloody thing for you. You don't need to paint me another picture. I need to get you to that clinic and Jock and Carol need to go back to their knitting and watching the antiques roadshow, so give me five minutes and I'll bring you your gun. You just sit there like a good little brat and I'll be back with your comfort blanket."

Telling Carol I was getting something Charlotte wanted from the car, I took the stairs down to the back of the building, opened the car and took the pistol from the glove compartment, taking another look at it for a few seconds, then spun the chamber, removing the rounds one at a time and slipping them into my inside jacket pocket. When all six were out, I snapped it shut again, tucked it into my waistband and went back, picking up Charlotte's handbag when I got into her room, dropping the shiny .32 into it with a theatrical flourish and placing the bag into her lap, giving a dramatic bow as I stepped away from the bed.

"There..," I mocked:" Feeling better now..?"

"Much..," she smiled, breathing a heavy, satisfied sigh.

"Good: Then would you please finish getting ready to leave. They'll be here to pick you up soon and they charge by the hour so I want to keep this as cheap as possible."

Ten minutes later, Carol came into the living room supporting a very pale, very fragile Charlotte under the arm, steered her over to a high-backed chair and sat her in it, fussing around her, making sure she was supported by cushions, all the time she was doing it Charlotte never once looking anywhere else but at the bottle of MacCallan's on the table with an intensity that made it look as if she was trying some Jedi mind trick on it to make it fly across the room and into her talon-like hands.

In keeping with my wish to have a quiet, compliant Charlotte when they came to take her away, not one that struggled and made a scene, ignoring Carol's disapproving looks, I made Charlotte a small whiskey and soda, handed it to her and watched her gulp it down her throat greedily, her eyes blazing with desperation, greed and pleasure.

Haughtily, she held out the glass for another but I shook my head and took it from her grasp, telling her firmly she'd get another treat when the car came but only if she went quietly and didn't make a fuss. For a few seconds she again locked eyes with me, her face taut and angry like before, but thankfully said nothing, just nodded and looked down at the floor, eyes gone back to being blank and vacant again. I exchanged looks with Carol but said nothing. Nothing needed to be said. We were both thinking the same thing: That Charlotte Dexter was in a bad way and it was a great shame.

Five minutes later, almost to the second, Jock, who'd been standing by the window keeping a look-out, said that a car had just pulled up at the front. I crossed over to the window and looked down into the street. A large black, top-of-the-range Mercedes was parking opposite the building. When it stopped moving, two people, a man and a woman, both dressed in smart, grey suits, got out of the back, the woman carrying a black-leather brief case. They looked very official and very efficient and could very well have been from the clinic.

They were.

When the intercom beside Jock's front door buzzed, Jock asked who was there, a woman's' voice answered saying that, as arranged, they had come to take Mrs. Charlotte Dexter to Kent, and I nodded for him to let them in, moving to stand on one side of the door, my back pressed to the wall, tensed and ready to explode into action if they did something they shouldn't when they arrived.

A minute later there was a knock on the door, Jock opened it and the woman, dark-haired, mature-figured, in her mid-forties, wearing heavy framed glasses entered, followed by a tall, blonde-haired, clean-shaven, well-built man, probably in his mid-thirties who looked more than capable of handling himself.

After introducing herself and her companion, the woman opened the briefcase, gave Charlotte an examination, asked her a few questions, wrote the barely audible answers down on a clip-board, took out a tan leather box which held a small syringe and three bottles clipped to the inside of the case lid, half-filled it with the contents of one of the bottles, injected Charlotte quickly and cleanly, put the syringe away, closed up the lid and stood up, asking Charlotte in a quiet, even voice to, please, follow them.

At first Charlotte seemed confused and looked from them to us, asking with her eyes what was happening, but a reassuring pat on the arm from Carol and a smile from me seemed to pacify her and she rose to her feet, a little unsteadily.

Jock and I followed them down to the car with the bags, put them in the boot, said goodbye to Charlotte, who looked tearful and miserable as hell, reassured her that she was going to be fine, stood back to allow her to be seated into the rear of the car, watched as it pulled away and walked back into the building when it had gone.

Jock asked if I wanted another drink but I declined, my body suddenly telling me that now Charlotte had gone it needed a rest, thanked them both for all of their help, told Jock to let me know how much I owed them, gave Carol a hug, went down to my car and drove in silence to my office, thinking about what I was going to do next. I also thought about Leonora Fitzpatrick and about how kind and caring Charlotte had said she was. Was I wrong about her? Maybe she was genuine and really did only have Charlotte's welfare in mind.

Still thinking about her, I climbed the stairs to my rat-hole, took off my clothes, swallowed a handful of pain-killers, curled up on the couch, pulled my thermal blanket over me and fell asleep.

THIRTEEN

The buzzing and rattling of my mobile on the wooden floor woke me and I groaned, rolled over, automatically looking at my watch.

It was just after seven: Roughly four hours sleep: Not really enough but I felt better for it.

Padding in my bare-feet into the tiny washroom just off to the side, I dipped my head in a chipped basin full of cold water, towelled myself dry, dressed and made a coffee, took the mug over to the desk and sat with my feet up on it, going back over the events of the last twenty four hours, thinking about what it all meant and why the fuck I was getting myself involved.

In all honesty I'd done what had been asked of me and what I'd been paid to do. It may not have worked out exactly the way my client had hoped it would, but I'd had a word with Dexter like she asked and as an added bonus, found Charlotte a safe place and put her out of Dexter's reach, at least for a while, which was something she didn't ask for. I'd also got a beating for my troubles and the pain in my side and down one side of my face was evidence of that, so why didn't I feel as though it was 'job done, beyond the call..? Why did I still feel the need to wade deeper in, maybe even beyond my depth? I knew the answer to my own question though. It was because I'm a stubborn, proud man who knows he's one of the best at what he does and does not like being outdone by a creep like Dexter. Being put onto the floor was a slur on my professional status: I had a reputation to protect and being slapped about without making a mark on my opponent could go a long way to denting that, not something a man in my profession can contemplate. My value would go down and there would be others who might consider me as a limping lion: Worth having a go at: Potentially beatable, and that wasn't going to happen, plus, and this was probably the main reason… I wanted that glossy-faced bastard to feel like I was feeling right then. Bruised and in pain. I needed to re-arrange those movie-star looks so that he resembled Quasimodo more than Al Pacino, and if it meant I had to go back down to Sussex and confront "His Sleaziness" again then that's what I needed to do, but first I had to eat something. It had been a while since Carol's omelette and I'd need protein, energy and carbs a 'plenty if I was going to take on the American again.

I walked across the street to the local 'greasy spoon', ate a large plateful of the most starchy food I could order so that my tank was full of the slow-burning energy I'd need for the next few hours, got back into the car and headed towards Knightsbridge, having decided as I'd been eating to take a look at Charlotte's place for myself.

Parking a few cars away from her building, I walked up the steps of the classy-looking red- brick mansion block, straight past the empty porters' desk and took the lift up to the third floor, getting out and looking for apartment twelve.

After taking a quick glance up and down the corridor, I let myself in, closed the door behind me, turned on the lights and stood taking in the first impressions.

It was a very nice flat indeed and I gave a mental whistle at the size of it.

There were seven rooms: An obviously expensive white-marble-everything kitchen, two bedrooms straight from the front covers of an interiors magazine, both with en-suite bathrooms bigger than my office, a living room I could park my car in, furnished with modern art on the walls and stylish, Scandinavian furniture, a study with a sofa that ran around three walls, surrounding a glass coffee table I could have lain spread-eagled on, and a small, pokey little room behind the kitchen which I assumed was the maids room: More like a bed-sit really. No sign of a maid though, or anyone at all. That room looked like it hadn't been occupied for weeks. It was a very stylish place but Jock was right. It was a fucking mess. Bottles of booze and glasses lay or stood everywhere; plates with remnants of food; cigarette butts; clothes lying where they'd been thrown and the wisps of coke trails on every flat surface. Charlotte was a very untidy little girl with far too much bloody money to play with, and as I wandered from one filthy room to the other any feelings of pity I'd had for her vanished like the coke up her privileged nose the moment I saw the squalor she played in. The flat was as fucked up as her mind and that was pretty fucked up.

I went back into the living room and had a closer look at everything, opening drawers, picking things up, riffling through any paperwork I found, opening note-books, trying to find something, anything, that might help me chop Marcus Dexter off at the knees but there was nothing I could use; nothing useful that is except for one thing: A leather- covered address book, full of names, numbers and in a lot of cases, actual addresses.' Might come in handy, if not in this job then certainly in future jobs. It's always good to have personal numbers and especially personal addresses. The less digging you had to do when looking for someone, the more time you had for getting on with what you'd been paid for.

I slipped it into my coat pocket, intending to go through it more carefully when I got back to the office. I didn't have time now.

The rest of the search through the chaos revealed nothing and I closed all the drawers, looking around to see if there were anywhere else to look and that's when I saw it. In the kitchen, on the middle of the central island, held down with a glass paperweight, was an unsealed envelope and on it was written the word "Charlotte". Obviously Marcus, or someone he'd sent, had been here after Jock and Carol had left or Jock would have easily seen the letter and brought it back with him.

Pulling out the smallest of one of a set of chefs' knives slotted handle deep into the marble-top, like Arthur pulling Excalibur from the stone, I slit the letter open, withdrew the single sheet of folded pink paper inside and read this:

"My charming, dearest, spoilt and very unhappy Charlotte,

How are you my poor darling? As pathetic and boring as ever? Of course you are. You simply wouldn't be you if you were in the least bit interesting.

Straight to the point before you fall over.

I've decided you no longer satisfy me in any way except maybe for your money, but as I've spent almost all of it and you are down to your last two million, I think it's time for me to lie between the tanned and lovely thighs of yet another stupid woman who has fallen in love with me and who has a lot more money than you now have. So I will be leaving for one of her late husbands' three islands in the Caribbean tomorrow and have chosen to grant you the wish I know you and your dreadfully snobbish family want so desperately: A divorce.

Come to the house tonight, no later than ten thirty, and you can pick up the divorce papers which I have signed, granting you all the conditions you wanted. Just bring some money as a 'Thank you' gift. Shall we say $ 10,000,000? I know you may not have enough left in your accounts my poor darling: My apologies. I can be a little greedy at times as you discovered, but your dear, dear friend Leonora has a lot more than that and I'm sure she would be only too willing to pay that minor sum to see us parted on amicable terms. Cash is preferable but Government Bonds are acceptable.

Make sure you arrive no later than ten thirty. I have business to attend to at eleven thirty and I want you gone before then. If you don't arrive, or are more than ten minutes late, I will tear the documents in half and kick your dull, skinny ass down the stairs, as I have grown accustomed to doing.

Until tonight then my dear, dull little bitch,

Your bored and dangerously disinterested 'husband',

Marcus x"

Nice guy: Charm itself: A catch for any woman with more than twenty million in the bank and no brains.

As I re-folded the letter, replaced it onto the island work-top and put the paperweight back over it, I wondered who the person or persons he was meeting at eleven thirty were and why such a late meeting? Was it because he was catching an early morning flight? To where? He'd said one of three private islands in the Caribbean. I could easily do a search and find out who the tan-thighed widow was but dismissed the thought. I'd never guess which one he was going to and I wasn't going to be able to follow him out there so what would be the point of knowing? I needed to focus my attention on making his ride in her private jet as excruciatingly uncomfortable as I could, if not impossible due to the extended stay in a private hospital his newly found money-fountain would have to pay for.

I looked at my watch: Almost half eight. If I wasn't held up and pushed the pedal a bit hard I'd get there by ten thirty but I needed to leave now. There was no time for a last look around, not that there was much to look around at. There was nothing to interest me. Tearing those signed divorce papers from Marcus Dexter's broken fingers after I'd knocked seven fucking bells out of the slick, arrogant bastard and putting several hard boots into his smug plans for continued abuse and the destroying of another woman's life was the only thing that interested me now.

I left the apartment to fester in its filth, locked the door, took the empty lift down to the still empty entrance lobby, walked casually to the car, started it up and pointed the shiny, black nose towards the A23 and the Sussex Downs.

FOURTEEN

Driving fast but carefully, I reached the North Downs by nine forty five and the single track road leading to "Devil's View" a couple of minutes later.

It was dark and I could barely make out anything beyond the head-lights as I drove cautiously between the hedges and trees lining the almost un-used road, not wanting to miss the turning up to the iron gates, and in the four or five minutes it took to get there, two vehicles passed me: A small, dark coloured van and what looked like a silver, fast saloon, probably a BMW but hard to tell because of the speed it was going and also because they all look alike these days. Give me a distinctive, old-style classic any day.

When I knew I must be close, I turned my headlights off, drove slowly on my side-lights until I found the entrance, slid past the gates, tucked the car into a small break in the hedge a few dozen yards further up the road, walked back, pulled myself up and over the wall beside the entrance and crept up the gravel drive, keeping close into the shadows of the trees.

 After about forty yards, I came to where I'd parked the car the last time I'd visited: The time I met Charlotte, and as I sneaked past it I thought a bit about her, feeling sorry for her. She'd had a pretty hard time lately, I thought. Sometimes life can be extra tough on a person, even a rich person like her; Someone you'd expect life to be a breeze for them because they had all the breaks there were going, but often they just seemed to get nothing but a finger in the eye: A slap in the face: A daily kicking in the guts. Money wasn't everything. It was good to have it, of course it was, but it wasn't everything. Okay so Charlotte had had a lot of it. Too much maybe, but apart from that she hadn't had much else, and now…? Now she was down to her last couple of million and however many apartments and houses around the world.

It's at that point in my thought process that I stopped feeling sorry for her and told myself to shut the fuck up. Who was I kidding..? She'd be fine: A couple of weeks at one of her villas in one of several paradises reserved for the wealthy, another couple of hundred thousand pounds in interest from her investments as she lay on her private beach and she'd be on the road to physical and financial recovery real soon.

I tossed her and any sympathy I might have had out of the window and instead concentrated on getting into the house which I could now see just around the corner of the drive, about fifty yards away: A big black box against a big, black sky. There were only two lights on: One upstairs, about the fourth window along, and one downstairs in what I worked out must be the main room: The room in which I'd had my balls handed to me on a plate by Dexter: The room he'd now be sitting in waiting for Charlotte to arrive.

I glanced at the dial on my luminous watch. It was nine fifty six and no sign of any other visitors: No cars out front. No people standing in doorways. Obviously Charlotte wasn't coming because she was at the clinic and his eleven-thirty appointments hadn't shown up yet. Dexter was alone, or I hoped he was. I was looking forward to giving that sleazy bastard a bigger beating than the one he'd given me, but didn't really want to have to work my way through a couple of his gooney henchmen to get to him. Might be fun though.

I crouched low in the shadows for a minute listening and watching, waiting to see if anyone came out of the house or more lights went on but nothing changed so I slipped through the trees to the rear of the building and looked for the back door, the one Charlotte had led me through.

To my relief it was unlocked, but then this was the countryside. People weren't as paranoid out here as they are in the city but still; I was slightly surprised. I had expected it to be locked.

I went in, closing the door very quietly behind me. Another glance at my watch told me it was now nine fifty eight. I was on time: A little bit early in fact. Dexter would be waiting, a drink in hand no doubt, and a smug, self-satisfied grin on his plastic-padded face which it would be my pleasure to punch off.

Padding down the long, black corridor I slipped out into the semi-dark hallway and, looking around to see if there was any sign of anyone else, I walked to the door of the drawing-room, glancing over my shoulder a few times to make sure I wasn't about to be jumped on by a hidden bodyguard.

Taking a deep breath, very carefully I gripped one of the double door handles, turned it slowly and, tensing my muscles, pushed, letting it open halfway.

Nothing happened.

There was no sound from inside. No condescending greeting, no push-back by a snappily dressed hired thug. I opened the door fully and stepped into the room, expecting to see Dexter standing by the fire watching me, or the hands of one of his men grasp my arm, but still there was nothing, only a heavy silence being warmed by the heat from the low-flamed log fire on the other side of the room.

Carefully, I closed the door behind me and stood scanning the room, looking for Dexter and anyone that might be lurking in the corners. Then, in a big, high-backed, wing chair in front of the fire, its back towards me, I saw him, or at least what I thought was him, reclining languorously, a half-full glass of whiskey on the carpet beneath his left arm, within easy reach.

I coughed but there was no reaction: No movement.

Frowning, I walked slowly across the carpet towards the chair, expecting him to suddenly sit round, pointing a gun at me, a nasty grin on his chiselled, handsome, All-American face, but he didn't and when I got within a few feet, it was easy to figure out why.

The top of his head had been blown off and there was blood, bone and brains splattered all over not just the chair but the ceiling above: Not a pretty sight and the all too familiar sweet tang of cordite mixed with the coppery scent of blood was not especially pleasant.

I went around to the front of the chair and took a better look at his slack-jawed, torn apart face. He wasn't very good-looking now, eyes rolled up into the top of the sockets, tongue out and dangling, hair spiked and matted with black, sticky, still-wet blood. Not really a catch anymore, unless you were into Halloween masks.

I took a step closer to the chair and saw his right arm hanging down over the other arm of the chair, the fingers of his hand only a few inches from the carpet and lying beneath them was what looked like a note. I would have picked it up and taken a look at it, but something else was grabbing all of my attention.

Between his shiny black shoes was a shiny .32 Snub-nose revolver with the letters 'M.D" engraved in the ivory handles.

The one I'd given to Charlotte nine and a half hours before.

FIFTEEN

Frowning heavily, I stepped closer to Marcus's grisly face and examined what was left of it.

Despite the shattered, cracked and bloody jaw, the internal pressure swelling that had blown out the cheeks, forehead and temples, and the unnatural tilt of the wrecked and dislocated skull, it was plain to see that the bullet that blew the top of his skull open had been fired from under his jaw: Classic suicide shot: I'd seen it before a few times but this time something about it didn't fit right.

I looked back down at the weapon lying between his feet. The random looking position of it seemed okay: It could have fallen from his opening fingers onto the floor like that, so no; that wasn't it. Something else was tickling at me but I couldn't place a finger on exactly what.

Taking a handkerchief from a pocket, I held it between my fingers, bent down, picked up the note and read it. It said:

"To my delightful wife, or anyone else unfortunate enough to find my body.

My apologies but I am suddenly weary of you, my life and the world in general.

I have decided to waste your time and create a situation that will cause real trouble for you and everyone involved with me. My death means nothing to me. I've been dead inside for some years now.

Goodbye Charlotte, Leonora, Nancy, Bernice, Carol and Barbera.

Its' been an absolute pleasure spending all of your money.

Your unrepentant husband, ex-husband and lover.

Marcus

P.S. You were all correct: I cheated on each and every one of you several times during our marriages and loved every minute of doing so. See you in hell my loves."

Short and not very sweet but definitely the man I'd come to know and hate, but why: What had made him put his gun beneath his chin, pull the trigger and blow himself directly to hell? Why would a vicious, mean-minded, nasty son-of- bitch like Marcus Dexter commit suicide? That didn't ring true. Dexter was the type of guy that took pleasure in driving others to kill themselves, not the type that did it themselves, and maybe that was it: Maybe that was what was niggling at me. It didn't make sense but then, I guess, maybe life made no sense either so…who knows?

I put the note back where I'd found it, stood up and took another long look at what was left of the man, an overwhelming sense of disappointment, with a bit of anger mixed in, rolling over me. I was sorry to see him like that, lying back in his favourite chair with only half his head left, because I'd wanted him to be alive when I came in: That was the disappointing part. I had so much been looking forward to beating him to the pulpy mess he was in now with my bare hands, maybe even putting a bullet in him myself if he'd forced me to, but that pleasure had been denied me. That was the angry part. But who had done it? I just couldn't convince myself it was Dexter himself, but, if it wasn't him then who would have come here and used Marcus's own gun to shoot him and make it look like suicide: Who could have got him to sit still while they did it and who could have gotten hold of his gun in the first place? The last time I'd seen it I was dropping it into Charlotte's purse and Charlotte was lying in a clinic in Kent somewhere now so it couldn't have been her.

I walked over to the drinks cabinet, wrapped my handkerchief around a tumbler and poured myself a large "thinking-drink", swallowing it in one long gulp. I needed time to work on this but not here and not now. Whoever he was due to be meeting at eleven thirty would be here pretty soon and I didn't want to be found in this house with Marcus's not-long dead, still warm body beside me. Besides: There was nothing else I could do right now anyway. I needed to leave so, taking one last, quick look around the room to see if there was anything that might be of interest, I walked out of the door, taking care to wipe the handles clean of my prints, turned left and began walking towards the back of the house but had only gone three paces down the hallway when another thought tickled at me and I stopped.

In my line of business you make a habit of mentally taking in more than you realise when you look at rooms and people: Things that get processed quietly in the background and then flagged up as being curious and worth looking into a bit deeper, and it was the tiny voice of one of my little 'observers' that must have been working on an oddity I hadn't noticed who spoke to me now telling me there was something about the set-up in that room I needed to go back and take a look at.

Glancing at my watch in the darkness, the glowing hands told me it was ten fifty: If I didn't fuck about, I had time to go back and take another quick look: Just. So I did and for a moment stood in the doorway taking it all in again, waiting for the little voice to tell me what it had noticed and when it did I nodded in understanding. The chair in which Dexter was lying was too close to the fire. My upper left lip lifted into a little half-smile. Of course: I should have realised it straightaway when I was standing in front of Dexter, examining his head and reading the note. The back of my legs had felt as though they were being roasted by the flames. No-one sits that close to a fire, not for long anyway.

I went over to the fireplace and stood in front of the chair again, this time feeling the heat instantly. Nobody, not even a frost-bitten Eskimo, sits that close to an open fire for more than a minute. I scanned the carpet for what I suspected I'd see and, now that I was looking for them, quickly noticed four imprints of the legs where they'd been pressed down into the pile over-time, three or four feet from where the chair was now. It had obviously been moved and judging by the drag marks in the pile, it had been moved with Dexter in it. There was only one reason I could think of why it had been done: To slow down the onset of Rigor Mortis. No doctor, or even a forensic scientist, could give an accurate time of death with a body that had been almost super-heated for hours as his was going to have been before it had been discovered.

The only conclusion I could come to was that Dexter definitely hadn't killed himself. Somebody had killed him, and with his own gun, then made it look like suicide, but knowing him as I did, I asked myself the same question again. How had they got him to sit quietly in his chair while they stuck a loaded gun under his chin? I doubt very much he would have just sat still and allowed that to happen?

Taking out my handkerchief again, I picked up the Snub-nose by the grips and spun the chromed cylinder slowly, counting the rounds: There were five: One had been definitely been fired. I sniffed the barrel: Not long ago either.

The longer I stood there thinking about it, the less this was beginning to make sense.

Puzzled, I put the .32 back where it had been, stood up and decided to look around the house, more specifically Dexter's bedroom.

I figured he would only use a couple of rooms when he was there alone: A bedroom and this room: The drawing room. I didn't have much time before whoever it was he was expecting turned up so I walked back out of the room quickly and jogged up the stairs, heading for the room that I'd seen lit up from the outside.

I'd been right: It was the fourth room along, the only one with a light showing under the door. When I got to it, with the handkerchief over my hand, I turned the handle slowly, pushed it open and stepped cautiously inside.

I needn't have worried because it was empty, and I began going over it quickly but thoroughly, opening and closing drawers, lifting up the mattress and pillows, searching through his extensive and very expensive wardrobe, patting down pockets and shaking out coats, looking for something: Anything. I had no idea what, but I knew I'd know when I found it.

I found lots of things, some of which I was very tempted to pocket, but I restrained myself and left them all as I found them. The last thing I needed to potentially be found with, should I for any reason be stopped, was anything that could be traced back to Marcus Dexter. I kept searching but nothing that might have had any connection with the murder came to hand: Nothing that is until I began to look through a long-legged Georgian desk pushed against the furthest wall, between one of the large wardrobes and the window. It looked like it had been used a writing table and the long, single drawer on the front was slightly open so I pulled it further out, rifling through the contents.

Amongst various bits of paperwork and random clutter I came across Dexter's passport, a letter sent from Nassau in the Bahamas, signed by a woman who was making it very clear exactly what she was looking forward to being done to her the moment Marcus stepped off the plane, and paper copies of his boarding passes onto a private flight from Luton airport the next day at 08:30: The Harrods terminal no less: Definitely not for the hoi-poloi. Dexter had been going to fly Premier class in a jet that I got a feeling his desperate-sounding new girl-friend had sent over especially for him. So much for his carbon footprint: Shame on him.

Finding an A4 envelope, I dropped the passport, the letter and the flight pass into it, sealed the flap, folded it, slipped it into my jacket pocket, closed the drawer and stood there thinking.

Dexter hadn't lied in his note back at Charlotte's place when he said he was going to the Caribbean to be with a woman that desired him and that made me even more certain that he hadn't killed himself. The letter and the passport were proof of that, and because of them, it got me thinking. What man with Marcus Dexter's appetite for money, women and depravity would pass up the opportunity of flying in a private jet to a private island in the Caribbean to fuck a very rich widow worth hundreds of millions of dollars in a private beach house overlooking a very private beach, just to piss of someone he was dumping anyway by shooting himself in the head? As I kept telling myself over and over again with increasing conviction…It made no sense. Somehow, some way, someone had murdered him.

I looked at my watch again and saw it was now ten minutes after eleven. His next appointment was due and I didn't think it would be a good idea to be in the house when the screaming or shouting started.

Checking to see I'd not left any clues that I'd been there in the room, I closed the bedroom door, went back down to the hall, half-walked, half ran to the rear corridor and slipped out into the now very cold night, my breath clouding around my face the instant I stepped into the dark.

I could have gone two ways: The quick way, diagonally straight through the trees for a short way and onto the gravel drive, then over the low wall beside the gates and out onto the road like I'd done in reverse when I first arrived, or through the woods and make for the small lay-by where I'd parked the car. It would take longer and be a trickier route in the dark, but the chances of being seen by anyone coming up the road were much less than walking along the main road.

I chose cutting through the woods and was just about to make my way across the muddy side-yard towards the outer perimeter of the trees when I stopped and stood looking down at the ground.

The reason it was so cold and that my skin was starting to freeze was because the night-sky was cloudless and filled with millions of stars that twinkled and shone like diamond dust in the freezing air, and that meant there was nothing to dull the sharp, silver-blue light of the moon that hung like an electric balloon high above the black trees, flooding the ground with a crisp brilliance, creating sharp shadows everywhere, and it was those shadows that gave me cause to stare.

There were two very distinct sets of tyre-tracks running in arcs through the mud. One set, wide, deep-treaded and heavy, went up to the garage doors, appeared to have reversed back out again, made a turn, then driven away towards the gravel drive: The other set, lighter in depth, narrower and with a less complicated tread pattern, crossing the first set in places meaning they were made after the heavier set, and those ones stopped beside the back door I'd just come through, also reversed, again cutting across the thicker set, then also arced around and made towards the drive. There was no frost yet on the second set which made me think it hadn't been long since they had arrived then left.

Based on the heavier depth of the tread and the width of the first tyre set, I made an educated guess that they had been made by a heavy, ostentatious, top-of-the-marque four-by-four such as a Range Rover, and that the narrower, lighter set belonged to a faster, sportier car.

I grinned.

A BMW possibly..? Silver..? Like the one that had passed me going the other way as I'd driven towards the house?

Yeah: Just like that one.

I took a dozen pictures of the tread patterns with my phone-camera, stood listening to the freezing silence for a few seconds, crunched across the grass into the blackness of the woods and was swallowed up instantly by the deep, dense shadows, carefully using the light from my phone-torch to pick my way through the thick branches and over the gnarled, twisting roots, trying not to trip and twist my ankle or crack my head open.

When I eventually got through and saw the estate wall, I turned off the light, looked over it, saw no headlights approaching from either direction, rolled over the top and dropped silently onto the grass verge on the other side.

Less than a minute later I found my car, clambered in, plugged my mobile into the charger, cranked up the heater, flicked on the lights and pulled out onto the road, shivering and thinking as the miles disappeared very fast under my bonnet.

SIXTEEN

Just on the outskirts of London, I pulled over and dialled the number of the clinic, looking at my watch as I waited for the connection.

It was 00:43.

An efficient sounding female voice on the other end of the line asked me how they could help and I apologised for calling so late but said I just wanted to check on the condition of Mrs. Charlotte Dexter: I was worried about her, I said, trying to sound it.

"May I ask who's calling..?" the woman on the other end said, brightly. She had a nice voice.

"My name is Mr. Carter..," I said:" I'm a personal friend. Your people picked Charlotte up from my flat in London yesterday afternoon."

"Thank you Mr. Carter..," the woman trilled:" I'll just put you on hold while I check for you."

After ten or fifteen seconds she came back.

"Hello? Mr. Carter? I'm sorry, but Mrs. Dexter is no longer a patient with us. She was discharged earlier this evening, at six fifteen to be precise."

I stared through the windscreen, eyes wide in genuine astonishment.

"What..!" I breathed:" She's left..? But why...? I don't understand...! She just got there..!"

The woman sounded un-nerved by my reaction but kept her voice professional.

"Well..," she said, obviously looking at a computer screen as she was talking:" It was at her own request it seems. Doctor Carrington came to see her at five, gave her a full assessment and seemed very pleased with her. She then requested a full discharge, under supervision: The doctor signed her out at five thirty and a car arrived for her at six. She actually left us at, let me see... six seventeen as I said."

"A car..? Was it one of your cars or was it a private car..?"

"I'm sorry Mr. Carter but I'm afraid..."

"Was it Mrs. Leonora Fitzpatrick's car..? Did Leonora Fitzpatrick pick her up?"

"I'm sorry sir, but I wasn't on the desk at that time. I only know Mrs. Dexter was picked up by a private car at..."

"Six seventeen..," I interrupted, my voice sounding angry and confused:" Yes, yes, you told me...Do you know where she was taken?"

"As I said Mr. Carter, I'm not at liberty to..."

"I understand..," I sighed, suddenly deflated. This was unexpected news: Unexpected and interesting:" Thank you. Thank you for your help."

I cut the connection and sat in the car thinking hard on what I'd just learnt, confused, my jaw clenched tight and hurting because of it, the rain that had just started running in a hundred silver rivers down my windscreen, trying to make sense of what I'd just been told but couldn't, not right then anyway. My tired brain kept over-riding my thoughts, telling me there was no way I was going to be able to come up with anything logical at one in the fucking morning with only a two hour doze to fuel it. What I needed to do was get back to my crappy room and try to get at least six hours of undisturbed sleep, then I might be able to see things in a fresher light.

It was right: I knew it was, so I stopped thinking, put the fan onto cold, started the engine again and carried on into the city. What else was there to do?

SEVENTEEN

I woke at nine, my brain feeling very grateful for the six hours I'd given it, dressed myself in something less crumpled and dirty, had a good breakfast over the road in the local "Spoon-de-Greasy", returned to my penthouse shit-house and made a call to someone I hadn't worked with for a few years but who owed me favours: Two distinct ones I could remember and probably more I couldn't.

Harry Taylor, known to everyone in our business as "Harry-the-Hacker" for reasons it's not good to go into, answered the 'phone gruffly but sounded happier when he knew it was me.

He'd worked for Cleaver for about thirty years, which is where I first met him, but also free-lanced with other 'agencies', and his work often took him abroad, more specifically America which was why I was calling him. I'd woken up with last nights' events and conversations still zipping around like bullets in an ambush at the front of my brain and I had decided I needed to do a little digging on Mrs. Leonora Fitzpatrick before I made her acquaintance again, which I was sure as hell going to.

I made a one o'clock lunch-date with him at a place we both used to frequent just off Regent Street and ended the call, leaning back in my creaky old chair and trying to make sense of what I'd been told by the nice sounding lady at the clinic.

I couldn't though, or at least what sense I did make had too many holes in it to make sense, if that makes sense, so I gave up trying and walked to the club to freshen up and put on some new clothes. Maybe after a long shower and a couple of strong coffees I would think better.

It worked, and after the shower, a fresh set of clothes and two cups of good coffee, I made my way to Regent Street, crossing the busy road and ducking down one of the small alleys that spur off it. Pretty enough in the day-time but dangerous when it was dark, as I knew only too well.

When I walked through the front door of the small, intimate, six-tabled restaurant that had been a meeting place for us 'meat traders' as we were known, Gino, the grey-haired old owner came out from behind the dated wooden bar and waddled over to me, rubbing his hands on his long white apron and sitting me down at the table that I always had, in the corner, facing the door, fussing around and smoothing the spotless gingham table-cloth down, shouting over his shoulder for a… "Speciale Americano for mistera A-Carta…!" as he made sure the cutlery was straight.

Two minutes later, Harry walked in and received the same waddling, gushing greeting, following the ruddy-faced, grinning Gino to my table.

Harry was a big guy: Somewhere around fifty years old, six foot two or three, wide-shouldered, thick-faced and still with a shock of greying hair that he kept well cut to go with the sharply tailored suits he always wore. He was old-school East End, deserved respect and got it, especially from the younger guys who had heard and well-believed the stories they'd heard about him, all of which were true, some of which even more gruesome than they needed to know. He was one of the meanest fucking bastards I'd ever worked with when he was in work-mode but soft as butter when it came to his three grand-children. Today he looked soft as granite but gave me one of his rare smiles when he saw me and shook my hand warmly.

"Army..!" he said, using the nick-name he had given me on the first day we'd met and gripping my hand like a bear grips your balls, his voice as deep and intimidating as I remembered:" 'ow are you boy? 'Been a few years ain't it..? Good to see you my son! You've lost your fuckin' 'air...!"

I hadn't lost my hair, or at least not all of it. I just kept it shorter these days, but it had been two years since he'd last seen me, so I let it pass.

We drank our complimentary coffees, ordered whiskies, drank those and shot the breeze for a while, reminiscing about the good old days, which I don't recall there being many of to be honest, and about how we met working for Cleaver on a long-standing debt collection task that the client needed concluding after being patient with his own client for more than two years. To this day the guy that owed the money still hasn't returned from the trip he took to the country, which is sad for his widow of course, but the debt was paid off nicely before he went, with the sale of one of the houses in France he'd signed over to our client and the gifting of a small Picasso which we found in a safe he gave us the combination to. I can't tell you where he went, but I can tell you the three places where his left hand, right foot and head are...

We ate a good lunch then both sat back, satisfied and relaxed, drinking more whiskies.

It was Harry that brought the conversation around to why I'd invited him for lunch.

"So "Army"...Is this lunch 'business', or are you just getting sentimental in your old age? What's the matter..? You dying of sum'ink..?"

I smiled and held my glass up for a re-fill.

"No Harry..," I grinned:" I'm not dying, don't worry. You'll get your lawnmower back. I just need a favour from you: Answers to a few questions."

Gino took our finished whiskies away and handed over two pre-prepared, freshly poured ones.

"I knew it..," Harry said, grinning, watching me with his alligator-like eyes over the top of his glass as he took a slow pull on his drink:" What questions..? If it involves the people I'm working for at the moment or their clients, I can't 'elp you. I'm not breaking client confidentiality old son, even for you: You should know that."

"I'm not asking you to break anybody's confidentiality..," I said, smiling, aware of his long, calculating stare:"…and you know I'd never put you in that position."

Harry put his tumbler down and smiled wickedly, his teeth appearing slowly as his lips split apart.

"That's okay then..," he grinned, his slow, gravelly voice curling around me the way a tigers slow growl curls around a cornered deer:" Just lettin' you know all right? What's the questions?"

"Were you working for Cleaver about a year ago?"

He nodded.

"Yeah: 'Course I was, off an' on, like you. 'Andling a few jobs for 'im…Why?"

"Did you ever hear of a Mrs. Fitzpatrick: Leonora Fitzpatrick..?"

He rolled the name around his mind for a few seconds, tasting it; searching his memory.

"Yeah, I did as it 'appens..," he said, nodding his head, a lascivious smile creeping into his cheeks:" I remember 'er well. She was one of Cleavers more profitable clients: Good lookin' woman: A lovely piece: Loads of fuckin' money!"

I'd struck lucky.

"Why was she a client of Cleaver..?" I asked, pushing the luck a bit more.

Harry shrugged his giant shoulders.

"Not too sure. Sum'ink about a divorce. She was in and out of the office a lot for a while, I know that. I remember it because Cleaver was very involved 'imself, which was unusual for 'im. Even went over to the 'States for 'er a couple of times, 'E didn't normally like to get out from behind his fuckin' desk to piss, never mind travel 'alfway round the fuckin' world, but he did it for 'er."

Harry was right about that. It was unusual for Cleaver to become personally or physically involved in a clients' case but for some reason he made the effort for Leonora Fitzpatrick: Why?

"Did you get involved with her..?" I said.

"Me..? No, I never get involved wiv' the women I work for. I got my Joanne an'..."

"I don't mean like that you old fucker..," I laughed:" I mean did you ever get involved in doing work for her? Did Cleaver ever use you on her behalf..?"

Harry nodded his big head again.

"Yeah, 'e did once..," he growled:" I remember he sent me over to New York to find some documents she needed. Nice trip it was: Four days in a big, very fancy 'otel, on the edge of Central Park. All the bollocks there: No mistake..!"

"What were the documents: Can you remember..?"

Harry sat forward in his chair and steepled his fingers on the table top.

"I can 'as it 'appens..," he gravelled:" like I said, I 'ad to get copies of some divorce papers from 'er attorney...What was their name..? Jewish sounding blokes they were: Nice fellers... "Goldbuck and sum'ink...'Ang on, I'll get it in a minute..."

He sat back, snapping his fingers, trying to recall the names.

"Gold" sum'ink an' "Werburg"...No...Wait..! "Goldstein, Rothsheimer and Warburg"...That was it! Yeah..! Goldstein, Rothsheimer and Warburg; Merrick Building, Fifth avenue, New York. A fuckin' big, very swanky building and they had two floors of it..," he gushed:" A lotta' fuckin' money tied up in that place. I tell you...There was some really interestin' people comin' in and out of those offices the few times I was there: Movie stars, a politician I recognised from the television and even one of our own clients who had an apartment in the city. He used Cleaver once to persuade his wife's brother to leave town for a couple o' years. Me and Terry Shepherd did such a good job on 'im 'e left the fuckin' country and never came back, the lanky tosser. We 'eard later e' only needed a coupla' operations an' his face was almost back to normal. Not good at walkin' too far though. Shouldn't live in a tall building if you don't wanna' risk fallin' on your face I say..."

I finished my drink and put my hand over it when Harry offered to have it filled again.

"Can't..," I said:" I've got a lot of stuff to sort out this afternoon and I need a clear head, but you have one. Put it on my bill: I'm paying."

" 'Course you're bloody paying my son..," Harry cackled:" You don't think for a minute I didn't suspect your sudden invitation to come all the bleedin' way into the middle of town from Eppin' was just so's you could 'ave a fuckin' lasagne for old times sake did' ya..?"

He picked up his glass, threw the remains of the whisky down his thick throat and slammed it back down onto the table cloth, a wide grin splitting his wide face in two:" Nah, nah..! I may 'ave a few grey 'airs these days but I still got a couple of brain cells left beneath them, and they are as sharp as they ever were."

He leaned forward and held me in a hard stare, still smiling.

"You're a nice lad Army, an' I like you: Always did: You got style and your dad was a good man, but you're a little bit of a cunt as well an' I knew you probably wanted to pick my fuckin' brains. Two years since we last met..? Not a Dickie until now..? Not even a bloody Christmas card then suddenly I get a call on the old bone askin' if I want to share a fuckin' pizza. Fuck me boy..! I 'ope you don't fink I was born yesterday. You're onto sum'ink an' you need infor-bloody-mation don't cha'..? Well, you got some an' all its cost ya' is a bloody lasagne an' a few Scotches..," he grinned, wagging a finger at me:" You're lucky I like you Army, uvverwise I might 'ave felt a bit inclined to throw you around Gino's a few times an' give you a bit of a slap for usin' me like an old tart. Gino wouldn't mind. It's happened before in 'ere an' you know it. Where do you fink' I put that smarmy bastards left foot and right 'and...?"

I shook my head and laughed, pleased not only with the information he'd given me, but the fact that Harry still liked me enough not to want to tear my ears off like I'd seen him do to others he thought were mugging him off.

I paid the bill, despite Gino's protests that the meals were on the house, told Harry it was great to see him again, thanked him for the information and walked back to my office, head full of more questions than I had answers to but glad I had a few more bits of the jigsaw than I'd had an hour before, the biggest piece being that Cleaver had been more than a bit economical with the truth as far as Leonora Fitzpatrick was concerned. It seems she'd been a long-standing and very important client of his, and more than likely still was: So important that Cleaver had squeezed himself out from behind that over-the-top desk of his and travelled all the way to fucking New York for her. Why would he do that and what was of such great consequence that he would risk the dangers of flying, something I know he hated, to look after personally? There was obviously a lot more to what was going on there than I knew, and the sooner I found out what that was, the safer I'd feel.

My primitive survival instincts were really tingling now and I was beginning to get the idea that maybe my first suspicions about all of this might have been right. Perhaps I was being set up for something and it was beginning to look like that 'something' could well be the murder of the late but not so great, Marcus Dexter.

EIGHTEEN

When I got back, I looked up the number and contact details of an old army colleague of mine who now worked as private detective, wrote down his e-mail address and sent him a message.

"Reference 'Old-Times sake':

Find all available records ref' intel' on Marcus Dexter, US citizen: Mid 40's: Possibly known to Californian police: Drug dealer: All background and known associates required: Also all intel' on Mrs. Leonora Dexter, now Fitzpatrick, UK citizen, Mid 40's, ref' marriage and divorce suit of both parties in California State, between 2020 and 2022.

Documents held at Goldstein, Rothsheimer and Warburg; NYC.

Within 24 hours appreciated.

Charge usual rates but detract for beers and Kurfürstenstrasse weekend still owed by you."

I sent the mail off into the ether, made myself a coffee, reclined back on the sofa and did more thinking, mostly about Charlotte being allowed to leave the clinic only a few hours after she'd been admitted, and the more I lay there thinking about it, the stinkier it all began to smell.

Why would the doctor pronounce her fit to leave when he'd told me she'd need to be in there for at least a couple of weeks to detox: Who picked her up and where did she go: Back to Leonora's place or to her apartment: Was she there now, and if she was, who was looking after her?

I flushed the cold, unfinished coffee down the sink, threw on my coat again and left the office, a few destinations in mind. The first was Cleavers' place, but not his office.

When I got to his street, I skirted the block and went around the back to the private car park where I knew his car would be. I was right: His car was there; a big blue Range Rover; armoured windows, all the security devices he could fit adding an extra ton to its weight, and parked beside it a BMW 8 series Gran Coupe: 'Nice car if you liked BMW's, which I don't: Fast, sleek, and more interestingly...Silver.

I whipped out my mobile, brought up the photographs I'd taken of the tyre marks at Dexter's house, looked around to check I wasn't being watched, quickly crouched down and checked the tread patterns on both cars.

The Range Rover was fitted with nice, wide, fat all-terrain tyres but it didn't match any of the treads but interestingly, the thinner, more sporty BMW tyres matched exactly and I stood up, a hot rock turning over slowly in my stomach. So… Some of Cleaver's guys had been at Dexter's place last night, leaving only a few minutes before I got there. Why? Were they backing up whoever had already arrived in the bigger, heavier car at least half an hour before them, judging by the layer of frost on its tracks? Had they been waiting up the road for a call to come and either kill Dexter, or arrange it so that it looked like a suicide?

I stepped back, fired off a half dozen or so shots of both cars and their tyres then left, my mind pumping on another gear as it worked on the next piece of the puzzle that had just been thrown into the bag, a bag that was beginning to fill up with pieces that was starting to make up a disturbing picture; one that might make be setting me up for a very nasty fall.

I strode back to my own car, slammed the door and pulled out fast into the traffic, ignoring the blaring of horns from cabs' and vans.

My next destination needed visiting and very, very soon.

NINETEEN

When I got to Charlotte's mansion block, this time there was a hall porter standing behind the desk who stepped forward when I entered: An older guy in his late fifties, grey hair well-cut, smart shoes, with a Veteran's pin on the lapel of his black blazer.

He asked if he could help, and I smiled.

"Yes you can..," I said:" I'm a friend Of Charlotte Dexter. I believe she may be home but isn't answering her telephone or my text messages. Do you mind if I just pop up and see if she's okay, or you could call up for me and let her know I'm here if you'd prefer. I heard she was going to go into a clinic and just wanted to know if she's all right."

"I'm afraid Mrs. Dexter isn't home today sir..," he said:" She came back yesterday evening, but left quite soon after she arrived. Can I leave a message if she returns?"

"So she was here last night? Can I ask what time that was?"

"About 19:00: Seven o'…"

"Thank you..," I smiled:" I understand what time 19:00 is. How did she seem: Tired? Anxious?"

The porter gave a small, embarrassed cough and lowered his voice.

"Well, it's not really my place to comment sir, of course..," he half-whispered:"…but as you asked me…I did think she looked rather ill: Very drawn and I couldn't help but notice her hands were shaking."

"Did you speak with her?"

"I did sir, yes. She asked me if I could let her into her flat as she had left her keys in her handbag, apparently at a friends' house. I was happy to help, of course and went with her up stairs. I have to say she really didn't seem well at all, and you're right to be concerned. She had to stop twice to get her breath. I was quite worried about her."

"Did you go into the flat with her?"

"I did sir, yes. I used the pass key and let her in. She seemed to brighten up a little when she got inside. Quite excited she was…"

"What did she do when she got inside?"

"She went straight into her bedroom and I could hear her moving about, opening and shutting drawers."

"Was she looking for something? Packing clothes maybe?"

"I couldn't rightly say sir, I'm afraid. I stayed in the drawing room as you'd expect. When she came out she seemed to have cheered up a little."

"Was she carrying any bags? Did it look like she was planning to be gone for a long time?"

"She had two bags which I offered to carry down for her, but only small ones. I did ask if she would be returning soon and she told me she didn't know. Not for the next few weeks at least she said."

"So she must have gone to stay with someone I suppose?"

"It would look that way sir, yes. There was a car waiting for her outside the building, I imagine to take her to wherever she was going."

"A car..? Did you recognise it at all?"

"I did as a matter of fact sir, yes. It was her friends' car: Mrs. Fitzpatrick."

My eyebrows were getting a really good workout today.

"Oh, really? What, the coupe..?"

"No sir: Not the coupe. The Mercedes saloon."

"Quite right..," I nodded:" Oh well: I'm glad she got away safely. Mrs. Fitzpatrick had said Charlotte might be staying with her for a while. What time did she leave by the way?"

"19:32 sir…It's in the movements' book."

"Of course it is..," I smiled, affably:" Very efficient. Well, thank you for your help. Much appreciated."

I turned to leave then turned back, as though I'd just remembered something.

"Sorry: One last thing. Did Charlotte go into the kitchen at all before she left?"

"The kitchen sir..? No, she didn't. I think she was quite anxious to get away."

"Hmmm..?" I said, casually, rubbing my chin as if turning something over in my mind:"…I just wondered if she'd found the note I left for her on the central island? It's quite important. If she's gone and hasn't taken it, do you think it might be possible for me to retrieve it, only some of the addresses and 'phone numbers are quite confidential. I couldn't just pop up and find out could I..?"

"There's no need sir..," the porter said, understandingly:"…There was no note that I'm aware of. I was in the kitchen for a brief period whilst I waited for Mrs. Dexter to pack and I didn't see any note on the central island."

I frowned.

"Really..? Then if Charlotte didn't take it, I wonder who did..," I mused.

"I imagine that might have been Mrs. Fitzpatrick sir. She arrived not long before Mrs. Dexter. She told me she needed to pick up one or two things in preparation for her friends stay."

I tried to stop myself from grinning. I knew it. The pieces were clicking into place.

"Mrs. Fitzpatrick..? She came here herself?"

"Yes sir. Like I said, she had rung a short time before to say that Mrs. Dexter would be staying with her for a few weeks and that she needed to pick up some things for her."

"What time did she call to tell you that and what time did she arrive? Were you on duty?"

"No sir, I wasn't, but according to the log book, Mrs. Fitzpatrick rang at seventeen thirty five and arrived at…"

He ran a finger down the page of the large week-to-view diary on his desk, stopped at a series of entries made the night before and looked up again.

"Eighteen fifteen sir, and she stayed for fourteen minutes it seems."

"That's interesting ..," I muttered:" Can I ask if she was alone?"

"The entry just mentions Mrs. Fitzpatrick sir. If she'd had a companion, it would have been noted."

"Of course: Thank you..," I said, taking out a ten pound note and offering it to him;" You've been very helpful."

The porter looked down at the money and shook his head.

"That's very kind of you sir..," he demurred:"…but there's no need. I was happy to help."

"You're a good man..," I grinned:"…but take it and either put it in a Legion tin somewhere, or raise a glass to absent comrades sometime. Either way, thanks for your help, and for your service."

He smiled graciously and, hesitantly, took the note, thanking me for mine and saying he'd raise a glass to the fallen on my behalf.

I winked at him, nodded, turned and walked back into the street, crossed the road and got into my car, thinking about what I'd just been told, my head now even fuller of meat to chew on than before. Okay… So, barely five minutes after Charlotte's being officially discharged from the clinic, Leonora rang the porter at Charlotte's apartment to say that Charlotte would be staying with her and that she would be coming over to pick up a few things for her. Then, at six fifteen she'd arrived, gone up to the flat and what..? Seen Dexter's note in the kitchen, read about him flying off to a paradise island to fuck some wealthy widow and demanding ten million dollars in bonds, taken it with her and then what…? Gone back home, called Cleaver and told him what was going on, asking, or demanding that he help her settle the Marcus 'problem' once and for all?

What about Charlotte? Was she part of the plan? That was doubtful. She was too sick to be able to think beyond the next five minutes, let alone get her head around the complexities of a murder plot, if that's what this was. As far as she was concerned, what happened must have been simple: Freed from the clinic but still in a bad way according to the old Vet', Charlotte had probably whined and whimpered all the way back, needing a hit desperately, asking the driver to divert to her flat, growing more insistent, finally broken his or her will, been dropped off at her apartment to grab her stash of 'H' and left as quick as she could, the driver relieved no doubt to be carrying on to Leonora's home.

For a few more minutes I sat tapping the wheel, staring out through the windscreen, working on the options then, my brain writhing around like freshly made bowl of spaghetti, started the engine, pulled out and drove back to the office.

TWENTY

I got back to the office around five, made a strong coffee and fired up the laptop.

I was feeling tired again and rubbed my eyes while waiting for all the bits to open up on the screen, still thinking about Charlotte, Leonora, Cleaver, The Doctor and the whole "clinic" thing, none of it, apart from it being a setup, made any sense, but why..?

The screen came to life and I'd just started tapping in the first strokes of my research when two things happened in quick succession, the first being when I'd typed in the name "Marco Dexter".

A "Breaking News" banner appeared on one of the news channels I subscribed to:

"AMERICAN BUSINESSMAN FOUND DEAD.

Mr. Marco Dexter, 41 years old, was found dead in his home, 'Devil's View', on the North Downs in Sussex, at eleven o'clock by Mrs. Marjorie Turner, employed by Mr. Dexter as a cleaner.

Mr. Dexter, from California, had been renting the house for the past year whilst negotiating several business deals in London, and his body was found by Mrs. Turner in the drawing room. It is believed that he may have committed suicide but although this has not been confirmed, Sussex police say they are not treating the death as suspicious."

I leaned back, staring at the screen...

So...That was how it was being seen was it? Suicide. Looks like Charlotte, or whoever had killed Dexter, might be getting away with it, at least for the moment, and why not? It certainly looked very convincing: Gun nicely dropped in the right place; a note and a good clean shot straight up through the jaw into the brain; No sign of a struggle...First impressions count and the first impression would be that Marco had sat down, written a note, put a loaded gun under his chin and pulled the trigger: Case closed. As long as no-one broke and talked under the influence of drink or drugs or maybe even simple guilt, the chances were good it would always be thought that a rich guy, alone in a big house, thousands of miles from home, had had a moment of remorse and darkness and couldn't take it anymore.

I thought about the hall porter at Charlotte's flat and The Doctor. What would they think when they saw or heard the story: Would they put two and two together and begin to make four..? The Doctor would have more than likely been involved in "suicides" like this before and probably wouldn't even start counting, but the porter might turn the events of the last few hours over in his clever old brain and begin to wonder.

It was at that point in my thought process that the second thing happened.

A notification in the corner of the screen glowed up telling me I had just received an e-mail from my private detective friend, so I clicked on it, opened it up and it read:

"Reference your request "All available records ref' intel' on Marcus Dexter, US citizen: Mrs. Leonora Dexter, now Fitzpatrick, UK citizen" As follows to date:

Leonora Fitzpatrick married Marco Dexter, Queen's County State Registry, NY State, 12th July 2019. Leonora Fitzpatrick brought divorce suit against Marco Dexter, 3rd January 2020. Suit served, 5th January 2020: No records of counter suit or of further proceedings: No records of hearings: No records of decree being granted: No records of second serving.

Used contacts to obtain information from Goldstein, Rothsheimer and Warburg: As follows...

Received instructions to stop divorce proceedings; 15th January 2020

Marriage registration...Still current

Marcus Dexter background:

        NY State......2 x charges blackmail: 1 x charge Intimidation...2011

All charges dropped. Divorce proceedings taken: Marriage ended: 2012

Florida State….I x charge Abuse: 1 x charge blackmail…2013

Proceedings stopped: Divorce proceedings taken: Marriage ended: 2014

California State….I x charge Intimidation: 2 x charges Assault…2016

All charges dropped: Divorce proceedings taken: Marriage ended: 2017

Conclusion: Marco Dexter…

Military Service…U.S. Marine Corps x 8 years; 4 x tours in Iraq & Afghanistan: Dishonourable discharge; 2010….Suspected gigolo/escort/living off immoral earnings….Suspected Narcotics dealing…No recorded drug offences….Licensed for fire-arms in eight states….3 x Previous marriages to women with individual net worth in excess of $15,000,000

Nice Guy.

Good Luck with this one…

All favours now paid…Thanks again for the weekend: Cheers!"

I read, re-read then read the mail again, a slow smile melting onto my face as I gradually took in the fact that Leonora Fitzpatrick was, technically, still married to Marcus Dexter! She may well have filed a suit against the bastard for divorce back in 2020, but, according to the records, nothing had happened: There'd been no hearings, it hadn't been served again and no decree had been granted, so that meant, officially, the woman was still Mrs. Dexter, and that meant poor bloody Charlotte wasn't and never had been.

I sat back, hands behind my head, looking into middle space.

Surely Leonora knew she was still married to Dexter? She'd paid Cleaver a probable fortune to send him and Harry over to New York to try and persuade him to sign the bloody second set of papers for God's sake, but failed again because Dexter was a twisted, sadistic fuck who enjoyed seeing women in pain, physically and mentally. So, when she came to see me and get me involved in taking the persuasion level up a notch she must have known she was Mrs. Dexter and she also must have known by then that her darling husband didn't give in to threats of physical assault, so why the lies: Why the big sob story? Was she really just hoping for third time lucky? What was I going to do about it though: Anything or nothing? What could I do? Nothing probably. My part in whatever it was had ended, so why should I bother? I'd been paid to scare off someone that didn't take kindly to me but I'd failed the task and someone had shot him instead, but that someone hadn't been me so why stay involved: What purpose would it serve? None really but I'm my own worst enemy when it comes to being left dangling like this. I have a natural and dangerous curiosity about these things and I need to know what's going on so, even as I was asking myself the question, I knew I was going to keep interested in this until I found out what it was all about, for better or worse.

The discussion won, I turned my thoughts to my next move and only one made any sense.

I had to go and have a chat with the lovely and obviously angry Leonora Fitzpatrick. She was at the centre of whatever was going on and I'd found out very quickly in my years of doing this kind of work that sometimes it pays to just go straight for the sucker punch: Go straight to the heart, and as far as finding out the truth about who killed Marco Dexter and why, the heart of this deadly dance was the woman that had come to my office at midnight and got me into all of this in the first place: Leonora bloody Fitzpatrick.

I'd cut a lucky break earlier when I'd found Charlotte's address book, because Leonora's address and even her private number were in there, so that saved me a lot of time and effort searching for it.

I closed the laptop, swung the chair round, grabbed my jacket and went down to the street.

TWENTY ONE

In the car, I sat and entered Leonora's post code onto the Sat' Nav on my phone, and when the location came up on the screen I could see it wasn't too far away: Richmond, right on the banks of the river: Maybe forty minutes' drive if the traffic kept moving.

I looked it up on Google Earth and saw there were three big, detached houses set in their own grounds, at the end of what looked like a private road: Nice neighbourhood, the kind that came with a very nice price-tag: If Leonora Fitzpatrick could afford to pay for a house like that in a place like Richmond, then she obviously had more than enough money to pay someone to kill Marcus Dexter and make it look like suicide, and I could think of two men that worked for Cleaver who specialised in faking suicides and they didn't work cheap.

Moving in on the image, I looked around for camera-free areas where I might be able to hide my car and possibly slip into the grounds of Leonora's house, but quickly decided there probably wouldn't be: People who owned houses like that in areas like Richmond were paranoid about security and could afford to have cameras and guards covering every angle and every square inch of their expensive property so I stopped looking, buckled up, indicated and moved out into the traffic, heading south towards the river.

Thirty minutes later, I arrived at the top of the private road and saw cameras high up on poles swivel around to watch me as I turned onto it, then follow me as I drove slowly towards Leonora's house. I was right: There would have been no chance at all of hiding the car and slipping over a wall anywhere. There was an obviously high level of security on show and I knew that someone in a building somewhere had already registered my arrival and was checking up on the car, its number and more than likely me as well. No point in trying to be cautious or sneaky so I kept driving, following the long, curving road around and down towards the river.

Leonora's place, when I found it, was big, white, romantic-looking, surrounded by trees and lawns, and had a definite air of old money about it. If the inside was as classy looking as the outside then this lady was living very comfortably indeed.

When I pulled up at the double gates and pushed the button on the intercom, the voice that answered sounded classy and indifferent. I told him who I was and that I'd come to see Mrs. Fitzpatrick and there was a slight pause as he checked in a diary to see if I was expected. When he discovered I wasn't, he sounded even more indifferent, dismissively telling me he was sorry but he didn't think Mrs. Fitzpatrick would see me.

I said, very politely, she would once she knew I was there, to which he replied that Mrs. Fitzpatrick was not expecting anyone at all and had retired for the evening: Perhaps I could return tomorrow.

I told him, again very politely, that I did not want to return tomorrow because when I said I needed to see her then I meant I really DID need to see her tonight and that what I needed to talk with her about was very important and that I would therefore be very bloody grateful if he would run along, tell her I was here and let her make her own mind up: Thank you.

The tone of my voice and the determination behind it must have gotten across to him because he sighed…"Very well sir…", went to convey my message to her and, less than a minute later, as I'd expected, the tall iron gates began to swing back slowly.

Following the drive around to the front of the house, I parked beside a large garage, got out and, out of curiosity, walked over to it, interested to see what cars might be in there.

The two up-and-over doors were electrically operated and locked, but there were small twelve inch windows in the centre of each one and through them I could see Leonora's sporty coupe and the black Mercedes that had picked up Charlotte from the clinic. Either it had returned from taking Charlotte to wherever she was now or she was here in the house, sleeping off whatever it was "The Doctor" had given her to make it look like she was well enough to be discharged from the clinic.

There was another car too: A large 4x4 Audi parked between the others, and the shaft of light that shone through the second window was falling across its near-side front panel, more importantly across the slightly turned tyre, and something about the pattern tickled at my retentive brain.

I took out my phone, opened up the camera and zoomed in as hard as I could on the tread pattern, taking three or four quick pictures, using the auto-enhance function to sharpen and contrast the images. Choosing the clearest of the shots I then pulled out the tyre patterns I'd photographed at Dexter's place and smiled to myself in quiet recognition. It was the same as the pattern beneath that of the Carter's BMW: The print made by the wider, chunkier, 4x4 tyres. The car that got to the house first: Leonora's Audi it seemed.

I stood turning over this new piece of the still picture-less jigsaw for a moment, stored it away in my head for future pondering, put the phone back in my pocket, turned and walked across the neatly crunching gravel to the house, mounting the three steps up to the porticoed entrance and pressed the door-bell, noticing the fixed eyeball camera set into the wall beside the door and the mobile globe camera above my head that covered the drive and the front of the house.

One of the tall white double-doors opened and the face behind the intercom voice appeared: An older guy, in his late sixties maybe; tall, handsome face; wearing a good suit and what looked like a military tie: The classic 'butler'. I almost expected him to say…" You rang sir..?" and was a tiny bit disappointed when he only said…"Please come in. Mrs. Fitzpatrick will see you in the lounge."

I followed him across a wide hall, along a carpeted corridor, then through another set of double-doors into a very tastefully furnished room with large modern art pieces on the walls and a long, panoramic floor-to-ceiling window at the far end, framing a very pleasant view across a well-kept lawn to a picture-box boat-house and the river. Indicating for me to take a seat, the butler left the room, closing the doors very professionally behind him.

When they opened again, Leonora glided in, wearing a floor-length, high collared, crimson house-coat buttoned all the way up to the neck, the colour accentuating the whiteness of her skin, the long-sleeves widening out halfway down the fore-arm, hemmed at the wrist in black fur. She looked casually glamourous and smelt gorgeous, bringing an involuntary smile to my lips and sending my mind straight back to the night I'd first met her in my office. As she came closer, the soft lighting caught the subtle highlights in her hair and made her skin look impossibly smooth but when she got to within a few feet of me I could see there were shadows under her eyes and that she looked tired...Worried.

"Mr. Carter..," she said, coldly, staring impassively at me:" This is a little unexpected."

"Is it..?" I smiled, an annoyingly unphased smile on my face.

She made no reply and her expression remained cool.

"You said you needed to talk with me..," she said, distantly:" Apparently you were quite insistent. What about, exactly..?"

"Why don't you sit down..?" I said:" I think you might need to."

"Please don't tell me what to do in my own home mister Carter..," she bristled:" I'll remain standing if you don't mind. You won't be staying long. Now, if you wouldn't mind just telling me why you are here..?"

"Okay then..," I said, pulling one of the chairs up myself and sitting down looking up at her, fixing her with a charming grin:" It's up to you, but I'll sit down if you don't mind. We've got a lot to talk about."

I nodded at the chair:

"Sit: Please..?"

She looked at me with frigid distaste on her beautifully made up face, her stunning eyes letting me know that right at that moment I was five levels beneath something she might have stepped on in her Louboutin shoes, but, with reluctant grace, she pulled up a chair and sat in it.

"That's better..," I said, my voice glowing with warm concern:" You're going to feel much more comfortable now: Much more relaxed: Give you time to think about what I'm going to tell you: Help stop your mind jumping around like a squirrel in a cage, which is what I can tell it's doing right now."

A sneer twitched at the corners of her gorgeous lips but she said nothing, just stared at me with ice-cold contempt. I brushed the sneer aside with a handsome smile.

"Two things..," I started, but she cut me off.

"Two..?" she scoffed:" I'm intrigued. What might they be..?"

"Yes..," I said, unruffled:" Two things. The first is the night you came to see me in my office."

"A night I now regret..," she snipped.

"Oh, I don't think you do..," I grinned at her:" I think you're actually very pleased you did. It may not have had the outcome you'd hoped for but it fitted in well with the general plan."

She suddenly looked beautifully confused.

"The general plan..?"

"Yes. 'The general plan'..," I repeated, still with my most dis-arming of smiles on my face:" The one that was probably intended to make me the patsy for a problem you'd already decided on the solution for long before you came to see me."

"I have no idea what you're talking about..," she said, a small frown creasing her otherwise marble-smooth forehead.

"Let's just say I think you do..," I said, crossing my legs, leaning back into the leather and folding my arms:" You see, in the light of what's been happening over the past couple of days, I've been thinking about that night a lot and the more I think about it the more I think you knew exactly what you were doing when you came to see me. Firstly...You came at midnight, which is a bit of a strange time to call upon a complete stranger, a probable meat-head, to discuss business don't you think...?"

"I was told..," she interrupted but I carried on, cutting her off again.

"You were *told*..," I said:"...that if you came to my office at midnight, I would very probably be very tired and very drunk and, being very tired and very drunk, I would probably just say yes to whatever you asked me to do for you, especially if you filled my whiskey-fogged head with that fantastic perfume and used your looks and womanly ways to flick my switches, but when you saw I wasn't going to fall for that old tactic, because the one thing I don't fall for anymore is feminine wiles, you then offered me money: The final temptation..."

"Which you accepted..," she said, snidely.

"Of course I did..," I grinned, opening my hands:" Why wouldn't I..? I'm never too tired or too drunk to say no to money: If a beautiful woman that can obviously afford it hands me thousands of pounds in an envelope I'd be a bloody fool not to take it wouldn't I? It's a weakness of mine."

She raised her eyebrows in an obvious reproach.

"And the second thing...?"she said frostily.

"Let's stick with the first for a while, shall we..? I haven't finished explaining when it was I first began to sniff the perfumed aroma of rat in the room."

Her eyes hardened but she held back whatever response she might have wanted to make and let me continue. I could tell she was becoming uncomfortable, which was what I wanted.

"You said you'd come to me because our mutual friend Cleaver had told you I was, to use your word, "unscrupulous"..," I said, watching her face for any kind of reaction:"...and, even though I was befuddled with drink, when you used that word, alarm bells began ringing in my head. Why, I thought, does this beautiful lady want someone "unscrupulous" unless she wanted them to do something that might not be very nice and that they didn't want anyone knowing about. Why would a classy looking woman like her come to a shitty little office like mine in a very naughty part of the city in the middle of the night, climb four floors of unlit stairs in very high, very expensive shoes and give a drunk like me thousands of pounds unless they want something doing that's very wrong."

"What do you mean..?" she said, tensely.

"I mean..," I elaborated, spreading my hands:"...you made me think you needed to hire some muscle: Someone with a bit of a reputation: Someone who had no qualms about using strong-arm tactics if needed, but I also think you already knew before you hired me that it was more than likely that however good I was, I probably wouldn't stand a chance against your low-life husband because, underneath all those fancy clothes and behind that fake-tan sophistication he was a combat-hardened, steely-eyed veteran who knew extremely well how to look after himself, something I discovered very quickly..," I grinned, rubbing my jaw theatrically:" But that didn't really matter did it? That wasn't the plan. No: What mattered was that I, or someone like me, would go and see him and that it would all go bad. That was what you wanted to happen. You wanted to use me as a stick to poke the bear in his cave: Make him angry and lash out in retaliation. I don't think you really wanted me to go and put pressure on your husband at all. I think you just needed a pawn in a game that only had a few moves left in it before you checkmated your ex-mate but...and this leads us neatly on to the second thing we need to talk about...it seems your ex-mate isn't your "ex-mate" at all is he..? Your ex-mate is actually very much still your 'mate', or to use the legal term...your 'husband'..."

There was an edgy silence as she absorbed my last sentence, during which she just sat staring at me, sizing me up, turning over what I'd just said.

Suddenly she stood up.

"Would you like a drink mister Carter..?" she said, tersely:" I would..."

I smiled charmingly, said I would love a drink and watched her walk across to a built-in cabinet at the end of the room, open one of the glass doors revealing three shelves of expensive looking booze, take two out, pour a long, tall measure of a very good single malt for me and a good measure of a stupidly expensive vermouth for herself, bring them back and hand me mine, all in silence.

I took my whiskey from her, sat back, raised it in a mock salute and swallowed some of the very smooth, peaty Scotch, watching her slowly drink hers, wondering what she was thinking: How she was taking what I'd said.

After a long minute she looked me in the eye and said:

"If you knew or even suspected that was what I wanted, why did you accept my money and go to see Dexter..?"

No mention of the '"still married" revelation which I found interesting.

"I told you why I accepted the money..," I said, evenly:" It was because I never turn down large amounts of cash: Simple as that, but as for deciding to go and see Dexter, it wasn't because you'd paid me to do it. No...I went to meet Dexter purely out of curiosity: I just wanted to meet the man: See if he was as bad as you'd painted him."

"And was he..?" she said, sarcastically, her voice low, looking at me with hooded eyes. They were nice eyes, even filled with malice like they undoubtedly were.

I threw back another gulp of the Scotch and moved the almost empty tumbler around idly in my fingers, keeping up the grin, even though it was beginning to wear slightly thin now.

"Yes..," I said, casually:" He was: Very..."

"What happened..?" she snapped.

"What happened after I'd disappointed you by not jumping in my car at one in the morning and driving all the way down to Sussex...?" I smiled:" Nothing. I fell asleep on the sofa as always, woke up, drank a lot of coffee, had a long shower, sobered up and then drove down to "Devil's View". Nice name by the way: Very appropriate..."

She shifted in her seat, impatiently, but I took my time, sipping the remains of the Scotch before continuing.

"When I got there..," I went on:"...I came across poor, dear Charlotte, dancing around in the trees, tripping out nicely on drugs and drink, interestingly carrying a loaded pistol in her bag and laughing loudly about shooting her husband...Or should I say, *your* husband because that's what he is isn't he? *Your* husband."

I could see her jaw tighten and there was a flicker of something on her otherwise mask-like features, but it was fleeting and she said nothing.

"Anyway..," I continued:" Charlotte said her little piece of nonsense, did a bit more dancing and then, unsurprisingly, passed out, so I put her in my car, wrapped her up nice and warm and carried on into the house to wait for Marcus. A couple of his very good whiskeys later he turned up and we had a chat, but it wasn't a very nice chat. After only a couple of minutes I wanted to slap the guy hard across his smug, arrogant face and I could easily see how Charlotte might want to shoot him. Anyhow...The chat got nowhere, fast, and it became clear very quickly that he wasn't interested in anything I had to say so I decided, just because I really didn't like him by then, that a light beating might make him begin to re-consider his attitude..."

Leonora's eyes widened when I said that and there was a shadow of interest in her expression.

"Did you thrash him..?" she asked, her voice rising and I could see her fingers weaving and un-weaving in her lap. I smiled, not because of how excited she had suddenly become but because she'd used the word "thrash". It was cute. No-one used that word anymore.

"I tried my best..," I said:"...but your husband.., (there was a definite wince when I deliberately used that word again)...quite casually just beat the living shit out of me, pardon the language. He did a pretty good job on me too..," I said, again rubbing my jaw theatrically:" When he'd finished, he left me lying on the floor with a note telling me to piss off when I woke up and not come back again or he'd kill me. I didn't like that or what he'd done, so all of a sudden I was no longer an amused bystander, I was on the team and all I wanted to do was come back and..."

"Why..?" Leonora said.

"Why what..?" I asked.

"Why was being beaten up by Marcus Dexter more important to you than helping me or Charlotte rid ourselves of him..?" she said.

I shrugged my shoulders.

"The reason doesn't matter..," I said:" Just take it from me I was more than a little hacked off."

She leant back and studied me with a look of curiosity in her eyes.

"No..," she said, raising a deliciously curved eyebrow:" I'd like to know. What made you so angry? Was it embarrassment: Did you feel humiliated..?"

"I *said*..," firmly:"...the reason isn't important."

"I really would like to know..," She persisted:" Tell me..? Please..?"

I looked at her for a long second, trying to decide whether she was just stalling for time, trying to divert the course I was trying to take the conversation in: "Gas-lighting" as it's called today, or really was interested and decided, looking into her eyes, that maybe she was. Obviously something deep inside me that I'd buried away for years had been woken up, probably by the "please", and, after a long sigh, I started talking.

"Okay..," I breathed, taking another sip of my drink:" Do you remember telling me that night when you came to my office, about your affair with a young officer? That he went off to the Gulf War, was ambushed, captured and had a very bad time in one of their prisons?"

"Yes..," she said, looking directly at me, her face set, her stare unwavering:" He was tortured and died of his wounds."

I sighed.

"Well, the exact same thing happened to me, except I didn't die. My unit was where we weren't supposed to be, doing something we weren't supposed to be doing and it all went badly wrong. Two of us were killed and the rest got captured, dumped into a bad place and treated very badly by people that really didn't like us..," I grinned, trying to make light of the story, but it was a weak grin and didn't do a very good job of masking the pain of the memories that were creeping back into my head from the dark place I'd been keeping them chained up in all these years. She could see that, I could tell, and it must have been the look of sympathy and encouragement she was giving me that kept the words coming.

"As well as not feeding us and urinating on our heads..," I said, clearing my tightening throat:"...we used to get a hammering every day, sometimes twice or three times a day: Nasty, random stuff: Nothing gentle like a slap or a kick as they walked by: No: Sustained beatings that broke things, and every time they did it, they laughed and told us they were taking bets about which one of us would die first."

I cleared my throat again and looked away, trying to keep a lid on my rising anger, the sound of cruel laughter, screams and wailings from the other rooms burning into my mind.

"I didn't like the beatings or hearing my mates being hurt..," I said:"...and I especially didn't like the feeling of helplessness it gave me listening to them being kicked to death. We were in that fucking hell hole for five very long, very dark months before the compound was taken by a bunch of Marines, and during those five months, between the beatings and the torture, I had a lot of time to think: About our situation, about my life and about what I was going to do to each and every one of those fucking rag-headed bastards when we got out of there. That's what kept me going: Gave me the reason to stay alive but we barely made it: What they hadn't broken they'd torn, bruised or ruptured and we spent another five months in hospital being put back together, slowly and painfully, and every operation and stitch I was given, I swore to myself that nobody was ever going to lay a finger on me again and if they did; if they fucking did…!"

I cleared my throat and bit back the stupid, stinging tear I could feel in the corner of my eye.

"I swore..," I snarled:"...on my life that I would make them suffer for it by breaking that fucking finger first before starting on the rest of them..!"

With a sudden realisation that my teeth were clenched and I was staring at her with a laser intensity, I stopped talking and pulled myself back into the room, the smile I slapped on my face tight and very self-conscious.

"So...There's the reason..," I quipped, glibly:" I guess I just don't like people beating the hell out of me and getting away with it."

Her hands were still now, her eyes had lost their coldness and there was a definite warmth in them.

"I'm very sorry to hear that Mr. Carter..," she smiled, softly:" Very sorry indeed."

The pause that followed was awkward, during which Leonora finished her drink and I used it to work out how I was going to get the conversation back in the direction I'd wanted it to go.

"I take it you've heard the news about..?"

"About Marcuse's suicide..?" she said, cutting me off matter-of-factly:" Yes, I have."

Her eyes had frozen over again and there was a steely sharpness to them that made me frown.

"Very good news for everyone concerned..," I said, watching her face:" Especially you."

She placed her empty glass down onto a side table.

"Why especially for me..?" she asked in a low, irritated voice, her expression neutral.

I interlaced my fingers in my lap and gave her a long, searching look.

"Because, as I said and what I came here to talk about, you never did get that divorce in the end did you, and until he decided to blow his face off last night, you were still Mrs. Leonora Dexter weren't you?"

She looked at me with cold distaste in her eyes, all the warmth there might have been for me a moment ago now gone.

"How did you..?"

"Does Charlotte know the truth by the way..," I interrupted:" Have you told her she's not actually married to him and that, theoretically, she's been having an affair with your husband all this time: That she *could* have just walked away from his abuse and his drugs whenever she wanted?"

Leonora said nothing, just looked at me, contempt and anger beginning to show itself around her eyes and the corner of her mouth.

"Let me take a guess about what happened between you and Cleaver the day you came to see me..," I said, returning her icy stare.

"Please..," she sneered, scornfully:" Do tell me what you *guess* happened Mister Carter..?"

"Another drink first though, eh..?" I said, rising from my chair and walking over to the drinks cabinet.

I poured myself a nice, long whiskey, made her another of what she'd been drinking and brought them back, handing hers down to her, returning the iron-eyed look she'd been giving me with a cheeky smile.

"Okay..," I said, settling myself back into my chair and taking my first sip of the malt:" Let's get started shall we? The night you came to visit me, you'd been to see Cleaver first, probably to ask him to help you settle your problem with Dexter once and for all, a problem he already knew you had because you'd used him in the past to try and persuade Marcus to agree to the divorce after he'd ignored the first serving of the divorce papers: The 5th of January, 2020 if my memory serves me right?"

Cold silence from the seat opposite, so I continued.

"My "not-really-a-guess" about what happened the first time was that, according to one of my happy-to-talk colleagues, at your request Cleaver went over to New York to liaise with Messer's Goldstein, Rothsheimer and Warburg about serving Marcus with a second set of papers, taking with him another of my loyal and happy-to-talk colleagues, in the hope that this time my rather burly and frankly quite intimidating colleague could 'persuade' your husband to accept the inevitable, sign the papers and step out of your life, but, because your loving husband sat right at the top of the "unscrupulous" pile, not possessing one single "scrupe" and not giving the coldest shit, he ignored them again but this time, probably because he was getting bored of the whole thing and just wanted to move on to hunt for other rich fish, he came up with an idea based upon his realisation that Cleaver was as nasty and sadistic as himself when it came to money, both of them led by their obsessions; Cleaver by his greed for money and Dexter by his twin greed for money and his dick."

She flinched slightly at that word because she was a sensitive, polite flower but I carried on.

"Knowing you were never going to stop serving him with papers, he made Cleaver an offer which, knowing the fat fuck as I do only too well, he accepted like a wolf with two heads accepts meat: Hungrily, and while they were hatching the deal between them, Cleaver had my colleague sit in the lawyers office every day for hours drinking their coffee, watching the celebrities and politicians coming and going, waiting to be told that the papers were signed and the decree was on its way, which was never going to happen because he and Dexter were cooking up a plan that would get Marcus Charlotte's money and body, strictly in that order, and reward Cleaver with bag loads of money."

I took a deliberately casual sip of my drink, watching Leonora's face, looking for her reaction to my guess but, like before, she gave nothing away.

"Well: This is fascinating..," she said, coolly, taking a sip of her own drink:" Please carry on..."

I threw more whiskey down my throat and carried on.

"I think what Cleaver did then was, as agreed between him and Dexter, go to your lawyers, tell them that as your spokesperson you'd changed your mind and decided not to continue with the divorce suit, then, using your money and the time that you were paying for, obtained an official Form of Decree, which you can get on-line if you want, used Dexter's network of bad guys to forge the New York Department of Justice Seal, stamped the form, filled it in with all the names and information you'd given him, sent it to you as evidence that he'd been successful and that you were divorced, accepted your grateful thanks and with gracious modesty pocketed the bonus you undoubtedly gave him. All done: Mission over. You thought you were free of Dexter and Cleaver was a couple of hundred thousand richer. Big cigars all fucking round."

This time when I paused for another sip, although there was no change in her expression, there was a distinct change in her eyes and I could see they were burning with a cold, blue flame. Had my guess been correct, and had my voicing it made her wary of me and my intentions?

"I have more guesses if you'd like to hear them..?" I said, taking another sip of the really rather good whiskey.

"More surprises..! How very "dramatic" of you Mr. Carter..," she said mockingly:" Please: Continue with my education."

"Well...My continuing guess would be that for a while you were happy, enjoying your long-fought for and very expensive freedom from Dexter, but when you found out Charlotte had returned to the States and your not-quite ex' was making moves on her, you were afraid for her well-being, realising he would try and hook her on drugs, make her miserable and drain her bank accounts like he'd done with other vulnerable young women and like he'd tried to do with you. But you also realised the only way you were going to be able to stop him ruining her life the way he almost had with yours was to play the way he plays, or should I say "played", and that was nastily, so, not knowing about Cleaver's deal with Dexter and the fact that legally you were still married to him, you went back to Cleaver believing he could repeat his success and throw a scare into him like he said he'd done, but because he was now in the pocket of Dexter, he gave you some cock-ass stories about not wanting to get involved again and passed you onto me, but only after you'd paid him even more money to get him to give you my address. He's generous like that."

"My, my..," she mused:" I do seem to be paying people a lot of money don't I..?"

I continued without comment.

"He told you that I was fussy about who I leaned on but would get involved if the money was good enough because I was, as he obviously put it, "unscrupulous", which is almost true but not quite. I do have a few 'scrupes left."

I grinned at my own joke but there was nothing from her, just that beautiful, dark-eyed, stony look.

"So...," I continued, unabashed:"...you came to me and you told me what you thought I needed to hear to get me interested enough to go and frighten Dexter, *except* that you knew Dexter wasn't easily frightened and it didn't matter because I was only a tactic: A set up to get him to react the way you wanted him to, and he did react didn't he? He reacted exactly as you knew he would: By sending a guy like me around to try and intimidate him, again, into signing the papers and going away, you made him angry because Marcus Dexter was just like me: Someone that didn't like being pushed around, taken for a piece of trash. You wanted him to send me back with a message stuck in my arse that told you to back off, possibly even threatening violence if you didn't: A message you could then use against him with the police to get him to back down and finally sign the papers and go away. Now... I think you had planned to do all of that over the next few weeks but when you found the note in Charlotte's kitchen and read his demand for money and the deadline of only last night to get it before he flew off to a private island to bleed some other rich woman dry, you realised you had to work very fast if you were ever going to end the cycle of his torment and vain cruelty once and for all."

There was silence and we both just sat there looking at each other, thinking different thoughts. I was pretty sure what hers were. She didn't look happy with what I'd just said but I was and I was just as happy looking at her. She was very nice to look at and I could have stayed looking at her for as long as she wanted but she broke the silence.

"Why would I want to do that..?" she eventually asked, coolly:" Whatever "that" is..?

I smiled back at her, a little arrogantly maybe but I was enjoying her disdain.

"Because..," I said:"...if Dexter did get out to the Caribbean, the web of laws and dodgy tax rules the super-rich like he and his besotted new girl-friend could weave around you would mean Charlotte and yourself would be tangled up for years trying to get free of him. Legally, you probably wouldn't have been able to do it at all and physically..?"

I gave her a 'God-father' shrug.

"Physically it would have been a very hard thing to do, trying to intimidate him on a private island, especially with someone who could afford a lot of security to keep you or anyone else you sent off the said island. So, no...You knew it would have been like trying to freeze hell over starting another divorce proceeding for Charlotte when you both lived here in England and he lived a few thousand miles away in a tax and legal haven, plus you thought you'd spent a lot of money so far and didn't want to spend a lot more trying to get him to sign on the dotted line when he was holed up in the Bahamas surrounded by some very cute law firms. You knew that and he most certainly knew that too, which is why he made the ultimatum. So, like I said, you had to act fast. You had to stop him getting on that plane and, amazingly, without you asking, he gave you a way to do it."

"Really...?" she said:" And how do you know that..?"

"Because..," I said, smugly:"...being the resourceful kind of guy I am, I "found" the key to Charlotte's apartment and had the chance to take a look around a few hours before

Charlotte returned. Charming place but she really has let it go a bit, don't you think? Could do with a duster being flicked around in the corners, here and there. Anyway, I had a wander around and came across the note Dexter had left for Charlotte in the kitchen; the one she told you about. Naturally, being nosy, I read it and it seemed to be the answer to your hand-wringing prayers. The arsehole-in-chief, your husband and Charlotte's lover as it turns out, was offering you both an olive branch. No idea why: Maybe I had got to him after all. Maybe he was a bit concerned I would come back and beat him to a runny pulp for no other reason than I very much wanted to, or maybe, which is more likely, he was just bored with playing with you both and wanted a new set of dolls to dance with, but whatever the reason, it seems he was willing to give Charlotte the papers, signed and sealed with a loving kiss in return for very nice farewell-forever, one-off, never-darken-my-doors payment. It also said she, or you, had better hurry up and find the money by ten o'clock, because if you didn't he would tear up the papers, catch a shiny private jet in the early hours of the morning to one of three islands in the sun that his new girlfriend owned, and let you chew his dust trying to get him to agree ever again. That didn't give you much time so you had to abandon the long-term plans you'd been making, think fast and come up with a short-term solution instead."

"I don't know what you mean..," she bristled, her voice low and tight.

"I mean I don't think Dexter committed suicide..," I said, sinking my voice:" I think your husband was murdered."

I saw her fingers tighten on the arms of the chair.

"Dexter was killed..," I said, matter-of-factly:" He didn't put a bullet into his head himself. Someone else did it for him."

TWENTY TWO

Leonora sat in her chair looking straight at me, her face tight, her skin flushed ice-white; eyes fixed on mine.

"Murdered..?" she said, distrustfully:" What do you mean "murdered"?"

"I mean I suspect Marcus didn't kill himself. I think someone killed him: someone we might know."

Her eyes opened and she looked elegantly shocked.

"Someone we know..?" she whispered, her voice sounding incredulous.

I nodded.

"Yes..," I said, taking a sip of my drink:" Someone we know."

"But who and...How?"

I noticed she didn't say "Why"...

I shrugged, nonchalantly.

"I have my theories..," I said:" but before you ask what they are...Another drink..?"

She nodded and watched me get up, walk across to the bottles and make us both another drink, the tension in the air very tight.

"Drink this slowly..," I said, handing hers down to her:" Relax."

She took the glass, drank a little and put it down, her eyes on me all the time, worried and unfriendly at the same time.

I lifted my glass.

"Relax..," I said, reassuringly:" It could be a lot worse."

"Tell me..," she said, sarcastically:" You've just told me that my ex-husband is still my husband, that he has been having what amounts to an affair with my best friend and that he might have been murdered: How exactly could it be worse?"

"Two ways..," I said, settling back into the chair, cradling the long, tall tumbler in my fingers:" First: Looking on the positive side, if Dexter were still alive, he'd be on his way to the Bahamas by now."

"And the other way..?"

"You might not have someone unscrupulous like me working for you..," I smiled, showing all my teeth.

"I see..," she said, suspiciously:" Are you still working for me then Mr. Carter..?" she asked.

"Of course..," I said:" I'm a man of principle, and if I take on a job then I do it to mine and the client's satisfaction."

"How very honourable of you..," she said, tartly:" Perhaps I under-estimated you and your alleged lack of scruples. Perhaps you are a man of integrity after all."

"I have a big blue streak of it running right down my back..," I said cheekily:" Put there by my dear old dad."

"I'm very pleased to hear that..," she smiled, this time less tightly:" You obviously inherited very conscientious genes. So…Taking into account all you've told me, where does this leave us now?"

"In what respect..?" I said, innocently, my smile still in place.

"In respect of the situation I, or perhaps now "we", find ourselves in. My dead, murdered according to you, husband still being my husband and his death being caused by someone you believe we both might know. Where does that put us?"

"Well, for a start lets' get it clear that there is no "us"..," I said:" there is just "you" and "they". I'm merely an interested party in all of whatever this is, but looking at it from over here, the "situation" as you call it doesn't look good. With any luck it may turn out all right. The police may be satisfied that Dexter killed himself. It certainly looked that way."

She frowned when I said that.

"You've seen him..?" she asked, genuinely surprised:" You've seen Dexter's body?"

"Yes and I doubt anyone would find him as attractive as he once was..," I said:" If he hadn't had plastic surgery before, he could do with a bit now, especially around the jaw-line."

My attempt at gallows humour was lost on her and she looked away, a look of cold contempt on her face.

I took another drink.

"Where's Charlotte..?" I asked.

The sound of my voice brought Leonora back into the room and she looked at me for a few seconds before answering.

"Charlotte..?" she said, her voice almost a whisper.

"Yes..," I said:" Charlotte. Where is she..?"

"She's…"

"Please..," I said, holding my hand up to stop her:" Don't say she's at the clinic because I know she's not. She left there last night, only a few hours after she was admitted. A bit odd that don't you think?"

"You knew she was at the clinic?"

"Yes I knew because it was me that put her in there, or at least that had her put in there. I saw her off from where I'd been hiding her that afternoon and a few hours later, she's gone. Signed out by the very doctor that admitted her."

"I had no idea…"

"Didn't you..?" I said, a look of disbelief on my face.

"No..," she scowled:" I didn't."

I grinned widely and shook my head. I held all the aces in this game and she was beginning to realise it.

"Oh I think you did..," I said:"…and I think she's here right now, in this house somewhere."

She looked at me, suspiciously and ruffled at the same time.

"Here..?"

"Yes, here..," I said, a little impatiently, turning over another card she didn't know I had:"…because, according to the people at the clinic when I phoned' to see how she was, your car, the one that's sitting in your garage at this moment, picked her up from there at seventeen minutes past six yesterday evening, so it makes sense she came here. She certainly wasn't in any state to go back to her own place and anyway… I already checked and she's not there…so…?"

I left the question hanging in the air, waiting for the answer, watching Leonora thinking, sizing me up, maybe getting her story straight, assessing the "situation" as she liked to call it, then, seemingly reluctantly, she said, in a defeated voice…

"She got here last night…"

"What time..?"

Her sigh was deep.

"About eight. Martin would know exactly..," she dismissed:" The poor girl was terribly ill: Almost unconscious. She's been sleeping for hours."

"Has anyone seen her since she arrived: Has a doctor visited her?"

"My doctor has been, but he says he really can't do very much for her. She ought to be receiving…"

"Clinical treatment..?" I said, raising an eyebrow:" Yes, she should and she was but for some reason she checked out of one, or was checked out, two hours after she was checked in and came here. Why would that be?"

The look Leonora gave me was angry and touchy.

"I don't know..," she snarled:" All I do know is that I got a hysterical phone call from her saying she couldn't stay there and that it was very important she got out. She sounded desperate. I was very worried and called her doctor…"

"Her doctor, or "The Doctor"..?"

"I don't understand..," she said, looking genuinely puzzled.

"Never mind. I do… What did the doctor do?"

"I have no idea. The next thing I knew I got another call saying she was being discharged and could I please send a car for her."

"Were you aware she stopped off at her apartment on the way..?" I said.

"Yes, I was made aware of it by my driver, but I had no idea she was going to. He had strict instructions to bring her straight here. I was furious with him."

"Do you know why she stopped there?"

"She told him she wanted to pick up a few things, but I suspect she..."

"Wanted to take a last hit of heroin before she got here..?" I finished.

Leonora nodded.

"Yes..," she said:" I'm sure that's what it was. I'd already told her I would be going to the flat myself to get her what she was going to need whilst she stayed with me so she would have had no other reason."

"Did she tell you about the note?"

"No..," Leonora sighed petulantly:" I wasn't here when she actually arrived. I only saw her when I got back and she was sleeping very deeply by then."

"Where were you..?" I said, quizzically:" Why weren't you here to meet her?"

She looked daggers at me.

"I was on my way back..," she breathed, irritably.

"From where..?" I said.

"From an appointment in the city..," she snapped, looking away.

I stepped back from asking who with. I would ask that later.

"Did she leave at all last night..?" I said.

She looked puzzled.

"Leave? Here you mean..? No, she couldn't have. She was very ill and still is. Martin would have stopped her if she'd tried. Why do you ask that? You can't think she had anything to do with Dexter's..."

Her voice trailed away.

"Death..?" I said:" I don't know what to think at the moment but someone went there."

She began twisting and untwisting her fingers again. Her eyes were dark and troubled, moving from my face to her fingers as she spoke.

"What am I going to do..?" she said, alarm rising in her voice:" What if the police decide it wasn't a suicide? Charlotte's his wife, or they think she is. What if they come here, looking for her to ask questions or find out what she knew? What could they do to her? What could they do to Charlotte? Could they...Could they...?"

"Don't lets' meet trouble..," I said, calmly:" There's a good chance the police will stay with the suicide theory. Unless they look hard there's no reason to suspect otherwise, and everyone gets out of this alive."

"Yes, but what if they do look hard? What if, like you, they begin to suspect that...?"

"I told you I still work for you..," I said: firmly:"...and if you want my help like you say you do then let me handle the "What if's", okay? I've had some experience of situations like this and I know how things work. Got that?"

She nodded, her face tense which gave her a different type of beauty.

"Good..," I said, more calmly and reassuringly:" Then what I need you to start doing now is telling me the truth, whatever that may be, okay? If you and Charlotte are going to get through this mess untouched, I'm going to have to feel sure that whatever you give me to work with is solid reality, otherwise the whole pack of cards I'm going to have to try and build is going to come crashing down around those well-heeled feet of yours. Understood..?"

Leonora's nod was imperceptible but I acknowledged it.

"Right'..,"I said, taking a last swallow of whiskey:" I'm going to go back over what I suspect and start making some educated guesses based upon those suspicions, and unless I make a mistake that matters whilst I'm working things out in my head, I don't want to be interrupted. Okay..?"

She nodded again, looking down at the floor, her eyes wide.

"Thank you. Let's start with the last time you visited Cleaver: The afternoon of the day you came to see me. You went to see him because you knew things had come to a bad place with Marcus and Charlotte: She was broken, bankrupt, badly addicted to his drugs, and miserable. Because of all that you were afraid she might do something very stupid like killing him, something she'd probably been threatening to do a dozen times at parties, social gatherings, amongst the few friends she had left: You were scared. Not just for her mental and physical health, but of what she might be close to actually doing. So you went to Cleaver because he'd worked on your behalf before and you figured he knew what a bastard Dexter was. You wanted him to put the scare on Dexter, like he'd made it look like he'd done before: Try to get him to force Marcus to leave Charlotte: Accept another generous offer and divorce her. What you didn't know was that because Cleaver was tied up in a deal with Dexter that had split the last generous offer you'd made to him about your own divorce between themselves, you were still married to Dexter and that Cleaver was conning you into believing you were free of him, so, obviously there was no way he could do that, which meant he gave you a load of bull-crap reasons for not being able to get involved again: Reasons that probably sounded good, but were lies. Then, to get rid of you, keep you off his back for a while longer and possibly get himself off the hook, he told you about me; suggested I might be useful: Said I was the ideal man for the work you had in mind: That I was the guy he used in difficult cases like your own: That I'd helped others in similar situations, etcetera, etcetera: "Bigged me up" as the kids say... but he warned you that I wasn't cheap and that I didn't take on cases I wasn't interested in: That you'd need to tug at the heartstrings a bit because I'm a cold bugger: You, being desperate, gullible and still trusting him, jumped at the suggestion and paid him even more of your money for my address which he happily gave you, telling you I was probably out on a bit of a bender right at that moment but would more than likely end the evening sleeping on the floor there in a pool of whiskey, a normal occurrence for me and unfortunately only too true, and so it was probably best to get there around midnight and wait for me to shuffle up the stairs. Am I right so far?"

"So far, yes..," she snapped, irritably:" He also asked me if I'd ever heard from Marcus since he'd married Charlotte. I said no."

I pouted and nodded my head thoughtfully.

"Probably checking to see if Marcus was keeping his end of the deal..," I said.

"Probably..," she whispered, staring down at her feet, sounding annoyed, obviously angry at being played for a fool.

There was silence for a bit as I almost finished my drink, looking at her as I drank. I could have looked at her for a long time. She was getting even more attractive by the minute, and that wasn't just the Scotch working its magic on my libido. She really was.

Her questioning voice shook me back.

"Do you honestly think the police will be satisfied that Marcus shot himself?"

"Yes..," I nodded, sagely:" I do. There's a very high chance they'll not look into it too closely..."

I was lying of course. I knew very well the police wouldn't take what they saw at face value. That's not what they did. They investigated things and I was pretty sure it wouldn't take much investigating to begin to suspect that maybe the millionaire playboy Marcus Dexter might not have put his shiny .32 Colt to his own head and pulled the trigger himself but, I couldn't bring myself to tell the worried looking woman in front of me that. It would have been like pulling the life-jacket away from a drowning child.

I finished the drink, looked at my watch and put the glass down on a side table. I now had the confirmation I needed on a few things and needed to go start the process of rectifying a situation which, if I didn't do anything about it, could, being selfish about it, see me deep in the crap I'd waded up to my knees in.

"Okay..," I said, rising to my feet:" That's all the guessing I'm going to do for tonight. I need to leave now."

She rose to her feet with me and smiled. It was a tired, worried smile but it was still a good smile and, stupidly, I wanted to kiss it.

"Thank you..," she said:" Thank you for everything. You've been very kind and very forgiving."

I took a long, deep breath, tore my eyes away from her lips and shook the slender, long-fingered hand she was offering.

"I have, haven't I..?" I smiled, disarmingly I hoped, and for a few seconds our eyes stayed locked and she smiled back, amused by my reply, her smile being definitely disarming.

"I've learnt a lot from this visit Mr. Carter..," she went on, not taking her hand from mine, which I found interesting.

"Well, I'm glad I could help..," I said, widening my smile, enjoying the subtle pressure of her grip.

"You have..," she said:" More so than you think."

Our hands finally uncoupled and she stepped to the side to allow me to head for the door, but before I did I slipped one of my cards out from my phone-holder.

"I'm not sure where I'm going to be over the next few days. I tend to move around a lot..," I said, handing her the cheaply printed, dog-eared card:" In my line of work it's often necessary. Always be a moving target..," I grinned.

She made no response.

"This is one of the numbers I can be contacted on..," I continued:" Call me on it if anything happens or if anything is bothering you. If anything happens or is bothering me, I'll do the same to you."

She took the card without looking at it, thanked me, dropped it into one of the red pockets on her housecoat and indicated the door with a graceful arch of her arm.

I had just reached the threshold when she spoke again and I turned to see her walking towards me, the scent of her perfume reaching me a few seconds before she did.

"Before you go..," she smiled, slowly:" If you are still willing to work for me...I feel its only right I continue paying for your services."

I smiled back and looked her up and down as slowly as she had smiled.

"You've already been quite generous..," I said, playfully.

"I know..," she said, seductively, her smile beginning to work its magic on my composure:"...but I get the feeling I am going to be highly satisfied with what you may end up doing for me and would like to continue rewarding you for your..."

She took a thoughtful breath:

"...Efforts..," she smoothed:" So please...Allow me to 'extend' that generosity further and show you that my gratitude can show very few bounds."

"In that case..," I smirked:"...I look forward to extending those bounds with you Mrs. Fitzpatrick."

She smirked back.

"Well then..," she purred: No other word for it: She purred: Like a cream-filled cat:" Here's to extended bounds and a very satisfying conclusion..."

I walked out into the hall, was shown to the front door by her 'man', went outside, started the car and headed back through the electric gates towards the centre of the city, unable to stop thinking about her refined-featured face, that crimson house-coat, her long, fragile fingers and the scared look at the back of her beautiful eyes, the real reason I was about to start taking the risk I was going to take becoming more obvious as I weaved my way through the traffic, my determination growing with each smile.

TWENTY THREE

When I got back to the office, I turned up the heat on the two old radiators, flicked on the kettle, made myself a strong, black coffee and lay on the sofa thinking about Mrs. Fitzpatrick and other things, not liking what was happening very much.

It was getting worrying now, scarily worrying, especially when I thought about how much I'd become involved and how that involvement could very easily be used against me.

As I lay there, thinking, my face, jaw and sides began to ache and throb again which told me all the whiskey I'd been drinking was reducing the efficiency of the pills the Doctor had given me. Whatever was in them was good and been masking the pain and discomfort I'd been feeling well, but now it was wearing off and it was all creeping back again, reminding me that it had actually only been two days since my humiliating encounter with the late Marcus Dexter and that my body was still recovering from the unexpectedly skilled beating he'd given me. A lot had happened in those two days and none of it was good.

I'd been beaten up; there'd been a murder; I'd drunk a lot of alcohol; done a lot of driving and met some strange people, the strangest of which was Charlotte.

The more I thought about her, and knowing now that Leonora had confirmed Charlotte was staying with her, the more a lot became obvious, the most obvious thing being that she'd never intended staying in that clinic.

It must have really worried her when I'd told her that if she didn't go there I'd hand her over to the police, so she'd kept me quiet by agreeing knowing that when she'd got there, she'd immediately call Leonora in a panic, beg her to call "The Doctor" and then pull the "Never-do-it-again" act on him, laying it on trowel-thick about not wanting drugs and drink anymore. For his part the act was probably unnecessary because no doubt he'd already been paid an extra-large 'consultancy fee' for his compliance by either herself or Leonora, but whoever it was, he had signed her discharge papers, told the slightly confused but trusting staff who knew him well that Charlotte would be leaving the clinic and staying in Richmond with daily nursing care, and that Mrs. Fitzpatrick's car would be picking her up later that night. All the time she'd been waiting, Charlotte would have been starting to come down fast from her last fix, lying in bed fretting, whipping her mind up into yet another fearful, distrustful, obsessive frenzy, convincing herself Dexter was looking for her to kill her for what she'd done, building up to a tornado of fear and anxiety that she knew only another fix of heroin would calm down. She would have needed drugs desperately and knew where some were; stashed away back at her apartment: Drugs she would have killed to get to, so when Leonora's car finally turned up she would have told the driver to take her to her place on the way so that she could pick up a few things she needed and when she'd got there, gone straight up to her bedroom, crashed about looking for her stash, found it and taken a small, quick hit that would be enough to settle her whirling mind but not to send her into a stupor, enabling her to come out of the bedroom appearing to be more settled and able to make the porter and the driver think she was okay, even though the porter told me he thought she didn't seem well.

I turned over the thought that she might have wanted to go straight down to Sussex to see and confront Dexter but quickly dismissed it. Why would she want to walk right into the monster's den, especially in that frame of mind? She was trying to hide from him, not offer herself up as a tasty meal. No, that wouldn't have made sense: She was too ill and too frightened to do any confronting: Dexter would have played with her like a tiger plays with a baby lamb before tearing her to pieces and spitting out her skinny bones. No: In the state she was in, she would have wanted to get to Leonora's, curl up in a ball and die, and anyway, it was very unlikely she could have convinced the driver to take her all the way down to the south coast. He would have been under strict instructions to bring Charlotte directly to Richmond and had already gone against orders by diverting to Knightsbridge, so he wasn't going to risk his job by getting into even deeper trouble and taking the parcel another hour and a half's drive all the way down to the coast. Leonora however..?

I started thinking about Leonora, concentrating on her motivations and strengths, both of which she had a lot of, trying to push her eyes to the back of my mind.

So it seems she did know about her still being married to Marcus but for some reason she appeared not to be doing too much about it, unless I was wrong. She must have been pretty upset when she found out and maybe she'd been trying to discuss "the situation" with her parasite-husband for months, trying to get him to give her back her life but, in true Dexter style, he'd just carried on ignoring her, even though he knew she had discovered his latest scam on her. If that was true, had Dexter's deliberate indifference and arrogant dismissal of her finally exhausted her patience, and was the final straw that pushed her over the edge the note she discovered in Charlotte's kitchen, making her realise a more drastic, possibly more final solution might be needed to be rid of him? I didn't like to think it but that possibility was making more and more sense the longer I tossed it around in my head, and it led me to start thinking about how she might have done it: How she might have killed Dexter, or had him killed, and that train of thought took me down a long, winding rabbit hole of conjecture starting with the gun. How had the pistol I'd dropped into Charlotte's purse yesterday end up lying between Dexter's feet a few hours later, when Charlotte had been at Leonora's all evening? How had it got there?

It was while I was making a second coffee that a probability crept into my head, probably the same way it might have crept into Leonora's.

A lot of people, or at least a lot of the people she knew and that knew Charlotte, would have heard her talking, rambling most likely, at parties and soirees or whatever it was the rich called a 'getting together', about wanting to shoot her husband: Wanting to kill him for the way he was treating her. It was probably talked about, laughed about more likely, in the circles they moved in. So, when and if he was ever found shot, logically the first name that would pop into the heads of her acquaintances would be Charlotte's. Had she finally made good her threats and killed the bastard that they all knew was treating her like dirt, they would think. She'd be easy meat for the actual killer to throw in the way of the police: An obvious suspect in his killing and one that was so brain-addled that she wouldn't be sure if she'd done it or not. A 'slam-dunk' as our American cousins like to say.

Now, I didn't like to think that Leonora would even consider using her friend as a patsy, but once that seed had been planted, it began to take root and grow fast in my mind. Could she have come up with the idea as well, and if so when would the idea have been planted in her head? After the third, or sixth attempt to get Dexter to stop being a prick and get his pen out or, and the thought suddenly hit me, when she was in Charlotte's apartment, going through her drawers, collecting things for her stay at Richmond? Had she, quite by accident, let's say in a small drawer in Charlotte's dressing table or hidden beneath a pile of underwear, come across a box of ammunition for the pistol that she knew Charlotte kept for personal security? Had she at first ignored it and carried on going through her list of items, but remembered it again when she'd found Dexter's note to Charlotte: The note that would have made her realise time was almost up to get Dexter out of hers and Charlotte's life and that it might need his actual death to once and for all end the torment they'd both been going through. Had the first very crude ideas, based around the box of bullets in Charlotte's bedroom, begun to form in her head and had she gone looking for the gun itself. Bullets are no good without a weapon to fire them from. She wouldn't have found it of course because Charlotte still had it in her bag but the thought might have taken a hold and, as she'd driven back home, a plan might have begun to formulate in her mind.

The sound of a notification coming through on my 'phone dispersed the crowd of thoughts that were vying for attention and I dropped an arm to the floor, picked it up and thumbed the 'messages' button.

There was only one message and it made me groan.

"The Doctor would be grateful if you would contact him as soon as possible."

That wasn't a good message to receive. I'd been hoping that the good doctor hadn't seen or heard the news about Dexter's death but it seems he had.

I sighed and finished my coffee, thinking about what kind of a man "The Doctor" was, and I came to the conclusion that he was a cautious man: A man with a reputation to protect and backed by people who would very obligingly protect it for him. I hoped I wasn't going to have trouble with him.

But that was later. I had more immediate trouble to consider right then and I went back to considering the scene at "Devil's View", visualising how it might have gone the night Dexter died.

In my scenario, he was sitting in his armchair, a whisky in hand, looking forward with sadistic pleasure to what he felt he knew was to come: Charlotte's humiliation when she arrived at ten o'clock.

He would be feeling totally sure she'd come. He knew that when she read his note, she'd want to come: That she'd want to find out what the hell was going on and who the new woman in his nasty cheating life was. He knew that if she thought he was running off to the Caribbean to meet and bed some other woman, she'd feel a mixture of emotions: Emotions that he'd put there: She'd feel despair, but at the same time he knew she'd feel glad.

Despair because she'd be worried about where she was going to get her regular supply of drugs from when he left and glad because at last she'd be free of his cheating, his lying, his threats; Of him spending all of her money, possibly even the violence he did to her, and of his humiliation of her on an almost daily basis, none of which he cared about.

So he knew she'd come, but...ten o'clock rolls around and she doesn't show up. Ten past ten and she still isn't there. He'd be getting unhappy, and that nasty temper of his, the narcissistic sadism that lurked just beneath the surface of his fake sophistication and smooth charm, would be beginning to rear its head because probably for the first time she hadn't done exactly what he told her to do. He had probably called Charlotte's flat to find out if she'd left or was still there, drumming his fingers on the arm of his chair, looking at his stupidly expensive watch as he waited for her to pick up, but there would have been no reply. His temper would have got worse. He'd be thinking about his next appointment suddenly, maybe getting a bit panicked. Maybe she hadn't read the note: Somehow it had been either lost or, (how fucking dare she..!), been ignored. He'd have no idea of course that Charlotte had been in a clinic all afternoon and was then at Leonora's place, her head filled with purple dreams. All he knew was that his demands were being ignored, and being ignored was not something Marcus Dexter was used to. It was at that moment of unaccustomed panic and loss of control that, in my imaginings, he heard a car coming up the drive, or possibly saw its headlights, and he would have been pleased. He was back in control. He was still going to have his little bit of sadistic fun, and he settled back into his armchair, almost preening himself, preparing for his favourite sport: Being cruel to women.

I imagined a smug, gloating Dexter, a fresh whiskey in a tumbler, waiting arrogantly for the knock on the door and for a meek and mild, simpering, hopefully tearful Charlotte to come whimpering through it, a briefcase full of money clutched in her pathetic hands, but when the door opens, it isn't Charlotte. To his utter surprise and momentary disbelief, it's Leonora that strides in, leaving him more than a tiny bit shocked. But, she does have a briefcase with her and seeing it brings a smile back to Dexter's confused face. Change of plans. Instead of being shitty to Charlotte, he'll be shitty to Leonora instead. Makes no odds to him: He hates them both.

So he starts in, saying how lovely it was to see her again after all that time and that he assumes she is there on poor, dear Charlotte's behalf: How was the now not-so-lovely Charlotte? Still ill..? Oh dear, how sad but no doubt the darling girl must have told her about the note and if she had she would know what he expects to be in the suitcase: Money and bonds, and if there is he'll sign the papers there and then and never darken young Charlotte's bank account again.

Now I'm only guessing here of course but let's say Leonora opens the briefcase, and there is actual money and bonds in there, just as he expects. She's rich so getting that kind of money and bonds together that quickly is possible for people like her. Who knows, but like I said, let's say there is enough in the case when she opens it to grab Dexter's attention, and he starts counting, trusting soul that he is.

He finishes, says he's happy with the amount, Leonora grabs back the case and demands he sign the papers, at which point, like the cat that's got the whole cream factory to himself, he leans back and with a wide, cosmetically perfect grin on his face, tells her "No…", he's not going to and starts laughing: Gloating: Enjoying the moment and the control, plus the fact he's now a few million dollars richer and can bring more than his dick to his new lovers bed. Leonora's face hardens and he's the recipient of one of the murderous stares I was getting earlier at her place, but, because he's drunk with malice and spite and thinking he's back to being king of the hill again, he carries on laughing, his cruelty fuelled by her anger. Furious with cold rage and triggered by years of frustration, she hissingly asks him why the hell not and he says, staring up at her anger-filled face with a grin wider than the Cheshire bloody cat, that she knows very well there were no papers to actually sign because there was no need for a divorce: There never had been: As they'd both known, poor, dear, sick Charlotte had been free to walk away from him for years he probably sniggered, because poor, dear, sick Charlotte wasn't and never had been Mrs. Marcus Dexter, had she?

And that, I decided, would have been the point when Leonora's brain probably turned to ice and she began to crack.

"Why the hell not..?" she might have asked him, already knowing the answer but waiting, like a deer in the headlights, for the words she had probably been waiting to hear for months to ooze from the lips of the man that she hated most in the world and hit her like a forty ton truck.

"Because my darling Leonora..," he probably scorned:" I'm still married to you…"

And that's when I believe she broke. Right there, on that admission. Her brain must have been shocked into action. She asked him exactly what he meant so, full of his own sense of invulnerability, he told her. He told her, with a laugh in his voice, that the decree that she had received from the New York court was a fake: A very good one because he'd spent a lot of money on a guy that was the best forger in the business to make the seal of the court look, feel and smell like the real thing but it wasn't. It was still a fake: a fake she accepted as the truth because she trusted her attorneys which was a reasonable thing to do, but the big mistake she made was in trusting the one man besides himself she should never have trusted to look after her interests….Cleaver.

That was too much for her. That was the last straw: The final insult. The ultimate grain of sand that tipped the balance between her being rational and her being very irrational. She couldn't put up with anymore of Dexter's shit, so she reached inside her handbag, pulled out Charlotte's shiny gun which she'd found when she was putting Charlotte's things away in her room, and pointed it straight-armed and cold-eyed at Dexter, nothing behind her glare but hatred for the man now sitting in front of her, scared for the first time in his life, his hands gripping the arms of the chair, his back pressed into the back of the seat, eyes fixed on the barrel of the pistol he hadn't even known was missing from his bedroom, taken by a terrified, paranoid Charlotte for two reasons: To stop him using it against her and as a defence against him should she displease him one day. I imagined him telling her not to be so stupid and to put the gun down. I can also imagine he tried to tell her she'd never get away with it and that her life would be ruined and so on and so on, but it didn't matter what he said because he was talking to a block of ice. Leonora had stepped over the line now and for once she had the power, not him: Not the man that had lied to her and cheated on her: Not the man who had tried to spend all of her money, get her hooked on drugs, probably slapped her around, treated her like a cheap whore in bed or wherever took his fancy, and not only humiliated her but ignored her and scammed her over the divorce, all the while at the same time ruining the life and health of her friend, Charlotte, now an addict, on the edge of bankruptcy and lying in her house writhing and squealing in mental agony.

But had she actually shot him? Had she been the one that pulled the trigger? She may have been stone-cold focused and filled with hatred for him but, in those ever-lasting few seconds between intent and actual action when most peoples' minds fight like cats in a bag about the rights and wrongs of what they want so desperately to do; the "God moment" as criminologists and psychiatrists call it, had she got what it takes to actually squeeze that trigger and end a persons' life? I wasn't sure, but if she didn't then who did? Someone put Dexter's pistol under his chin and blew a hole through the top of his head, and that set off another train of thought in my mind. Under his chin..? How had Leonora been able to walk up to Dexter, even with a gun in her hand, kneel down, stick it under his chin and shoot him through his teeth and tongue without Dexter trying and probably succeeding in knocking it from her hand and then using it on her? The man was a combat veteran: He was trained for Close Quarter fighting. The odds were very much in his favour that he could have disarmed her within seconds and knocked it flying across the room. No, that didn't work for me. There had to be someone else that kept him sitting in that chair. Someone that knew how to make a guy like Dexter do as he's told and make him afraid enough to not even attempt to disarm him. Someone who knew exactly what they were doing and would have no qualms whatsoever about pulling the trigger. But who..? Whoever was in the second car maybe: The BMW that arrived after Leonora's: Cleaver's car? That made a kind of sense but still didn't seem quite right. Why would Cleaver get himself involved in helping her get rid of Dexter with all the risks of a link back to Leonora, when he'd already turned her down before he'd sent her to me? Unless when, or if, she had come to him again for his help, he'd seen a way of shutting Dexter up for good and preventing him ever trying to blackmail him about his deal over the divorce, which at that point Leonora knew nothing about. It's certainly the way his mind would have worked.

Whatever had happened though, and whoever was involved, it was over for Dexter and Leonora must have walked out of that room and back to the garage in a daze, the money and bonds still safe in the briefcase, made her way back to London, knowing, or at least hoping that her and Charlotte's nightmare life with Dexter was over.

I made a third coffee and lay back, going back over the scenario, working on some parts but generally satisfied. All I needed to do now was prove it and to do that I needed actual facts, but getting actual facts was going to be tough and I might have to be prepared for all kinds of surprises.

I drank the last of the coffee, pulled my thermal blanket over me and fell asleep within five minutes.

TWENTY FOUR

I woke at eight, went downstairs to the steamy, warm café, ate a good breakfast, walked to the club, had a hot and cold shower, changed into fresh clothes and called "The Doctor's" to make an appointment, telling the snooty receptionist that it wasn't me that wanted to see him but her boss that wanted to see me, was asked to arrive in just over an hours' time and started driving.

When I walked into the reception, interestingly I was told to go straight to his room, was greeted by the dapper man behind the big desk with a handshake, sat down and, trying to sound as casual as possible, asked him why he'd asked me to come.

He looked surprised.

"I take it you haven't heard the news..," he said.

"About..?" I replied, again, casually.

"About Mr. Dexter committing suicide..," he said, a trifle irritated by my nonchalance I could tell.

"Oh that..," I grinned, callously:" Yes I read that. A bloody good thing. Good riddance as far as I'm concerned. He was a bastard and the worlds a nicer place without him."

He looked slightly taken aback by my seeming nonchalance.

"Anyway..," I continued, airily:" Looking on the positive side it means you can get on with helping Charlotte now without having to worry about him anymore. How's she doing at the clinic by the way? Early days I know but..."

He didn't reply, just sat there in his expensive suit staring at me, sizing me up. Then he leaned forward, the professional smile he'd worn when I first came in, gone.

"I'm afraid I'm rather worried Mr. Carter..," he said:" I don't like this development at all."

"Development..?" I asked:" What development? Dexter killing himself? Don't tell me you're sorry he's dead?"

"I'm not in the least concerned about Mr. Dexter's death..," he said, tightly:" He was an appalling man and dangerous for his poor wife's health. I've had the misfortune to talk with Charlotte on too many occasions about his unsavoury and ungentlemanly 'habits' and his mistreatment of her and I'm more than aware of his damaging influence on her, so no...I have no pity for him. I know quite a few husbands like him and I loathe their existence equally, and would wish the same fate to befall them, but that is not what is worrying me…"

"Oh..? Then what is..," I said:" Why did you ask me to come and see you?"

He leant back again.

"I have been practicing medicine for more than thirty five years now Mr. Carter..," he said, slowly:"…and during those years I have come into contact with all sorts of people, in the process learning to recognise and assess personality traits quite quickly: Character flaws: Deviative disorders: Psychological imbalances and so forth, and because of that skill I was able to weigh up Mr. Dexter and his proclivities immediately. He is, or was, fundamentally psychotic, without empathy, violent by basic temperament, avaricious, self-centred and naturally abusive. In other words, in my professional opinion, Marcus Dexter was man I would have said was the least inclined to commit suicide I have ever met."

I let the sentence hang for a moment, its meaning growing in the silence.

"Okay..," I ventured:" I would be inclined to agree with you on that, but what are you saying? What are you suggesting..?"

"I'm not suggesting anything..," he interrupted:" What I'm saying is that I don't like it."

"What..? His suicide? Why not..?"

"Because Mr. Carter, if you recall, a few days ago you were telling me that you found Mrs. Dexter, Charlotte, in the grounds of Mr. Dexter's house in a highly neurotic condition, waving a gun around and threatening to kill her husband, on the strength of which, and at your request, I placed her in a clinic to undergo intensive detoxification. However, that very same evening I received a call from Mrs. Dexter asking, no *begging* me, to give her a temporary release into the care of Mrs. Fitzpatrick, a past patient of mine, whom she assured me would be a guarantor of her safety and care. I was naturally doubtful and consulted with a trusted colleague at the clinic who confirmed to me that Mrs. Dexter was in fact displaying symptoms of acute stress and anguish at being there, and upon whose recommendation I decided to make an examinatory trip to assess for myself her condition. Before I made the journey to Kent I spoke with Mrs. Fitzpatrick to substantiate Charlotte's assertion of her proposed medical care and received her assurance that, if I allowed Charlotte to be placed in her hands, the greatest nursing care would be taken of her friend. Based upon those two calls and my subsequent examination of her, I reluctantly made my decision to allow Mrs. Dexter a temporary suspension of treatment, its final cessation subject to my appraisal of her progress, if any, in two weeks' time. However, it seems that within less than twenty four hours of her release Mr. Dexter allegedly committed suicide."

I pouted and opened my hands in a gesture of…"And..?" which clearly annoyed him.

"Mr. Carter..," he said, heavily, a serious expression on his high-cheek-boned face:" It is my considered opinion that Charlotte Dexter never intended to stay in the clinic more than a few hours. I believe she deliberately and with forward planning, made a fool of both you and of me: Used us as mere facilitators in her well-thought out scheme."

"To do what..?" I said, trying to sound slightly astonished:"…Kill her husband?"

"Yes Mr. Carter..," he said:" To kill her husband. I believe she may well have been going to kill him the morning you first met her, but the combination of you interrupting her train of addled thought and the amount of drugs and alcohol in her system prevented that happening so she had to think of an alternative which she was able to do once she had been 'cleaned up' by your nurse friend and by the drugs the clinic gave her upon her arrival."

"That's quite a supposition doctor..," I said, calmly:" Very difficult to prove."

He looked reprimanded.

"I'm not saying that she did intend to kill her husband..," he said, quickly:"…but I am saying the whole business does sound and feel very odd and that makes me feel I may have to do or say something about it."

"Oh..? Who to..: The police..?" I asked, a hint of mockery in my voice.

He nodded, apologetically, his face showing the inner battle that he must been having with himself since hearing of Dexter's death. It would have been a very difficult decision for him to make, the consequences of doing so weighing heavily on his obviously troubled mind, but despite what he did to make his extremely lucrative living, he was a decent man and knew he needed to cover himself in the event the police came knocking on his very tasteful doors which, in this case, they might very well do.

I smiled at him and gave him a very 'knowing' look, putting on a 'thinking' face as if considering what to say next about something I actually *didn't* want to say anything about at all, then, after staring at him for a while longer, said:

"Listen doctor. Like yourself, I didn't like the man and I know for a fact he didn't like me and him being dead puts me in a very delicate, very awkward and complicated situation, so I know how you must be feeling right now. You've been good to me and put me back together more times than I care to remember, and because of that I really do want to relieve your concerns, but because of the nature of my work, there are some aspects of my clients business I can't discuss or disclose to you, which I'm sure you understand. However, what I can tell you is this: As far as the police are concerned, Marcus Dexter committed suicide, but if that turns out not to be the case then I can assure you Charlotte Dexter didn't kill him. That I know for a cold, hard, stoned fact. How I know that I'm not at liberty to tell you, but I can promise you it couldn't have been, and it wasn't her."

"You really mean that..?" he asked.

"I really mean that..," I said, smiling, sitting back and lacing my fingers in my lap, looking for all the world a confident, relaxed man:" Why would I tell you if I didn't?"

The Doctor looked into my eyes, searching for the sincerity behind my words then nodded his head slowly, the tightness around his cheeks and temples gradually slipping away. He smiled, tightly.

"I'm very glad to hear that Mr. Carter..," he said, the relief obvious in his voice:" As I've said, the fact of Mr. Dexter's demise, by whatever method, causes me no sorrow or regret but what does concern me are the findings of the coroner who will be called in, by law, to determine the cause and the means of his death. During his examinations and investigations he will want to know if there are any relations, by marriage or family, which means he will find out about his wife and want to ask her some possibly very difficult questions, and it was the state of her mind and the fragility of her health that made me worried her answers may lead him to call upon me to act as an expert witness to his investigations and, as you are fully aware Mr. Carter, there are many of my patients who would not wish me to be in such close proximity to the scrutiny of the law. The difficulties that such close proximity may cause to my position and credibility could be, shall we say, injurious to my continued well-being."

I smiled slowly at him. He was good with words and his mind was as sharp as a velvet-sheathed dagger. I liked that. It meant he watched the angles. That kind of attention to detail and forward thinking keeps you healthy, but the guy was nervous, I could tell. Underneath the smooth, unflappable exterior, he was flapping and that hint of panic made him a potential threat to my plans. I couldn't have that so, if I was thinking strategically, I needed to remove or delay that threat but for obvious reasons I couldn't remove him so it had to be delay, at least just for a couple of days.

"However..," he continued:"...now that you tell me Mrs. Dexter couldn't have been involved in his suicide, and I believe you, that possibility becomes less troublesome to me. Nonetheless, my concerns are not wholly allayed. There will be those, like yourself, who will have heard her publicly or in private, possibly both, wildly stating her hatred for her husband, no doubt whilst deep in drink or drugs, threatening to kill him, and it is more than possible someone might inform the Coroner of that fact. If that happens, he will have to place to one side the verdict of suicide and investigate further the possibility of murder, and if that becomes the case and my involvement with her as a doctor comes to light, the coroner may feel, and perhaps rightly so, that I have not done my complete duty of care to her. They may say that I should have contacted the police with any concerns I might have had about Charlotte, her state of mind and her threats towards her husband, and perhaps worse than that, decide to look into my general patient list as a matter of course."

"I see your point Doc'..," I said, frowning in agreement at the seriousness of his last observation:"...and I agree with it. The last thing you need is for the old Bill to come clod-hopping about in this lovely office, going through all your files, confiscating computers and asking compromising questions. I get that, but there's no need for you to go giving them the excuse to start doing that, at least just yet. The harm it could do to Charlotte in her present fragile state might be irreparable and I know you wouldn't want that either, especially when its' proved to you later that all the trouble you'd caused her and your patients had been unnecessary. I don't think you could forgive yourself, but what's probably more important is your patients more than likely wouldn't forgive you either and take it from me, you wouldn't want to upset some of the people you have on your books."

"Of course not, but..," he began.

"Then my advice would be to just hold your fire for a while..," I continued, keeping my tone calming and reassuring:" The inquest won't be for a few days yet..."

"Saturday..," he said.

"Saturday..," I said, gratefully:" Thank you. That's a while away and between now and then, I'm hoping to be able to work out for certain who, if anyone, might have been involved in, or even responsible for Dexter's suicide. You can wait until then I'm sure."

He nodded.

"Of course..," he said:" I wouldn't like to cause Charlotte or anyone undue stress or concern."

"Good. Then please: Don't worry. Let's just wait and see what the Coroners' verdict is shall we? In the meantime, I will keep working away at proving Charlotte had nothing to do with our nasty friend's untimely and tragic decision. If the decision isn't suicide, which it will be of course, and you feel you have to contact the coroner with any information you feel you have then go ahead and do what you have to do."

He looked sheepish.

"I'm not trying to cause any sort of trouble Mr. Carter. You do realise that."

"Of course..," I said:" I'm in the same position you are. Charlotte Dexter isn't a client of mine but she is a very close friend of someone I know and am working for, so I feel almost responsible for not only her welfare but her position within the messy and tangled picture that Marcus Dexter seemed to have painted around himself and everyone that became involved with him. The man was a vicious bully and made a lot of people's lives hell but no-one you or I know are in any way involved in his death, believe me."

"Thank you Mr. Carter. I feel more assured of the situation now and will put aside my concerns at least until the coroner's verdict after Saturday."

We stood up, shook hands and I left, breathing a sigh of relief out on the pavement. I'd managed to side-step a possible fatal complication in my plan but only for a few days.

I had until Saturday now to get all the pieces of the picture I'd told The Doctor about clicked into place, which wasn't a lot of time, and some of those pieces were going to be very dangerous to try and make fit. I'd need to be very, very careful from now onwards because it was looking like I'd let myself be led into a scorpions nest and at any moment I could be very badly stung.

TWENTY FIVE

I had a good lunch in a good hotel not far from Cadogan Square that I'd done the owner of a few favours; drank two good whiskies, went into the guests lounge, ordered a third and telephoned Cleaver.

"Carter..," he mumbled, probably because he had another big fat cigar stuck in his fat mouth:" What you calling me for now?"

"I need to see you..," I said:" I'm worried."

"Who isn't these fucking days..," He grunted:" What's the problem and what have I got to do with it?"

"I don't want to talk about it over the 'phone. It's about the Fitzpatrick woman."

"Her again..? Jeez Carter. You got your little panties in a bit of a fucking twist about her haven't you? What the hell..?"

There was a pause then...

"Okay. Come and talk to me. I need a good laugh, the morning I've had. Make it an hour. I'm busy till then."

The line went dead and I sat back, waiting for my third whisky to arrive.

TWENTY SIX

When I got to Cleaver's office I was let in by a stone-faced goon I'd never seen before: No sign of Kenny or "Clubber".

I asked about them and was told, grudgingly, that they were "resting". I grinned widely, gave the ape a wink and told him to give them my personal regards, then went on through to Cleaver's office.

When I entered Cleaver was standing by the fireplace, his big hands in his pockets, a very large cigar clamped between his mean, pudgy lips.

"Carter..!" he grinned, taking it from his mouth:" Get yourself a drink: Cheer me up. It's been a fuck of a morning and I need you to make me smile."

I walked over to the big, glass-fronted drinks cabinet and poured myself a long shot of his twelve year old Chivas Regal which I hadn't had for a while and suddenly fancied a tumbler of.

"You know, I was in a bad mood until you called..," Cleaver said behind me:" The usual thing. People not doing what I tell them to do: Making decisions of their own: Not seeing the big picture: Causing unnecessary complications, but you Carter? You're a good man. You are "uncomplicated". I can always rely on you to do things right. You can be fucking pain in my arse at times but I don't dislike you. You..."

"I have a problem..," I said, turning around and taking a sip of the brandy, cutting of his flow of shit:"...and I need your advice."

Cleaver stopped waving his cigar around and looked me dead in the eye, wondering whether or not I'd disrespected him enough by shutting him up mid-flow to have me slapped around a bit or to let it go and listen to my problem. It was fifty-fifty but his sudden wide grin told me the coin had fallen on "heads".

"Straight to the point Carter..," he smiled:" Good. I like that about you. Luckily I'm in a good mood otherwise I'd have you…"

"Taught a lesson..?" I said, taking another sip of my drink:" Who by: The missing link out there? I doubt that. His nose has been broken so many times he can barely take a breath. One swing and he'd be struggling to take another…No: Apparently "Clubber" and "Jail-Boy" are still resting from the last attempt to teach me a lesson."

For just a second, he gave me a hard look and his mean little mouth tightened but he stopped himself from saying or doing anything that might have been hasty and smiled again, jabbing playfully at me with his cigar-filled hand.

"You my lad, are a very cheeky cunt..," he said, giving me a sly wink.

"Don't worry..," I grinned back:" I come in peace. I'm not here to toss your furniture around."

"Good because if you did you'd get a bill for it jammed right up your arse..," he said, only half threateningly:" Now, sit down and tell me what your problem is."

I sat down and finished off the Chivas.

"I'm worried..," I said:" I think I might have made a bloody fool of myself with the Fitzpatrick woman."

Cleaver sat down himself and stuffed his cigar back into his mouth.

"Oh yeah..? Well, we all do stupid things sometimes..," he mumbled:"…but what's it got to do with her? Don't tell me you've tried it on with her?"

He chuckled indecently and took a long drag on the cigar, blowing a blue column of smoke out of the side of his mouth.

"If you did, you're wasting your time lover boy. She's way out of your league. Beauty, brains *and* money, none of which you've got. What happened..? She catch you trying to dip your hand into her personal assets..?"

Again he laughed crudely and took another drag on his cigar.

"No, nothing like that..," I said, smiling: Humouring him:" I'm a gentleman. You know that."

"You're an idiot if you think you've got a chance with a woman like that..," he chortled:" You're nothing more than a servant to her: Same as a waiter or a bloody gardener. Your grubby hands aren't going to get within a mile of her fucking Dior's my son."

"Like I told you, nothing like that..," I said, letting him have his moment of fun at my expense.

"Then what's the problem? What' you done?"

I lifted up my empty tumbler. I didn't need another drink but I needed a minute to get my words right.

"Okay if I have another..?" I said and he nodded.

I got up and went back to the drinks cabinet.

"Pour me a Scotch while you're there..," he said, casually, leaning back into his big chair, looking and sounding very relaxed.

I made the drinks, giving Cleaver a generous amount, and brought them back to the desk, handing the big man his.

"All the fucking best..," he said in mock salute.

I returned the gesture and sipped a tiny amount from my tumbler.

"Look..," I said:" I've got a feeling I may have dug myself into a bit of a hole over the past couple of days and to be honest I'm a little worried it might be a bit too deep for me to crawl out of."

Cleaver looked at me dubiously over the rim of his glass.

"You..?" he said:" Worried..? Christ..! This must be something serious... Go on."

I made a deliberate thing of taking in a deep breath as if preparing myself for an embarrassing confession.

"Okay..," I said:" I told you I wasn't sure about taking on the job she came up to my place to talk about..?"

"Did you though..?" Cleaver feigned.

"Not to begin with. I told her I wasn't interested, she got a bit upset, offered me more money, crossed her legs a few times but I said I still wasn't interested and showed her the door. After she'd gone though, I got curious and started thinking about what she told me, and the more I thought, the more curious I became until, in the end, I decided, in my drunken way, to go and see this guy Dexter for myself. Just out of nosiness, nothing more. I was going to be a messenger boy, just delivering a message: Say the words and go back with his answer. Job done and money taken. I wish I hadn't now."

"Oh yeah..?" Cleaver said, uncertainly:" Why: What happened..?"

"So I drove down to his house, "Devil's View", and, to cut a strange story short, I met Dexter, the guy Leonora Fitzpatrick said she married a few years back but divorced soon afterwards..."

I looked into Cleaver's eyes when I said that to see if he would react to the mention of the divorce and all the money he'd made by lying to her about, but there was nothing: Not a flicker.

"The story she'd told me..," I went on:"...and you probably, was that while they were still married, he began playing naughty games with a young woman friend of hers called Charlotte, feeding her drugs and bleeding her dry just like he'd been trying to do to her."

Cleaver shrugged.

"She might have done..," he said, off-handedly:" I don't recall. I wasn't really listening. So anyway: Keep going. Tell me about this Charlotte. I'm interested."

He was, I could tell, and that was good. I gave him a long look that said I doubted he didn't know about her but it was like throwing water at a wall: It just slid off and didn't get through. He knew her though. Of course he did.

"Charlotte was younger and weaker than Leonora..," I continued:"...and she fell for Dexter's charms. All the way it seems. Hook, line and syringe. According to Leonora, pretty soon she became dependant on him and he took full advantage of her naivety and addiction, and when the Fitzpatrick woman finally divorced him, the besotted, addicted girl jumped into her best friends' still warm bed and quickly became the next Mrs. Dexter, opening everything for him, including her bank accounts. Now it seems, financially, health-wise and mentally, she's in a pretty bad state and it's the mental part that's worrying the first Mrs. Dexter. What with the drinking, drugs and physical abuse, she said she's become very unstable and has been telling everyone who cared to listen that she wants to finish him off and put an end to all the misery he's been putting her through. That's what Leonora came to see me about. She wanted me to go down there and frighten Dexter away."

Cleaver pouted and shrugged.

"And did you..?" he said, in a "dis-interested-but-slightly-curious" kind of voice.

"Not exactly..," I said:" When I got there, I found Charlotte dancing about like a drunken fairy under the trees, with a fully loaded .32 automatic in her purse."

"Naughty girl..," Cleaver grinned, taking another puff on his cigar.

"Very..," I went on:" So I took the weapon off her, pocketed it and tucked her up warmly in my car to let her sleep it off."

"You're a real gentleman..," Cleaver chuckled, crudely.

"I try to be..," I smiled, carrying on with my story:" When she was settled I went into the house and waited for Dexter to show up, helping myself to his expensive Bourbon while I waited. Nice Bourbon it was too."

"Lucky you..," Cleaver said, looking deliberately at his stupidly big watch:" I assume there's an end to this story, only..."

"Oh, there's an end..," I said:" There's definitely an end."

"Good..," he said, disinterestedly:"...because I'm not a great one for stories."

"You'll like this one. So, after the second drink, just as I'm about to try a whisky instead, Dexter arrives. He's surprised to see me of course but tries not to show it. Asks me who I am, what I want, and I tell him about Mrs. Fitzpatrick and her wanting me to have a quiet word with him about her friend and his wife, Charlotte. I don't tell him she's curled up in my car, coked out of her head and that I have her gun in my pocket."

"A wise decision..," Cleaver says.

"I thought so. Anyway, we exchange a few words, toss scenarios around, it all gets a bit heated and we mutually agree that we don't like each other. He asks me to leave: I say I need to know he understands what's been asked of him: He says he doesn't care: I decide to give him a lesson in manners..."

"I'm betting he didn't like that. You can be very persuasive when you need to be."

"I didn't get the chance to do any persuading I'm afraid."

Cleaver's eyebrows shot up.

"Oh..? Why's that..?" he says.

"Because he beat the crap out of me that's why."

"Jesus Christ Carter..," Cleaver bellowed, jabbing a stubby finger at me, cigar in hand:" You..? You had the fucking crap beaten out of you...?! That's' not fuckin' possible..!"

I nodded in embarrassed but magnanimous acceptance, smiling ruefully.

"Yes..," I said raising my hands in mock defeat:" Hard to believe I know, but it happened, all right? I'm not very happy about it, but there it is. What can I say? The man was fast and knew exactly what he was doing: Barely broke a sweat."

Cleaver's laughter died down into a chuckle and he took a calming puff on his cigar.

"Fuck me..," He sniggered to himself:" I think I might have to reconsider how much I pay you Carter. 'Looks like the king might be losing his crown, and it was a Yank that knocked it off. Christ, I needed cheering up and you've done it!'"

"Very funny..," I said, suddenly a little angry but not enough to cloud my focus:" I'm pleased I've managed to cheer you up but never mind all that. There's more..."

"Go on..," he grinned:"... but don't make me laugh again, all right? I might choke on my cigar...!"

"I'll try..," I said in a sarcastic tone, throwing him a look before continuing:" When I woke up, Dexter had left and I somehow managed to crawl and stumble to my car. He'd done a professional job on me, I'll give him that. When I got there, Charlotte was still out, bless her so I knew I needed to get her help but I also knew I couldn't leave here there. After my conversation with her husband, I doubted she'd be very welcome, so I took a deep breath, which hurt like hell, and drove back to London."

"What' you do with her when you got back: Drag her up those ratty stairs to that dump you call an office and drop her on the sofa..?"

"No..," I said, patiently:" I took her to some friends place and left her with them. They've helped me out before when..."

"When a woman has passed out on you..?" Cleaver chortled, naughtily.

"Sometimes…Yes..," I said, not so patiently this time:" Have you finished or are there a few more snappy "Get Carter" jokes in the magazine…?"

Cleaver leaned back into his chair and waved his hand about like the Queen.

"Go on: Go on..," he said, imperiously:" I'm still awake."

"Thank you..," I said, graciously and continued:" Well, I couldn't leave her with them long. She was falling in and out of consciousness and needed help they couldn't give her so I had to find a doctor."

"Which doctor…?" Cleaver said.

"That might have been an option but I decided to go for a regular one first…"

Cleaver grinned and winked at me.

"You're a funny man Carter..," he said with a wide grin across his pudgy face:" Not a great fighter but you're a funny man."

"I'm an idiot for getting mixed up in all the crap that was starting to fill up my life..," I snorted:" So…I called our mutual friend."

"The Doctor…You called The Doctor?"

"I did and he was his usual helpful self. Turns out, as I half suspected, he had treated her before for her drink and drug addiction and wasn't a fan of Marcus Dexter. He agreed to put her in a clinic he knows and she was picked up by his people a few hours later."

"The Doctor's a good man..," Cleaver said, nodding his head wisely.

"The Doctor's a worried man."

"Oh..? Why's that then?"

"For reasons that'll become apparent."

"Well make them "apparent" quickly Carter, all right? I've got a life to carry on living and this is losing me some of it."

"Understood..," I said:"…but light another cigar and just sit back. There's a bit to go yet."

"I'm all fucking ears..," Cleaver grunted impatiently:" Just get on with it."

I re-crossed my legs and shifted in my seat, pleased to be getting under the bastards heavy, pink skin.

"The morning after I sent Charlotte to the clinic..," I continued:"...I woke up and decided I needed to go and talk to Dexter again."

"Why's that then? Had he missed a bit?"

"Personal reasons."

"What: A re-match? Your pride hurt as well as your ribs..?" he sniggered, but I ignored him.

"Something like that, yes..," I said, dryly:" Anyway, after a day jumping around like a flea on a blanket asking questions, I get in the car and drive down there. By the time I arrive, it's dark, so I park up out of sight and creep into the house by the side door."

"You didn't want to ring his doorbell then? Worried he might knock your bails off this time..?"

I sighed and shook my head.

"You're even less funny than you were six wise-cracks ago..," I said wearily:" No, I just wanted to have a recce' around first before I had another chat."

"And did you find anything?"

"No. Not in the rest of the house but I found something very interesting in the living room."

"What? A book on how to beat up Brits'...?"

"Fuck me..," I breathed, giving him a hard look:" You crack me up, you really do."

"Not as much as Dexter it seems..," Cleaver laughed, obviously enjoying himself:" He cracked you up very nicely."

"I thought you wanted me to hurry up..?" I growled.

"Okay: Keep your bandages on..," he snickered, pulling more smoke into his mouth:" What did you find in the living room that was so interesting..?"

"The top of Dexter's head stuck to the ceiling..."

Cleaver stopped smiling but showed no emotion: No shock: No amazement: Not even disbelief: Nothing.

"That must have been very interesting indeed..," he said, calmly. No jokes now...

"It was..," I said, coldly, watching his face for some kind of reaction:" He was dead: He'd blown his brains out in front of the fire. Seems he'd committed suicide."

"I know..," Cleaver said, evenly:" I read it in the papers. Heard it on the news too. Shame...Nice guy."

We looked at each other for a few seconds, not saying a word, both searching each other for something.

"A pity when a man gets to such a state he feels the need to blow his own head off..," Cleaver eventually said, dryly, not taking his lidded eyes off me.

"Yes..," I said, squarely, my eyes boring into his but getting no more than half a fuck deep:" A big shame and that's what it looked like but I'm not so sure."

Cleaver took a long suck on his cigar.

"Really...?" he said, blowing a column of smoke in my direction, his voice low and a little sinister:" What d'you mean? You don't think it was suicide?"

"No..," I said, thoughtfully:" Once I'd gotten over the sight of his face falling down his chest and the smell, I took a look around. There was a note of course: There's always a note. Nothing strange there, and his gun lying between his feet, but something didn't seem right and it took me a few moments to figure out what."

"And what was that..?"

"The heat from the fire, on my leg. I was standing next to the body, studying things and I began to realise the back of my leg was burning. I looked around and I noticed how close I was to the two bar electric fire that was on in the grate. We were almost on top of it and it was throwing out a fair old wave of heat. I'd only been standing there for a minute and was singeing, so how Dexter had managed to sit there in that heat I don't know."

"Maybe he knew he was about to blow himself to bits so it didn't matter..," Cleaver said.

I nodded:

"Possibly but why get *that* close? A few feet further back would have been a more comfortable place to sit and contemplate eternity don't you think? No loss of focus due to the extreme discomfort of having your skin seared off while you're trying to think."

"Okay..?" Cleaver asked, rolling the cigar between his fingers, his attention fully on me:" So what do you think happened..?"

"I think..," I said, off-handedly:"...someone might have moved his chair closer to the fire."

"Why would they do that..?"

"To keep the body warm: Stop rigor mortis setting in: Making it difficult to be precise about the time of death."

Cleaver just stared at me so I carried on speaking.

"...And if that's the case, it can't have been suicide. It must have been murder."

"That's a very big word..," Cleaver said deliberately, his previous endless vat of humour run dry suddenly:" Can you prove that?"

"No, I can't prove it but I can put what I saw and felt together and come up with a pretty accurate conclusion. Did I mention I saw grooves in the carpet pile where the legs had been dragged through it..?"

"No..," Cleaver said, looking at me warily:" You didn't."

"Well I did..," I said, lightly:" Long curves, about two to three feet from where the chair ended up."

"That's very fucking interesting..," Cleaver agreed, looking down at the tip of his cigar:" Okay Sherlock. Since you're in fucking detective mode at the moment, and since you think Dexter didn't top himself, any idea who might have pulled the trigger for him..?" he said, lifting his eyes from studying the wrapper on the cigar and looking me right in the eye.

I smiled inwardly, knowing the bait had been taken, keeping my lips detached from my face muscles for a few seconds.

"No..," I lied:" I don't but I can make a pretty good guess."

"I bet you bloody can..," Cleaver said, slowly:" Go on then. Give me your best guess."

"Charlotte..," I said;" Charlotte Dexter."

Cleaver replaced the cigar between his teeth and chewed on it, hard.

"Nice guess..," he said, to himself more than me I felt:" I can tell you another name that comes to my mind..," he smiled, nastily:"...but don't go getting all offended and start crying when you hear it."

"I'll try not to..," I said, knowing the name he was going to say:" What name is that?"

"Thomas Edward Carter..," he said, unsmilingly, holding my eyes with his own:" Your name."

I allowed my lips to form a wide grin.

"Whys that..?" I said, giving him a little more rope to try and trip me up with.

"Easy really. You were there, on your own. No witnesses. The first person to find his body it seems. I'm just tossing a few thoughts around you understand, but what's to say you didn't go there carrying a fucking big chip on your shoulder and a gun in your coat pocket? You get into another fight and, because you know he's fast and this time might do you serious damage, you put a bullet through his head, then drag the chair close to the fire yourself."

I tilted my head to one side and pouted, as if giving the idea serious thought.

"True..," I said:"...but if I did do it, why would I come and tell you about it and why would I mention the chair being dragged closer at all? It'd be pointless. No..," I said, politely but firmly, shaking my head:" Sorry about that but I didn't kill the bastard, although I'd like to have been given the chance to. Someone else did though. I'm certain of that."

"It was just a thought Carter..," he shrugged, his eyes remaining menacing:" Don't get upset: First thing that came into my head, that's all. The kind of thought that might come into the heads of the police as well if they somehow happened to find out you were the first person to find the body and had been beaten up badly by the deceased only a few hours before..."

He looked at me very hard as if nailing the obvious and barely concealed threat to my eyeballs and giving me time to register its seriousness. Then he smiled:

"Given all that though..," he said, opening his hands in a "there-you-have-it: Threat-made" gesture:"...I still don't see what you've got to worry about. If it wasn't you, what's the concern?"

I smiled at him knowingly, letting him see I understood the subtly planted threat he'd just made.

"Me..," I said:" I'm the concern. I'm a fist for hire. A fist with brains of course and worth every penny, but still a hired gun. If, as you so nicely say, I "somehow" get mixed up in a murder case, I'm not only going to have to keep two steps ahead of the law, I also become persona-non-grata to you and all the other employers in the city. My livelihood goes through the window. That's my concern."

Cleaver pursed his fat lips and considered what I'd just told him, staring up at the ceiling as if weighing up what he'd just heard like some kind of wise old Solomon.

"That's true..," he finally said:" But, apart from them "somehow" discovering you were first on the scene and had a grudge against the man, how else would the law decide to add you to their list of suspects?"

"Leonora Fitzpatrick..," I said:" She might decide to mention my involvement if she were questioned herself."

"Why would she do that..?"

"To divert their attention from her. They'd be far more inclined to believe Dexter might have been killed by a professional bad guy with a reputation for violence and a grudge the size of Florida on his bruised shoulder, than a sweet-smelling rich woman with friends in very high places. She might even throw Charlotte into their heads as well to double the deflection. Then there's The Doctor."

Cleaver frowned.

"The Doctor? What about him..?"

"He's got a lot of very naughty names on his prescription pad, including yours."

I let that hang in the air between us like a gentle poke in the eye and it had obviously registered.

"Go on..," he said, suddenly interested.

"When I first went to see him about Charlotte, he wasn't very keen to help me. "Reluctant" is probably the word I'd use to describe his attitude. I made a very strong plea to his better instincts of course to get him to even consider the thought, but in the end it was my telling him that if he didn't I'd be forced to leave her outside a police station with the gun in one hand and his name and phone number clutched in the trembling fingers of her other hand that finally persuaded him to re-consider."

"You can be a very persuasive man Carter..," Cleaver said.

"Thanks..," I said:" I try my best. Anyway, with that thought in the front of his head, he decided to listen to my story, heard me out and agreed to keep her tucked away in that clinic of his. All good: Job neatly done, or so I thought, until, not long after the news of Dexter's death is made public I got a text from him saying he needed to see me, which I did. I've just come from meeting him in fact."

There was a distinct look of disquiet on Cleavers face now.

"Why did he need to see you..?" he asked.

"Because he said he'd heard about the suicide and was worried he might become involved through his connection with Charlotte, aka Mrs. Dexter. He was worried that she might be flaky enough to let that connection out during questioning by the Coroner, who, doing his due diligence, would call him in to give a statement about her mental condition and any help he'd given her vis a vis medical treatments, detox' courses, etcetera."

"Would they do that..?"

"Because..," I said, a little testily:"...it's the coroner's job: He has to, and what with him having to admit to her being his patient, it might, in fact it probably would, lead the police to lift the lid on his other connections, and if they did that they'd find me and Leonora Fitzpatrick on his files, work out that she was the previous Mrs. Dexter, begin to put two and two together, make six and call us both in for questioning. Like I said, before that happens she might decide to divert attention away from herself by throwing me and Charlotte to the wolves; mention her many threats to kill Marcus, her "naïve" visit to yourself to get help in "persuading" Dexter to leave Charlotte alone, your referral to myself and before you know it, a lot of very private people, including yourself, get the light shone on them and the whole ball of wax begins to melt..," I said, crossing my arms and sitting back, watching his features closely for a reaction.

"Bit of a long-shot isn't it..?" Cleaver said, calmly inspecting the end of his cigar:" Even if the police do decide it isn't a fucking suicide and start looking around for suspects, it's one thing for a woman to go around threatening to shoot her husband but it's a whole other thing to prove she did it. I mean what proof would they have? It'd be purely circumstantial."

"Yes..," I agreed:"… it would but there's a hell of a lot of circumstantial evidence surrounding Charlotte to get them more than a little interested in her. If they start asking Leonora and the doctor, they'd find she was put into a clinic the day of his killing, then discharged a few hours later. If they talked to the porter at her apartment, he'd tell them she returned there and exactly the time she arrived, and he'd also tell them she was only there for a few minutes during which she went into the bedroom, because he's ex-army and writes all this sort of thing down in a book. That might make them think she went straight to a drawer and found a gun; the very gun that was used to stick the top of his head to the ceiling. If Leonora wanted to implicate her even deeper, she could tell them that yes, her car picked Charlotte up and brought her to her house as arranged, but that Charlotte disappeared soon after she arrived, reappearing, again according to Leonora, late at night in a very distressed state. Leonora's guess, or lie depending on how you look at it, would be, quite justifiably, that she had probably been scoring with her dealer but the seed of thought that she might have somehow gotten down to "Devil's View", killed Dexter then got back would have been very successfully planted in the minds of the police, which, as Leonora knew, would mean all their focus would be switched to finding out how and when she did it, narrowed even further down by Leonora throwing our names, yours and mine, into the pie."

"And what would your story tell them when they come asking you..?" Cleaver said, giving me a long, slow look through the blue smoke he was letting curl out between his lips.

"I'd tell them that Leonora came to me in a very anxious state, worried about her friend Charlotte's mental health, telling me about how she'd been married and badly abused by Dexter who, after she divorced him, was doing the same with the poor, delicate heiress to a banking fortune and how that drugged up junkie heiress was going around in a purple haze threatening to kill her husband, and that she wanted me to go to see Dexter and persuade him to back away before it all went horribly wrong."

"Would you mention me..?"

I had expected him to ask that, but I still didn't like the menacing way he asked it.

"Probably, yes, because when they turned up on my doorstep I would have guessed that the police wouldn't have come to me before they'd seen Leonora first and she, like I said, wanting to spread the seeds of suspicion across a wide and diverse field, would have mentioned you as her first port of call and that you recommended she ask me to help instead of you, all information I feel sure Leonora would have happily given them in order to leave her out of their enquiries, at least for the immediate future, so there would have been no point in lying to our friends and making their antennae stiffer any further than it probably would already be."

There was a pause during which Cleaver continued looking at me like he was wondering how many pieces he'd have to cut me into to fit into his top drawer, then he spoke.

"I see what you're worried about now..," he said, deliberately:" You think anyone of those three might start talking and make the old bill think that someone killing Dexter is a much more interesting idea than just a fucking lonely businessman having a bad moment."

I drained my tumbler dry and placed it onto the desk.

"That, in a nut-bloody-shell, is my biggest concern..," I said:" If the Doctor gets summoned to give evidence at the inquest, or Leonora decides to cover her very attractive arse, I could find the Met' being very rude to me and threatening to throw the old "withholding evidence" bit right between my eyes. That's what I think."

The next pause wasn't as long because I could tell Cleaver had already made his mind up about what he thought ought to be done about the solution, but I let it go on then ended it by saying…

"You know, it's a funny thing about Dexter's killing…"

Cleaver looked at me like a fat lizard looks at a bug before flicking out its tongue and snapping it dead.

"Funny..?" he said, slowly:" What's so bloody funny..?"

I shrugged my shoulders, casually which I could tell he found annoying.

"I don't know but I can't shake off this feeling that someone went down to Dexter's place after Charlotte left and before I arrived."

I might have been wrong because it was only a flicker but I felt certain I saw a corner of Cleavers' mouth twitch when I said that.

"I just get a tingle in my gut, that's all..," I went on:"...and that tingle tells me that when, or if, Charlotte went to see him, Dexter wasn't sitting that close to the fire when she arrived. I reckon whoever came to see him later, the ones that might have actually killed him: I reckon they moved him. I wonder how the investigating officers would take to that as an idea..?" I mused:" At the moment, as far as they're concerned, it's a ninety nine percent certainty that it's a suicide. If my theory gets planted in their heads, it could well change their whole way of thinking: Cast a shadow of doubt over everything and make them go looking for other suspects."

Cleaver eyeballed me, drew another long haul of smoke into his lungs, let it out purposefully and gave me a look that had the words "You-are-a-fucking idiot" written in it in big letters.

"My advice, for what its' worth, which is a fucking lot..," he growled slowly and with meaning:"...is to keep very, very quiet about that fucking chair. Don't mention it at all to anyone. Let the bastards think of it themselves, which I'm pretty certain they won't do."

I opened my hands and made a deliberate thing out of clearing my throat guiltily.

"That would be very good advice and I'd most certainly take it without a doubt except…"

"Except..?" Cleaver said, coolly, his eyes still fixed on me like a rattlesnake on a hiker's ankle.

"Except I did a stupid thing…"

"Another stupid thing…?" Cleaver asked, darkly:" How fucking stupid..?"

"I moved the chair back to its original position..," I said, clearing my throat again, looking away to one side; deliberately not meeting his eyes.

"You did fucking what..?" Cleaver said, raising his eyebrows, the look in his eyes and the raised tone expressing the thought that he considered me to be a complete and total half-wit.

"I know, I know..," I said, raising my hands in contrite apology, still not meeting his eyes:" It was a stupid thing to do and I don't know why I did it, but for some reason I pushed it back to where the marks in the carpet began, which wasn't easy with Dexter literally a dead weight in the seat. Looking back on it, I still can't think why I did it."

The pause that followed was so heavily pregnant I expected to have to fetch hot water and towels any second, and during it Cleaver looked at me like I'd just urinated on his desk but when he spoke, his voice was threatening but calm.

"I understand..," he said, affably, spreading his hands:" You began to suspect that maybe what you were looking at wasn't what it looked like, so you thought, "if the police see the chair's been moved then, somehow, they get an anonymous call suggesting you may have been there at the time of his death, they're gonna' think you moved it closer to the fire to cover up what you did, so you pushed the thing back. I get that. Of course I do. When people are in a tight spot they don't think straight, or if they do think, they think too fast and make mistakes they regret later. If you'd stood and thought about it for a minute you'd have probably realised it wasn't so clever a thing to do but it's a thing that happens so forget about it. It's done and you can't undo it. All you gotta' do is hope the cops don't look too close at the carpet or get that anonymous phone call."

The look we exchanged said more than words and said we both understood exactly what had just been threatened.

"You're right..," I said, not breaking the eye contact:" You're right, but I'm still in a spot if they do look close. That's why I'm here. To ask what you think I should do?"

Cleaver shrugged his big shoulders, washing his hands of me, content that his implied warning had gone in.

"I don't' know..," he said, off-handedly:" It's your problem, not mine. I wasn't there and I'm not involved so why would I know what to do? You have to decide what you're going to do yourself. You're a big boy now."

"Gee, thanks Dad..," I mocked, but it bounced off his humour-plating.

"You're welcome..," he said, haughtily, waving the cigar around in a small, tight circle:" Like I said, it's got nothing to do with me but, for what it's worth, and because I like you, I'm gonna' give you some free advice. Seems to me you've got two choices. One: You go tell someone the truth. All of it: Get yourself off the hook: Throw other people, a lot of people, straight under the fucking bus, but if you decide to go do that you need to make fucking sure that fucking bus runs them down flat: Kills them dead, because if they survive and they find out who pushed them under those fucking tyres, you are going to be alone and naked in this big, nasty city and will probably be dead within twenty four hours. Or two...You say and do nothing: You keep fucking quieter than a fucking mouse with no tongue and just hope the suicide option is the only one the police choose to pursue, but that option only works if the Doctor or Charlotte or the fragrant Mrs. Fitzpatrick don't start talking and one, or all three of them don't bring your name up if they do, because if they do put the finger on you, you become the focus of a lot of very unwanted attention."

I nodded thoughtfully, as if turning over the options in my grateful head.

"So which of those options would you choose..?" I said, knowing my question would irritate him.

"I already told you..," he sighed, heavily:"...I wouldn't know. You're the man on the spot. You decide, but, again because I like you, I'll give you the benefit of some personal advice for free."

He shuffled around in his chair so that he was facing me.

" I would sit yourself down, pour yourself a very big fucking drink, start working out who the biggest potential threat to your continued freedom is, and begin deciding how or if you can persuade them to never mention your name if they are questioned."

"How do I do that..?"

"How the fuck do I know..!?" he said, slapping his hand on the desk top, giving me an exasperated expression:" That's your bloody job. You're the one that's supposed to be good at "persuading" people! You do it for a fucking living: Do it for yourself for once. Go see them all. Be your most charming self but make it very fucking clear that they don't know you, they've never heard of you and they've never met you, and that if they do let slip that they do or that they did, your next visit to them will be less polite. You know...All the usual shtick."

"You're right..," I considered:" Maybe I should have a talk with them. I'll start with..."

"I don't care who you bloody start with..," Cleaver snarled, dismissively:" You can start with the man in the fucking moon for all I do care. What I do care about is not getting a knock on my door from some cocky bloody Detective Inspector Old Bill of the fucking Yard wanting to know about my involvement with all this shit, just because someone dropped my name into their ears. If that happens, you will get a much bigger and noisier knock on your door and it's all going to go very black for you, very quickly...Understood?"

The threats weren't veiled anymore and I smiled inwardly knowing I'd achieved what I came to do which was to rattle Cleaver's expensive cage.

"Understood..," I said, reflectively.

"Good..," Cleaver said, the anger gone from his voice:" Now, if story time is over I'd like..."

"You know its' funny..," I said, contemplatively, cutting him off.

"What's so fucking funny about it..?" he growled, impatiently.

"It just occurred to me..," I said, pensively, ignoring his rising irritation at my words and my presence:" Ever since I got into this line of business, I've managed to keep my nose clean: Not a spot on me: Never even got mud on my shoes. I've made good money out of the jobs I've chosen to do. I've never taken on jobs I didn't want to. Now, I go against my gut and take on a job I didn't really want to and suddenly my nose is bloodied and I'm in mud up to my balls."

"Yeah...Fucking hilarious..," Cleaver sighed:" You just make sure none of that mud flicks in my direction, you hear me..?"

I smiled, stood up, thanked the cigar-smelling, murderous pig for his time and his advice, left the room and nodded to the goon who opened the door onto the corridor for me on the way out, waiting until I was out on the street before I smiled.

I'd done what I came to do and it had worked. Despite his air of casual indifference, Cleaver was worried, I could tell, and that was a good thing.

He was in this murderous thing right up to his corpulent neck and he could sense that the gold-plated house of cards he had brutally but carefully built up over the years might be on the edge of falling down and that was making him angry, and angry people sometimes could be made to do stupid things if they are played right. I was a good player of people, and bringing down houses of cards was my speciality.

I'd started one big, thick plate spinning and as I walked along the pavement I worked on the others I needed to start, thinking about how I was going to do it and in what order, knowing that as long as I could keep them all spinning in carefully timed synch' I was pretty sure I was going to be all right.

TWENTY SEVEN

Feeling a bit peckish and being close to Bond Street, I went into a small but respectable café I know well, ordered a sandwich and two coffees to counter the whiskies I'd had earlier, and sat watching the normal people go by, idly turning over my next move in my head: A return visit to Leonora Fitzpatrick.

I was just finishing my second coffee when the 'phone vibrated. It was a London number but not one I knew, so I stared at it for a few more rings, wondering whether or not to answer. After three more rings I thought "what the hell…" and pressed the answer button with my thumb.

The voice that spoke was male, middle class, efficient, but friendly, and it asked if I was Thomas, Edward Carter.

I told it I was and asked who he might be. Apparently his name was Steven Shepherd of Shepherd, Cunningham, Wright and Carmichael, and that he hoped he hadn't interrupted anything important.

I said only a sandwich and asked what he wanted.

He thanked me for my kindness in speaking with him and informed me he was calling me on behalf of his client, a Mrs. Leonora Fitzpatrick whom he believed I knew.

I put down my coffee cup and sat back in my chair.

I did know her, I said, the sudden hearing of her name bringing a frown to my forehead: What was he calling about?

"I'm not sure if you are aware Mr. Carter..," the clipped voice said:" but there has been a very recent and rather tragic occurrence that may have involved both Mrs. Fitzpatrick and, it appears, yourself"

What tragic occurrence might that be, I said, my thumb playing idly with the handle of the cup.

Shepherd cleared his throat and said that Mrs. Fitzpatrick's former husband, Mr. Marcus Dexter, had been found dead at his home: A suspected suicide.

I told him I had read about his death but in what way did it involve myself.

It would appear, the very polite solicitor said, that from what his client Mrs. Fitzpatrick has told him, I had acted on her behalf in an on-going dispute she was having with the late Mr. Dexter and that I also knew the unfortunate widow, Mrs. Charlotte Dexter, on behalf of whom I may also have been working.

I admitted I knew Charlotte but denied I was working for her. Could he please get to the point of his call, I pushed, intrigued and a little alarmed. Was that the sound of an approaching bus under which I might be about to be thrown I could hear?

Again, the well-spoken, very pleasant Shepherd cleared his throat and said he felt it might be better if we met in his office to discuss the...'ahem'..."situation" rather than over the 'phone, in perhaps an hour's time?

I told him that might not be convenient, which wasn't true but I needed time to think about how this sudden left-field move by Leonora might affect my plans, and suggested another time: The following day in fact, but that brought a quick reaction from Shepherd who stressed that any delay in our meeting would be unfortunate and that it was important, if not essential, that we spoke as soon as possible. If it was inconvenient and it meant having to cancel or postpone other commitments, Mrs. Fitzpatrick had authorised him to offer more than adequate financial recompense.

That did it. Not just the offer of money but the fact that he, and therefore Leonora, felt it was "essential" I talked with him. I was intrigued now and perhaps a tiny bit worried. Was I being led to the edge of the pavement inches from the wheels of the rapidly approaching bus?

I agreed to meeting, wrote down the address of Shepherd's chambers in Lincoln's Inn Field's, and told him I would be there in about an hours' time.

I was thanked for my understanding, the line went dead and I sat staring at the blank screen for a minute or two, weighing up the possibilities, assessing the risks and deciding on how I might deal with what could be an expensively perfumed trap I was being led into.

TWENTY EIGHT

Lincoln's Inn Fields is a very old, very elegant, ivy-covered hive of legal chambers on the banks of the river and I drove through the archway leading into the neatly-lawned 'Fields', found a parking space as close to the chambers as I could and walked up the wide stone steps into the reception of Shepherd, Cunningham, Wright and Carmichael: Very old fashioned and very respectable. Lots of wood, stained glass and leather chairs: I felt right at home.

Stephen Shepherd was a kind-looking, upright, decent, type: Early sixties with white hair, a sharp nose and keen, penetrating eyes. Every inch the dark-suited, wise old lawyer.

He thanked me for coming at such short notice, indicated a high-backed leather armchair opposite him on the other side of his desk and offered me a drink from a row of crystal-cut decanters nestled amongst rows and rows of dusty, dry-looking legal books behind him.

I accepted a very nice whiskey and settled back as he himself took a few sips of his own.

"Mr. Carter..," he started in that nice, respectable voice I'd heard on the phone:" I'm not going to waste your valuable time with long explanations. I will come to the point as quickly as I can."

I raised my tumbler to him.

"Thank you..," I said:" I'd appreciate that."

He smiled. It was a bit of a patronising smile but it was a nice smile and I smiled back.

"Briefly, the situation is this..," he said:" Mrs. Fitzpatrick, whose solicitors we are, has instructed us to represent her friend, Mrs. Charlotte Dexter, who, it would seem, may very soon come under the suspicion of having murdered her husband, Marcus Dexter at his home, "The Devil's View" I believe, near Brighton."

That piece of news rocked me on my heels when I heard it but I kept my face straight and tried not to show it. Already? What had made them think it was murder, or more likely, *who* might have made them suspect his shooting wasn't suicide? I knew I had to keep a grip on things. Events were running ahead faster than I anticipated and I could be in danger of having to play catch-up and second-guess, both of which were losing games.

"We have had only vague instructions from Mrs. Fitzpatrick..," Shepherd continued:" In fact she has been unable to tell us very much about the matter at all. All she can tell us is that Mrs. Charlotte Dexter is at present very ill at her home in Richmond and that she is slipping in and out of consciousness most of the time. Her doctor considers her to be in a very poor state of health and will not allow her to questioned by the police, who are, of course, respecting his wishes and those of Mrs. Fitzpatrick, at least for the time being, but there is a detective constable at the house at all times in the event Mrs. Dexter recovers sufficiently to be able to answer some enquiries. Naturally Mrs. Fitzpatrick is extremely upset and perturbed about the whole situation. She only instructed us less than thirty minutes before I telephoned yourself and we are now in the process of collating as much information as possible with a view to full and effective legal representation should it come to that. I hope you understand and appreciate our position Mr. Carter?"

"Yes..," I said, my mind still working on him having only been instructed thirty minutes before he'd called me at the coffee shop, which had been about the time I left Cleaver's office:" It can't be a very satisfactory one for you. You must be working virtually in the dark I imagine?"

"Almost entirely Mr. Carter. I have been in touch with a Detective Inspector Cherwell who is in charge of the case and he has very kindly informed me of the areas of initial suspicion that he and his team feel are appropriate."

"That's good of them..," I said, sarcastically:" Do they know much themselves?"

"At this stage, I am not privy to the lines of investigation that he and his colleagues are exploring, but there is communication between us and certain facts have come to light."

I bet they have, I thought.

"That sounds interesting. Anything of interest?"

"Nothing I can go into I'm afraid but what I can say is that Mrs. Fitzpatrick believes you may be more than helpful to us, and possibly the police, in the pursuance of this investigation, especially where it pertains to the very harsh circumstances which seem to be pressing on Mrs. Dexter at the moment so, in compliance with her wishes, I requested we might have an informal chat about this unfortunate affair and in the process try to find out more about you and your involvement. Naturally, anything that is said in this office between ourselves is and will remain completely confidential."

"Of course Mr. Stephens..," I said, taking a sip of my whiskey:" Please feel free to ask whatever questions you'd like."

"Thank you Mr. Carter. I appreciate your co-operation."

"Potential co-operation…," I corrected, with a tight smile.

"As you say..," Shepherd conceded:" Your *potential* co-operation."

There was a moments' pause whilst he studied me carefully, then…

"Mr. Carter. In your considered opinion, do you believe it possible that Mrs. Dexter may have killed her husband?"

I extended the moment by studying him this time, my mind working on the reasons for the question and the consequences of how I answered it. Rather like working out my moves in a game of chess, trying to think two ahead.

"Yes..," I said:" I think she was capable of it."

"In that event, do you think her actions would have been accidental or deliberate and pre-meditated?"

"I don't know..," I said, fixing my eyes on his:" I wasn't there."

"But you do believe she may have killed him?"

"I didn't say that and I wouldn't admit to it in a witness box. What I said was I think she was capable of it. Not the same thing as saying she did it. To be able to say she did it with any authority I would have had to have seen her do it, and, like I said, I didn't see her do it."

Shepherd nodded, considering my answer.

"I understand that Mr. Carter..," he said:"...but would it be correct of me to say that you believe there to be enough circumstantial evidence involving Mrs. Dexter that would lead you to believe she might have killed her husband?"

I took a long swallow of my drink.

"I believe there is a lot of potentially negative circumstantial evidence that might suggest Mrs. Dexter may have killed her husband, yes..," I said, carefully.

Shepherd steepled his fingers and mulled over my reply and, no doubt, my deliberately evasive responses to his direct questions. I carried on drinking his rather good whiskey as he mulled, thinking my own thoughts.

After a long minute the bespectacled man opposite un-steepled his fingers and sat back into his big, leather chair.

"Mr. Carter..," he said, purposely:" I wonder if I could ask you, just between ourselves, to speak openly, freely and a little less guarded with me on this matter?"

"You can ask..," I said.

Shepherd's smile was thin.

"Thank you..," he said, rigidly, clearly uncomfortable with my disinclination to be as open and direct as he'd hoped:" Perhaps you could tell me more about the circumstances that led to your involvement with both Mrs. Fitzpatrick and Mrs. Dexter."

"Of course..," I said, putting my empty tumbler onto his desk top:" Happy to...Okay: Lets' see... Last Monday night, very late, Mrs. Fitzpatrick came to my office. She told me she was very worried about her friend, Mrs. Dexter, because she, Mrs. Dexter, had been drinking heavily and taking a lot of drugs, supplied she believed by her late husband, Mr. Marcus Dexter, whom she had married not long before, after having previously divorced Mrs. Fitzpatrick. All very complicated as you can tell. Anyway, Charlotte, Mrs. Dexter, was in a very bad state and it had been reported to her, Mrs. Fitzpatrick, through mutual acquaintances, that, whilst under the almost permanent influence of both drink and drugs by now, she had been threatening to kill her husband."

"A very important point Mr. Carter..," Shepherd said.

"Very..," I said:" May I go on..?"

Shepherd nodded.

I went on...

"Mrs. Fitzpatrick made a big thing about telling me how bad and nasty the late Mr. Dexter was as a person: How nasty he'd been to her whilst she was married to him; how terrible he was being to Charlotte and how evil she thought he was as a man: The worst type: A sadistic blackmailer who preyed on rich women: Bled them dry then moved on to others. In her very considered opinion he had only married Charlotte for her money but that now he had gone through most of it he was bored with her and was seeking fresh prey. She told me she was desperately worried that Charlotte, in her worsening state, might actually make good on her drunken threats and do something very stupid."

"Such as murdering her husband..?" Shepherd asked.

"She didn't say so, not in those words..," I said, correcting him politely:" but the implication was definitely there. I discovered for myself that she might not have been wrong in her assumptions."

He raised his eyebrows above his glasses.

"I see... And what was the discovery that led you to that conclusion..?" he enquired.

"Well...At Mrs. Fitzpatrick's request, I went down to "Devil's View" purely to try and convey her concerns to Dexter and ask that he be a good chap for once, stop supplying his wife with drugs, not bleed her totally dry and just walk away: Agree to a divorce and go live his life somewhere else."

"Why did she think you might be able to succeed where she had plainly failed?"

"Because..," I said, matter-of-factly:"...I have a reputation as a very persuasive negotiator on behalf of others."

He considered me for a long moment.

"Indeed..," he said, having come to the conclusion that I wasn't lying:" And how "persuasive" were you prepared to be Mr. Carter..?"

"I had no idea until I had properly taken stock of the circumstances and the personalities involved. I had met Mrs. Fitzpatrick, heard her side of the story and formed my opinion of her from an actual meeting, and so I wanted to do the same with Marcus Dexter: He might have been a real sweetie when I'd got to meet him."

Shepherd smiled the same cynically doubtful smile I was smiling.

"From what I understand, that would be a gross misunderstanding of his character..," he said.

"As it turned out, that was my conclusion too..," I grinned:" I drove down to the house on Tuesday morning and unexpectedly got the chance to make an assessment of Mrs. Dexter's character at the same time because she was there as well."

"Oh..? With her husband?"

"No: I found her staggering about the woods beside the house, blind drunk and out of her head on drugs, worryingly carrying an automatic pistol in her handbag."

His left eyebrow rose sharply at that.

"Is that so..?" he said.

"It was so..," I said:" Not long after I came across her dancing beneath the trees, she collapsed in a heap, and whilst I carrying her back to my car, her handbag fell to the ground and I found the gun when I picked it up. I asked her why she was carrying it and she had enough control left of her brain to burble out that she'd come to kill her husband because he deserved it. For a while longer she rambled on incoherently about what an awful man he was then, thankfully slipped into unconsciousness. I left her wrapped in my coat and went back to the house to meet her husband."

"Do you feel she might have actually killed him if you'd not been there to prevent her?"

"No..," I chuckled:" In the state she was in, she couldn't have lifted the gun out of her bag let alone aimed it and pulled the trigger. She was flat out drunk and flying high on drugs. There is no way on this God's earth that she could have killed her husband when I found her."

He jumped in on that one.

"Do you feel she could have done so if she'd been sober?"

"I don't know..," I said, firmly, giving him a look that said "please don't keep trying to put words into my mouth":" I've never seen her sober."

"Please go on Mr. Carter..," he said:" This is most illuminating."

I continued with my version of events, choosing my words tactically, carefully omitting what I didn't feel he needed to know or that could be used to snare me with.

"Later that morning, through a doctor I know, I arranged for Mrs. Dexter to be placed in a discreet rehabilitation clinic somewhere in Kent and she was taken there in the afternoon. However, later that night I called the clinic to check on her condition only to find she'd checked herself out of it at..."

I didn't hesitate but I didn't go on telling the truth beyond that point. If there was any throwing-under-buses to be done it wasn't going to be my me...Not yet anyway, and besides I couldn't be sure my suspicions about Leonora were correct. I might need her in the future.

"...ten. When I asked how she'd left, it seems a private car had come to pick her up."

I didn't mention that it was Leonora's car or that she'd been taken to Leonora's house. He probably already knew that.

"Do you know where Mrs. Dexter went from the clinic..?"

I tried not to frown even though I instinctively wanted to. Was he still trying to trip me up?

"No..," I said:" I don't. I imagine she went to Mrs. Fitzpatrick's'. You told me she was convalescing there just now."

"I did, indeed..," he conceded:" Do you have any reason to suspect she may have been elsewhere that night?"

"Elsewhere..? You mean at "Devil's View"..?"

He nodded.

"I do have evidence to suggest she might have..," I said.

His ears seem to prick up at that and he sat up, attentively.

"I see. And may I ask what that evidence might be?"

I could see I had him hooked.

"You may ask but I'm not going to reveal that just yet..," I said teasingly.

He leaned forward, his fingers steepled in front of his mouth.

"Have you mentioned that evidence to any other persons Mr. Carter..?" he said, eagerly.

"Yes..," I said, enjoying the man's sudden interest."

"Again, may I ask who..?"

"And again you may ask, but I'm afraid I'm not going to tell you."

He didn't like that and went quiet. Then he said:

"Why can't or won't you disclose what the evidence may be or who the person or persons you mentioned it to are?"

A shrugged casually which I could sense annoyed him.

"I can't tell you that either. Let's just say it might be prejudicial to me and my state of health if I were to reveal too much of what I know at this stage in the enquiries."

Shepherd sat back, disappointment in his eyes.

"Mr. Carter..," he said after a few considering seconds:" Perhaps it might be beneficial to our discussion if we adopted a theoretical basis upon which to progress."

"Perhaps it might..," I agreed:" Let's try shall we? See how it goes…"

Shepherd's smile was taut and false.

"Quite..," he breathed:" Very well. Let' us start with the assumption, purely for the sake of hypothesis, that Mrs. Dexter did go down to "Devil's View" on Tuesday night and that, whilst she was there, accidentally or not, she did kill her husband. I shan't use the word 'murdered' as that implies pre-meditated fore-thought of action."

"No: Let's not use that word..," I said, mockingly:" It's a bit presumptuous don't you think..?"

He nodded graciously and continued.

"Do you think, taking into account the mental and physical condition that Mrs. Dexter was in on that evening, she could have been responsible for her actions?"

I smirked and I could see he knew why I was smirking. It wasn't me that was going to be shoved under the metaphorical bus after all, it was Charlotte. Leonora, or whoever was pulling the strings here, wanted it to look as though, under the influence of drugs and drink, she was mentally unstable and therefore not responsible for her actions: Manslaughter or diminished responsibility was what they were going for, which meant that whoever had killed him was setting Charlotte up to be the unwitting and drug-confused patsy that would get them off the hook, and she wouldn't be able to deny it because her brain couldn't remember her own name at the moment, let alone where she'd been and what she'd done during the past forty eight hours.

"I'm pretty bloody certain she couldn't..," I said, going along with the narrative:" I don't believe Charlotte Dexter was responsible for putting one foot in front of the other during the whole time I knew her: Certainly not on Tuesday morning. Tuesday night is debatable because she might have been cleaned out a bit by then by the clinic, but I personally can't attest to anything because I didn't see her after I put her in the car taking her to the clinic. All I can say is that when I last saw her she was mentally and physically very ill. As I've just said, she may have been given stimulants at the clinic which improved her mental capacity but, again, I don't know. Mrs. Fitzpatrick would have a better idea than me about the state of her mind because she would have been the next to see her when she left the clinic."

Shepherd looked pleased with my answer.

"Quite..," he said:" And by the sound of it she would clearly have had to have taken a large dose of something to try and steady herself had she gone down to confront her husband."

"I should think she would have had to..," I agreed.

"And if she had taken such a large dose of 'something'..," he pushed:"...she still would have been under its influence and not in a rational or stable frame of mind?"

"Not my place to assume. I'm not a doctor or a psychiatrist. I'm not qualified to say."

He nodded, sagely.

"Why do you think she might have decided to go to see her late husband Mr. Carter..?" he asked.

"How should I know? Maybe she just wanted a quiet chat: Maybe she just missed his magnetic personality."

"A hypnotic attraction possibly? A compulsion..?"

"Call it whatever you like. If she did go down there, it had to be for a very good reason."

He steepled his fingers again. People who think a lot seem to like doing that.

"Continuing with the hypothesis, would you say she might possibly have taken her gun with her: For her own personal protection? As you said yourself, the late Mr. Dexter was a rather sadistic man. She could have been afraid of his reaction to her visit."

I stared at him for a whole five seconds, my mind suddenly focused on what he'd just said: How had he known about her pistol being there? I hadn't said anything about my finding her pistol there, or what kind of pistol Dexter might have used to kill himself. Why was there an assumption that hers had been there at all and that it was hers that had killed him, unless either they knew already or because someone I'd told about it had told someone else who told someone else, etcetera.

"It's a thought, yes…" I said, quietly, looking into Shepherd's eyes.

"And..," he continued:"…do you think that's why Dexter would have attacked her? He was frightened of her?"

"No..," I said, coldly, still staring into Shepherd's eyes:" From what I knew of the man, through my one and only meeting with him, he may have been a very shifty, manipulative, intimidating character and a mean-hearted sadist, but he was also a very smart guy. I don't believe he would have physically attacked her. He went in for verbal and mental abuse. He got off on hurting people emotionally. He was a bully but he wasn't stupid. If she had pulled a gun on him, he wouldn't have risked giving her any reason to claim she had to fire it in self-defence. If she pulled that trigger it was because she wanted to, not because she needed to."

"I see..," Shepherd pouted, looking away and considering what I'd just said:" That is a very interesting analysis Mr. Carter. Thank you. Tell me: If I asked you to describe Mrs. Dexter in your own words, based upon your having met her, albeit for only a short time and under rather extreme circumstances, what would you say?"

"I'd say she was a sad, pathetic, poor little rich girl that has never been given the chance of any real happiness in her whole life and that her descent into an extremely pampered hell of her own making was completed by her meeting and marrying the cold-eyed, black-hearted bastard that was Marcus Dexter and choosing to marry him. I also think that after he'd started working on her vulnerabilities and naïve vanity with the precision and coldness of a surgeon, all hope of any recovery was gone. He wrecked her mentally and physically not just for the money but for the sheer pleasure he got from doing it, then, when he'd got bored with the dried out husk he'd created, he threw her away and went looking for another stupid rich woman to play with."

"That's quite a brutal assessment Mr. Carter..," Shepherd said:" Tell me. Do you think her husband might have already found another companion..?"

That was a cute and very middle class way of describing Dexter's next conquest but what amused me and chilled me at the same time was the question: Did he already know about the flight to the Caribbean and was he trying to tease out my knowledge of what had been going on, pushing me even further and more firmly into the narrative someone, probably Leonora, was writing?

"Very possibly..," I said, cautiously" A man like Dexter doesn't leave one bed or bank account before having another to crawl into. It's his life. It's what he does. He goes from one sad, lonely rich woman to the next and he's very good at it, or he was."

Shepherd got to his feet and re-filled both our glasses, obviously thinking about my answers and more than likely about me. What his conclusion was I had no idea but I liked to think he realised I wasn't the slow-witted heavy he had imagined I'd be.

When he'd sat down he raised his glass in a salute, took a small sip and leaned forward, putting his elbows on the edge of his desk.

"Let me tell you what I think Mr. Carter..," he said, as if he were a judge summarising a case to the jury:" It's my firm and honest opinion that, based upon what I've learnt about Mrs. Dexter from Mrs. Fitzpatrick, and from what you've just told me, that when, or even if, she recovers from her medical ordeal, and she is arrested for the killing of her husband, no jury in the land, or indeed anywhere in the world, would find her guilty of anything other than aggravated manslaughter through mental harassment and intimidation and she would receive a much reduced sentence, very possibly a secure hospital placement but certainly not a sentence for murder. I am convinced that if a court hears the story you have just told me, it's very doubtful they would pass anything more than the most nominal sentence on her."

"Maybe you're right..," I said, non-committaly, sipping my drink.

Shepherd smiled a self-satisfied smile as though congratulating himself on a job well done.

"I'm very glad I've been able to talk with you Mr. Carter..," he said:" Thank you for coming in at such short notice. I'm very grateful and so will Mrs. Fitzpatrick be. You are a strong and eloquent witness, and I feel we can confidently call upon you should Mrs. Dexter's case come to court. Not only are you an impartial and trained observer, but you have seen at first hand her state of health both physically and mentally and can therefore attest to her lack of rational and pre-determined capabilities with regard to physical violence. You appreciate her lack of cognitive reasoning and would be able to confirm to a court that in no way could she be considered responsible for her actions. It is my firm belief that your evidence will save Mrs. Dexter from receiving anything but the lightest of penalties from the courts."

"If I give it..," I said offhandedly.

He sat back in his chair, genuinely surprised by what I'd just said.

"I'm sorry. What do you mean…"IF you give it"?"

"I mean "If I give it..," I replied, stone-faced.

"I don't understand. Why would you not give evidence Mr. Carter..? You would be a perfect witness for the defence."

"I'm sorry..," I said, my face still stony:"…but I don't think I would be."

"Why not..?"

"Because..," I said, leaning forward myself and speaking slowly:"…I'm not as on-side with Mrs. Fitzpatrick and Charlotte Dexter as you might like to think Mr. Shepherd. Like the police, I too don't believe Marcus Dexter killed himself. I believe he was murdered and much though I didn't like the man, in fact it would be fair to say I openly disliked everything about him, I'm not a fan of murder and, being old-school, I would want to see whoever murdered him brought to justice and if it turns out that Charlotte or anyone else close to her was responsible for putting a bullet through his head then I would try to ensure that he, or *she*, goes to prison for a very long time because of it. Call me old-fashioned but…"

I let the sentence hang there and sat back into my chair, taking another sip of my drink and looking at the grey-faced, confused looking man across from me through the bottom of the glass.

"I must say I find it very difficult to understand your attitude Mr. Carter..," he said, shaking his head slightly in bafflement.

"To be honest..," I said, finishing off the whiskey:"...quite a lot of the time I find it difficult to understand my own attitude Mr. Shepherd."

He shook his head and sighed.

"I must also say I am very disappointed and more than a little surprised..," he said:" Mrs. Fitzpatrick assured me I would receive the fullest and most sympathetic co-operation from yourself."

"Well, I hate to disappoint you but it looks as though Mrs. Fitzpatrick was wrong, doesn't it?"

"I'm afraid it does..," he nodded.

I stood up, pushed back my chair and extended my hand.

"Well, if that's all Mr. Shepherd, I'll say it's been very nice to meet you and goodbye..."

Shepherd remained seated, left my hand hovering in mid-air and looked up at me with a serious expression on his pasty, pinched face.

"I wonder if I may ask you something Mr. Carter..?" he said.

I remained standing and dropped my hand.

"It rather depends on what you want to ask Mr. Shepherd..," I replied, politely:" Go ahead though. Ask what you like..."

"Is it the money that worrying you? I am not privy to the dealings you had with my client prior to this conversation and it may be that you feel Mrs. Fitzpatrick was not as generous as you might have wished. I can assure you that if that is the case, or you had any doubts as to the fee you might be offered, any figure you have been paid in the past can and will be doubled, if not trebled. I have full authority to agree to whatever financial terms you may demand."

I grinned at him.

"That's very nice to hear..," I said, my smile barely hanging onto my cheeks.

"I can guarantee that your recompense will be far more generous than you can imagine Mr. Shepherd..," he finished.

"I have a very rich imagination Mr. Shepherd..," I grinned.

"And Mrs. Fitzpatrick is a very rich woman Mr. Carter. You needn't worry about the size of the settlement you would be paid for your continued services to her."

I dropped my grin and stared down hard at him.

"Did I say I was worried about it..?" I said, acidly.

He sighed, looked away and rubbed his hand across his mouth. I got the feeling from the way he did it and the look in his eyes that he was starting not to like me very much which didn't really surprise me to be honest: I had that effect on people sooner or later. My attitude towards rich peoples' attitude sometimes showed and I could sense it was beginning to show now. I didn't want her money and I didn't want to be paid to say what someone else wanted me to say. I was sorry for Charlotte and I could see how bad it would look for her if the case ever came to court, but two things had always held me back from being as successful as I knew I could have been in this dirty game I was a player in. One: Despite what Leonora and Cleaver thought, I did have scruples, lots of them, and two: I didn't care enough about money. Not enough to lie or kill for it anyway and I got the feeling I might be being asked to do both for it in this case.

Shepherd sat up in his chair, put his elbows on the desk, inter-laced his fingers and gave me a serious look.

"Mr. Carter..," He said, a hint of impatience in his grammar school voice:" Let me try, one last time, to change your mind. I and my client believe that you alone can save Mrs. Dexter from a great deal more misery and unhappiness in her already more than miserable life. I believe that if you are able to bring yourself to tell me, openly and candidly, about the events that led up to this tragic situation: About Mrs. Dexter's state of mind, your conversations with her and your conversations with Mr. Dexter himself: About his character and about your inter-actions with him, I can build a very strong case for poor Mrs. Dexter's defence and will be able to present it to the police and the Crown Prosecution pre-trial which would make it plain to the prosecution that our lines of defence would be so strong as to make it impossible for a jury to convict: So strong that they would be willing to come to a pre-trial agreement which will greatly reduce the punishment they might otherwise have had in mind and give her the opportunity to rehabilitate herself and lead a happy, contented life beyond her sentence."

He paused to take a breath and I smiled down at him. He was making a very good case on behalf of his client and I had to admire him for it.

"Would you not consider it to be your duty as a decent human being to offer the chance of freedom and a better life to one who has suffered so badly at the hands of another and was not responsible for her actions? Please Mr. Carter. Will you not re-consider your decision?"

"No..," I said, calmly:" Thanks for the drinks and the nice chat, but I'll pass on the offer. I'm sorry I can't be of any more help to you or your client. I hope Charlotte recovers and that she gets all the help I'm sure you can give her, but it will be without my specific involvement I'm afraid. Now...If that's all, I'll be going."

Shepherd shrugged.

"I'm very disappointed to hear that Mr. Carter..," he said, dejectedly:" After my 'phone conversation with Mrs. Fitzpatrick, I honestly thought we could rely on you for support. You'll forgive me for saying that I don't understand your decision or your attitude and I am mystified by your lack of compassion."

"Well..," I said, self-deprecatingly:"...if it makes you feel better I don't like me much either sometimes. I can be a bit of a bastard when I want to be. Good day Mr. Shepherd."

Shepherd didn't get up.

"Good day Mr. Carter..," he said, the look on his face and the tone of his voice making it very clear that he thought I was a complete son-of-a-bitch.

I left and stepped out into the grey, bleak afternoon, wind-blown bullets of rain stinging my cheeks, knowing that Shepherd would be calling Leonora now, telling her about what I'd said and how I'd turned down her offer to pay me to be a pawn in her game of "Let-your-sick-friend-take-the-rap".

She wouldn't like it. She'd be very upset about it in fact and I felt sure I'd be hearing from her again, one way or another, very soon and that from now onwards I'd have to watch my back as carefully as I was watching my feet on the rain-soaked steps of the Chambers.

I drove back through the rain-blurred traffic to my office, made myself a strong coffee, took off my clothes, lay on the sofa, pulled the thermal blanket tight around me, drank some of the coffee and fell fast asleep.

TWENTY NINE

When I woke up three hours later, it was dark outside, but the rain had stopped and I lay under the warmth of the blanket for ten minutes just thinking, mostly about the meeting with Shepherd but also about the whole state of affairs.

It was getting messy now and the speed with which the police had contacted Shepherd and warned him that Charlotte may be brought in for questioning about the death of Marcus was ringing alarm bells in my muzzy head.

It could have been of course that they had come to the conclusion all on their own. They have some very bright sparks in the C.I.D., and it wouldn't have taken even a relatively sharp-eyed individual to begin to see things might not be as straight forward as it first appeared, but my suspicious mind was steering towards them having had the seeds of doubt sprinkled in their little minds by an anonymous voice down a telephone line, and it was whose anonymous voice that could have been that I was using precious brain-cells on trying to work out.

Suddenly my phone pinged and I fumbled around on the bare-wood floor trying to find it. When I found it I opened the message box to find I had a mail from Cleaver of all people. There were no words, just a link and when I thumbed it, a news headline appeared, with the story scrolled beneath it.

"BUSINESS MAN SUICIDE NOW BELIEVED TO BE MURDER....ARREST EXPECTED IN SOUTH DOWN TRAGEDY"

So that was it: It was out and official. Dexter's death was now the result of murder not suicide which meant the investigation would be in the public realm and the resources used to work on it would be increased. Doors were going to be knocked on and questions were going to be asked, and I was pretty sure my door would be one of the first to feel the knuckles of Scotland Yards' finest.

I scrolled down and read the text.

"Scotland Yard detectives investigating the shooting of American businessman Marcus Dexter, found dead at his home on the South Downs on Wednesday morning, are now treating his death as murder.

Mr. Dexter's body was found in the early hours of Wednesday morning by Mrs. Turner, a cleaner, and at first it was believed that Mr. Dexter had committed suicide using an automatic pistol.

However, after closer and more intensive investigations, and the receiving of some important information, Detective Inspector John Cherwell, leading the investigation, has said that there is now sufficient evidence to be certain that Mr. Dexter had been the victim of a deliberate murder, for which it is expected an early arrest will be made."

Things would start moving fast now.

They'd talk to Leonora who would feed them only the crumbs she wanted to feed them and set them off down a road that would lead them away from her and straight to others, which meant she would probably bring The Doctor into the conversation. That would lead to the clinic who would tell them where they picked her up from, and that would see them knocking on Jock and Carol's door.

I grabbed a cup of coffee, threw my clothes back on, called Jock to ask if it was okay to come around, went down to the car and drove to Sloane Street.

THIRTY

When Jock opened the door there was a look of curiosity on his big, rugged face.

"Come on in..," he said, stepping to one side:" To what do we owe the pleasure of yet another visit so soon after the last? You nae' got another wee damsel in distress in the boot of your car have yae..?" he smirked:" We've barely changed the sheets from your last girlfriend."

I shot him a look and headed over to the drinks cabinet, pulling one of the bottles out from it and filling two tumblers, Carol shaking her head when I offered to pour her one.

"Help yourself why not..?" Jock said, accepting the glass I'd half-filled for him:" Make yourself at home, eh?"

He raised his crystal cut tumbler to me and nodded to the chair I was already headed for, sitting down in his own and leaning back, staring at me questioningly.

"Are you all right son..?" he said, kindly:" You look a wee bit troubled if I may say so."

I downed a third of the whiskey and took a deep breath.

"I'm good thanks Jock..," I said:" But I need to bring you up to speed with some developments."

"Oh aye..?" the big man frowned:" And what exactly might these "developments" be?"

"Do you remember Charlotte..?" I said:" The spaced out woman I brought here and who was taken off to a clinic?"

"Of course we do..!" Jock chuckled:" I may be getting on son, but I'm no' fuckin' senile yet! It was only a few fucking days ago..!"

"How is she..?" Carol asked.

"Not great..," I said:" Worse than before if anything. I discovered she checked herself out of that clinic we sent her off to just a few hours after she arrived and came back to London. From what I've heard she's in a bad way."

"I'm sorry to hear that..," Carol said:" She was in a bad enough way when you brought her here."

"Why did she check herself out..?" Jock asked:" Wasn't it her idea to go there in the first place..?"

"No..," I said, sipping on the drink:"...it wasn't. If you recall she wasn't exactly keen to leave."

"Aye..," Jock smiled:" I do recall that. So what's happened, and why do we need to be kept in the loop?"

I took another breath.

"You remember the reason I brought here in the first place?"

"Another question..?" Jock sighed:" Why don't you just answer my bloody question first, eh?"

Carol gave him a look that shut him up and she turned her face back to me.

"She was full of drugs and booze..," she answered:"...and carrying a gun which you said she was threatening to use on her husband?"

"That's right..," I nodded:" It was complicated...Still is"

"When isn't it..?" Jock mumbled.

"Well..," I continued:"...it seems she, or someone, might have actually used it... Her husband was shot through the head a couple of nights ago."

Jock sat back into his chair and shook his head in disbelief.

"Jeez..!" he growled:" When you pick a fight son, you pick a good one..!"

"Was it that American businessman who committed suicide..?" Carol asked, her eyes widening.

I nodded.

"Yes..," I said:" It was. Charlotte is his wife, or his widow now."

"Did she kill him..?" Jock asked, stroking his big, heavy moustache thoughtfully.

"I have no idea Jock but I very much doubt it. She could barely stand up when I last saw her and according to a very reliable source I have, she's pretty much comatose again. I doubt she would have been able to pull the trigger let alone shoot in a straight line. It was obvious that whoever put that round through her husbands' head had a steady hand and it was even more obvious it wasn't the man himself."

"And you know that because...?"

"Because it was me that found him Jock..," I said, throwing back the last of the whisky:" I was there, and probably not very long after the shot was fired."

"Fucking hell son..!" jock grinned:" You need to learn to walk away from trouble once in a while, not run towards it. You're not in the fucking army now. Those days are over."

"What were you doing there..?" Carol asked, gently.

"He and I had some unfinished business that needed clearing up..," I said:"...so I was going to ask him a few questions."

Jock shifted in his seat, awkwardly.

"I have to ask this..," he said, uncomfortably, sipping on his drink:"...so don't get all fucking angry now, okay?"

I knew what he was going to ask.

"That's okay Jock..," I smiled, wearily:" It's the same question I'd ask if it was you telling me the same story. Go ahead: Ask it."

"It was' nae' you that killed him was it..?" he asked, a frown creasing his wide brow.

I shook my head.

"No jock…It wasn't. I might have wanted to because he was a total fucking bastard and deserved all he got, but it wasn't me. You know I don't do that anymore. I honestly just went down to have a friendly chat about a few things and found him, faceless in his chair, still warm: Too warm actually, which is what made me begin to realise he might not have done the deed himself."

Jock waved my answer away.

"I don't need to know the details son..," he said, dismissively:" You telling me you didn't do it is good enough for me."

I thanked him, lifted my empty glass from the arm of the chair and indicated the drinks cabinet with it. Jock nodded and I got up, crossed over to the bottles and poured myself another.

"So why are you here telling us these things..," Carol asked when I'd sat down again:" Do you need a place to stay for a while?"

I shook my head.

"No..," I said, insistently:" Don't worry about that. I don't need to hide, but thanks for offering."

"Well..," Jock gruffed, looking at me steadily, his expression stony:" If y'did'nae come here to get your head down for a wee while and you've told us y'did'nae kill this Dexter guy, what was the other reason you came here, apart from drinking ma' whisky?"

I didn't answer him for a few seconds then…

"Okay Jock..," I said slowly:" Here's the thing. When I heard about Dexter's killing being treated as murder not suicide, and that Charlotte was being considered as the main suspect, it occurred to me that once the police start digging down a little and they find out about the clinic and how she got there, they might want to come and ask you a few questions."

"Aye..," he said:" They probably would: So...? Are you worried that'll lead on to you?"

"No Jock: I'm not worried about that. I'm pretty sure they'll have tied me in nice and tight already by that time: No...What I'm worried about is what you might say if they ask about the gun."

Jock's expression didn't change. I could see his mind working.

"Oh aye..?" he said, taking a sip of his whisky:" In what way?"

"Well, you remember when we were all waiting for the people from the clinic to arrive?"

Carol nodded

"Aye...Of course..," Jock said.

"And you remember when she asked me for her gun?"

"Yes, yes. Of course we do..," Jock grunted, shaking his head:" Just get to the bloody point..!"

"Well, that is the point..," I said, meeting his stare directly:" I want you to forget what you remember."

They both exchanged glances and I could feel the air in the room suddenly sharpen. They weren't happy with what they'd just heard, I could tell.

"You want us to forget about her asking you for her gun..?" Carol asked.

"Yes...Please..," I said, a thin, slightly guilty smile on my lips.

"Not mention it to the police..?" Jock said.

"In one Jock...You got it."

He stared at the carpet for a moment, turning over my request in his mind.

"Forget about you saying she shouldn't have it because they don't take kindly to having patients high on drugs taking pot shots at the staff..?" he said.

"Christ Jock..! Yes..!" I hissed, impatiently, regretting it instantly:" Please forget about my saying anything to Charlotte Dexter about her having a gun. In fact please forget you know anything about a gun at all. If they get around to asking, what I'd like you to say is that you have no recollection of a gun ever having been mentioned."

Jock's sly, slow grin made me shake my head in both relief and understanding. He was ribbing me: Playing with me: Twisting my balls:

"For fuck's sake…!" I breathed…

"Okay laddie..," Jock chuckled, winking at me:" I won't say a word about her having a tantrum about you not letting her have it or you going down to your car and giving it to her to shut her up."

I shook my head and smiled long-sufferingly.

"Thanks Jock..," I smirked:" I'd be very grateful if you didn't."

Jock's face hardened suddenly and he leant forward.

"Just as long as you know what you're doing son..," he growled:" You could be playing a dangerous wee game here, you know that?"

"Yes Jock. I do know that but I there's a good reason why I'm doing this."

"I'm sure there is..," he said:" All I'm saying is just be careful. The police are not stupid. Never go underestimating them like some of those clowns do."

I promised them both I wouldn't, thanked them for their understanding and left, kissing a concerned-looking Carol at the door, my tight little smile meant to reassure her I was going to be fine, but somehow failing.

That over, back in my car, I called Cleaver and told him I hated to be a nuisance but I needed to see him again.

I seem to have caught him at a bad time because he sounded very angry, telling me he was not a happy man right now and that there had better be a bloody good reason why. I told him there was and he said well it doesn't matter: It would have to wait because he had a dinner date to go to and there was no way on this fucking earth he was going to be late for it, so if I wanted to see him it would have to be half eleven. If that was no good then I could find a large pole, insert it and start swivelling on it.

I said I understood, apologised for calling, graciously accepted his offer, closed the phone and drove back to my office.

THIRTY ONE

By the time I parked outside my office building, the rain was coming down like a tax bill; fast, hard and heavy and, in the glowering, torrential downburst, the street looked even more miserable and third rate than ever, if that was possible.

Blipping the car locked, I turned my collar up and splashed across the chromed tarmac, fumbling with the key to the main door, cursing when, as usual, it wouldn't turn the first or second time, fell inside when it did, shook myself and began climbing the dusty, dingy stairs, my footsteps echoing in the gloomy emptiness.

I was tired of the place, tired of my office: tired of the area: tired of the set up: tired of myself, tired of this case: Just plain and simple 'tired', and the lack of speed with which I trudged up to my floor was the physical evidence of those feelings.

Closing the door, I flung my top coat onto the sofa, opened the bottom drawer of my desk, pulled out a half-empty bottle of the cheap stuff I kept for days with a "Y" in them, moved a few piles of paper work, lifted my aching feet up and onto the desk top, gripped the cork between my teeth, pulled on it and was pathetically grateful when it came clear from the neck in one clean 'pop'. Standing it upright and smack-bang in the centre of the desk, I lifted the bottle in mock salutations to a crappy day and threw back the first of the dark brown gut rot, planning on there being several more when I distinctly heard footsteps in the corridor outside.

I swallowed the mouthful, listening to their approach, half filled the glass with another and swung my feet back onto the floor, quietly re-corking the bottle.

The footsteps were getting closer and my trained ear told me they weren't the heavy clomp of men's shoes: They sounded more like the light tapping of high heels.

I leaned back in my seat and waited for the knock on the door, and when it came I was even more certain I was right. It was a knock that told me the odds were very high there was probably a woman standing on the other side of it and I was proven right when it opened and Leonora Fitzpatrick stood framed there.

She was wearing a long, expensive looking, fawn-coloured raincoat and on her head she had a wide-brimmed hat with a feather tucked into the band, the sort country gals wear when they trudged through a muddy field watching horses crashing through woods and over fences on some Viscounts estate. Actually, she looked like she owned the estate. She looked good: Very good indeed, and instinctively I smiled, half-rising out of my seat.

"Well, good evening..," I said:" To what do I owe this honour?"

"I'm not sure I want to sit down..," Leonora said. Her voice was cold and unfriendly.

I shrugged, genuinely not interested.

"You choice..," I said, just as coldly:" Sit or don't sit. Stay or don't stay. You obviously wanted to see me though. I doubt you drove all the way from Richmond through Noah's flood to just to stand in my doorway."

She stared at me with the eyes of a viper, stepped into the room, sat down and crossed her long legs, her eyes boring into mine. For my part, I sat back and let my eyes move from her knees, down her nicely shaped calves to her very expensively shod feet then travel back up to her very lovely face.

"I came here..," she said, injury and outrage in her voice:"…because I wanted to find out the reason for your extraordinary attitude today..."

"My attitude..?" I said, amused and confused:" What attitude was that?"

She drew in a deep breath which seemed to fuel the furnace burning nicely behind her eyes.

"The police came to my house this morning to interview Charlotte which was a terrible shock to me..," she said, the anger in her voice elegantly contained.

"Was it..?" I said, inquisitively:" 'Couldn't have been that much of a surprise, surely? I got a call from your Mr. Shepherd this morning, charming man by the way; nicely spoken, asking me to visit him in his chambers for a chat, and according to him you were half-expecting it to happen. He told me he was in touch with some very friendly sounding detective involved with the case and that this very friendly detective had promised to keep him, and therefore you, in the loop about any developments. He said, as soon as the decision to treat Dexter's death as murder not suicide was made, your pet policeman would drop the bone right at his feet so that he and you would have been nicely fore-warned of their visit."

I could hear the intake of breath and see the flash of fire in her eyes.

"The fact that they came to my house wasn't the shocking part mister Carter..," she hissed:" As you say, I was expecting that they might want to interview Charlotte, even if it had just been a suicide, because she is, or was, his wife. No…The shocking part to me was the speed with which they came to see her after the decision had been made to treat Dexter's death as murder. Less than half an hour to be precise. Fifteen minutes after you had left your interview with Mister Shepherd in fact and, based upon what

Mister Shepherd had told me, it almost instantly crossed my mind that you might have been responsible for contacting them and making them think that Charlotte could possibly have been his killer."

"Really..? I said, raising an amused eyebrow:" "Why would that make you think it would be me..?"

"Because..," she said, firmly, her jaw tight:"...Mister Shepherd told me that your response to his questions and your general attitude was highly unsatisfactory."

"Unsatisfactory..." A cold word and coldly delivered.

"Unsatisfactory..?" I echoed, holding her stare with mine:" I think what you might mean is I didn't tip my forelock and thank him for giving me the opportunity to serve his mistress as you'd hoped?"

There was a tense few moments during which she visibly bristled and gave me a sharp look.

"Mr. Shepherd telephoned you at my perhaps rather naïve request..," she stiffened, her voice clipped:"...in order to try and gain your help in keeping Charlotte safe, something I thought you might want to do as much as myself, but he told me that far from wanting to help you seemed actually quite hostile."

I nodded slowly: Understandingly.

"I can see how he might have felt like that..," I agreed.

That annoyed her I could tell.

"Why..?" she said, her angry coldness replaced with amazement:" What were you trying to do? Do you not think that Charlotte needs all the help we can give her..?"

"We..?"

She sat back and stared at me, hard.

"Yes; "We..," she bridled.

I shrugged nonchalantly and opened my hands.

"I wasn't aware there was a "we"..," I glowered:" I thought there was only you and the people you paid."

That made her angry.

"And you led me to believe that you and I were working together for the benefit of Charlotte..," she growled, sarcastically:" My mistake obviously."

"What gave you that idea..?" I asked, casually.

"The trouble you took to get Charlotte help and then finding her the clinic..," she said.

"Which she signed herself out of within an hour of arriving..," I replied.

"She should never have done that, I know..," Leonora said regretfully:"...but she was confused and frightened. She just wanted to be amongst friends: People she knew."

"Maybe she did, maybe she didn't..," I said:"...but it did rather complicate matters didn't it? 'Might have been good if her "friends" had sent her back there, then all of this might not have been an issue."

There was a short pause and when she replied, her voice was less hostile.

"Hindsight is a wonderful thing I agree..," she said:"...but that didn't happen and we need to deal with what's happening now..."

"There's that 'We' thing again..," I said.

"I thought you'd been very kind and gone out of your way to do all you could to help her..," she went on, deliberately ignoring my snarky comment:"...and to help me. I thought..."

"I always do my best for my clients..," I said, tiredly.

"Do you? It doesn't seem that way at the moment."

"Just because I didn't sit up like a little puppy at the sound of its mistresses' call..?" I said, taking a short swig from the bottle and looking her dead straight:" The trouble is with you, and people like you..," I said, cynically:"...is that because you have money you're all used to having things done your way and when you don't get your way, like now, you become angry and stamp your expensively wrapped feet if anyone dares disagree or does it another way."

I saw her eyes widen and her lips tighten when I said that and I enjoyed the moment.

"The last time I saw you..," I continued:"...back at your place, when you were all teary eyed and asking for my help, I told you that if anything happened, if anyone called or if anything was bothering you, you were to ring me and let me handle it because that's what I'm good at and you said you would, but you didn't did you? You carried on with your own plans. You reverted back to type, got your man Shepherd involved, had him contact me and got him to bring me in like a leashed dog. Why did you do that? Why didn't you just do what I asked you to do?"

"After what Shepherd told me, I didn't think I could trust you..," she said, haughtily:" He certainly doesn't think I should."

"And what am I supposed to say to that..? I'm so fucking sorry you don't trust me anymore: I'm sorry your tame lawyer thinks I'm hostile: Which pier would you like me to jump off the end of..?"

Another swallow of whisky which she sat silent through.

"Tell me something..," I said, glaring at her, the bottle gripped in my fingers:" Why did you ask Shepherd to talk to me? What did you think he would be able to get me to do?"

"If the police ever charged Charlotte with Marcus's murder..," She said:"...I wanted him to make a case for poor Charlotte acting under diminished responsibility, which he agreed with. He seems to think her state of health, her state of mind, is so fragile that if she ever came to court, the prosecution and any jury, even if they found her guilty, would recommend that the worst she be charged with was manslaughter and ask for a nominal sentence to be passed on her. When I told him about you and your involvement with the events up to now, he told me your help would be invaluable. I assumed you would be glad to support him."

"There's a lot of assuming going on here isn't there..?" I snorted:" The main assumption being that Charlotte killed him in the first place, which I'm not sure she did but for the sake of argument let's go along with it. If she did kill him, why would Shepherd need my help to push for that? He's a clever man. He should be able to build his own case for her being too stoned to know what she was doing."

"Because..," Leonora said, petulantly:"...he believes your personal experiences with her and your past professional encounters with others like her would be key and central to her defence."

"I can understand that..," I said, nodding in agreement.

"Then why won't you give him a statement..?"

"Because..," I said, sighing heavily:"...I'm not ready to make any statements to anybody yet. Not him, not the police: Not anyone..!"

"Why not..?"

"Because..," and said again, this time with meaning:"...there are still a lot of things about all this I'm not sure about and until I am, I'm not prepared to discuss anything with anyone or give any kind of statements. Not yet at least."

Leonora crossed her legs again and looked at me with interest.

"What aren't you sure about..?" she asked, her voice suddenly calmer; more measured.

I looked at her for a few seconds, trying to work out whether or not I actually cared. When I gave it, my answer was guarded and deliberately provocative. I wanted to see her reaction.

"A lot of things but, like I said, the biggest thing is whether or not Charlotte actually killed him. I don't think she did."

"Oh..?" she said, her voice low, her long, dark, delicious eyebrows high:" That's interesting. Why not..?"

"Simple really..," I smiled, deliberately annoyingly, my voice fuelled by a sudden wave of genuine exhaustion. I'd done a lot of thinking and talking since the woman in front of me had first walked into my office like she had just now, and I'd heard a lot of stuff that made me tired just trying to work it all out and, all of a sudden, right at that moment, I decided I'd had enough. I wasn't in the mood to argue or explain myself anymore. I just wanted her to go away, think what she liked, and for me to get whatever sleep I could:

"Because..," I forced myself to continue:"...she was coked out of her head and couldn't have hit the end of her bed with a bazooka that night, never mind an ex-Marine in a chair who didn't want to be shot. What I am prepared to believe is that she might have been taken down there by someone and the gun placed in her hand to leave fingerprints for the police to find, but I'm not at all happy with the idea that she did the deed herself. That's what I'm not sure about, and until I have something I am damned sure about, I'm not helping anyone defend or prosecute anyone. So...Now you know why I was 'hostile' with your man, what I'd very much like you to do is use those lovely legs of yours to walk back down those stairs like before and let me get on with finishing this bottle and trying to work out to my own satisfaction, not yours or anyone else's, who shot Marcus Dexter and why."

I picked up the bottle again, drank another mouthful, saw her face flush white with anger, watched her rise to her feet, fix me with a look that was meant to tell me she'd kill me right there and then if she could, swallowed some more of the fire-water, listened to her say..."I made a mistake coming here mister Carter. I can see that now. I thought that when I first came here but I was desperate and needed someone unscrupulous so I swallowed my doubts, just like you are swallowing that cheap whiskey, and asked you for help but now I know I was right. You are nothing more than you are, despite your high opinion of yourself. A thug for hire. A man without scruples!"...saw and heard the door slam, swallowed the rest of the mouthful, heard the high heels clack angrily along the wooden corridor and vanish then, lifting the neck of the bottle to my lips one last time and muttering a toast to "scruples", whatever they were, slammed the almost empty bottle down on the desk, lifted my feet up onto the top, crossed my ankles and fell into a deep, heavy sleep.

THIRTY TWO

By the time I got to Cleaver's place, the rain had stopped trying to drown the city and I stood on the wide doorstep of the Mayfair mansion block he lived in, staring into the small camera and waiting for my ring on the doorbell to be answered.

When the buzzer went, I entered, took the mirrored lift to the third floor, walked right to the end of the blue-carpeted hallway I'd trodden down many times before, stopped outside Cleaver's door and rang the bell.

Surprisingly, this time the door wasn't opened by one of his usual gorillas. Instead, Cleaver himself came through on the small speaker and told me to come in. There was a click and the door opened slowly, allowing me to push and enter, moving back silently into place behind me when I'd entered.

I walked along the corridor past expensively furnished, tall-ceilinged rooms, got to the door at the end, waited for a grunt from the other side that told me I could go through, went inside and was greeted by a widely grinning Cleaver wearing a black smoking jacket and smoking his usual dick-sized cigar, looking very pleased with himself for some reason: Dinner must have gone well. He was obviously getting his money's worth from that escort agency.

"Come on in son..," he grinned, pointing to a large leather armchair by the fire and going over to the drinks cabinet, pouring us both a large whiskey, adding a dash of soda from an ornate siphon and placing mine on a table at my elbow. The man was in a good mood tonight and prepared to be generous. I laughed inside. That wouldn't last but it was worth milking while it did.

Taking his own drink over to the fire, he stood with his back to it, warming his burly arse, looking down at me like a cheerful, slightly dodgy uncle.

"So, what's the trouble..? Still the Fitzpatrick woman or maybe the news the police are probably going to come looking for you now they're treating Dexter's death as murder..?" he said, mischievously.

"Not really..," I said, rolling my glass between my fingers casually, acting unconcerned:" Once they'd spoken with his wife, it's a pretty fair bet they'd come. My name would probably be the first one out of her mouth."

"Some mouth..," Cleaver scoffed:" I doubt they'd get much sense out of that. Her brain must be fried to a fucking crisp by now, what with all the stuff she's shoved up her fucking nose. She's probably still sitting on a purple cloud somewhere holding hands with God or some other fucker. Not a lot of use to the Plod really. She shouldn't be a worry to you."

"She's not..," I said, sipping on my whiskey:" It's the other wife I'm worried about."

Cleaver's face flickered suddenly.

"The other wife..?" he said:" What other wife..? He's only got one."

"No, he hasn't..," I said, giving him a direct look which I could tell un-nerved him:"...He's got two hasn't he?"

He looked straight back at me with hooded eyes, his whiskey-coated smile now more like a knife-cut, watching me like a snake. The fire might have been roaring in the grate behind him, but it had suddenly become distinctly chilly in the room, as I knew it would.

"I have no fuckin' idea...Has he..?" he replied, darkly, staring into his glass, nodding to himself; mind working, the good humour he'd been filled with before all drained away now.

"Yes..," I carried on, taking a long pull on my drink:" He has. He's got two: One legal, one very *un*-legal."

It was Cleaver's turn to take a long pull on his drink, using the time it took to size me up. I could tell he knew I knew and I was telling him through my neutral expression that I knew he knew I knew.

"So, if that's true..," he eventually said:"...which one are you worried about: The legal one or the illegal one..?"

"The legal one..," I said, calmly:" Leonora."

"Why..?" he said, tightly, something about the way he said it told me we weren't friends anymore. I knew it wouldn't last.

"Because I've got a theory about her..," I said, keeping my cool in the face of the heat from his stare.

"Have you now..? What kind of a fucking "theory"?"

I put the tumbler down on the table and laced my fingers together, looking up at him, reflecting back his growing anger with a deliberately aggravating smile.

"A theory that makes her the prime suspect for the killing of Marcus Dexter, her husband..," I said, firmly, amused to see his mind twisting and turning behind his nasty little eyes, wondering what direction this conversation was going to take:"...And we both know, don't we, that he is still her husband because you and I both know they were never actually divorced, don't we?"

THIRTY THREE

If the atmosphere had been growing chilly before, suddenly it was Arctic, and I could see Cleaver's eyes become hard as diamonds and sharp as razors.

"What the fuck are you talking about..?" he hissed through clenched teeth, the venom with which he coated it showing me he knew exactly what I was talking about: It was strangely satisfying to see him squirming like that and I could feel the adrenalin begin to seep into my veins, preparing me for the confrontation I was deliberately engineering. The confrontation I wanted to have. This must be how a hunter felt when he's pushed a wild lion into a corner, not knowing what the outcome would be, and I loved it. Fucking loved it..!

"I'm talking about your little deal with the dear departed Marcus Dexter..," I said, coolly:" The one my colleague "Harry-the-Hatchet" told me all about over a very nice plate of pasta at Gino's the other day."

His look was murderous now and I could see any control he might have had left was slipping through his pudgy fingers. Finishing his drink in one gulp, he slammed the empty glass down onto a sideboard and looked at me like I was a pile of runny shit that had just come pouring through his letterbox.

"I've told you I have no idea what the fuck you are talking about..!" he snarled:" What deal...!"

"Not just the deal..," I carried on, deflecting the aggression.

"Oh really..?" he sneered, beads of sweat beginning to prick out on his shiny, pink forehead:" Something else is there: What's that then?"

"You calling the police."

That made his eyebrows slam together just above his thick nose and for a fleeting second I got the feeling he was genuinely confused about what I'd just said. I took a mental step back assessing his reaction, the tiniest hint of uncertainty slipping into my mind.

"Me..?" he said:" "What the fucking hell are you talking about Carter? What do you mean *me* calling the police? You know talking to the filth brings me out in a fucking rash."

"Yes, you..," I repeated, a little less sure of what I was insinuating suddenly but knowing I had to continue with the assault. If I stumbled now, I'd be on a back foot and I needed to be the one on top in this increasingly dangerous game:" I suspected you would be the first one to tip them off about me, especially after what I told you the other day. I don't blame you of course. You had to. The second you heard about them treating his suicide as murder, you knew you'd have to start covering that nicely burning backside of yours. It's only natural. You've got to protect yourself so, as soon as I left you yesterday, knowing I was there at the house not long after he was killed and that I have more than two brain cells to rub together, I'm betting you started worrying that I might have begun to put everything I saw together and come up with the theory I now have. The theory that puts you firmly in the picture and that, if I did go to the police with it to protect *myself*, you knew would turn everything you'd managed to cover up over the past year or so into rat shit and make them come here to talk to you about how and why you framed his killing to make it look like suicide."

His face suddenly turned grey and the skin around his mouth tightened. I was on dangerous ground now and I knew I needed to take the next few steps very carefully.

"I fucking told you..," he growled, slowly, with all the building anger of a cornered bear, but I didn't let him finish, needing to keep control of the conversation:

"So the obvious thing to do..," I said, magnanimously:"...would have been for you to call them and, anonymously of course, say that you knew Marcus Dexter had been killed, that you knew who killed him, and give them my name and where I could be found as a piece of meat to lead them off your scent. I understand that: Almost respect it in fact. It's what I would have done if I was in your position, but the thing that made me scratch my head a little when I was coming up with this theory was how you got wind so quickly about them changing their minds in the first place: Do you have a tame copper in your pocket? I didn't doubt you might well have but like you said, talking with the filth brings you out in hives so it was more likely you knew someone who did, but who? It baffled me for a while until I had a very interesting meeting with a man called Shepherd, and something he said made me realise you *do* know someone who has: Leonora Fitzpatrick..."

I picked up my drink, took a sipping-break; ignoring the..." You must be fucking mad...!" mutterings Cleaver was spitting at me, wiped my lips with my fingers, put the tumbler back down and continued:

"Mister Shepherd is Leonora's lawyer, and during our meeting, he informed me that he knows one of the detectives that happens to be working on Dexter's killing, and that this said detective had promised to keep him up to date about any developments in the investigation ahead of the press, which immediately made me think that when he let Mister Shepherd know about the official change of mind, Mister Shepherd rang Leonora who then rang you..."

"Why the fuck would Leonora fucking Fitzpatrick ring me..?" Cleaver said, his eyes stabbing into me like bayonets.

"Because..," I continued, with a calmness I wasn't really feeling:"...you owe her a very big favour don't you; one she finally decided to call in."

"A favour..?" Cleaver repeated, his voice rising as his temper heated up:" A fucking "favour"..! Why would I owe fucking Leonora Fitzpatrick a fucking favour?"

I could always tell when Cleaver's threat level was rising because his swearing became faster and louder and his swearing was becoming both those things.

"Because..," I said, meeting his raging-bull eyes with as steady a look as I could manage:"...I think, and as she probably revealed to you, she's known about your seedy, secret deal with her now deceased husband for quite some time but, being the astute, forward-thinking woman she is, she'd decided to keep that piece of information up her elegant sleeve until the time came when she could use it. A time when either she or you, probably both, were deeply in the shit and she would ask, no not ask...*demand*, you help her."

"Help her do what..?" Cleaver snarled impatiently.

I took a long breath...

"Help her kill Marcus Dexter and make his murder look like suicide."

Suddenly Cleaver's eyes blazed with a white fire, his mouth set into a spittle-rimmed rictus of hate, loathing and murderous intent and he glared at me with a face I imagined a lot of people had seen seconds before their lives ended, and I have to admit it was a bit intimidating.

"You must be raving fucking mad, you slimy piece of shit, coming here, accusing me of murder..!" he hissed, the curling of his fingers telling me he wanted to rip my throat open and eat my heart:" You stupid fucking cunt..! I ought to..."

I shut him up with a harsh look.

"You ought to what..?" I said coldly, fixing him with a long, soul-sucking look:" Shoot me? Kill me with your bare hands? Stab me through the face with that knife I know you keep in a sheath under the desk?"

His jaw tightened but he said nothing.

"You ought to and you want to, but you won't..," I said quietly:"...because you know I'm not going to let you. You know, because you pay me more than any of the others to be as good as I am, that if you move one fucking inch from that fireplace I will get up from this chair and do you a lot of damage before you've put one foot in front of the other you fat prick."

He didn't like that one bit, I could tell. Cleaver was looking at me like there was nothing more in this world he wanted to do than skin me alive and eat me but I didn't care. This is what I'd come here to do and I was going to make him listen:

"Now shut up, stand there like a good little bastard and let me tell you what I think happened to Marcus Dexter the other night and what I think your part in it was."

THIRTY FOUR

The air in the room was so thick with tension it was like trying to breathe treacle and I knew in Cleaver's eyes, right from that moment, I was a dead man talking. There was no going back now, only forward, so I took a mental deep breath and went forward.

"I think you got a call from Leonora telling you to get down to "Devil's View" around eleven..," I said, holding his stare with my own:"...so you got hold of, oh I don't know...Marty "Angel" and "Savvy" Gillman? They're specialty is suicides isn't it? Yes: It is, so you three got into the BMW and drove down to Dexter's place like good little killers."

"Prove it..," Cleaver said in a slow, steaming hiss.

I reached into my jacket pocket, took out my mobile and waved it at him.

"You know what I like about cold, clear, frosty nights..?" I said:" The cold, clear, silver light: It makes things look a lot sharper: You can see much more detail, especially on tyre treads: 'Brings the patterns out really crisply, and that night there were three sets of really identifiable car tracks around the house, each one telling a very interesting story. First of all there were Dexter's tracks leading up the drive from the road, straight into the garage but not coming out again. 'Makes sense. After leaving a politely worded invitation in Charlotte's flat to join him for drinks and a few laughs at ten, he would have come down from London and made himself comfortable for the night of fun ahead. The other two were a bit more interesting. One set was wide and deep and were made by 4x4 tyres. Very good tyres: The sort you might find on say, a Range Rover or, as I found out when I visited Leonora, an Audi Q8. Very expensive tyres with very distinctive treads. Treads that still had mud in them. You don't get much mud in your tyres driving around London."

Cleaver looked like he was chewing a hot wasp.

"The second set, the ones that had obviously arrived after the first because they ran over the top of the Audi's, were more the sporty coupe type..," I said, bringing up the set of photo's I'd taken of the BMW tracks and holding them up for Cleaver to see. Oddly enough, he didn't look at them, choosing instead to give me the full laser-eye treatment, never once wavering his stare from me:" An Audi maybe or possibly a Mercedes? Turns out it was a BMW 8 series Gran Coupe, very much like the one you have parked next to your Range Rover, in fact exactly the same. Again, very expensive tyres and again, highly distinctive tread pattern."

I put the phone away.

"Based upon which tracks were on top of the others, I'd say, after Dexter's car, the Audi was next to arrive, close on ten I'd guess, then the Coupe which parked itself at the side of the house making a neat three point turn so that the nose of the car was facing out ready for a quick getaway if necessary: The mark of a true pro'..," I smiled, cutely:" Well done."

Cleaver didn't return the smile and it was obvious he wasn't going to say anything witty or profane in repost, so I carried on.

"There were also shoe prints: A lot of them..," I went on:"...all headed to and from the house, and all telling an equally interesting story, but for the moment I'm going to stick with the tyre tracks. Much more enlightening."

There was a very uncomfortable silence while I took a swallow of the excellent whiskey that I would have loved another tumbler full of, but that might have been pushing my luck a bit too far so I carried on with my theory.

"Like I said, knowing what I now know about your New York dealings, I should think you were very fucking pleased to be given the chance to shut the mouth of the one man in this world who had any kind of a hold over you forever, and there he was, just as she had told you he would be, sitting in his chair, waiting for you, Leonora standing next to him with a briefcase full of money and bonds in one hand and his gun in the other. She'd kept her part of the deal somehow, knocking him out, ready for you, but one thing puzzles me..," I said, genuinely puzzled:" How had she had got him to sit still and take what was about to happen to him without a whimper? I mean, when she walked through the door instead of Charlotte, he must have been very confused and bloody, fucking angry and his first instinct would have been to rise up and confront her, but somehow she kept him in his seat and submissive enough to wait for you lot to turn up...? Drugs maybe? Yeah... It had to be drugs and if it was, I'm guessing they had to be just powerful enough to paralyze the poor bastard...Make him aware of what was coming next. Christ..! If they were and he couldn't move, he must have been shitting himself when you and the two fucking stooges walked in, which may very well have been exactly what Leonora wanted..," I chuckled:" It doesn't matter right now though...I'm just painting the bigger picture here..," I continued, brushing the problem away with a flick of my hand:" I'll Let the police work that one out: So...there he was, slumped in his chair waiting for you to do something horrible to him, or rather for "Angel" and "Savvy" to do it for you by doing what they do best: Making it look like he'd shot himself. They dragged the chair with his paralyzed body in it a few feet closer to the fire to keep it from going stiff too soon, took the .32 from Leonora, wiped her prints from the butt, assuming she hadn't been wearing gloves which she might well have done, probably slipped it into that very clever device they carry around with them that positions the weapon either against the temple or under the jaw, placed Dexter's fingers around the handle and the trigger, moved it up under his chin, worked the mechanism that pulls the trigger, waited for the bang, let it drop out of his hand onto the carpet then removed the equipment. All very neat and professional, as usual, but this time they made a mistake."

Cleaver's frown was momentary and almost imperceptible but I saw it.

"…and the mistake was..," I said:"…when they dragged the chair across the carpet, they didn't brush the pile back smoothly afterwards. That's what made me first begin to suspect the chair had been moved: That and the heat on the back of my legs as I stood looking into what was left of his face. Both dead giveaways. Never mind..," I shrugged:"…Clever idea though, using the warmth from the fire to stop him stiffening up and making it look like he shot himself later than he had so as to give you all time to get away from there and back down to London. The suicide note though..?"

I sat forward in the chair, warming to my theory.

"If I'm being honest, when I read it, it wasn't very convincing. Having met the guy, it certainly didn't convince me. Not really the kind of note a nasty piece of work like him would have written: Not the kind of words he would have used but then that's because I knew what a nasty cunt he was. The police didn't of course, so they had to assume they were his own words written in his own style."

There was another silence during which Cleaver's face changed from barely controlled anger to cold contemplation of my words and, slightly surprisingly, it ended with a laugh, or at least a noise that attempted to sound like a laugh.

"You know what Carter..?" he said, grinning and pointing the end of the cigar at me:"…You've got imagination boy. I'll give you that. That is a fucking great theory you've just told me: Very bloody interesting. Only one thing wrong with it…"

"What's that then..?" I said, intrigued by the sudden change of attitude.

"It's not true, and it's not true because of one thing..," Cleaver winked.

"Oh yes..?" I said:" And what would that one thing be..?"

"The fact that it wasn't me or any of my guys that killed him. It was Charlotte Dexter that did it. She murdered her bastard of a husband."

There was a silence during which I said nothing, just sat there staring at Cleaver, turning over what he'd said, then…

"Cut it out Cleaver..," I said at last:" Charlotte Dexter was nowhere near that house and I know that because over the past few days I've been doing what I do best: Checking things out: Asking questions and seeing things for myself. What I've just laid out is, a few fine details aside possibly, essentially true and I know you know you know it, but can't admit it because you and Leonora have got a nice little story concocted between you, ready to tell Scotland Yard's finest if you ever get asked. About her being an old client of yours that you helped with her divorce proceedings some years back, because of which she trusted you, so much so that when she has another problem, concerning her dearest friend and Dexter's second wife Charlotte, she comes to you again to help because, knowing the kind of man Dexter was, she was terribly worried that if poor Charlotte stayed with him much longer, she might become so desperate and afraid of what he might do to her that she might kill him out of fear and frustration, and therefore she needed to get Charlotte away from him. You however, being the fine, up-standing citizen you are, didn't want to get involved so instead, you put her onto me, someone you told her was the perfect guy to put the frighteners on Marcus. Fearful for Charlotte's state of mind and what it might drive her to do, Leonora persuaded me to go down there and use my talents to induce Dexter to grant poor, dear Charlotte a divorce, just like you'd done on Leonora's behalf before but I told you that when I got there I found Dexter dead and Charlotte standing over him with a smoking gun, just like she'd threatened publicly she would do one day. Nice story except I know different and what I know happens to be a lot more believable."

I paused to allow him to say something, but Cleaver just grinned at me, which was a little disconcerting.

"D'y'know what..?" he said, waving his cold, almost-out cigar at me:" I always thought you might not have all your screws tightened up Carter, and what you've just said proves it, but because it's you and I like you, or used to anyway, I'm not going to follow my instincts and have you murdered slowly over the next couple of days. No…I'm going to take a chill pill and admit something to you. I'm going to admit I've been a fucking fool..," he said in what was intended to be a cheerful, warm voice but sounded a little strained:" I'm going to admit that I've been holding out on you: Keeping you in the dark on a few things that I realise now I should have been including you in on. If I had it would have saved all of this…"

He paused theatrically, as though struggling to find the word he was looking for...

"...Unpleasantness: I should have made you part of the picture: You'd have been far less dangerous that way."

"Well, I'm happy to hear I haven't got a few days of fucking pain and torture coming up..," I said, noting his change of mood:" I'm also glad you're going to admit something. That's progress and shows you're not the knuckle-dragging cunt I always thought you were. What are you going to admit?"

Cleaver's laugh wasn't a very successful one but it was an attempt. He grinned at me, and this time I felt it was genuine which was good because it meant he might be coming around to giving up trying to hide the truth and might tell me what had been going on in the background.

"It's an admission that you're right..," he said:" What you said just now was correct. At the Fitzpatrick woman's request, I did go down there that night and when I got there I have to confess I was pleased to see the two-faced piece of shit that had been Marcus Dexter lying in a chair, as helpless as a new-born baby and fucking terrified, unable to move a muscle, just whimpering and shaking a lot."

He brought the cigar back up to his lips and spent a few seconds re-lighting it, blowing a cloud of aromatic blue smoke out in my direction:

"Christ..!" he chuckled, smiling at some inner memory:" His eyes! You should have seen the size of them! When I walked into that room, that bastard knew exactly what was coming to him. He'd been blackmailing me for two long, fucking years about that deal we made in New York. A deal I thought we'd agreed on keeping quiet about but which lover boy decided he was going to hold over my head like that fucking sword some Greek king had swinging over him."

"Damocles..?" I ventured.

"That's the cunt..," Cleaver laughed:" Damocles: Him... Anyway he kept threatening to tell Leonora and the New York police department about our arrangement and, in exchange for his silence, got me to help him out with some of his preparations for setting up business in London, using Charlotte as his social in-road into the wealthy and connected, and me as the muscle with the local knowledge to smooth his dealings: Un-ruffle some of the feathers he was going to ruffle: You know the score. I got nothing out of it apart from his fucking silence of course, which was the part that raised my dander to even higher levels. So yes...When I saw him pinned to that chair with a look of sheer fucking panic on his sweaty face, I admit I was a happy man. Even happier when I saw the briefcase full of money and bonds she was carrying in her hand, because some of that cash was going to be mine, as payment for my part in Dexter's demise."

He drew a long, deep pull on the cigar and again, blew a stream of blue smoke up towards the ceiling.

"To be honest with you..," he continued, strangely calmly:" I would have quite happily blown his face off for nothing but you know I never turn down an offer of good money so I didn't. Two million for getting rid of the guy that cheated me out of millions more? Too fucking right son!"

I sat coolly smiling at him.

"Nice confession..," I said:" Just a pity it's still not quite the truth."

He looked at me, his face smiling but his eyes taut.

"What do you mean? Of course it's the truth. Why would I lie?"

"Because that's what you do..," I said, returning the smile:" You tell lies. Sometimes only half lies but they're still lies. You lie for a living and you make a very good living which means you must lie a lot."

Cleaver took another long drag on his smoke and stood in front of the fire, just a few feet away, looking down at me, still smiling.

"You better be very fucking careful my son..," he grinned:" Ever since you walked through the front door of this building you've been stepping on thin fucking ice and now it's thinner than a fucking razor blade and it might just be about to crack and cut you in half."

I smiled up at him and gave him a side-ways grin.

"I don't think so..," I said, quietly:" I think I'm standing on pretty solid shit to be honest. No ice, just shit and you're the one that's been dropping it everywhere in nice big piles."

He laughed, just like the old Cleaver I knew and loathed.

"What do you want Carter..?" he said:" Why did you come here? Money? Is that what you're after? You want a share of the action? What have you got in your pocket? You got your phone switched on have you, recording all this? You plan on getting my admission so you can twist my bollocks and get me to fill your pockets with cash? Is that the plan…You getting half of what I'm getting: A million? Or maybe you want to try and blackmail me for a lot more? Chisel money out of me every month for not going to the police with your theory?"

"No..," I said, shaking my head:" I don't want your money. I want to see you where you fucking belong. Behind bars. Locked away: Rotting. Paying the price for what you and she tried to do to me."

"Fair enough..," Cleaver said, magnanimously, shrugging his big shoulders and nodding in mock submission:" I'll give you that. Pity though. You were one of my best, that's why I paid you so fucking much but it doesn't mean you're indispensable. You might well have my confession in your pocket but it don't mean anyone's going to get to hear it."

"Oh? And why's that..? Are you going to take it off me..? You know you can't do that. You're not good enough."

Cleaver took another deep draw on his cigar and nodded in agreement.

"Maybe not..," he said, casually:"…but he is..," and pointed over my shoulder.

Instinctively I whipped around to see a figure standing in the doorway: A man with a familiar face but not one I had any time to try and recognize before something thumped into the side of my neck and the world went black.

THIRTY FIVE

I don't know how long I'd been out but it can't have been more than a minute because when the thick black curtain began to lift from my brain and I opened my eyes, Cleaver was still standing in front of the fire, a whisky in one hand and that damned cigar in the other, staring down at me, wearing a big fat, greasy smile on his big, fat, greasy face that said… "Who's the wise guy now eh..?"

Slowly, raggedly, slumped in my chair, I began trying to piece together the moments before the darkness from the fragments of vaguely recalled conversations slipping around my head like snakes in the mist, then suddenly one of the snakes became the man in the doorway and I spun my head around to see if he was still there, or at least I tried to, but for some reason my neck and my head wouldn't move: Neither would my hands, fingers, legs, feet or any other part of my body. I tried opening my mouth to speak, or yell, but when I couldn't do that either, a cold, bony hand squeezed its icy fingers around my heart and a flood of ice water ran through every vein in my rigid body. For some reason not one single fucking muscle in my body seemed to want to work: I couldn't move: The only thing I could do was breath in and out and move my eyes left and right; up and down. That was it: Nothing else. Apart from that I was totally paralysed and for the first time since the Gulf I felt genuine prickles of fear begin to crawl around my stomach and up my spine as I realised I was alone in a room with a man that really didn't like me and who I got the distinct feeling would very probably like to do me a great deal of harm if he could, but who I literally couldn't lift a single finger to stop if he tried.

Seeing the confusion in my eyes and sensing my panic, Cleaver took a long, deep pull on his cigar, stepped forward, pulled back the sleeve of his smoking jacket and, smiling widely, slapped me hard across the left cheek which to my surprise and alarm I didn't feel: No sensation at all: No pain, no sting; Nothing, just the weight of his hand rocking my head and rattling my teeth.

He slapped me again, harder this time, right across my jaw, but there was still no pain, just a dull numbness.

"Fuck me, I love this drug..," he chuckled, stepping back and flexing his knuckles, which I saw had blood on them. He must have cut my cheek or opened a lip but I didn't know which because I couldn't feel anything:" I want a truckload of it."

From somewhere behind me, a man's slow, educated voice said..." I'm afraid you can't have it: It's for my personal use only..." and again, instinctively I tried to look around to see who it was but like before, nothing happened: Not one bloody muscle responded. All I could do was stare ahead. If I could have frowned I would have. I'd heard that voice before somewhere but where and when..?

"Pity..," Cleaver said, looking down at me like he hadn't eaten for a month and I was a twelve ounce steak covered with onions:" There's a few cunts I'd like to use it on."

"I'm sure there are..," the voice chuckled coldly:"...but I only have enough for the cunts I want to use it on."

The owner of the voice stepped forward from behind me and stood beside Cleaver, and as soon as I saw the guy I knew who he was: It was the man with the military tie and the handsome face: The guy that had showed me into Leonora's living room: Her fucking butler...

"Good evening Mister Carter..," he said coldly:" Nice to see you again."

Maybe it was the sudden rapidness of my breathing and the look of fear in my eyes that gave away my attempt at gaining control over my body, but he raised the palm of his hand:

"Please..," he smiled; a tight, disinterested smile:" Don't bother trying to move. I assure you its' completely futile."

Another shadow appeared in the corner of my left eye and the instant I heard it speak, my blood froze.

"It's quite true what my uncle says Mister Carter. It really would be a pointless waste of energy trying to speak or move."

It was Leonora Fitzpatrick.

Fuck..! Now there were three people in the room that hated me and my stomach rolled over.

Dressed to kill and smiling a slow, self-congratulatory smile, she stepped into my line of vision and, stopping between Cleaver and her uncle, stared down at me, her eyes roaming over my face and body taking in my vulnerability, nodding her approval at what she was seeing.

"Well, well, well..," she said, smiling in the way a cat smiles at a cornered mouse:" We meet again Mister Carter. I do hope you were in a comfortable position when the dart hit you. It will make the next few minutes much more bearable if you were because you see, as you've probably realised, the toxin that's just been shot into your bloodstream has rendered you completely and utterly paralysed. I'm afraid you really won't be able to move at all for at least the next hour or so."

Sitting herself down opposite me, in one of Cleavers big armchairs, she crossed her long legs and without taking her eyes from mine, took a languorous sip from the drink she had in her hand, looking me over, giving me the distinct feeling as she did so that seeing me helpless in a chair and at her mercy was actually turning her on.

"Do you know Mister Carter..," Leonora continued, her voice low and erotically breathless, settling back into the leather, making herself comfortable, obviously enjoying her "villainess" moment:"...there is nothing more sensual and arousing then seeing the terror in a man's eyes whilst he is helpless and about to experience intense pain, something I discovered some years ago when, to my deep pleasure and delight, I realised I have a very extreme and deep-seated passion for inflicting torture."

As she took another sip of her drink, I tried hard to flex my thighs, my eyes flicking between all three of them, but still nothing moved. It's as if I'd been carved from stone.

"Something else I discovered..," she continued, her voice returned to its normal educated, soft but cruel tone :"...was that there are an awful lot of very wealthy, very powerful men who are quite prepared to pay an awful lot of money to have me inflict such exquisite and absolute pain on them, although..," and her eyes glittered in the firelight:"...not perhaps the amount of pain and fear my dear, unsuspecting husband was forced to endure during the last few minutes of his nasty, miserable little life however..," she smoothed, taking another sip of her drink.

Feet, toes, fingers, knees and elbows: I tried them all but nothing even twitched:

"Before we start, perhaps I should explain a little about my clever uncle...," she purred, smiling contemptuously:

Start..? Start what..?

"...He spent fifteen very productive years in the Royal Marines, then another five living deep in the Amazon with various indigenous tribes, becoming a highly respected jungle warfare specialist and eventually coming to have an intimate knowledge of a wide range of obscure but rather deadly drugs and poisons completely unique to them and, fortunately for me, totally unknown to the rest of the world. One of them, the one now flowing around your veins and solidifying your muscles making you entirely helpless, is made from the venom of the blue lipped viper and is used by the N'Awatack people to instantly paralyse their game but not actually kill it. Really quite effective as you've discovered."

So that's how they fucking did it, I thought: That's how they got Dexter to sit still and let them make his death look like suicide. The old "Blue Lipped Viper" trick..! Stupid of me..! Suddenly I could see what must have happened. Using Leonora's key to the house, uncle Fester must have let himself in, taken up a position from which he could wait until Dexter turned up, waited until he had sat down to await Charlotte's arrival, shot this viper-juice into Dexter's neck, paralysed him like he had me, then called Leonora to say it was safe for her and Cleaver to walk through the door instead of the expected Charlotte. Bloody simple really. You just needed to have spent a few years in the Amazon jungle eating Piranha soup and learning how the natives killed their enemies, that's all. I kept trying to tell my legs to flick up and kick her straight in her expensive teeth but the message just couldn't get through. I had to hand it to those N'Awatackians: That blue-lip stuff was good. No matter how much my brain told something to move, nothing did.

"Well done for getting this far with your little attempt at private investigation by the way..," she went on, condescendingly:" I have to admit, rather grudgingly of course, from what I was hearing on the other side of the door, you have proved to be far more intelligent and inquisitive than I assumed you would be."

I tried to raise an eyebrow to let her know I appreciated the compliment but even that little muscle wouldn't work.

"When I first walked up all those dusty, filthy stairs..," she sneered:"...I thought you would be nothing more than yet another thug for hire. No better than any of the others Mister Cleaver employed, but his insistence that you would be the perfect man for what I needed persuaded me to stay."

Another sip of her drink and another attempt by me at flexing something but moving nothing, all the time unnervingly aware that Cleaver was looking at me like a butcher looks at a fresh carcass, weighing up where to start slicing.

"You see..," she continued"...all I needed was someone who could meet with Marcus, see and understand how intimidating he was, so that when asked, they would concur with the idea that poor, delicate, pathetic little Charlotte, under the influence of drugs and drink, could very well have been driven to pulling the trigger on him, pushed to the edge of her drug-induced madness by his infamously sadistic and manipulative behaviour. It was no secret that she feared and hated Marcus and, she had openly declared her desire to murder him. It had become the whisper of all the social circles..," she continued:"...which meant that her having shot him in some drunken stupor would have come as absolutely no surprise to anyone who knew the background to their marriage, sham though it was, and all I needed was an outsider to be able to affirm his character if or when the police came calling."

She finished her brandy and held it up for her uncle to refill, seemingly unaware of my continuing attempts to get any part of my anatomy working

"And Charlotte's marriage was a sham Mister Carter..," she went on as Uncle Fester stepped back to stand beside Cleaver again:" A marriage of pure convenience, all planned and arranged by me, with the direct and deliberate purpose of using my dear, sweet, simple, tragic friend as a means to avenge myself on Dexter for his cutting me out of the highly lucrative business we'd built up together over the past few years using my contacts..!" she said, angrily, her eyes hardening:"...MY contacts! Together we created a network of incredibly rich, powerful men who, through their own sense of self-importance and entitlement, were not only customers for the pain, humiliation and degradation it was my utter delight to inflict on them, but his best customers for the exotic range of recreational drugs he could provide."

Why was she telling me all this..? What was the point? Was she getting off on having a captive audience? I really didn't care about her "Network" or her plans for revenge...All I cared about at that very moment was getting some kind of control back over my body so that I could leap up from my chair and end this rambling, self-important monologue by inflicting the maximum amount of damage whist kicking the living crap out of all three of them.

"Without me..," she snarled:"... none of that would have been possible. All I wanted in exchange was my share of the proceeds, but one day, without any warning or discussion, that arrogant, selfish, conceited bastard made it very plain that he didn't need me as a partner anymore and, just like that..."

She snapped her fingers:

"...I was no longer required..," she hissed:" Shut out. Closed down..."

She set the glass down on the table, and looked me up and down, like a spider eyeing up a fly caught in its web before continuing.

"I wasted months trying to persuade him to let me back in, but he continually ignored me: Treated me like one of his whores: Once he'd fucked me..,"she hissed:"...physically and financially, he discarded me like trash. It was clear nothing I did to threaten him was going to work so I stopped and decided instead to use my brain instead of hired brawn and that's where our mutual friend came into the story."

She threw a cold smile back at Cleaver who raised his cigar to me in a mocking salute. In return I shot a withering look back at him, wishing it were a 9mm bullet instead.

Leonora continued...

"You can't have been aware of it Mister Carter, but Mister Cleaver and I have been associates for quite some while: Since the early stages of my original business venture in fact..," she said.

Cleaver winked at me cheekily and, using two fingers and his thumb, made a gun gesture at me with his right hand, as if to say "Gotcha." In my head I pointed a real gun back at him, and blew his fat, grinning head clean off.

"He has helped me with certain situations that arose every now and again, a service he continued to provide for Marcus when required, some of which, ironically, you may very well have been involved with yourself..," she grinned, obviously highly amused by the idea:"...and because of that involvement, and our mutual dislike of the way in which Marcus conducted himself, I knew I could trust him."

I really, really wished I had control of my mouth right then because I would have laughed out loud at the words "Trust" and "Cleaver" being put together in one sentence, but I couldn't and she carried on with her fucking monologue while I shot hard looks at Cleaver and the cold-eyed uncle, trying to control my breathing which was becoming faster.

"And the reason I knew I could trust him..," she said, almost as if she'd read my thoughts:"...was because I knew that like me, he had been screwed over by Marcus on more than one occasion and that he too had his own list of very good reasons to hate him."

Cleaver took the cigar out of his mouth and nodded.

"Too fucking right I did..," he growled.

Leonora smiled, took another sip of her drink then continued.

"So, we met secretly and came up with a plan that would get us both what we wanted: Control of an enterprise that is worth many millions of pounds a year and that could be worth many millions more if I were running it. I would pretend to Dexter that I'd given up and he had won and that if he agreed to a divorce from our frankly embarrassing marriage, I would, for a sum far less than he owed me, waive all rights and claims on the business and leave London which, of course, he said yes to straight away but, being the greedy, uncouth bastard that he was, I knew he would still keep stalling, ignoring all the legalities, which he knew would be costing me money, taking pleasure from watching me dance to his tune: He would be laughing at me Mister Carter, and those who know me, know that I'm not someone that allows any man to laugh at her, so.., on the pretence of his acting as a mediator between both parties, I sent Mister Cleaver to New York to re-start divorce proceedings, both of us knowing Dexter would use the chance to try to cook up a neat little scheme between the two of them when he got there and, just as we predicted, he did, isn't that right Mister Cleaver?"

"That's exactly right, yeah..," Cleaver grinned:" 'Two fucking hours after I'd landed, he gives me a call, has me picked up from my hotel and taken to some fucking fancy, expensive place on the East Side where he "suggested" that, while I sat around the pool doing nothing at Mrs Fitzpatrick's expense for a few days, telling her we were having meaningful discussions, he would use one of the finest forgers in the city to fake a

"Form-of-Decree", forge the City Seal and Stamp, get it filled out with the information my lovely friend here gave me, sign it and send it back to her, making her think he had finally decided to give her what she wanted. She would then counter-sign the fake papers thinking she was finally rid of him and send them back. In the meantime, I would have instructed her attorneys that, after private talks and for personal reasons, Mrs. Fitzpatrick had decided she wanted to drop the divorce. They would assume that was the end of it, stop the legal proceedings, close the files, step to one side and leave him free to marry Charlotte who he'd been liberally sprinkling his finest Colombian fairy dust all over for a few months, and who we both knew was bat-crazy about him."

"The deal for Mister Cleaver was..," Leonora interrupted:"...that he would be given a generous share of the takings for helping get rid of Marcus and for keeping quiet about the fake divorce. Several million a year I believe was the figure mentioned: A not insubstantial sum, wouldn't you say?"

I had to agree with her there. It was indeed a very substantial sum, and one that Cleaver would have killed his grandmother for, if his weird fucking uncle hadn't already done that ten years ago so that they could sell her house in Fulham for a thousand times more than she and his dad had paid for it in 1936.

"So, that was that..," Leonora smirked:" My plan worked. I "accepted" his decree absolute, the only thing "absolute" about it being that it was an absolute fake, and Dexter came back to England with Charlotte tucked neatly between his legs..."

She laughed at her own joke, which was quite a good one to be honest, and Cleaver laughed too which is something I hadn't seen before and didn't really ever want to see or hear again, but I noticed her uncle's expression didn't even flicker. He looked as bored with the whole fucking thing as I was. Apart from the blue-lipped viper bit which was a real surprise, I didn't need to hear all these details: I'd already guessed most of what she'd told me, but she was obviously getting some kind of narcissistic thrill out of telling me everything and I couldn't exactly get up and leave so I had to sit and listen.

"Within days..," she continued and I groaned heavily, or at least I did in my head, Christ..! She's off again:"...Within days he carried on exactly where he'd left off, spending her money like it was spare cash, buying houses, yachts, art and cars, keeping her permanently high on Coke and whatever else he could stick between her toes or up her nose, pouring drink down her throat, making sure she was out of it most of the time. Now he was married to her and had all of her contacts in his pocket, I knew as soon as she became of no further interest or use to him, his plan would be to get rid of her, file for divorce and dump her, just as he'd done with others in the past and I was going to use that callous indifference to my advantage: I was going to make her angry and heart-broken: Desperate enough to start telling everyone that she was going to shoot Marcus which I knew they'd all believe. Why wouldn't they? They knew he was an arrogant pig: A total bastard. No-one would have blamed her for shooting him. I don't doubt quite a few people would like to have shot him themselves."

She finished off her drink and set the glass down on the table, looking into my eyes intently.

"But it wouldn't be Charlotte that actually shot him Mister Carter. It would be one of Mister Cleavers associates. The plan was they would make it look like a clumsy, amateur killing and leave the gun lying in the room as if she had dropped it and run away in panic. Her fingerprints would be found on it, the police would come looking for her, find her shivering and strung out in her apartment, question her, come to find you because you were the last person she would remember meeting at the house, you were going to tell them that yes, you had met him; that you thought he had a vicious temper, was a very nasty piece of work and that it wouldn't have surprised you at all to hear that Charlotte had shot him and I and everyone they also asked would act shocked and would say how awful it was but that it was more than possible she had killed him because he was a pig and had made her life a misery, addicting her to his drugs and spending all of her money. The icing on the well-prepared cake: The final nail in her coffin, so to speak, would be me, collapsing under the weight of my emotions and from the shock and horror of what my poor, abused friend had done, revealing the fact that I'd discovered Marcus had faked our divorce: That I was still married to him and that when I'd told her, Charlotte had gone berserk, saying that he had humiliated her once too often, etcetera, etcetera. All of that was the plan Mister Carter and it was a good one but it fell apart because of two things."

She leaned forward, her eyes glittering in the flames of the fire, her perfume clouding around me:

"The first thing was you Mister Carter. You were supposed to have acted like the gun-for-hire I'd assumed you would be when Mister Cleaver gave me your address and I came to see you in your nasty little hole of an office. You were supposed to take the money I offered you gladly and with a cold glint in your eye, jump into your car and roar off into the dawn to confront Marcus like the killer I'd been told you were, but you didn't. Instead you threw the first of a series of increasingly annoying spanners into my plan by refusing to go until the next day which meant Charlotte would be even more the worse for wear than I'd already made her a few hours before, going to her filthy apartment, sympathising with her, listening to her whinings for the hundredth time, giving her more drink, letting her cry on my shoulder, waiting for her to, as always, threaten to kill him if he left her, then…"

She flashed another cold grin at Cleaver who grinned back and puffed on his cigar twice.

"…making her even angrier by telling her the reason I'd come to see her was because I'd discovered Dexter hadn't really divorced me therefore her marriage was illegal, and that he was planning on leaving her for someone else, just like he had done to me and several other women before. That worked perfectly of course, just like I knew it would, and the gullible, befuddled idiot was all ready to go down to Sussex right there and then to shoot the bastard, even though she could barely stand, but I stroked her precious hair, calmed the stupid bitch down and told her to wait a few hours because I didn't think Marcus would be back until the morning. Of course she had no idea what I was saying: She just kept staring at me, her eyes rolling up into the back of her head, but it didn't matter. Mister Cleaver was supposed to have two of his men take her down there before you arrived, leave her staggering about in the woods for you to find, shoot Marcus helped by my uncles drug, wait for you to arrive, watch you find Charlotte and take her into the house, discover the body, come back to London and wait for the whole, seemingly fool-proof plan to unfold."

She leant forward and smiled a secret smile.

"By the way..," she half-whispered:" Just in case you were wondering.., it was me that put Dexter's gun in Charlotte's bag. I knew where he kept it so I gave Mister Cleaver Charlotte's set of keys to the house and he sent some of his men down there to find it and bring it back so that whilst I was comforting her, I could slip it into her little clutch. Simple really."

She sat back and carried on.

"It was all going to work so perfectly, but because you were too drunk and too obstinate to go straight away, I had to call my uncle, stop him travelling down to Sussex and instead get him to go to Charlotte's flat and use his invaluable knowledge of drugs to keep her on the edge of oblivion for a few more hours without killing her, which wasn't an easy thing, even for him, then I had to call Mister Cleaver to tell him you wouldn't be leaving until you'd slept off your hangover, and to let me know when Marcus was on his way back from his damned party or his latest rich little whore, probably both, so that the plan could continue, albeit half a day late. But that didn't work either did it Mister Carter, because my darling Marcus stayed longer at his party or inside his bloody whore than he was supposed to have done and didn't return to the house until after you got there. That really tore up the plan. There was no possibility we could have shot him when you were there was there!"

She sat back with a look of barely restrained fury on her face and just stared at me with a loathing I really didn't think I deserved.

"My God, but you and my dear, late husband were pains in my arse that night Mister Carter..," she said in an exasperated, irritated voice:" I just wanted her meet you in the grounds of the house at the house, be awake enough to recall meeting someone and be able to give the police the description and name of the man she'd met: Your description Mister Carter..," she smiled, pointing at me with one long, red-nailed finger:"...and even though you weren't going to be the one that actually killed him, your name was going to be the one she would drag out of the fetid depths of her drug-softened brain when they came to question her about Dexter's death."

Out of the corner of my eye I saw Cleaver take a step towards his desk, bend forward and place his hand on one of the drawers but a sharp look and a shake of the head from Leonora stopped him and he shrugged then stepped back to his original place in front of the fire, grinning a snakey, sideways kind of grin as if he knew something I didn't.

I didn't like this. I didn't like this one fucking bit. I'd seen that grin on his ugly, fat face before and it had always meant someone was in for a very painful time, and I had the growing, nasty feeling that tonight that someone was me. Leonora's long-winded confirmation of everything I'd suspected from the moment she'd walked through my door: That I'd been used as a sacrificial bull by the back-stabbing, main-chancing Cleaver for his own personal gain, and that she was using Charlotte in a cold, calculating game of murder and deceit, suddenly filled my stomach with a heavy, icy ball of fear and I could feel my blood coursing through me like an adrenalin-fuelled bullet train, every nerve and sinew now on fire. I tried to calm my mind, taking deep calming breaths, sending increasingly frantic demands to bits of my body for just one fucking muscle to at least twitch or jerk but still nothing happened. I was a statue and very worried one now.

Leonora's voice tore my eyes away from Cleaver's leer and I concentrated on her face, trying, as she continued with her homily, to focus my now screaming demands for movement on just one part of my body: My arms. "One adrenaline-powered fucking twitch", I repeated: Just fucking one...

"I'll admit to you Mister Carter..," she said, deflatedly:"...for a while I completely thrown. I didn't have a plan B and it looked as though all my careful, meticulous planning had come crashing down because of your stubborn refusal to do what you were supposed to do, and Marcus's refusal to ignore a pretty face, but ironically it was Marcus himself who re-booted the whole thing."

She leant forward conspiratorially.

"It was the note..," she said quietly and confidentially, as if it was just between us:" The note he left in Charlotte's apartment telling her he was divorcing her and leaving for the Caribbean that night."

The smile returned to her face and she sat back in triumph.

"At first it totally blind-sided me..," she said:"...and for a few moments in that kitchen I just stood, frozen, convinced the whole thing was over: That he was going to get away scot-free: That he wasn't going to get the bullet in the head he so richly deserved, but suddenly it came to me that actually, his giving Charlotte an ultimatum and demanding she come grovelling to his feet meant I knew exactly where he was going to be and when. It was exactly the re-boot I needed and I began to revise the plan which in the end worked out far better than the original would have done. Without realising it, Marcus had just sent out the invitation to his own execution."

I felt a twitch..! In my left wrist..! I felt a fucking *twitch*..! My heart surged: I demanded another one but didn't get it. That was okay though. Something was getting through. I had a chance, slim though it was.

Cleaver suddenly took his cigar from his thick lips and blew out a long column of blue smoke, clearing his throat loudly.

"Listen..," he snarled:" Let's just cut out all the fucking bull shit here shall we..? This is all very fucking interesting, but he's heard enough. I know I fucking have..! You heard what he said just before he got that fucking dart in his neck. He's already worked all that shit out for himself. He's a clever little fucker is our Mister Carter. Good with his hands and even better with his head. Too fucking clever for his own fucking good sometimes but he's a clever little cunt nonetheless. Just like his fucking dad was, which is why he had to go..."

My eyes widened suddenly and my heart thumped against my chest like a demon in a coffin. What did he just say..! "Had to go..?" What the fuck did he mean..."Had to go..?"

"I thought that was a good thing once..," Cleaver went on, twisting the cigar between his fingertips:"...Having brains as well as brawn: Having this fucker gave me an advantage in a very competitive game, but now..."

He jabbed his cigar straight at me...

"*He's* just dangerous..! Everything you've just fucking told him..? He already knows most of it..," he guffed, shoving his smoke back between his lips and puffing angrily:"...and now, thanks to your endless fucking monologue, he knows even more..!"

Suddenly there was a lot going on, and I flicked my eyes from one to the other, trying to keep track of the conversation and gauge what everyone was thinking.

Leonora was sitting calmly looking up at Cleaver, an almost amused expression on her porcelain smooth face as if humouring a ranting child, giving him the chance to blow hisself out before carrying on. I couldn't see the expression on Uncle Fester's face because he'd either left the room during Cleaver's tirade or he'd stepped away and was standing somewhere behind me, but as I couldn't turn around to find out, I had to guess that's where he was.

"Why d'ya tell him all that..?" Cleaver went on:" What's the fucking point..? It might be giving you a thrill having him sit there all 'elpless, forced to listen to you giving with all the wanky, soul-clearing, self-confession speech, but what's it achieving apart from you getting a bit wet between the legs knowing you've got a fucking tiger sitting two feet from you who would normally rip you apart with his bare fucking hands but he's stiff as slab of concrete and you can do anything you want with him or to him because there's not a fucking thing he can do to stop you?"

"Have you finished..?" she said quietly.

Cleaver let out a long breath, still angry but weighing up his answer, his eyes on me as he considered his reply.

"Yes..," He replied but in a more measured voice:" I'm finished, but I'm still fucking angry. I don't get why you couldn't just let me have him killed when he told your fucking lawyer he wasn't going to be a witness. It would have been a lot fucking simpler than all..," and he waved his cigar about:"...this. One shot to the head, like with Dexter, and there you go. Simple: He's dead and everything he knows is dead with him. Then, we get on with making all those millions you fucking talked about."

There was a long silence during which my heart tried to crash through my ribs, my eyes swiveled from one face to the other, my brain sweated and I yelled in my head for something, anything, to respond to my increasingly frantic screams.

Leonora broke the silence.

"I'm very sorry if I've bored you Mister Cleaver..," she said evenly, that enigmatic half-smile still on her ice cool face but a chilly edge to her voice:" I merely wanted to let Mister Carter know just how important a role he's played in our little game and how very disappointed I am in his performance but..."

She fell silent again, wrinkling her perfectly smooth brow in thought as if considering the question, then looked up again.

"Maybe you're right..," she said, smiling sweetly, like a child making its mind up about which toy to play with:" Maybe we should just kill him now."

My throat closed and I could feel the bile rising up from my churning stomach, anger mixed with fear making it taste bitter.

She turned away from Cleaver and looked somewhere just behind my back.

"What do you think uncle..?" she asked:" Is Mister Cleaver right? Have I indulged myself much too long? Maybe we should just do what we came together to do?"

Her uncles' educated, clear-voiced answer came from just behind my left shoulder.

"I really have no concerns my dear..," he said, calmly:" By all means, carry on. Continue to indulge yourself if you wish. Mister Carter is a very fit man and his constitution is no doubt strong, but I'd be quite confident in saying we have at least another thirty minutes before the drug even begins to wear off. You have plenty of time. It's entirely your choice."

Again a silence, during which I continued sending waves of adrenaline powered demands down my central fucking nerve system like lightning bolts, begging a whole arm, a leg or even one single, useful muscle to wake up and give me the chance to turn the tables on these bastards, but not a thing happened. Only my thumping heart, my flaring nostrils and my aching lungs were working.

"No..," Leonora said, firmly:" Mister Cleaver is quite right. I've enjoyed myself for far too long. Forgive me. I think it's time we completed the plan and moved on."

Cleaver snatched the cigar from his lips.

"Thank the fuck for that..," he breathed, opening his arms in exasperation:" Let's just get on with it then shall we?"

He leaned towards his desk.

"May I...?" he said sarcastically, indicating the drawers.

For the briefest of seconds, Leonora's eyes flicked back to her uncle and her fixed smile dropped, then back again to Cleaver who was bent sideways, hovering over his desktop, an expectant grin on his flubbering cheeks.

"Of course Mister Cleaver..," she nodded:" Please: Continue."

"Thank you..," Cleaver grinned, wickedly:" I think I fucking will..."

He pulled open one of the top drawers and slipped his pudgy, veined hand inside.

"At long fucking last Carter..," he said, chuckling like an asthmatic pig:" I've waited fucking days to do this you cocky little cunt."

He stood up straight, leering down at me, his wide, pudgy face red and sweating in the heat from the fire, and in his left hand he had a 9mm, long nosed, Smith & Wesson, pointed directly at my face. I couldn't move, but evidently I could sweat because that what I was doing: Sweating hard.

"Not so fucking clever now are you Mister fucking Carter..?" he sneered, the fingers around the butt flexing, adjusting their grip:" Not so full of dis-respectful shit anymore, eh? No...This is where you learn about knowing your place in the order of things. Unfortunately, you've learnt it too fucking late you smug bastard..!"

He lifted the gun level with his shoulder and held his arm out straight, the small, black, perfectly round hole of the barrel less than four feet from my pounding forehead.

"Do you know what's going to happen now, eh? I'll fucking tell you shall I..? Might as well: My lovely new business partner has just told you everything about our plan to kill Dexter and Charlotte for some fucking reason I do not understand so I might as well let you know what I'm going to do after I've put a bullet straight through that overconfident fucking head of yours."

He licked his lips and winked at me, leaning in closer.

A finger moved..! A fucking finger..! What the hell use was one single finger when I couldn't use my arm to stick it through Cleaver's eye like a bloody knife-blade..! Come on..! Give me an arm...! Give me a fucking arm..!

"After I've spread your brains all over my walls..," he half-whispered, looking for the fear in my eyes:"...I'm going to call the fucking police and tell them that you came here to try and blackmail me by saying when the police came to arrest you for killing Dexter, you'd tell them I'd ordered you to kill him unless I gave you...ooo I don't know...what shall I say...Two million fucking quid? How does that sound? I of course, told you to fuck off, you pulled a gun on me and I had to shoot you in self fucking defense...That should keep the fuckers off my back for a while, eh? In the meantime, poor little Charlotte goes and bloody overdoses, isn't that right Mrs. Fitzpatrick, or shall I call you Leonora?"

He looked at Leonora and smiled impishly.

"...We are partners now, after all..?"

Leonora smiled, indulgently.

"No..," she breathed, slowly, like she was bored suddenly:" That's not actually quite correct."

Cleaver's face clouded over and he frowned in confusion.

"What do you mean "That's not quite fucking correct..?" It's exactly fucking correct. I shoot Carter and you kill Charlotte. Both witnesses dead..! That's the fucking plan..!"

"That's *our* plan, yes..," Leonora smiled, wearily:" But it's not *my* plan..."

She looked up and around, somewhere over my head.

"Is it uncle..?"

"No Leonora..," her uncle said, coldly:" It's not..."

There was the "tump, tump" of two suppressed shots fired only feet from my left ear, and instantly Cleaver fell backwards into the fire, sending the logs tumbling left and right and a shower of sparks flying up the chimney, one hole in his forehead and another in the sternum: The classic "double tap" we were all taught...

"Well done Mister Carter..!" Leonora laughed:" Perfect shots: Just as you were trained to do when you were in Special Forces. The police will be very impressed, won't they uncle..?"

"Uncle" stepped forward and stood astride Carvers body, the smell of burning cotton, silk and flesh beginning to fill the air, a small but powerful Heckler & Koch P7 M13 in his hand, a three inch suppressor fitted to the short barrel.

"Highly..," he said, dryly, looking down at Carvers body, no doubt checking that he was dead, and then turning to face me:" Well placed if I may say so. Perfectly in keeping with your military records. You were quite the shot I was told."

He ran his cold, ice-blue eyes over my useless body.

"Unfortunately, you weren't quite quick enough to prevent him getting in the first shot were you..?"

He raised the HK and aimed at my knee.

"The leg I think..," he mused:" A random, believable, amateurs' shot."

There was another cough from the muzzle of the pistol and I felt a numbing blow just below my left knee like a kick from a horse and I could see and feel my lower leg fly back and sideways, the skin, flesh, muscle and bone exploding in all directions but apart from a violent, slamming sensation, there was no fucking pain. It was as if someone had turned a switch off inside my brain that cut pain, the way you do a light. I wanted to scream and I could feel one gargling in my throat but nothing came. My mouth wouldn't open and my jaw wouldn't move. Christ..! He'd shot my fucking leg off..!

"Oh dear..," Leonora gasped in mock-horror, her eyes theatrically wide, unable to take them off the shattered remains of my left shin, a wide, sadistic grin on her lips." You've been shot Mister Carter. How awful for you! So much blood...!"

She leant forward, reached down, dipped a fingertip into the stream of dark crimson running into my socks, brought it up to her lips and very delicately rubbed it across her teeth, wiping it away with a highly suggestive lick of her tongue.

"Mmmmm...Delicious..," she moaned, eyes closed, head back:" And so fresh."

She looked at me and smiled, her teeth slightly pink.

"You have very tasty blood Mister Carver. If only I'd known sooner...Oh well, perhaps I'll take a bottle of it when we leave."

"Shall I continue..?" her uncle asked, his dead, pitiless eyes looking at me with utter disinterest:" The shock to his system of those broken bones and the loss of blood flow might cause the drug to be over-ridden by a wave of adrenaline. I'd hazard a guess that we might have less than ten more minutes before he regains his muscle co-ordination and that would upset the scenario if he started thrashing around like a landed fish."

Leonora studied me for a minute like a Roman emperor trying to decide whether a defeated and bloodied gladiator should live or die, an amused little smile of triumph on her face.

"Yes..," she said, huskily:" Let's continue. I'm tired of this now and it's time to visit Charlotte. She will be missing me."

She turned to me and raised her eyebrows, tilting her head to one side, coquettishly.

"I'm sorry Mister Carter, but my uncle is right. We can't risk you beginning to feel pain suddenly and starting to scream and thrash about. You see, we have a scenario we need to create that makes it look as though you and my late business partner had a terrible argument and shot each other. It's very well thought out and I feel more than sure the police will believe it when they see it. My uncle again..," she twinkled, proudly:" He really is very clever."

She sat back as if that were a signal and watched as "Uncle" sent a bullet tearing through my jacket and shirt and deep into my stomach, the explosive kick throwing me back into the chair. A gut shot… Fuck..! He'd gut shot me..! The nasty fucking bastard..! I could take hours to die from a gut shot and he knew it. Seems like Leonora had inherited her sadistic genes from his side of the family. My hands fell off the arms of the chair and hung down over the carpet, my head suddenly becoming impossibly heavy and lolling to one side.

Again I wanted to scream but no sound came out of my throat, mainly because it was blocked with a sudden rush of hot, iron-tasting blood that was filling my mouth and that I could sense was pouring through my teeth and out the corner of my lips, dripping onto my right arm.

Thankfully there was still no sensation of pain. All I felt were tears stinging my eyes and the sensation of slipping down a black hole into the mouth of a scorching volcano.

Leonora rose from her chair and bent over me, looking down at me, her lovely eyes searching my face.

I looked up at her through eyelids that felt like warm lead. I could see the tiny hairs along her upper lip and the whiteness of her teeth. They were beautiful teeth. Very expensive teeth. I'd liked to have kissed those teeth once but now..? Now I didn't care…

"I'm sorry we had to kill you Mister Carter..," she said, low and gently, her lips just inches from mine, her long fingers stroking my left cheek almost tenderly:"…but Mister Cleaver was right about you. You really are…were…much too clever. You became just too dangerous to keep alive."

She sighed quietly and smiled, brushing a strand of hair out of my eyes.

"You really shouldn't have thought too much you know, you silly man. Look where it got you."

Another soft smile, a light, slow kiss on my bloodied lips then she stood up, looking down at the hole in my shirt and the thick black blood pumping rhythmically out onto my stomach in waves.

"Goodbye Mister Carter..," she breathed, almost in pity:" You were a very interesting man. It might have been nice getting to know you but…"

She shrugged.

"Have a pleasant death..," and left the room without a backward glance.

The flow of blood into my mouth was making it difficult to breathe now and darkness was starting to creep across my eyes. The outer edges of my vision were blurring and the light from the fire was dimming. I was dying: I knew it but strangely I wasn't afraid or even concerned. I didn't care anymore. It was a sense of relief and if I could have smiled I would have done because it really didn't matter. I was tired now. Tired of everything and just wanted to sleep.

Leonora's uncle was standing over me, a look of professional indifference on his stark features, using a cloth to wipe the trigger and body of the Smith & Wesson he'd killed Cleaver with, and I watched him take my right hand, curl my fingers tightly around the trigger and butt, then let it go, feeling and hearing the thump the gun to fell onto the carpet, a few feet away from my open fingers, the all too familiar smell of cordite mixing with the smell of burning Cleaver tickling my nose.

I felt incredibly weak now and the room seemed to flatten out around me, all the colours draining away leaving a vague, grey blurriness instead.

With a last, dead-eyed look around, Uncle Fester stuffed the cloth into an inside pocket of his well-tailored suit, straightened his cuffs and tie, threw me a cursory last look…and left, the sound of his footsteps heading down the hallway and the front door closing being the last earthly sounds I knew I would ever hear.

I felt relieved though. This was the end of my road and I was very okay about it. Suddenly I was content. Leonora had been right, bless her. Dying wasn't really unpleasant at all.

My heart thumped loudly in my chest, but I ignored it. My mouth was full of blood now, making me choke, and pouring onto my chest but I didn't care.

I began to float up towards the ceiling and knew my brain was closing down but it really, honest to God's truth was okay. I was going to go smiling, at least in my head because one last comforting thought was running around my closing down brain and it was making me very happy.

Leonora's cold-hearted, bastard uncle had made one mistake. Only a small one and one he couldn't have known he'd made but it was one that might just make anyone who knew me well doubt that I had shot Cleaver.

You see, he had put the gun in my right hand and let it drop onto the right hand side of the chair but...I'm left-handed.

My heart thumped again and I choked on the blood that it forced into my mouth.

This was it.

Time to die.

At long, long last, it was time to die.

THE END

Printed in Great Britain
by Amazon